LOVE

WOLVES OF WALKER COUNTY

KIKI BURRELLI

CONNECT WITH KIKI

Join my newsletter!
And stay up to date on my newest titles, giveaways and news!
Want a free—full length— wolf shifter Mpreg novel? Join my newsletter when you get Finding Finn!

———

Join the Pack! Awooooo!
Come hang out with your pack mates!
Visit Kiki's Den and join the pack! Enjoy exclusive access to behind the scenes excerpts, cover reveals and surprise giveaways!

EXPERIENCE THE WOLVES OF WORLD

Wolves of Walker County (Wolf Shifter Mpreg)

Truth

Hope

Faith

Love

Wolves of Royal Paynes (Wolf Shifter Mpreg)

Hero

Ruler

Lovers

Outlaw

1

AVER

I kept to the shadows. Standing. Watching. Waiting. The black concrete glistened from the evening rain. The drops had stopped, but this was Seattle, so it was only a matter of time before they fell again.

Shedding the mask of my day-to-day life wasn't as difficult as it had once been. It dripped from me like blood from an open wound. At home I was Aver Walker, spineless son of two conniving parents. My cousins looked at me with pity. Their mates looked at me with pity. When I looked in the mirror, I saw only disgust. Who was this person?

What had started as vengeance had since transformed into something I didn't recognize anymore. My life felt like a huge mistake, like I'd gone to the store and had accidentally been given the wrong costume. When I was younger, I hoped the solution could be that simple as well. Just walk in and say, *excuse me, I've been given the wrong life. My life is this one over here.*

I wasn't young anymore. I'd observed enough of other people to realize they didn't have to pretend to be the people they were every moment of the day. That wasn't the status quo. Other people were who they wanted to be. Or they were stuck like me.

The person I really was, the Aver in my soul, had spent so long locked away, being set free was a process. There wasn't a personality switch I could flip. Transforming felt more like a series of locks, unboxing the real me took time. Like pulling out a favorite shirt that had gotten lost in the back of the closet. And once it was out, I couldn't wear two shirts. I didn't know how to take some of one and leave the rest. It was all or nothing.

Which was why I snarled when my phone chimed. I should have already turned the damn thing off—and I would—just as soon as I made sure there wasn't an emergency at home.

Branson, and everyone else back at home in Walker County, thought I was in Seattle to meet with a supplier. That wasn't a lie. I was. I had. Walker Construction officially had a new gravel, boulder, and stone provider and at rates that were cheaper across the board than what we'd seen with our original supplier. Today had been a successful day for the business Branson and I had built from the ground up, but right now, I didn't give two shits about it.

Still nothing, but then, my mother is too devious to leave the evidence needed to convict her laying out in the open.

Branson's mother had been taken in by the shifter council weeks ago. At first, it had looked like a slam dunk case. She'd been caught in the act of selling a blessed omega. Since then, Delia had done what Delia did best: wiggle out of tight spots. Ever since Branson had received a call from the representative tasked with presenting the case against Delia, he'd spent his extra time combing through the home he'd grown up in.

I found a floor safe under my old bed. Will the things I learn ever cease to freak me out?

It was an emotion the four Walker cousins shared. From the night we were asked by our parents to fight each other to the death, we'd ran and spent the following decade unpacking childhoods of baggage. When I was at home, in helpful, gentle Aver mode, I was all for listening and unpacking right along with him. But right now, that wasn't who I wanted to be.

Across the street, the entrance to the club had a line that wrapped around the block. This was the type of place where the young and sexy stood in line for hours hoping to get a taste of what was inside. I was at least ten years older than most the hopeful partiers, but that never mattered. Not for my purposes, anyway. I quickly typed and pressed send.

Crazy, man. I'll take a look when I get back.

Branson must have had his answer ready because he replied before I could turn the phone off.

I bet Nana would know the combination.

My heart squeezed like twisting the last bit of moisture from a towel. We all missed Nana, but she missed her dead son, and she wouldn't come back until she was finished with this stage of her grief. No one had thought we'd still be wondering where the woman was weeks after she'd left, but Nana wasn't as frail as most people were picturing. It was almost as if her absence had made people forget the tough-as-nails woman she'd been. I sent back a smiley face, growled at myself, and shoved my phone in my pocket after finally turning the damn thing off.

Yes, the conversation with Branson was important, but that wasn't who I wanted to be right now, and since I couldn't do both, I had to choose. Spineless, agreeable Aver was who I was most of the time, I could only be the alpha I felt within when I carved the time to get away. And that time was rapidly ticking by.

I rolled my shoulders back, shaking away the tension Branson's texts had tried to bring in. My breathing evened out, my lungs expanding and deflating at a steady, cautious pace. Normally, I kept my senses close to my body, but now, I let them run wild. The effect was like taking off sunglasses after a long day and realizing the world wasn't at all how you saw it.

I could hear and smell farther than that which was in my immediate area. There was a couple fighting in their apartment at the end of the block. At the far end of the street, a man ate a hotdog with relish and ketchup. I couldn't see him, but I could smell him.

Directly in front of me, the scents coming from the nightclub were enough to bring my alpha bounding out. Sweat-soaked skin, a relentless, pounding dance beat, and laughter.

I took the first step off the curb and crossed the street taking such wide steps I was on the other side before I finished exhaling. Those in the front of the long line eyed me. A few scowled, clearly upset that I believed myself more important than them.

I bypassed the line, stopping in front of the bouncer, Sai. The handful of times I'd been to this place before, Sai'd had no trouble keeping the masses back. He painted an imposing picture at seven feet with a body of solid muscle and a bushy beard as black as the waves of hair on his head.

"Mr. W, it's been a while." I never gave out my name other than Mr. W and always paid in cash. I didn't need anyone following a paper trail.

"Too long," I grunted. "What's it look like in there?"

He nodded. "Ripe. You picked a good night."

"Any night I get out here is a good night." I sounded arrogant, but I was fine with that. I wasn't back home where arrogance was a slippery slope.

I slipped Sai a folded hundred dollar bill. I wasn't stupid. I knew he was only so casual with me because I was one of the few people he'd met in his life who could kick his ass and because whenever I went out, I paved my road to a wild night with money.

I wasn't crying over it. The money was mine to spend. Walker Construction had been turning a profit for years, and there weren't a lot of home expenses. I didn't have a mate or child to spend my money caring for. I wasn't into fancy cars or any other habit—other than Lawrence—that would happily lighten my pockets.

This was my hobby.

I went out to the city, let loose, and blew a shitload of money in a single night. At the end of the night or the next morning—as the case usually was—I made sure to leave behind smiling, happy faces.

When it was time to go out again, I never chose the same lover twice, and I was *always* careful. Things were too messy otherwise, and no matter how much fun I had, no matter how *free* I felt, that part of me always needed to be shoved right back in the closet when the night was over. And, at least this way, I wouldn't accidentally get anyone pregnant—a worry we hadn't had to concern ourselves with until recently.

At least, that was the reason I told myself for why I always used condoms. The sadder, more pathetic explanation was at least this way, I could claim ignorance. I could tell myself I didn't lack whatever masculine magic had made my cousins able to impregnate their mates. I was simply more cautious.

Bullshit.

Sai leaned to the left and opened the door while simultaneously giving the line a glare that dared them to say something about it. No one did, but more than one gaze sized me up. Those who didn't already know who I was were probably memorizing my face for when they finally made it inside.

I winked at a cute preppy guy standing in front, his eyes twinkling beneath my attention.

He was definitely a contender for *Aver's Partner for the Evening,* but I'd have to get inside before I knew for sure.

"See ya later, Sai."

"Yeah, yeah, save some for the rest of us," he called back, but I was already inside the narrow dark hallway.

At the coat check, I sloughed off my jacket and handed it to the man behind the counter. He was extremely thin with long, sleek, red hair and wore a slinky black dress that hugged every angle. He handed me my ticket with a demure smile.

"I was wondering when we'd see you back," he purred, letting his fingers linger in my palm.

My lips stretched into an arrogant grin. "Here I am."

He propped his other elbow against the counter and let his chin sink into his hand. "There you are." Every word dripped sex. Clearly, the man imagined the two of us wrapped around each other. But I hadn't waited weeks for this night just to stop at coat check.

"See you inside," I shot back over my shoulder as the other man fanned his face. The hallway opened to the main room, a wide square space with a dance floor and a few tables around it that were always stuffed full with far too many people than the table had been built for. There was a bar on this level as well that ran along the length of the room. Customers stood three and four people deep, waiting for their chance to catch the bartender's attention.

At that moment, there was a curly-haired red head draped over the bar top, commanding the full attention of all three of the bartenders. He said something while twirling a thick ringlet in his fingers. I smirked, and the sexy redhead's gaze turned to me, like I'd called his name. Our gazes collided, and I had the strangest suspicion that I wasn't the only person playing pretend tonight.

By then, the bouncer who manned the VIP level had either spotted me or been informed that I'd arrived because he appeared by my side, smoothly waving his arm, creating a wide berth for me to continue forward. "Mr. W, we have your table ready."

I had a similar table at every high-end gay nightclub in Seattle. That hadn't always been the case, but it had taken only a few nights of competing over the music and the other patrons to realize I couldn't do that every time. My nights out were too infrequent to waste a single moment.

My table was in the corner in a corded-off section that also included a sofa that looked out over the dance floor. Up here, where the shadows kept much of the space cloaked, I could do whatever I wanted. Some nights I spent hours just watching the dancers, writhing and rolling over one another. The sight never failed to arouse. I didn't know the people dancing, would never speak to most of them in my life, but in those moments, it was as if they'd joined together forming a single, throbbing, carnal beast for me to enjoy.

I wasn't in the mood to just watch tonight. Back in Walker County, the recent pack-related squabbling had made keeping my aggressive side hidden more difficult than ever. There'd been moments when I'd failed and had let the cracks show. Blaming Wyatt for Alpha Walker's illness had been one of those times. And if I wanted to keep that side of me back, then I needed to find someone tonight to help me take out those aggressions in a way we'd both enjoy.

There was only waitstaff in the VIP level, and my server for the night sauntered forward. His tan chest was bare. Rainbow suspenders, attached to a pair of black booty shorts, stretched and bunched over his nipples as he walked. He flashed me a smile, and I had no doubt he'd practiced grinning in the mirror to find the right intensity to make his dimples pop.

"Grey Goose on the rocks."

I'd disappointed him, skipping over the part where he got to flirt, but he'd get tipped all the same.

My attention transitioned to the dancers below. From this viewpoint, there wasn't a corner that I couldn't see. I spotted the cute preppy guy from outside. The interest I'd had in him faded, my gaze drawn to the energy coming from the dance floor.

Sometimes, I wished things were easier or that I could find someone like my cousins. I'd watched over the months while each of them had found the men they were meant to be with. I'd been happy each and every time, but the truth was I could never live like they were allowed to live. The need to prove myself had gone on for too long, I couldn't give it up now. More reason why I shouldn't waste a single moment of this night.

I looked back over the rolling mass of limbs on the bottom floor. The mess of motion and chaos made singling out any one dancer difficult.

But I had no problem seeing *him*.

My thighs tightened, attempting to coax me to my feet. I

remained seated, giving a sharp nod of gratitude to the server when he returned with my drink. My gaze never budged, not even when I reached forward to grab the glass from the table. I took a sip, letting the crisp vodka pour down my throat. The man on the dance floor moved with a freedom I'd never experienced. My heart pounded in my ears, drowning out every other sound. I sucked in a sharp breath, exhaling on a low growl I couldn't put a stop to.

He didn't wear anything especially tight or flashy: whitewashed jeans and a blue dotted button-up. He wiggled in a half circle—laughing at something one of the other dancers had said—and stuck his ass out, revealing a strip of neon fabric at his waist.

My fingers tightened around the glass. Though there were many in that very room who wore far less, I found that tiny peek of his thong to be more arousing than any of the other flesh on display.

The man beamed, his chin-length, wavy blond hair swaying with the beat. Every alpha instinct I possessed rose to the surface. It wasn't clear from the man's outfit what he was here for, but the joy on his face as he danced was clear.

I didn't know what the man had come for, but I knew who he'd leave with.

2

HOLLISTER

THE ATMOSPHERE in the room sharpened, and I sat straight, attempting to find the cause. In any other instance, I would've assumed someone had brushed by me and that my skin had come in contact with something of theirs without me knowing. But, I didn't feel the rush of emotions I would have expected if that were the case. The feeling was more subtle, like unlocking a door I hadn't known was closed until it wasn't.

My head turned, my gaze like a divining rod attempting to locate the source of the feeling. A man with his back to us took the stairs that led to the second level and the VIP tables. He had dark blond hair and wore an expensive suit. That was all I could tell from so far away. For as many times as I'd come to this place with my friends, we'd never made it to the second floor. More than half the times we'd come to this club, we bought drinks to share, pooling our meager funds to make the most of the night. None of us were VIP-table people.

"It doesn't count as cheating if you're tired," Jorge said to Sprinkles, bring my attention to the conversation at hand.

Jorge couldn't pass a chance to impart some of his wisdom on the newest and youngest member to our friend group.

Sprinkles was the youngest, but it wasn't an easy life that had brought him to where he was. When Sam and I had found him, Sprinkles had been huddled under a paper grocery bag he'd torn open to use as a blanket. While he wasn't as clueless as the others seem to think he was, he always took the others' constant mentoring in stride.

This time, Sam was quick to jump in. "Don't listen to Jorge, Sprinkles. It's always cheating if you're in a committed relationship and the other person isn't aware and hasn't given their consent. All the time, *even* if you're tired."

Jorge leaned over the table so he could be heard over the pounding music. "You mean to tell me if I fall asleep with a man, and he starts touching me in the middle of the night, and I respond to those touches, and then we make dirty, filthy noises all night, that's somehow my fault?" His words slurred together. Not only was Jorge a lightweight, but he hit these nights out like a racehorse sprinting toward intoxication.

Sam pushed the empties from the center of the table to the side and leaned his narrow face into the space he'd created. The light overhead made his bushy eyebrows even bigger. "Yes, even then. That is cheating."

I sat back in my chair to give the others more room to square off. I didn't know why the club lined the dance floor with these small circular tables. They were only big enough for two, but there was always a group that ended up huddled around each one. The table was already cluttered with empty glasses—and Jorge's elbows—and was about to get a lot more cluttered as Jazz worked his way from the bar back to us. His red curly hair bounced with each step.

Jazz carried a tray with several shot glasses full of

brightly colored liquid on its surface. He caught my gaze and shot me a wink cheesy enough for a toothpaste commercial. Jazz was so unapologetically and authentically himself that I always had a great time whenever he was in town. Tonight, he'd declared the drinks would be on him and had kept the booze flowing at a rate I would feel the next day. I wasn't too tipsy yet but only because I'd started skipping every other round.

Most nights, my friends and I hung out at a place closer to where we all lived and more suited to our prospective incomes. We didn't always drink a lot, or at all, but down in the city at night was one of the best times to find people in trouble. Sam had founded the You Belong Outreach when he had been in high school. At that time, his outreach was just him, walking around and passing out items he'd been able to collect to those in need. In the time since, Sam had grown his one-man operation into a city-wide movement. He'd opened a physical shelter that specialized in offering LGBT youths a safe, clean place to sleep at night and, with the help of employees and volunteers—like myself— canvassed the streets on a daily and nightly basis, handing out information, hygiene products, and food to those in need.

But, while the mission was important to us both, not every night was for outreach. Especially not nights when Jazz came into town. It was too hard telling the boy no for one, and for two, a night out with Jazz was guaranteed to be an amazing time. In comparison, this night had been fairly tame.

That man swam into mind. The feeling I'd gotten when he'd come in the room hadn't been tame. Not at all. It had felt like...being seen. Like that moment when you're dreaming and realize you've gone to school without your pants on again. I bit the inside of my cheek hard. I had no reason to think of that rich douche again.

Especially since we were out with Jazz. He didn't live in the Seattle area like the rest of us. He floated around the country, which wasn't so odd compared to the lifestyles of the rest of my friends. The one quality that united us was that we all lived our lives marching to our own drummers. The true miracle had been finding so many people whose drums pounded similarly to mine.

"Who's ready to taste the rainbow?" Jazz sung the question like he was in a campy musical.

Sam glared at the drinks. "These all keep looking like drinks I'll be tasting a second time tomorrow morning."

"Nonsense. You'll pee it out first. Then you'll throw up bile." Jazz smiled. Only he could make the word bile seem sort of charming. He had one of those big mouths that could smile incredibly wide. I liked to think he simply had a face that was meant to be happy. "Good thing that's a problem for future Sam to worry about."

Sam tried not to smirk, but it was useless. The world was putty in Jazz's hands.

"When you were at the bar, did you see that guy?" I asked Jazz, pointing my forehead toward the VIP steps.

"What guy?" Jazz followed my gesture to the second floor. "Oh. Yeah. I saw him. Why?"

That hadn't quite been the response I'd expected. Jazz normally effused with a tad more vigor. I'd seen him nearly faint over men not even half as attractive as that guy. I shrugged. "I don't know. He felt..." I shook my head.

I couldn't always trust my feelings. Not when they weren't always my own.

Sam and Jorge turned their heads toward the VIP

section while Sprinkles lifted his hand and pointed. "You mean that guy?"

I lunged over the table to rip Sprinkles's arm down or off —whichever would stop trying to kill me by way of utter mortification. "No, not that guy. It was no one, actually. Let's move on—"

"If he's got you this worked up, there must be something special about him," Jorge added. "Want me to relieve him of his wallet, and you can work your mojo?"

Jorge's journey to his present self had been colored and included several years of stealing what he could to survive living on the streets. He'd since given up his life of a pick-pocket, but I had a hunch he went out to keep his skills sharp every once in a while. I didn't approve of the stealing, but I understood being backed into a corner. I also under-stood how, having gone through something like that, he'd never believe the life he had at the moment would be the life he'll always have and wanting to make sure he had his survival skills to fall back on.

My mojo. Sometimes it felt more like a curse. But on most days, it was my blessing. One day when I was very young, my life changed. When I touched things that belonged to other people, things that they'd had around or on them during particularly emotion-packed moments, I *felt* the emotional history of what I touched.

I thought it had something to do with sensing energy waves or auras, but it was easier to describe to my friends by just calling it my mojo. It wasn't a skill I was ashamed of. I'd be a hypocrite if I were, since reading auras from people's things was how I afforded to live at all. I offered fortune telling to the tourists on the sidewalks. The schtick was they would ask a question. Then I would ask them to give me something of theirs. Most people handed over a watch or an umbrella. It didn't matter. The emotions were almost always enough to make an educated guess.

It was a gamble each time, and I just had to hope an item didn't carry a bad aura. Objects that had been present during horrible events were the worst. The negative emotions clung to me like memories refusing to fade. It was the same when an object had a happy history too. Basically, I was tofu, and there were some flavors, some emotions, that I *did not* want to soak in.

I bit the inside of my cheek again. I couldn't seem to concentrate, but I remembered Jorge's question a second before it could seem too obvious. "You promised your life of crime was behind you," I said with a smile.

Jorge grinned, leaned to the side, and planted a chaste kiss on the tip of my nose. "Only for you, Holly Golightly."

That was one of those nicknames I had, whether I wanted it or not. Personally, I didn't see any connections between myself and the main character of *Breakfast at Tiffany's*, but my friends liked to pretend they did. And there weren't a lot of other ways to get a nickname out of Hollister anyway.

The energy in the room seemed to pulse and gather, funneling directly into my limbs. It buzzed through my veins, making staying put impossible. "I have an idea better than petty theft." I got to my feet, prompting the others to copy me. "Let's dance."

"I'm gonna have to sit this one out," Jazz shouted before any of us could get too far.

"What? You're leaving?" I navigated through the maze of pushed-out chairs to get to him. "Why? Is everything okay?"

Had Jazz gotten a weird feeling too? Was that what this was? But, if he had, why not admit as much? It wasn't like he could think I would have a problem with it.

"But the night was just getting fun!" Jorge slurred.

"And yours doesn't have to end," Jazz said, patting his face with honest affection. "They've been instructed to keep your drinks flowing, but I'm afraid it's time for me to move on."

"Oh, cool! Night, Jazz!" Jorge shouted as he walked away.

At the same time, Sam tugged Sprinkles away with him. "See you next time! Thanks for the drinks!"

Jazz's mouth dropped open with shock. I was close enough to hear his little squeak of indignation. Before his feelings could grow really hurt, they turned around laughing.

"Your face," Jorge squealed, pulling Jazz into a hug while the others piled on top of him. "We love you. We know you're slumming it when you come hang, but we still love you."

I added my arms to the hug pretzel.

Jazz's cheeks went pink. With his red curls, it wasn't his best look. "Thanks, guys. Even if you truly have no idea who I really am." He said the last bit like he was auditioning to be the next Batman.

I let the side of my head fall against his. "We don't care. We'll still love you."

"Awww—okay—enough sap. I'm going to throw up. Get away from me. Go dance. But...wait for me." His face went solemn. "Save yourself for me?"

Sam, Sprinkles, and Jorge booed, but I could only laugh. I waved him away like a loved one sending someone to war. When he disappeared down the hallway, I spun on my toe. That was always more impressive when I wore something with tassels. "Let's dance."

This sort of scene still made Sprinkles a little nervous.

He swore he was ready to get out and try, so he wanted to be here, even if it sometimes brought memories back. He'd be staying close to Sam's side while we were on the dance floor. Jorge, however, had been descended upon immediately. I caught his eye while he was surrounded by three burly men. Jorge fanned himself and sent me a smirk that said he was exactly where he wanted to be.

I spun in the other direction, closing my eyes as I felt nothing but the beat, rumbling through me. That was until I felt a finger tap my shoulder. My look of confusion turned into one of delight when I saw who stood there. "Lee! Hey!" I pulled him into a hug. I'd first met Lee a few years back at one of the You Belong fundraisers I'd helped Sam with. "Was this the club you got a job at?"

"Yeah. The tips are even better than I imagined." Lee took a step back. "I'm swamped, but I heard you asking about Mr. W."

I frowned. "Who?"

Lee jerked his chin to the upper level. "Mr. W. I haven't been here long, so I haven't seen him in action, but the other employees talk about him all the time. Rumors say he's old money. I think he has a touch of the serial killer myself, but anyone who ever goes off with him spends the weeks following whispering about their night with him. It's like they come back possessed."

I shuddered, but I didn't think it meant the same as when Lee did it. Lee's reaction seemed steeped mostly in desire. To hear Lee describe the man, he was like a demon or the Devil himself. No thank you. I'd come face to face with enough demons. I didn't need to invite them into my life.

I waved to Lee as he rushed to the bar with his notepad in hand. It was nice of him to warn me, even if he'd assumed my interest in the blond demon had been stronger than it was.

After checking in on Jorge and the others, I closed my eyes again, determined to clear my mind and let the music move me. When I opened my eyes, I realized I'd *followed the rhythm* to the stairs that led to the VIP level.

"What the heck? No, Hollister." Great. Now I was talking to myself. I shuffled away from the stairs, deeper into the mass of people and tried to lose myself. Thankfully, I was able to keep a reasonable bubble around me so I wasn't bumping into anyone's emotional baggage. My eyelids still flew open, and my head turned as if tugged by an invisible rope toward the far corner of the second-floor lounge.

When our eyes met, I saw a spark. I didn't mean I recognized an attraction, but that for a brief second, something in the air between our bodies illuminated. I licked my lips if only so I could prove I remembered how. My body continued to sway on autopilot as the demon lifted the glass in his hand to me in recognition. He brought the drink to his lips, and when he swallowed, I couldn't help but swallow along.

I brought my hand to my throat, caressing down the side of my neck while continuing to hold complete eye contact. He brought the drink back down, resting it casually against his knee as he stared without blinking. My hips wiggled and rolled with the movement, which wasn't so odd, since I liked to dance. I didn't always like dancing sexy, but when the music moved me, I didn't often feel like I had complete control. I felt that way now, out of control, like my body was responding to the other man's attention—enticing him—without me expressly telling it to.

I bit my lip, my teeth sliding to snag a chunk of my inner cheek instead. Dull pain throbbed in my mouth, and I was able to rip my eyes free from the man, spinning in a circle. Even then, I didn't spin all the way around as I'd wanted to. I danced with my profile to the man—Mr. W.

As someone who survived by reading auras and energy from other people, I knew some people were just too charismatic. Jazz came to mind, when there was something about a person that made it impossible to do anything but follow blindly. At least with Jazz, he was good, so you knew you'd never get into too much trouble around him. But this man... he didn't strike me as all that good. The way he let his eyes climb over my body like he owned it already shouldn't have made my dick twitch as it did. Plus, he was on the second level. A guy like that wanted me for one thing, which was normally fine too. I'd had memories from wild nights I cherished even though there was no chance of it ever being repeated.

The difference now was that I'd felt like a moth hypnotized by this man's flame from the moment he stepped inside the club. And for what reason? The most interaction we'd had was just then, when he'd tilted his glass at me. I had no reason to feel as I did, like I'd been dancing for him alone, trapped and helpless beneath his gaze.

I *wasn't* helpless—had worked pretty hard at not being helpless, actually, and I wasn't going to start now. I kept dancing, keeping my movements distinctly non-sexual. I channeled the dance of my youth, when I'd been so happy to be out and free that my arms and legs had moved without concern for what they looked like but filled to the brim with joy.

That kept my attention for about ten seconds, but when my gaze flitted back to the darkened corner of the upper level, the chair Mr. W had been sitting in was empty. I didn't have time to wonder where he'd gone. In the next moment, a pair of hands settled on the swells of my hips as the body standing at my backside rolled against me in time with the music. I grinned, and a feeling of triumph lifted my smile wider.

"Couldn't resist?" I purred, leaning my head back. I peered up, fluttering my eyelashes with coquettish innocence. My gaze landed on a stranger. I jerked forward, out of his grip, but he resettled his hands on my hips and pulled my ass back into his crotch. Now that I knew it wasn't my blond demon thrusting against me, the feeling of the man's erection on my backside felt more like those moments when the city bus was overcrowded and you had to ride the whole line with some jerk's elbow in your ribs.

"Not when you move like that," he replied. I felt bad for the man. There was nothing wrong with trying to dance with someone. He didn't know I'd been hoping for someone else. But, it wasn't my responsibility to accept his advances simply because he'd made his attraction known.

"Thanks, but I'm more into solo dancing tonight." I wiggled out from under his palms a second time.

I waited with my breath caught in my throat. My head turned back to the dance floor, where Sam was dancing with Sparkles. The younger man twirled with his hands in the air having the time of his life while Sam watched me. He lifted his eyebrows, and I waved his concern away.

This was always the moment when the true nature of a man was revealed, those seconds after rejection. With my back to him, the man reached forward, snagging my hips again and pulling me against him so hard I stumbled into his chest. "You don't dance like that if you aren't looking for someone to manhandle you."

I frowned. This guy must have picked up his dating habits from old romance novels. "Incorrect," I huffed, wishing the music wasn't so loud for a second, only so I could explain to this man all the ways he was wrong. If he didn't let up on his fingers pressing against my hipbone, he was going to get an elbow in his gut.

"Let me go." When he didn't, I recalled the self defense classes I'd taken at the Y. I cocked my arm and sent the point of my elbow flying back. The bony tip made impact, but the body I'd collided with was rock hard, and pain blossomed out from my elbow.

What the hell? Was this guy made of stone? I whirled around to ask just that, and my breath whooshed out from my mouth at the face of Mr. W. He was so much more handsome up close. From far away, his features had been masculine but cold. Close up, he looked like a man who could smile. If that made any sense.

But he certainly wasn't the dude who had been standing there. I rubbed my elbow with my other hand. My eyebrows furrowed and stretched to look around him. "Where's the other guy?"

"He had to go." Mr. W stepped to the side smoothly, blocking my view from a group of people crowding around something on the floor. He offered me his hand, palm up. "I enjoyed watching you. Have you had enough dancing?" he asked, like we'd come to the club together and I'd spent the night dancing for him.

A part of me bristled against his arrogance, but only a small part. The rest of me wanted to take his hand. At least he'd done what the other guy hadn't—asked me. I checked out his hand, looking out for a watch or ring that I might touch accidentally. I didn't always have to worry. If I touched something with no strong emotional ties, like a shirt or pair of pants a person wore every day without incident, then I'd feel close to nothing. If that person happened to murder someone while wearing that shirt or pair of pants, that was a different story.

At the least, I'd be able to give Lee more insight into his serial killer theory.

"What did you have in mind?" My voice came out breathier than I'd intended.

The man pinned me with his glittering green eyes. They weren't flashy or bright but a dark, muted green that reminded me of the forest. His lips curled like I'd asked a question far more carnal. "Let's talk first." He leaned back, letting his gaze rake up and down my body. "If I tell you what I have in mind now, you're liable to give me a second elbow." He massaged the spot on his ribs I'd hit, though I had a feeling my elbow hurt more than he did.

Laughter bubbled out of me, and I took his hand. If he was a killer, I'd find out before I fell too hard. I brushed his sleeve with my fingers, but the only thing I felt was lust, pure and unbridled. It wasn't all mine either. I gasped against the sudden supercharged flow of passion. He pulled me in, wasting no time latching me to his side. I inhaled his fresh, clean scent, and his hand tightened around my waist.

He was in control as he navigated us out of the crowd and toward the stairs. I looked over my shoulder at the crowd of people and spotted the man who had trouble taking no for an answer. He sat up on the floor, looking around like he was confused about where he was. I felt bad but not bad enough that I didn't smirk. Next time, he'd listen to a person's words.

My stomach fluttered, rolling with each ascending step up the stairs. There'd been a bouncer at the bottom manning the rope that divided the stairs from the general public. He closed it behind us as we passed, and even though we were still in a crowded club and my friends were within sight, a small thrill of fear shivered up my spine. With his warm hand cupped around my side, I didn't have to worry about where we were walking. He led the way. I had a feeling, if I stopped walking, he'd have no trouble carrying me away like I was his prize to be enjoyed.

He led me to the corner and sat on the couch instead of the chair I'd spotted him in earlier. The thought occurred that I should take the chair, but when he patted the cushion next to him, that thought disappeared.

I took a seat, leaving a half foot of space between us. Mr. W smirked at the narrow expanse of cushion that divided us. He leaned forward, snagging one of the drinks from the table, and took a sip.

I frowned. "That's dangerous." I didn't care how much money you had or how powerful you were in your regular life; anyone could get drugged. He'd left these drinks when he'd come down the stairs.

Mr. W arched a single brow. "You worried someone slipped something in?" he asked.

I nodded, aware I was killing the mood. But what good was flirting when you were going to wind up knocked out in an alley later anyway?

He frowned. "Has that happened to you before?" He growled the words out, but rather than feeling intimidated, the sound made me want to press into him like a cat happy their owner was home.

Out of instinct, I reached for his sleeve again, fingering the hem between my pointer and forefinger. For a second time, I felt a tsunami of lust pour from him. I'd never felt anything like it before from any other person or object. My head felt light while all the blood in my body flowed directly to my dick. "No, but because I'm careful. I've heard of it happening often enough that I know it does."

That seemed to relieve the other man. I'd been expecting frustration. Men like him were used to getting what they wanted exactly when they wanted. But though Mr. W seemed exactly like that type of man, he didn't act upset at all. He lifted his hand in the air, and a server rushed to his side of the couch. It wasn't Lee, and I didn't recognize them, but that didn't matter since they didn't look at me anyway.

"Take these and bring me two cups of ice and an *unopened* bottle of Grey Goose." Mr. W turned from the server like he was impatient to be alone with me again.

I exhaled a worried breath and sunk into the cushion. "That was pretty slick."

Mr. W's lips curled in the corners. "Thank you."

I narrowed my eyes. It was impossible for me to get a good read on the man. His confidence was undeniable, but just then, it was like I was seeing a different part of him, no less confident but a little less arrogant. The server returned with his order and left the items on the table without a word.

As Mr. W poured our drinks, I stretched my neck to look over the railing. My friends were down there dancing still. Jorge shot me a thumbs up. I looked over at Mr. W to see if he'd noticed. His eyes were on me. He handed me a glass, and my fingers brushed over his skin. I didn't even touch something of his, but that same surge of desire reared up nonetheless. I wiggled, attempting to give my dick a little more room. I was leaking so much precum. If we kept this up, it would be impossible to hide the wet spot that threatened to soak through the front of my pants. My butt muscles clenched, reminding me of how long it had been since I'd seen any action.

I exhaled slowly, hoping Mr. W wouldn't notice how

worked up I'd gotten from simply *sitting near* him. Our legs weren't even touching.

His grin was knowing when he lifted his glass to his lips. I copied him, if only so I had something to do. What was wrong with me? I'd danced this little dance before, but now, it was like I was stumbling through the steps for the first time. Mr. W unnerved me at the same time he made me feel...*protected*.

The vodka didn't burn too badly. Not only was it a higher quality than I normally sprung for, but the ice had melted just enough to take the edge off.

I still winced when I swallowed. "You have a reputation." It would be best to get that part of this night over with.

His eyebrow arched a second time. "A good one?"

I didn't want to say Lee's name, in case this guy wasn't happy about the employees gossiping about him. "A mysterious one. They say no one knows who you are, that you're known only as Mr. W, you come and go as you like, and anyone who ever spends a night with you talks about their time in hushed whispers." I'd given him enough ammunition to keep his head big for years to come, so it was odd when he frowned.

"I suppose that's all true. Except the hushed whispers part." He took another sip, bouncing his index finger along the rim as he balanced his glass back on his knee. "Does that bother you?"

I tilted my head to the side. How could he still manage to seem vulnerable while also looking like he ruled the world and everyone living in it? "Why would that bother me? We're just talking."

His smile matched mine. "Good boy."

Hearing that slight praise shouldn't have made me feel as good as it did. I was a young gay man who had made it a point to spend my early years exploring every facet of my sexuality. I'd played around with kinks in the past, but it had always felt just like that—playing. Cuddling up against this man and purring in response to his slight praise felt nothing like playing; it felt natural.

"Since we're *just talking.*" Mr. W's tone dipped low. "What's your name?"

I'd been drinking slowly all night, so I knew it wasn't the burn of the vodka that made me smile like a cat who caught the canary. "I don't know. That feels a little personal. We should start with questions that are a little less invasive." I enjoyed being in control of information that this man wanted a little too much.

He leaned in, bracing his elbow over the top of the couch. I hadn't expected the playful smirk that played over his lips. "Are we talking a negotiation?"

"Don't negotiations usually require both parties to have something of worth to the other? I have information. What do you have, Mr. W?"

A sultry fire burned in his green gaze, but he nodded and kept the pretense of the game going. "That is true. Who would've guessed I'd chosen a sharp businessman for the night?"

I didn't think he meant anything he said as an insult, but it felt close enough that my back stiffened.

Mr. W leaned in, fluidly cupping my chin and cheek with his warm palm.

I wouldn't sink into his touch, no matter how much I wanted to.

"My intention wasn't to tease you. I'm enjoying this." He let his thumb graze over my lips.

The feather-light touch sent tendrils of excitement further down my body. Forget the vodka. All I needed was his hands on my body, and I was drunk with lust. No man should hold this much power.

"It's a far cry better than the usual banal small talk. Where are you from? What's your favorite movie?"

"You've never heard of it and *Twilight*."

This time, it was Mr. W who stiffened. "Please don't tell me you're a sparkly vampire lover." He'd leaned in so close I heard and felt his words tickle the wild pulse pounding in my neck.

I didn't know if it made me a stereotype, a cliché, or unique, but I knew I didn't care. I was over letting people tease me for the things I enjoyed. But it didn't feel like Mr. W's teases were anything more than playful. "Proud of it. Firmly Team Edward. Don't even come at me with any of this Team Jacob bullshit. He ended up with her *daughter,* and if you think I would ever let something like that fly..."

I'd intended for Mr. W to laugh, but he suddenly got a strange look on his face, and I forgot what I'd been going to say. He recovered quickly, sliding closer as he replied. "You'll get no argument from me, but because I don't know what you're talking about. I've heard of the movies, but we've already surpassed all that I know of them. I do know vampires shouldn't sparkle. Nosferatu, now that's a creature of the night you can get behind."

I snorted, and after a second, Mr. W did as well.

"I can see now how I should have rethought my wording."

I couldn't help my laughter. My head tilted back, resting lightly on the cushion behind my head. When I could look at him again, his eyes tilted down in the corners, and he had a small smile on his face. "What? Do I have drool?" I wiped my chin.

"No." Mr. W shook his head. "No drool." There was a

sweetness in the curve of his lips that had my tongue darting out to moisten my own dry lips.

Suddenly, I didn't want to tease anymore. I *needed* this man to know my name. "I'm Hollister. My friends call me... well, just call me Hollister."

"You know my name."

I frowned, and the motion felt odd after so long smiling. "That's all I get?"

He smiled, but I didn't believe it. "That's all *we* get."

I didn't understand the change in words, but I wasn't sure if I was supposed to. I realized I had a choice: either accept this limit and let the night continue or decide it was too weird and cut and run. But choosing the latter meant not being in this man's presence anymore, and when I looked at it that way, I didn't really have a choice. My skin sung from simply sitting near him. He'd barely touched me, and I already felt like putty in his hands. "I'll just have to come up with a nickname for you then."

His lips twitched. "What are the contenders?"

Only one. "Blond demon," I whispered.

That time, Mr. W was the one to laugh. He looked delighted at my suggestion, and I didn't know what that said about him. I wasn't used to not being able to read a person. With tourists, it was almost too easy to tell what type of a person they were. Being on vacation only heightened the best or worst in people. Shitty people became utter assholes on vacation. But Mr. W was all over the place. Arrogant and confident one moment, unassuming and kind the next. And, when I did meet a tourist who was more difficult to read, touching something of theirs filled in the blanks. Touching anything on Mr. W just made me wildly and uncontrollably horny.

Mr. W had wiped the laughter from his face. "I don't

think I've done nearly enough to earn that sort of name," he murmured. His face swam nearer, and though I prided myself on being a quick-witted, unflappable young gay of the world, my spine sunk into the cushion as I sat pinned beneath his ever-growing closeness.

His lips skimmed over mine in the lightest kiss that could still be called as much. It wasn't enough, and yet the rush of adrenaline made me gasp. Mr. W took my parting lips as an invitation for his tongue. He wasn't tentative or hesitant, but he didn't demand anything of me as well. His kisses felt inevitable, and thank the Goddess that was true because now that I'd had one, I never wanted them to stop.

There I'd been, wondering if he was the pushy one, and yet I was the one who sprang up. I was the one who straddled his lap, and I was the one whose tongue thrust into his mouth with wild abandon.

I knew after the fact what I'd been doing: testing Mr. W's boundaries, whether he'd take control back or let me run with it.

He did not let me run.

One moment, I was in the dominant position, straddling his lap and squeezing his legs between my thighs. Then he made a growling sound, and suddenly, my back was against the cushions again. Our positions hadn't reversed, but I felt very much nestled beneath his considerable weight. Mr. W was a large man, both by height and muscle mass. That fact had never been more obvious than right then, as he sheltered me between his arms. All the while, our lips never parted.

My dick throbbed. The hard shaft pushed against the zipper. I had no doubt Mr. W could feel my erection as plainly as I felt his, insistently and firmly nudging my waist. I pumped my hips, too turned on to care we were still in a public place. If Mr. W reached down my pants and pulled me out for the whole club to see, I'd let him. And not because I was into exhibitionism; that normally wasn't my thing. But if Mr. W was the one asking...

His lips wrenched from me so abruptly it took my brain a few extra seconds to catch up. My heart dropped as my eyes fluttered open again. We were done with the kissing?

When I peered up into Mr. W's handsome face, the desire raging in his eyes told me we weren't. But then why were we getting up?

"Where are we going?" I asked, still in a daze from his kisses.

"Someplace I can enjoy this without anyone watching you move like that," he snarled, but there was no anger, only masculine determination.

I dug my heels into the ground, and Mr. W bounced against my backside. He caught me before I could trip forward. I spun around and looked up into his face. At the moment, the arrogant, confident side of him was winning. He looked a second away from draping me over his shoulder and carting me away, with or without my permission.

I pressed my hands against his chest, realizing my mistake the second my fingers curled to grip him closer instead of holding him away. "I'm not going to just leave with you to wherever you say. You're a stranger." He had to at least see how not even having his name would make disappearing with him a stupid decision.

His chest rumbled like he was half animal. "What are you saying, Hollister?"

For a crazy second, I wondered what he'd do if I said I was putting a stop to our time together completely. The rational, reasonable part of my mind said that he better accept my decisions or face the consequences. But the less rational, less reasonable, hornier side of my mind wanted to push him just to see what he'd do.

Until I knew his boundaries better, that was a very stupid thing to do. Besides, I didn't want to be done kissing him either. "We just met. You could be a killer! I'll take you to my place." I regretted suggesting it the moment the last word came out of my mouth. I didn't even bring my friends back to my place. There was no point when we would all have to crowd into my bedroom the entire time. But I didn't think either of us had anything planned for the night that would require leaving a bedroom, so I went with it. "I don't live far. It's just one bus over." I recognized a small part of me was also still trying to shock him. He was VIP lounge, while I was general public. Maybe he liked the idea of picking up a young, eager friend for the night, and I wasn't above being that for him, but that rebel in me still wanted to show him how very different we were—let him leave *before* things got to a point where I felt left.

Self-sabotage at its finest.

He frowned, and I thought he was going to reject my suggestion. Part of me wanted him to. I wasn't proud of where I lived. But it was a room that I could lock myself inside of and sleep without facing the elements or waking up with some stranger attacking me. And it was all I could afford at the moment. More important than all of that, did I want to spend time with a man who didn't listen to my wants and needs?

I didn't end up needing to answer that question. "Okay, we'll go to your place."

I beamed and grabbed his arm. "Awesome! I'll just go say bye to my friends."

We walked back down the stairs arm in arm. I found the guys back at the cluttered table.

"Heading out?" Sam yelled teasingly over the music. Sprinkles didn't lift his head from where he had it, resting on his arm on the table. I wouldn't be the only one leaving soon.

I nodded.

Jorge narrowed his eyes at Mr. W. "Be safe. Have fun." To Mr. W he used two of his fingers to point at his own eyes and then at Mr. W in the universal sign for *I'm watching you.* "I know what you look like."

I tightened my arm around Mr. W's and tugged him away before Jorge could issue any more threats. My stomach jumped, doing a gymnastic act that would've won golds across the board. Was I really taking an incredibly sexy, altogether intimidating man back to my house after knowing him for less than twenty minutes?

3

AVER

HOLLISTER'S HAND remained in mine the entire trip south. The Uber stopped finally in front of a squat two-story home. The remnants of a cyclone fence sat in the small, patchy yard out front. The path to the door wasn't so much a designated passage as it was simply where the ground had been packed and condensed enough to form a smooth, dirt surface that I was sure turned into mud at the first hint of rain. As the owner of a construction company, I was appalled. As the man who'd lain claim to Hollister for the evening, I was disturbed. A man stood hunched at the corner segment of the crumbling fence. His back was to the street while his hands clearly fumbled with his crotch. Somewhere on the street someone had their music blaring. I couldn't decipher what kind, only that it had a lot of bass.

"Is this it?" The driver looked from myself back to Hollister.

Good. So I wasn't the only one wondering where the hell we were. The neighborhood had suddenly transformed a few blocks back as if we'd crossed an invisible boundary. I'd spotted no less than two prostitutes in as many blocks and was pretty positive the two gentlemen at the end of the block south of us were currently exchanging drugs for money.

This was where Hollister lived? All the time?

Granted, the Uber ride had officially doubled the amount of time I'd known Hollister, but he was so vibrant and full of joy. Even after knowing him a short time, I knew he was sexy, sweet, and loyal—and he didn't deserve to live inside a home where people pissed in his yard every night.

"Yep!" Hollister chirped, releasing my hand to grab the door handle. I had to fight my urge to lunge across him and keep the door closed. I understood Hollister's reasons for not wanting to follow me blindly out of the club just like I'd appreciated his caution in accepting drinks from strangers.

But this was pushing the limits.

"This is where you live?" I asked, hoping I kept the judgment from my tone.

Despite my efforts, Hollister's head hung between his shoulders. "Yes. It isn't so bad inside though!"

I thanked our driver and climbed out, all while fighting my urge to pick Hollister up and run him out of this neighborhood.

"Hey, you got any change?" the man who had been peeing in Hollister's yard asked.

Hollister tightened his grip on my fingers and tugged me faster down the dirt path. The window next to the front door was cracked, the bottom corner covered with layers of cardboard and plastic garbage bags. He pulled out his key to unlock the front door, but the pressure of pushing his key inside the lock was enough to swing the door open. That was one mystery solved. The house blaring music loudly for the block to *enjoy* was Hollister's house.

A man crossed the hallway from one doorway into what

looked like a living room. Five other people already occupied that space, sitting where there was room among the mess.

I arched a brow at the man as he walked by without acknowledging Hollister's presence. He wore only jeans that hung off his hips. He had a round stomach that hung over the waist of his pants. "Your roommate?"

Hollister pressed his lips together, making it look very much like he was trying not to cry. "One of them."

One?

"I have six. I think. Cameron mentioned bringing his girlfriend to stay since she recently lost her job."

Six, going on seven, in a home that did not look fit for one.

"C'mon, my room is upstairs." He grabbed my hand and pulled me up a set of rickety stairs. I noticed Hollister didn't use the railing and, as I set my hand down on it, realized why. The entire structure shifted beneath my hand. "Oh, no, we don't use that. It's loose."

"Hm." I couldn't say anything else. I wasn't having sex with Hollister in this house. But I also wasn't about to *leave* Hollister here either.

The top of the stairs brought us to the mouth of a short hallway. I wrinkled my nose against the sudden new smell. This was when being a wolf shifter with enhanced senses was annoying.

On the second floor were three doors, one of which was closed with a combination lock. Hollister reached for the lock, spinning the dial as a sharp clucking sound came from one of the other two rooms.

"I, uh...I don't know what that is." Hollister looked over his shoulder.

The two of us peered into the dark sliver where the door

hung open. I didn't think Hollister could see inside without the light, but I could. "Chickens?"

Hollister frowned. "What?" He stomped just inside the room, flinging the light on as he opened the door all the way.

The light must have spooked the rest of the chickens because they began to cluck, squawk, and shake their bodies, sending tiny white feathers into the air.

"These are new," Hollister said without looking at me. His shoulders fell forward, and I couldn't help my urge to pin Hollister against the hallway wall, blocking him from the dirt and danger of this house. His head hung down, and I slid my finger under his chin, turning his face toward me. "This is a disaster, isn't it?" he whispered when our eyes met.

I kept his gaze on me. "You are smoking hot and sexy, and I still want to fuck you," I murmured.

Hollister gasped, sliding his bottom lip between his teeth. "But?"

"No but. That's all I have to say. Well, that and we're both getting the hell out of here right now." At last, I let myself do the thing I'd wanted to do since we got here. I hooked my arm around Hollister's waist, keeping him so tightly to my side his feet lifted off the ground. "Do you need anything from your room?"

He shook his head.

"Good. We're leaving." Our journey down the stairs and out of Hollister's house took only seconds, and yet it wasn't fast enough. His roommates didn't call after us, asking why some stranger was carrying their friend from his home. If I didn't already dislike the people based on the types of things I'd seen strewn over the coffee table, I would've then. I wasn't being a snob; this place wasn't safe.

The cool, outside air felt even more refreshing after breathing in the mix of stale beer, body odor, and animal smells from the inside of Hollister's house. Hollister's lip stuck out in a pout that reminded me how young he was. In his twenties, yes, but his early twenties, while I'd crested closer to forty than thirty. He probably felt embarrassed, but I hadn't left that house only to have the house follow us.

I lifted his frame, leaving Hollister with the choice of either pushing me away or winding his legs around my hips. He chose the latter, and our lips collided with brutal force. My hands molded against his ass, a cheek in each palm. I kneaded the soft flesh, a growl rumbling low in my throat. That hadn't been the first growl to sneak out while in Hollister's company. He had a surfer's charm and a bohemian innocence, but it was his fire, his passion, that I couldn't look away from. I wasn't sure if I'd blinked a single time since spotting him dancing in the club.

But if I wasn't careful now, before my beast took over completely, I'd end up rutting into him against a tree. And Hollister deserved so much more than that.

I broke the kiss, cupping Hollister's face. I had to hold him in place as he strained forward to kiss me. His eyes were still closed, and I smirked, not at his exuberance—that was sexy as fuck—but at the fact that Aver Walker was currently fighting off a gorgeous man's advances in the street. Except I didn't want to fight Hollister's advances. I just didn't want us to get thrown in jail for indecent exposure.

Hollister's eyelids fluttered open while his lips still searched for purchase. Finding only my thumb, he sucked the finger into his mouth as his tongue licked circles around it.

"*Very* good boy." These trips out of the closet and into the city were always about me letting my inner beast roam wild, but Hollister managed to bring him out without any interference from me. My cock throbbed, and I wanted nothing more than to kiss him again, but I needed to get him out of public. I'd meant what I said at the club. I didn't want anyone seeing Hollister as he writhed against me. I knew I needed to put a stop to my possessive thoughts, and I would, later, when I had Hollister safe and secure and *out of this fucking neighborhood.*

I blew out a harsh breath and put Hollister's hand in mine before heading down the sidewalk. "Why don't you tell me about your friends while we walk?"

And help me figure out which one of them is going to take you in.

"Where are we walking?" Hollister settled into a pace that put his steps down at the exact same time as mine. I didn't think he even noticed what he'd done. His body had simply obeyed.

I tightened my hand over his. "A few blocks over."

Hollister tried to slow, but I'd prepared for that already. "Why?"

He didn't need me to tell him, and I wouldn't fall for his trap.

His obstinate chin lowered in surrender. "You're right. They don't stop on my block." He took a deep breath that lifted his shoulders and then exhaled, shaking his breath out. "My friends are...my family, actually. We aren't always close. We go through waves, but we always find each other again."

I liked hearing him say that but had to wonder how his friends let him stay in the type of place he lived.

"I didn't so much as move to Seattle as I did find myself here. Things were tough at first, but Sam helped me and later Jorge—he's the one that gave you the I-see-you eyes— and now we're doing the same for the next generation.

Sprinkles hasn't been with us for very long, but he's making leaps and bounds in terms of finding stability inside and out."

Having ordered a car to our location, I checked the surrounding area before leading Hollister to the bench to wait. "Sprinkles is an interesting name. Is there a story there?"

Hollister smiled, but I knew the affection in his face wasn't for me. "Yes, but it isn't very interesting. I think the story is more proof of how we suck at giving members of our group nicknames than anything else. Sprinkles's parents owned one of those ice-cream-slash-sandwich franchises, you know, for those times when you want a meatball sub and a cookies-and-cream parfait." Hollister's lips twitched and he let out a sharp puff of air from his nose.

When Wyatt or Nash laughed at their own jokes, it was annoying, but when Hollister did it, it was the most adorable thing I'd ever seen.

"But Sprinkles's parents were also utter shit heads, so Sprinkles developed a thing with ice cream shops. When Sam and Jorge found out, they insisted on doing exposure therapy because, to them, nothing should ruin ice cream. Well, the first time we all went out to a shop with him, he couldn't do it, but he didn't want to leave." Hollister started laughing in preparation for whatever came next. "It was his turn at the register, and he panicked, ordering an entire cup of sprinkles. We didn't want to make him feel bad, so we all ordered cups of toppings too. Sam nearly threw up trying to eat a bowl of hot fudge."

His happiness was so thick, I felt like I'd been there and had witnessed the same moment. I settled back against the bench, looking out onto the street with a smile. When I'd been Hollister's or his friends' age, I could've used people like him. I'd been confused as a teen, and by the time I *knew* what was going on with me, my mother and father had made their stance on the matter clear. They used to call Branson and the others horrible names after they'd all come out.

By the time I'd found my own spine, it was already bent into the shape of the box my parents had shoved me into. To repress my sexuality, I'd had to repress my alpha nature. I couldn't have one without the other, just like I couldn't be two people, Aver and whoever this person was. When I tried letting one out, even just a little, the other came with it, hand in hand.

The car showed up, and I had the transition to occupy my thoughts. The drive back into town was longer than the one out, due to the late-night traffic going downtown. I was eager to get Hollister back to my hotel room, but I found unexpected contentment sitting silently next to him in the back of the car, his hand warm in mine as we watched the scenery whiz by our windows in comfortable silence.

"What about you?" Hollister asked the moment we got out of the car at my hotel. It was as if we'd ridden under an unspoken agreement, and the conversation started up again exactly from the point we'd left off. The man holding the hotel entrance door open nodded as we approached.

I had a strict no-private-information policy that usually always came up once during these nights and then never again. My regular reply was locked and loaded. *Let's keep this casual. Not knowing is half the excitement...*The words tasted like dirt in my mouth. "My cousins," I blurted out.

Hollister's bottom lip puckered as he nodded. "That wasn't what I expected." He looked around the elegantly furnished hotel lobby. The fountain in the center of the marble room tied the look together while also providing the soothing sound of burbling water.

It was a very nice, very expensive hotel, but I didn't give two shits about the fountain, not when I had my own work of art walking beside me. I noticed the looks Hollister got from those lingering in the lobby: some curious, others laced with desire. I draped my arm over his shoulders, laying my claim. It was an arrogant, domineering action, but this was why I couldn't let any part of my alpha nature free back at home. That guy was a dick who did exactly what he wanted.

But right now, I *was* that guy, which meant nothing but Hollister could stop me from turning him to me once we were inside the elevator, cupping his ass, and kissing his lips softly. I drew my head back to look in his face. Like on the sidewalk, his eyes were still closed as if he was stuck in time a few seconds ago when our lips had still been pressed together.

I liked that he seemed to need a few extra moments to go from kissing me to not.

His eyes opened eventually and focused on my face. "I'll give you one thing—your place is nicer than mine," he said with a smile.

I grinned. At least we were joking, and he wasn't still embarrassed. There wasn't anything to be embarrassed about when it came to living within your means. Branson, Nash, Wyatt, and I had camped on the land where our home now stood. Tents had been preferable to the glittering mansions mocking us from the other side of the bay. I clearly didn't have a problem with him sharing a house either. My only issues with Hollister's situation were the dangers I saw lurking there.

"I'd have to tell a lot more fortunes," he said, but I didn't think he was talking to me at that point but to himself.

Already, I knew his name, where he lived, and what he did to earn his money. If I let this continue, nothing would stop me from trying to find him again the next time I was in town. These nights out of Walker County were about living without limits, ignoring that quiet voice that ruled my day-to-day actions. I couldn't make ties or connections. But I didn't want to stop what we were doing, not yet. "Will you tell me my fortune?"

The elevator doors opened onto a long muted hallway lined with doors on either side. Our room was the first on the left. I already had my key card out and tapped it over the mechanized lock. The lights were out inside and the window curtains shut like they'd been when I'd left earlier. That gave me an idea that made me glad I'd left the room shut up. I flipped on the light at the door and stepped to the side to let Hollister in first.

He looked around for a few seconds but then back at me. "I can't tell your fortune."

My eyebrows dipped. "Why?"

He frowned, his face scrunched into an expression that made me believe he was thinking very hard about what he said next. "You're too distracting."

I could handle that.

We were now several hours and many topics of conversation away from the possessive desire that had compelled us to leave the club in the first place, but it was as if Hollister realized at the exact same time as me that we were finally alone in a room with a door that locked. I flipped the lock over and flicked the bottom latch closed.

Hollister stood facing me, his arms relaxed at his side in

the center of the dark room. The on[i]
from where I stood by the door.

"You have me where you want me
worrying the sleeve of his shirt betwe
other hand.

I did indeed. My steps from the doc
stood turned predatory. Hollister's eye ___, and he
backed away from the animalistic gleam he surely saw in my
gaze. When I was close enough, I tugged his sleeve from his
other hand. Hollister's lips trembled.

"Are you cold?" I asked, cupping his cheek at the same
time.

He closed his eyes, shook his head, and leaned his face
into my palm.

"Nervous?" I had him in my arms again, but this time,
there was nothing to divide us. No one was looking on,
seeing moments and emotions from Hollister that were
meant for my eyes only. I tucked a long strand of blond hair
behind his ear.

"A little. Were you going to turn on some lights? Or are
you trying to add to the whole 'beast in a dark castle'
appeal?" He was likely joking, but he didn't know how close
to the truth he'd come.

Being this version of myself, a proud gay man, dominant
and self-assured, it felt as natural as breathing in his presence. "Will you let me blindfold you?"

Hollister searched my face. He put his hand out, laying
it flat against my chest before suddenly tightening his
fingers over the fabric. His breath came out as a hiss, and his
eyes burned with carnal fire. "Do you plan on hurting me?"

The thought of someone hurting this man had my chest
expanding, my muscles tensing in preparation to defend
and protect. "Never," I growled.

shivered, and the next thing I knew, I had both
_____und him. He snuggled into my embrace, his arms
____d tight against himself while he burrowed deep against
_y chest. "I shouldn't trust you as much as I do."

No, he shouldn't. For as connected we felt, I'd still
known Hollister for hours. I assumed I knew things about
him, based on what I'd observed of him so far, but I didn't
really know him. The same went for him about me. When I
thought about Hollister in the same situation with any other
man on the other side, I squeezed my hands into fists to
push back the fury that image caused.

That made me a hypocrite, but I didn't care. Hollister
was with me now. I'd make sure he stayed safe in my care.
Later, I'd deal with what happened after.

"Is that a yes?" I asked. I needed to hear him say it.

He sucked his lips between his teeth, nervously
gnawing at the tender flesh. When he released them, the
skin was red and glistening. "Yes."

His lips called to me so sweetly. I lowered my face to
his. Kissing him hadn't been part of the plan at the moment,
but I'd been unable to resist. The kiss was brief, and I spun
him around gently so his back was to me.

"I'm sure you paid for your view. Why don't you have
the windows open?" Hollister asked, his voice shaking with
his nerves.

I loosened the knot at my neck and tugged my tie free.
"I'll open them in a minute."

"After I've been blindfolded?" he asked quietly over his
shoulder. I focused on his steady breaths, quickening in the
moments when I brought the tie over his eyes. He might
have been apprehensive, but he didn't move a muscle as I
pulled the thickest section of the tie over his eyes, tying the
ends together high on the back of his head. His blond beach

waves stuck out from under the tie. The hair was long enough for a bun. Hollister was the only man in the world I would like in a bun.

I stepped a half foot back, and he turned his head, eyes angled up while he tested the thickness of the fabric. His tongue flitted out nervously. "I can't see anything."

My lips tugged up. "That's the point."

I stepped around him, and when I grabbed his hand, he gasped. "You aren't going to take off my clothes and trick me into going into the lobby naked, are you?"

Leading him toward the curtains, I slid my other hand down his spine, making him shiver. "I'm going to do half those things."

He sucked his bottom lip into his mouth as his feet tread carefully over the carpet. "Wh-where are you taking me?"

"To the window."

Hollister smirked. "I'm only barely not singing that song right now."

I knew the one he was talking about and was surprised he knew it. He had to have been a toddler when that song came out. I wouldn't dwell on how old I'd been. Besides, rap wasn't really my thing, and singing wasn't in the agenda. Unless it was Hollister singing out my name as he climaxed.

Checking to make sure his blindfold was secure, I pulled one side of the ceiling to floor curtains aside and then the other. Hollister hissed when I lifted his arms, setting his palms flat against the glass.

"How does that feel?" I murmured over his shoulder.

Hollister licked his lips. Some people held their emotions in their eyes, but for Hollister, it was his mouth. "Cold, hard."

As he responded, I undid the button of his white jeans, peeling down his pants like I was unwrapping a present. I hadn't once forgotten about that thong I'd spotted at the club, but I'd been successful in not dwelling on it until right this moment. It shone out at me now, a bright neon green against his tan ass.

I dropped to my knees behind him, sliding my nose between his cheeks as I inhaled. "I saw this little thing when you were dancing at the club." My words were whispered, uttered solemnly as if in prayer.

Hollister's slow exhaled shuddered through him. "You did?"

I nodded, letting my nose glide between his cheeks. "I did. While I watched over you."

"Is that what you call it?" Hollister arched his ass out, truly putting himself on display.

"Yes." I nipped his left cheek, and he yelped sharply. "That's what I call it." I licked the reddened skin, savoring the sweet flavor and blossoming warmth under my tongue.

"You're driving me crazy," he moaned.

I smirked, continuing my attention around to the front of him. His dick stood out from his body proudly. The neon fabric straining over his cock head darkened with his precum. "I can see that."

His whimpering continued, but I was in no hurry. I explored his body, keeping my touches light but far reaching. There wasn't a part on him that I hadn't caressed, and by the time I removed his shirt, leaving him in nothing but his thong as he stood blindfolded, hands braced against the window, he trembled from head to toe. "I knew it," Hollister mumbled, barely loud enough for me to hear.

"You knew what, pet?" The name felt right rolling off my tongue.

Hollister let out a sharp whine and popped his ass back.

He also didn't mind the name. "I knew you were a demon," he rasped.

I chuckled and stood up. My lips brushed over his ear as I spoke. My chin balanced over his shoulder while I stared out at the glittering downtown Seattle skyline. I didn't mind the pet name he'd come up for me either, but teasing him was too much fun. "Oh, come now, that isn't very nice."

I popped open the slim travel tube of lubrication, drizzling the transparent stream of liquid down his ass crack. My hand split his cheeks, tugging the strip of the thong aside so I could tickle his fluttering back hole. He was more than ready for my touch. His hips twitched back, so aroused he twerked on my hand, attempting to drive my fingers inside of him. My pet was ready.

I slid in one finger, the only hesitation coming at the very beginning when I probed the tight ring of muscles. His moans turned husky as I added another, and though he kept his palms flat against the glass as I'd asked, his hips gyrated. His body trembled and shook. His breath fogged the glass in front of his face, all while his inner muscles tightly clamped around my hand.

I kissed down his cheek to his lips. "You're going to feel so good around my dick."

He turned his head, frantically latching his lips to mine. "I agree. Let's test that theory now." His fingers curled, lifting slightly from the glass.

"Tsk. Hands flat, pet."

Hollister groaned in frustration. He dropped his forehead against the glass, his fingers straightening as he worked to obey. I would've loved to continue this game, teasing him until he was a shivering, sweaty mess. He'd done as I asked, though, and such obedience should be rewarded. Besides,

I'd held my own urges back for so many hours. I wanted to see him come nearly as much as he wanted to.

I stroked his rigid length. He wasn't far from climaxing. I barely had time to get my teeth around the tip of the tie, tugging the knot free and allowing the tie to fall from his face. "Come for me," I growled.

"Oh my Goddess!" Hollister's eyes flew open. The exact moment he took in the sparkling skyline, his dick opened, spurting cum over my knuckles.

His knees buckled, and I quickly caught him, allowing his body to slump into mine while I guided the two of us down. My back hit the cool glass as Hollister collapsed on top of me. His shaking groans continuing for several more moments. "That was..." His eyelids fluttered open, and it took him a few seconds longer for his eyes to focus on my face. "That was a very dramatic way to show me the view." He smiled and leaned upward, kissing the bottom of my chin.

There'd been nothing particularly sexual about the kiss, but the familiarity with which he stretched up into me made my heart pound. I felt a power unlike anything I'd experienced. It wasn't like the adrenaline rush I felt when called to protect my cousins, their mates, or children. It was something new and a thousand times as forceful. "Wait until I show you the bathroom."

I was surprised I could speak at all with my head so full of snarling, primal grunts and growls.

Hollister closed his eyes, sighing in a contended sort of way. He leaned the side of his head against my chest. "That moment might have to come sooner than you anticipated."

I wasn't always the brightest tool in the shed, but I could take a hint. I lifted him as I got to my feet. "Take your time. Freshen up. You may use anything you find in there." I brought him to the bathroom door and stood at his back with my hands on his shoulders. "I'll make us drinks. Unless... ?" I wouldn't be offended if he still wasn't comfortable.

He stepped out from under my hands, and even then, when he would only be a room away, I yearned to pull him back by my side. He turned around, the bathroom light illuminating his blond waves like a halo as he batted his eyelashes at me. Shyly, he said, "It's okay. I trust you."

It was a good thing he locked the bathroom door immediately after. If he hadn't, I wouldn't have been able to resist claiming his mouth again. And this time, when I let Hollister go, he would *know* who his mouth belonged to.

And every other part of him too.

I frowned as Hollister turned the shower on. My frown remained while I washed my hands and made our drinks from the wet bar, sticking with Grey Goose on the rocks. At the last minute, I add a splash of orange juice into Hollister's. He'd been enjoying those crazy colored drinks with his friends and likely preferred it a little sweeter. I was still frowning after I set the drinks down and changed out of my suit into a pair of black sweatpants. My aching erection appreciated the extra room, though only one thing would cease the throbbing.

That one thing was still in the shower, and...yep, he was singing.

Listening to Hollister's off-key warbling made me smile, but my possessive thoughts from earlier were still troubling. I had three rules for my secret nights out: always use protection, stay as anonymous as possible, and *never* get attached. I frequented the same establishments, returning until I was too well known and had to switch to a new club for a few months. Even just meeting with a man for a second time would allow them to come to conclusions about who I was.

Would that be so bad?

Before, that thought would've been answered with a resounding YES. Now, that was a more difficult question to answer.

"Hey there," Hollister said softly. The light was still on in the bathroom, and steam billowed out, but Hollister was right next to me, clutching the knot that held his towel in place. He'd walked across the room without me noticing.

He cocked his head to the side. his damp hair drying in blond waves. "Big thoughts?" He brought his hand to the side of my face.

I grabbed it, holding his palm against my cheek as I kissed his wrist. "Just wondering how a person could take so long in the shower."

Hollister snorted. "Perfection takes time."

"But you make it look so effortless."

He beamed. "That was smooth, Mr. W, I'll give you that."

I frowned. I didn't normally mind the name but not on Hollister's lips.

Aver wasn't that uncommon of a name. I could tell him that mu—

No.

There wasn't much of a difference between telling him my name and then my last name too. And since he knew that much, why not go a little further and tell him what I did, and how perfect he felt in my arms, and how the only times I ever truly felt awake was during these stolen moments in the city?

It seemed like Hollister took my frown to mean something else because he suddenly cast his eyes around the room like he was looking for a way to change the topic. "Please say the orange one is mine."

I nodded. "It is." I lifted both drinks and brought them to the head of the bed.

Hollister crawled quickly behind, still dressed in only a towel. He sat with his legs folded beneath him and the towel twisted loosely around his lower half. "So, is this your thing? You...go out randomly and choose to give some needy soul a mind-blowing orgasm?"

My lips twitched into a smile. "I don't know if I can call this my *thing*. You make me sound so philanthropic." I was the one getting everything from these weekends. "I'm not out there saving orphans or anything."

Hollister's eyelashes fluttered as he cupped his chin with his free hand. "I'm open for adoption."

A growl ripped from me.

Hollister's eyes widened. His pupils dilated, and he licked his lips. "I like that sound. But it isn't normal."

I brought the rim of my glass against his. They collided with a clink. "Sounds about right."

Hollister took a drink, and my eyes fell to his neck. His muscles contracted, and I wondered how the same motion would feel beneath my tongue.

My cock hung full and heavy, still hard and aching. By now, I was confident I'd live the rest of my life erect. Every sense I possessed felt heightened, every strength increased. It was as if every primal element that made me more animal than man had suddenly increased exponentially. I didn't understand the change, but I also wasn't going to question it. I felt *right* in a way that was entirely unique.

"I want to fuck you." I should have said that more kindly than I had.

Or, if Hollister's immediate lust response was any indication, I'd said that like I was Goldilocks. His bottom lip stuck out, plump, red, and ripe for the taking. There simply wasn't a way to resist kissing him, so I didn't try. I set my drink down—positive I'd only succeeded in dropping it on the carpet—and leapt on top of Hollister. He squeaked, giggling as my lips pressed against his. As we rolled, I kept him plastered to me. My back settled against the mattress, and my head found the pillow. I grabbed two handfuls of his damp wavy hair and tugged his face closer, using the leverage to control every aspect of our kiss.

I loved the way his smile felt on my lips, but it wasn't long before they straightened as his mood sobered into something more passionate. He draped over my chest, whimpering as he writhed against me.

I cupped his face, and he stilled, pulling back to look into my gaze.

"You. Are. Perfection," I whispered, kissing Hollister before he could see just how much I meant what I'd said.

Hollister smiled in return, but it was such a curious-looking smile, I had to know the thought that had caused it.

"What? You can say it. I'm tough. I can handle it."

Hollister threw his head back and laughed. "I was just smiling because I thought about how I could say the same thing for you, but then I remembered you aren't even real. There's no way you can be. Your perfection is at a level that simply isn't possible."

"Not real, eh? Clearly, I need to up my compliment game. That was poetry."

Hollister winked.

I melded my mouth to his, holding him with a hand at his waist and the other at the small of his back. I spun us around, cradling his toweled body beneath me. He blinked rapidly, looking up at me with a look that was two parts desire and a million parts something I couldn't quite name, but knew that it was important. I kissed the very tip of his nose, and Hollister sharply sucked in air between his teeth.

"Put your cock in my mouth, please," he whispered. "I have to taste you." He lay his head flatter against the pillow as he opened his mouth wide to the ceiling.

There was no substitution for clearly stating what you wanted in the bedroom, and I wasted no time in rising to my knees, cradling Hollister's head between my thighs as I fed my dick into his waiting mouth.

His lips wrapped around me with enthusiastic zeal as he bobbed his head. The pillow kept him from getting the leverage he wanted, and he grunted, his eyes narrowing in the cutest expression of irritation.

I pumped my hips, going shallow at first as Hollister raced to catch up with my rhythm. He moaned as his eyelids fluttered. His throat opened, and I slid down his throat, groaning at the way his tongue rolled up and down my shaft. My thrusts were relentless. I should have let up, been gentler with this precious angel. But I believed Hollister would speak up if he wasn't comfortable, and the look he gave me wasn't one that left anything up for interpretation. He was loving this. When my cock filled his throat, his eyes rolled back as his groans deepened. His dick stuck out from his body, the towel having fallen open long ago. A river of precum flowed down his shaft, and I reached back, pumping his length twice.

Hollister squealed his pleasure around my cock. His nostrils flared, working double time to bring in oxygen while his throat was blocked. His cheeks were rosy, and his eyes glistened with happy tears. My dick pulsed, spilling precum down his throat. I was too close, and though a condom wasn't negotiable and I wouldn't be able to truly fill his sweet hole, I wanted to be balls-deep in his sweet heat when I came.

I pulled free, needing to actually tug my dick from his mouth. His vacuum-tight lips released my cock with a lewd, wet *pop*. Hollister moaned out his frustration, silencing when my fingers found his ass. One more packet of lube and I made short work of stretching his hole. When his whimpers turned into squeaks I rose, quickly sheathing my dick before plunging the tip inside of him.

Hollister hissed and panted. He breathed deeply, moaning before he slowly pumped his hips, my sign my boy was ready for more.

As I fed my dick into his tight channel, he clenched the sheet on either side, squeezing tight. His tight channel was as hot and snug as I'd anticipated. I would climax quickly. This round.

"Yes! Oh fucking hell, yes!" he howled, his body opening to receive me.

I sucked his lip into my mouth, bottoming out at the same moment I nipped the soft flesh.

If an earthquake suddenly struck, splitting the ground beneath us, I was positive I'd be able to muscle the sections of earth back together. While buried inside this amazing man, I was stronger than ever. "You're *mine*," I snarled.

Our bodies collided with sharp smacks, faster and faster. My hips pumped into him. My balls tightened, and my vision sharpened. It was as if I'd been looking at the world through a film that had suddenly been lifted. The air had changed, the scents dividing into pieces of themselves. Instead of being able to smell the cotton towel beneath them, I could smell the detergent used to wash it, the scent of the person who had folded it, and another who had brought it to this room. Rising above it all, a single scent called to me like no other. Hollister's scent.

My dick pulsed, and I came in a sudden, unavoidable wave. I filled the condom, the liquid heat a brief regret in an otherwise perfect moment.

Hollister twitched beneath me. He'd painted both of our bodies with his release. His breath came in huge gasps that he needed a few moments to calm from. He gripped my arms, hands kneading my biceps. "Next, you show me the closet."

———

HOLLISTER COLLAPSED TO THE MATTRESS, and I pulled his back tight against my chest. I balanced my head in my hand, my elbow propped up against the pillow as we looked out the window. The sky had changed in the time we'd spent together.

We'd filled every second of that time making love, fucking, and doing everything in between. I'd lost count of the number of times I'd held him as he'd climaxed. He liked to cuss when he came, and I found every foul word made me smile that much wider.

But as the dawn rays crept over the mountain, we were both very much spent. I'd fucked Hollister long after he'd been able to push back into me. He'd lain beneath me, nearly exhausted until I told him I'd fuck him like my personal fuck toy. At that, he'd climaxed immediately. Hollister's sexual appetite rivaled my own. He was ready for anything I threw at him, and as the sun brought a new day—and my time in Seattle to a close—I drew him as close as was physically possible, wondering how I was ever supposed to leave him.

"Let me see your hand," Hollister mumbled. "I promised you a palm reading."

Hollister told fortunes, read palms, and practiced tarot, though he claimed it was mostly about reading the room than anything else. He'd shied away from my questions of clarification, but considering that was the only part of him he'd purposefully kept private, I'd decided not to pry. For now.

"I see here you're going to have a long life." Hollister drew a line diagonally across my palm. "And you are a fantastic lover," he continued. He gasped and cocked his head. "And this line here says you really know how to wield a meat sword."

I snorted, loving how Hollister could be silly and serious all at once.

He popped his bottom lip out. "Hm."

"What?" I asked, tugging my hand back.

"These are working hands. You have calluses. Why would a businessman have so many calluses?"

I said nothing, fighting an inner battle I'd likely lost the moment I'd spotted Hollister. I had to go home; that was an unavoidable truth. But why couldn't Hollister come to Walker County? I kept the two sides of me separate now. Why couldn't I do the same at home?

Hollister worked hard, both to pay his bills and to help those in need. Despite his hard work, it didn't sound like he'd taken a single vacation in all the years since coming to Seattle. Not because he didn't deserve one. He'd jokingly described himself as a guardian gayngel, but though he'd said it like a joke, it was true. The man worked long hours, and when he wasn't working, he was volunteering, trying to help young people who were lost, lonely, or needed help. My pet was an angel, but he deserved a break.

"Hollister." His name rumbled out of me.

"Hm?"

"My name is Aver."

Hollister's eyebrows furrowed, and he spun in my arms, turning his back to the dawning sun. "Hi, Aver." He smiled. "Why are you telling me this now?"

He sounded suspicious. The man was sexy and smart.

"I've got to go back home today. The ferry is leaving, and I have to be on it. I don't want to say goodbye to you yet, and I'm pretty sure you aren't ready to say goodbye either. But I can't stay longer in Seattle. I have to go home."

Hollister frowned, his chin dropped as he burrowed his forehead against my chest.

I leaned back, wishing I could allow him to hide in my embrace as he wanted. "Come with me, Hollister. It will be like a vacation. I'd cover everything. You don't have to worry about paying for a thing."

Hollister stiffened, and I had to strangle my alpha's urge to tighten my arms around him. I had to know that if Hollister wanted to go, I would let him. I couldn't kidnap him and convince him he'd wanted to go with me all along—even if I wanted to.

Hollister searched my face. "I get to go on this all-expenses-paid vacation in exchange for what, Aver?"

I frowned. That wasn't right. He wasn't meant to say my name with that level of suspicion. "In exchange for nothing, Hollister. I've enjoyed my time with you, more than I can describe. I don't want to say goodbye. I already have a cabin. It's nice. We could stay out there, live the rustic forest life. At the very least, you'll get time to rest. You deserve that much."

4

HOLLISTER

I SHOULDN'T HAVE NEEDED to think his offer over. Running off with a man I'd just met to a place I wasn't familiar with was just about the stupidest thing I could think to do. Though my tongue pressed against the back of my teeth, readying to spit out the word that would put a stop to this madness, I couldn't pull the trigger.

What if I did agree to go away with him? With precautions, of course. I'd tell my friends exactly where we were going, and Jorge and Sam would check in on me. If they didn't hear from me or if something happened, I trusted them to sound the alarm. But should I go away with a man when these sorts of thoughts were at the forefront?

If any one of my friends had approached me saying they wanted to run away with a man they'd just met, I'd—well, after I'd made sure the man wasn't a killer in disguise—I'd wish them well and make sure they stayed in contact. So then why was the situation different when it was me poised to spend a few days laying around in a bed in the middle of the forest getting fucked?

Jazz came and went as he pleased. Sam left on conferences a few times each year, and Jorge visited his sister in southern California as often as he could afford the trip down. Even Sprinkles was known to disappear for days at a time, always popping up the moment before we could report him missing.

During all that, I remained in the city. How long had it been since I'd gone a night without being lulled to sleep by the soothing sounds of sirens and traffic?

"Say something, Hollister. Let me know how much convincing I need to do."

I smirked. Mr. W—*Aver*—sat up but didn't let that put space between us. He tugged me into his lap. "It's a beautiful cabin. Surrounded by green all year around."

"Seattle is green."

Aver frowned and scratched the bristles at his cheek. "There's a creek nearby. You can lose yourself in its gentle babbling."

My smirk curved into a smile. "I've gotten lost in Seattle."

Aver hugged me, gently shaking me. "Hollister," he growled, and though it sounded like a warning, I didn't bristle against him.

I didn't do a lot of the things I normally did with Aver. Every domineering look and possessive touch would have normally set my alarms off. My mind, body, and desires were my own. Always. So what did it mean that I didn't mind as much when Aver had started saying that *mine* stuff?

I'd heard several men claim that I was theirs. With Aver, for the first time, I believed it.

That is crazy, Hol. You just met the man.

Yeah, I'd just met him, but touching him was like stepping into whatever circle of hell was filled with nonstop orgies. Call me crazy, but I didn't want to say goodbye to Mr. Orgy Skin so soon.

And all that physical stuff aside, Aver was so much more than the arrogant businessman I'd first pegged him for. He could be sexy and sweet, cunning and kind. "Are there lumberjacks around for me to ogle?"

Aver made that sexy chest rumbling noise. "No. You'll ogle me."

See, domineering and possessive, and yet I was exactly where I wanted to be. "Can you dress like a lumberjack? Put on a flannel? Carry an ax? Ravage me against a tree?"

"All of that can be arranged," Aver said quickly. "Does that mean yes?" He tightened his arms briefly before relaxing his hold. He kept doing that, almost like he had to force himself not to hold me as tightly as he wished.

"That means maybe. It all depends on one very important thing."

Aver's forehead pressed against mine. He puckered his lips to kiss my nose. "Anything you want and I'll give it to you."

A thrill of desire skittered down my spine and settled between my legs. His confidence was hypnotizing. "Will there be pancakes? I require pancakes. And bacon."

"Every morning." Aver smiled. The playful curve of his lips was one I hadn't seen—yet a new side to this enigmatic man.

How many sides did he have? If I was really considering running off with him to the middle of nowhere, I guessed there would be time to figure that out. "When do we leave?"

———

THE FERRY's horn blasted our arrival. I plastered my face against the window of our first-class cabin. I hadn't even known ferries had first-class options. We had the square space entirely to ourselves, and there weren't benches but comfy swivel chairs that faced each other.

The island grew before my eyes, steadily emerging from the twilight fog. It was as lush and green as I'd been told, and though my excitement grew with every minute, Aver had gone quiet about an hour ago, and I'd only been able to get one-word answers from him since.

He'd been all over me all morning. When we'd gone back to my place to pack a bag, he hadn't let me out of his sight and had encouraged me to keep packing. By the time he was satisfied, I'd packed most of my belongings. I probably should have anyway, since I didn't trust my roommates or that my room would still be mine after leaving it for so many days, but that wasn't the point.

All that time, Aver had kept me close, always touching me, *until* we'd boarded the ferry. Now, he just stared out the window, his hands shoved into the pockets of his designer jeans.

I sighed, slumping back in my chair. That hadn't taken long. I should have known when a gorgeous man whips you away for a night of carnal pleasure and then offers you a free vacation, it was too good to be true.

"Are you tired?" Aver asked.

"No." There, let him learn what it felt like.

"Are you hungry? I'd planned on stopping by the grocery store on our way up, but we can get you something now."

I crossed my arms. "No."

Aver leaned forward. He kept his hands in his pockets, but now they were balled into fists. "Do you regret coming with me?" He didn't ask his question very loud, but there was a subtle intensity that made the small hairs on my arm stand straight up. Aver's gaze slid to my goosebumps, and he leaned back. "I'm sorry," he said quickly.

I wasn't sure what he was apologizing for, but I believed his remorse. He couldn't hold my gaze for very long before his eyes twitched away.

"What's going on with you, Aver? You were so excited for me to come, and now you aren't."

"I am. I want you with me." He held his hands out in the space between us.

He was offering me the choice, but it was one I took immediately. "Then what happened? I know we haven't known each other long, but you can talk to me. I'm a world-renowned listener."

Aver met my gaze, and the torture I saw there took my breath away. It didn't make sense. Nothing had happened, and yet he looked torn apart. He sighed heavily before bringing my knuckles to his lips. "It's the transition, going from the city to...home. It's...jarring." He'd chosen his words so carefully I knew he was holding things back.

For some reason, seeing his inner conflict only made me more confident that I'd made the right choice in coming with him. Much of him was still clouded in mystery, and a few times, I'd convinced myself he was more than human. This proved he was just a man like me. And sometimes, men needed to be coaxed into sharing the things that ate at them. "I understand. I haven't heard a siren in hours, and my eye is beginning to twitch."

"No, it isn't."

He would know. Though he'd spent most of this ferry distant, I'd felt his gaze on me whenever I wasn't looking. If I'd noticed him watching me that much, odds were there were also times he watched me when I hadn't noticed. I had a crazy hunch if I asked him how many times I'd inhaled since sitting down, he'd be able to at least ballpark a number. I pouted. "It was a comical exaggeration and my attempt at relating."

"You did a very good job. I feel very related."

I tugged my hands, but Aver's fingers tightened. "Eww," I squealed, continuing to tug.

Aver pulled me so fast I gasped, afraid my face was about to slam onto the floor between us. He caught me, tugging me up like I was nothing more than a feather that he lifted into his lap. "I really am sorry," he said between kisses. "I shouldn't have let my negative mood affect you. And if you will accept a bribe to forgive me, I swear to get chocolate chips to go with our pancakes."

I snorted. "You are forgiven...but only if you get bananas too."

He cupped my face, kissing the corners of my lips before claiming them entirely. In between the kisses, he whispered something so quiet, I couldn't be sure of what he said. But I thought it sounded like he repeated two words: "Thank you."

THE RAIN HAD STARTED the moment we drove off the ferry. Since we were first class, we'd been able to get into our cars and off the ferry first, so we didn't have to wait in a line of traffic.

A few minutes later, Aver pulled us into the parking lot of a Village Market. The moment he cut the engine, the skies opened, releasing rain in streams.

"Why don't you stay here?" Aver suggested, needing to

talk louder over the sound of the rain hitting the car. "I'll run in. We both don't need to drown."

I smiled and pretended I had to think about my answer. "Are you sure?" I cocked my head to the side to increase the confused puppy look.

Aver narrowed his eyes. "Uh-huh. Wait here, my prince." He leaned in and gave me a quick kiss.

I caught his wrist before he could open his door. "I thought I was your pet?" That moment, when he'd first called me by that name, I'd nearly orgasmed on the spot. I loved it, but it wasn't one that you could admit to loving, was it? You had to pretend to hate it, at least until it'd been long enough for you to convince his dick it couldn't live without your mouth.

"Yes, you are my pet prince." He leaned in, and I thought he was going in for a kiss when he suddenly lifted my hand to his lips. "I'll be quick." He grabbed the handle, pausing as a woman ran by his door toward the entrance. Aver's fancy wool peacoat was about to get soaked, but he didn't hesitate. He opened the door and exited quickly.

I watched that tight ass run. Each downward step, the ass muscle on that side clenched. After he disappeared inside, none of the other asses could compare, so I stopped ogling and grabbed my phone. As they had required of me when I told them where I was going, I sent Jorge and Sam my exact location so if I disappeared later they could give a timeline of my night. I'd done this at their request every thirty minutes and had promised to until we got to the cabin.

Jorge's text came first. **Was I right? R u his sex slave now?**

I shook my head. Jorge said sex slave like that would be a bad thing. **Not yet, but there's time.**

Sam's name popped up next. **Be serious for a second. You're okay? Everything is how u thought?**

Most of the ferry ride had been confusing, and I'd kept feeling like Aver regretted asking me to return with him. But everything else that he'd said and did convinced me otherwise. **Things are perfect, guys. Really. He's not real. I mean it.**

Jorge sent a vomiting emoji while Sam sent a heart with a question mark. I was pretty sure he meant for me to be cautious and to question things that didn't feel right. Though I loved that he cared, I had a sudden urge to defend Aver. I wouldn't; he didn't need defending. **How are things there?**

It felt safer to keep the conversation on things happening in Seattle.

Sam's name popped up with three dots. They pulsed there for a moment before disappearing. Moments later, there were three dots again. I could almost picture him fighting with himself, sitting behind his desk at the You Belong shelter. He wanted to protect me, but he also wanted to support me. **Things are exactly the same as they were. You've been gone hours.**

I know, but life can change in a moment!

Remember that, Holly Golightly. Sam sent seven heart emojis and two lines of kissing faces.

Jorge jumped back in. **Ok, onto the actually important things. U send us a pic of his dick ASAP. I need to witness this Rod of Wonders.**

I looked up and all around me as if worried someone had seen Jorge's text and would tell on me or something. **I** *won't be taking a pic of him without him knowing. Srry.*

I don't believe ur actually sorry, but I accept the apology all the same. Have fun!

Sam sent a waving hand, and I sent back as many hearts as the text box would allow. Before I could feel too homesick, Aver came out the exit, carrying shopping bags on both arms as he sprinted across the parking lot. He opened the back door first, unloading the wet bags in the back seat before jumping behind the wheel

"You've returned. My hero!" I clasped my hands beneath my chin.

Aver smirked and started the car. Minutes later, we were on a winding highway, thick forests growing on both sides. The sun had fully set while Aver had been inside, and with the fog drifting between the trees, the view was both beautiful and creepy. Great to photograph, a bitch to get lost in.

When he turned down an unmarked gravel driveway that seemed to appear out of nowhere, I prepared myself for a charming little cabin with no electricity and a toilet located in a small hut outside. At least the rain had stopped, the clouds breaking up to allow patches of stars to shine through. The winding driveway went on for a while, but as we ascended a steep hill, a gorgeous log cabin *mansion* lay ahead. The only way to describe the sprawling home in front of me was to say it was rustic charm on steroids. Several huge windows faced the front of the house, each illuminated with a warm glow. A covered, wraparound porch had a bench swing next to the front door on the left. The right side had a wide rocking chair, big enough for at least two.

"This place is..." I didn't know what to say. Never, in my wildest dreams, had I expected a place like this. I hadn't known places like this *existed*. It was obviously handcrafted, top-of-the-line luxury. And yet, the home had been built in a way that complimented the forest around it. Between the trees, I thought I saw the moon's glint reflected from a watery surface. "Is that...?"

"A lake, the creek feeds into it." His lips twitched. "Walker Lake, actually."

I kept seeing that name. Someone had certainly been compensating for something. "Walker County, Walkerton, Walker Lake, other names exist." I found his gaze. "Who can we report this to?"

He looked like he was fighting the urge to laugh. "I'll look into it."

He parked in front of the door, and the motion sensors illuminated the space around us. I'd watched his face as he parked. Each time he looked from me to the mansion he'd called a cabin, his eyes softened. This wasn't just an epic find of an Airbnb. It meant something to him. "Tell me about this place."

Aver looked shocked for half of a second before smiling. He cut the engine and rubbed his hands in half circles around the steering wheel. "I built this."

I suddenly didn't understand English. That answer made no sense. This man was wealthy, fit, with a huge dick that he knew how to use, *and* he was an artist? "She's beautiful, Aver. What do you call her?"

Aver's lips twitched. "She's a he, actually, but his name is Lawrence."

Now that he'd said it, I could see there simply wasn't any other way it could be. "Lawrence is impressive."

Aver looked at the wooden structure with so much

adoration, I felt a flicker of jealousy. So far, I'd only seen him look at me that way. "He is my *second* greatest secret."

He had to know saying that would only make me want to know what his first greatest was. I waited long enough that if he'd wanted to offer the information voluntarily, he would have spoken up. I wasn't here to push him, but I did hope he pushed me repeatedly against a flat surface, so getting inside and freshening up was in order.

I got out of the car, meeting Aver at his front bumper. "Are you going to carry me...or...?"

Obviously, I'd been joking, but the moment I spotted that gleam in his eye, I knew he would make me pay for my sass. He lowered his head, effortlessly lifting me around my waist and draping me, ass up, over his shoulder. "Of course I will carry my pet prince." He slapped my butt, gripping a chunk of flesh as he kneaded it in one hand. "I'll take any excuse to finger this sweet hole." He ripped my pants down before sucking one finger in his mouth, coating it with his own saliva.

I bounced like I was trying to escape while Aver carried me up the steps and through the front door. My head hovered over his butt, and I wiggled and winced as my erection poked Aver in the chest.

"I *know* you *want* it," he said, driving his finger in deeper with every other word.

"Fuuuuck! Shit, you fucking..."

Aver laughed, and I couldn't remember what I'd been saying. The way I felt when I touched him hadn't lessened. It was a desire that never ended and had started affecting me in unpredictable ways. The world was clearer, literally. I was nearsighted and had worn glasses until they'd been smashed during a stupid fight that had broken out between two tourists. I'd been too close and got knocked down. The lenses had been shattered, and though I wore them for a few days longer, the shattered glass slowly fell out. I hadn't been able to afford another pair, and now, for some insane, sex-fueled reason, it seemed like I wouldn't need to.

I could make out every detail of the rustic, exposed log walls with crystal clear clarity. Decorated with beautiful, poignant, and sometimes funny wildlife photos scattering the walls, even though we were inside, it felt like we hadn't stepped out of the forest.

He tossed me down on a dark gray leather couch.

"Lawrence has seven rooms, a two-car garage, and a basketball hoop. There are mountain bikes in the shed, but if you are going to explore, take me with you. We're in the woods here, and there have been signs of bears. You can fish the lake anytime you like. There's wifi and cable, and the smart TV is subscribed to several streaming services." He paused, nuzzling his face into my neck. "I'm so happy you're here."

I didn't need to see his face to know he told the truth—I *felt* it. "What about something with hot water, maybe some bubbles? You got anything around here that can do that?"

Aver picked me up again. This time he carried me like we'd recently married and were walking through the doorway for the first time. He brought me through a sunken entertainment room with a wet bar, a huge stone fireplace, a big screen TV, and a pool table. Ahead, a wall of windows opened in segments to the outside. Aver carried me through an open portion, bringing us outside the house to the deck. He set me down in front of a hot tub large enough to fit at least fifteen people. The water bubbled softly as steam rose from the surface.

"You asked for hot water and bubbles," Aver reminded me.

And he'd delivered. Despite the cold air and wet deck, I ripped my shirt off, letting it fall to the wood as I reached for my pants. Aver's hands twitched toward me, but he stopped himself at the last moment, clenching his hands into fists as he swayed back to watch me undress. With his hot eyes on my body, my movements slowed, drawing the moment out as long as possible. I unbuttoned my pants and turned, bending with my ass to him as I slowly slid the pants down my hips.

There was a growling snarl, followed by the sound of fabric tearing, and the next thing I knew, I was completely naked and in an equally naked Aver's arms. I tried looking over his shoulder at our clothes rumpled on the deck, but he spun me around and took the first step into the hot tub.

The combination of hot water and cold air had me simultaneously sweating while I clung to Aver's body. "Don't you drop me," I told him, my arms tightening into almost a death hold around his throat. In actuality, being ducked into a tub of pleasantly warm water wasn't that bad, but there was just something about being ducked in water against your own will. Even when the plan had always been to get into said water.

Aver tightened his hold around me. "Why would I do that to my pet?" He nuzzled my neck as he sunk down to sit.

Goosebumps erupted on my arms, and I shivered against him as my body fought the conflicting hot and cold.

"I'm here to take care of you." He kissed my neck, drawing the tender flesh into his mouth where he let his teeth scrape slightly over the skin. "Tell me what you want, Hollister. Anything, and it's yours."

That was a dangerous thing to ask someone. Though it was clear that between us, Aver was the more dominant one, a possessive, protective feeling grew within me. For as controlled and confident as Aver seemed most of the time, moments like this one let me see through that mask to the vulnerability within. That had been real gratitude in his voice. He was thankful I'd agreed to come with him, and I felt like much of this generosity stemmed from that appreciation. A lesser man than I might have seen that gratitude and taken advantage of it.

But Aver hadn't chosen a lesser man. He'd chosen me, and I would protect him. "I'm a simple man to please. I think you know what I want."

His expression darkened. He reached out of the hot tub and grabbed a tube of lube. Bracing my body, he propped me up so that my knees were on either side of him, my ass arched just high enough to pop out of the water. I already felt relaxed, but Aver still went through the steps, making sure my body was ready before he sheathed his dick and lowered me slowly onto it.

I was glad he hadn't tried taking the long way to getting inside my ass. I knew he could play my body like a guitar, teasing me to the edge over and over. But he didn't tease me now. He gave me exactly what I wanted, when I wanted it.

Gripping my hips, he controlled the pace and depth, but as I got my balance on my knees a little more, he gave up that control. He leaned back, folding his hands under his head as he smiled up at me like a conquering king enjoying his spoils.

His dick felt like royalty, and I rode him slowly at first, gathering speed as the skies opened.

I shrieked, but Aver held me tightly, letting out a sharp growl that I thought meant I was supposed to stay. After the initial shock of rain, I realized though the drops were fat and splashed against the surface, really, the rain was redundant. I was already wet, and the parts of me that weren't pressed

71

against Aver or underwater were already cold. I let go of the instinctive urge to find shelter at the first sign of rain and lifted my face to the sky.

Aver groaned, his hands returning to my hips like it had already taken all his will to give me the control for as long as he had. His cock plunged into me at the perfect angle to nudge my prostate. Like a wild animal being rutted in the woods, I threw my head back and howled. Aver was relentless now, pounding into me so forcefully the water in the hot tub started to resemble a stormy ocean. The churning water was a good metaphor for the feelings churning inside me. Some cautious, some wary, but only a little. Mostly, I felt a love too powerful for as little as we'd known each other. It was a destructive love, the kind that left you broken, but I'd be damned if my journey to heartache wasn't paved in orgasms.

Nothing good lasted, not forever. I'd accepted that truth long ago, and even though this time it felt like I'd found something truly special, I had to remind myself that, as all vacations must end, my time with this man would come to an end as well, and I'd be back in my real life in the real world. But with this gorgeous man between my thighs, bringing me the best orgasm of my life while his own release exploded out of him, I'd at least enjoy the ride.

5

AVER

THE GRAVEL FLUNG out from under my tires. If I didn't slow down, I'd only be out here later, raking the rocks back into place. It had been three days since Hollister and I had arrived at my home away from home, and though this was my first time leaving him, I was eager to return.

Lawrence was a secret I'd kept even from my cousins. I hadn't been sure how it would feel inviting another into my sanctuary. When the confines of my personal prison caved in, I escaped here. I'd built every part of this home, from foundation to roof. And when I'd finished, I'd perfected what I'd made until I was left with a forest oasis.

I'd thought I'd been successful in making the perfect house. Until Hollister walked inside. At *that* moment, I knew I'd truly succeeded. This house was a home.

But what would happen when Hollister left? Would I ever be able to look at this place again? I simply had to keep him so satisfied he couldn't dream of leaving.

So far, the shortest path to Hollister's heart was through his dick, but as I'd quickly replenished our shopping supplies, I'd stopped to buy Hollister a present that I looked forward to giving him.

I'd been able to give both my father and my cousins sufficient reasons for my prolonged absence, but it was only a matter of time before I had to go back to the office or answer my father's phone call. As interim Alpha for the Walker Bay pack, he was in way over his head.

I hadn't forgotten how being Alpha had been my father's lifelong goal. But Alpha Walker had died of natural causes, and since there'd been no alpha prepared to take his place, my father did the job in the meantime. The pack needed a true leader, though. They needed someone who they could rally behind, and as much as Glendon Walker wanted that person to be him, I didn't think the shifters of the pack would follow him.

And since Delia Walker had singlehandedly brought every neighboring pack's eye on us, it was only a matter of time before someone came sniffing for control.

I parked and spotted Hollister through the open window, reading on the couch. I smiled and pulled out my phone, checking the messages before I turned the thing off for the foreseeable future. I had a text from Wyatt, asking if he could drink my almond milk. That meant he definitely had already.

Riley had a question about some materials he needed to build the kids an outdoor play area, and Branson had texted saying I'd owe him after taking so long off work. We had several employees, but one of us spearheaded each project we were contracted to do. While I was with Hollister, Branson had needed to do the brunt of that work.

I'd make it up to him later.

My stomach clenched. *Later.* I'd thought convincing Hollister to come with me had won me the war, but really, it had only been a battle. I'd brought him here under the pretense of a vacation, but it was a vacation I had no intention of ending.

Except, at some point, I would have to. Even if I told everyone about Lawrence and said I was moving in full time to have my own place, they'd want to come over. And it wasn't like I could keep Hollister inside forever. He was used to a bustling social life, and though he seemed to be enjoying his time around me, he'd crave those interactions again.

The last text was from my father saying Leann had been asking for me. I'd gone on a single blind date with the young woman; she was the daughter of an Elder family from a pack out east. My father had met her parents through his job as a political consultant, and I assumed a relationship between us would be advantageous for my father's dealings. Otherwise, he wouldn't have pressured me so much on this one person. The number of blind dates I'd gone on to please my parents was a running joke with my cousins.

Each time I agreed, I felt less and less like myself.

I looked up, sensing Hollister's eyes on me. He'd spotted me out the window and stood inside, directly in front of it giving me a curious smile and slow wave. My worries vanished, and I turned the phone off without ever looking back at the screen.

Miraculously, Hollister looked as excited for me to return as I'd been to return to him. He met me at the door, wearing boxer briefs and one of my sweatshirts. He worried the right sleeve between his fingers, tugging at the ribbed cuff. I liked seeing him in my clothes. A lot. Not only did it rub my scent off on him, something my inner alpha definitely appreciated, he looked adorable.

Hollister narrowed his eyes at me. "Your note said you left for groceries."

Leaving him while he'd still been asleep had been unforgivable, but it had also been the easiest way to get out of the house alone. "They are in the car, along with a present. But then I saw you and..."

I shrugged, and Hollister stepped into my embrace, seeming as if he understood me completely. While I'd been out, the urge to return to Hollister had been intense, but it was a feeling I believed I alone experienced. Could Hollister have felt the same? Was there any way he could be as obsessed with me as I was with him?

I loved how tightly Hollister squeezed me back, but I didn't like the way he trembled. He'd been reading when I first saw him, and I'd assumed that meant he'd had a peaceful morning, but now I wasn't sure. "Did something happen?"

Did he want to go home? I had to let him...if he wanted to leave...I had to let him.

"Not really." He pressed the side of his face against my chest. "I checked in with Sam and Jorge. They still haven't spoken with Sprinkles. He's been missing since the day I left." As loyal of a friend Hollister was, I was lucky he wasn't already in the car demanding I take him back to the city.

I hated to see him so worried. "Didn't you say Sprinkles did that sometimes? Disappeared until you were sure something bad had happened?"

Hollister nodded, pressing his face back into my chest. "You're probably right. I just...things have been so perfect since we got here, and then I woke up without you and had all those texts from Sam." He shivered before inhaling deeply through his nose. If I hadn't known Hollister was a human, I would've believed he was taking in my scent.

As my affections for Hollister grew, I'd wondered what it all meant. Had this been what my cousins felt when they'd met their mates? I didn't want to think about it for very long. While Hollister and I remained safe in the bedroom, there was no chance of him becoming pregnant, which had seemed to be the catalyst that started everything with my cousins. As much as I hated the thin barrier between our bodies, as long as I was safe every time, everything would be fine. Unlike all three of the other mates, Hollister had no hint of an extra, unexplainable ability. I'd been within close contact with him for so long. If he could compel someone to tell the truth with his touch like Riley, heal a wound like Phineas, or suck the energy from my body like Kansas, then I would have noticed. Hollister did have a superpower, but it was his ability to get hard at the slightest touch, to come with the smallest provocation. At least this way, I couldn't have my heart torn in two when I discovered Hollister wasn't my mate.

"It might sound stupid, but the world looks darker now when you aren't around," Hollister whispered.

It didn't sound stupid at all. "For me as well." I kissed his lips gently.

I understood how that could have been troubling, so I didn't ask Hollister to explain why he'd suddenly looked away. His eyes fluttered open a few seconds later. "Did someone say something about a present?"

I smiled. "Yes, I did. I have a present for you. And I have more syrup." The man ate syrup like Will Ferrell in that Christmas movie, *Elf*. Riley had rented it over the holidays for one of our movie nights.

I'd watched the comedy from the corner of the room.

But when I pictured the moment now, Hollister was in my lap, laughing along while I held him tightly.

Could a moment like that ever exist? I didn't see how. The Aver I was with Hollister would be like a stranger to my cousins. They'd think I'd been taken over by aliens.

Hollister's face brightened with a smile, but worry still made his eyes tilt.

"Do you want to talk more about your missing friend? I could help you brainstorm places he might be." I knew a thing or two about wanting to disappear from life for a while. As much as I didn't want to talk about anything that could lead Hollister to wanting to go back to Seattle, I didn't want him worrying.

He didn't look excited to brainstorm, so I pivoted.

"Or I can explain the terms of my present."

Hollister arched his brow, his natural curiosity chasing away his worried thoughts. "Terms? That doesn't sound like a present. Gifts aren't given with stipulations."

"You're obviously correct, but when a gift is this epic, the rules may be bent. Wait here. I'll bring in the stuff—"

Hollister frowned.

"I change my mind. Help me bring the stuff in, but no peeking."

His frown disappeared, and he jumped up, content to walk outside in his underwear and my sweater.

"Hold on. You need shoes." I caught his wrist before he stepped out the door. On second thought, now that I was touching him, I didn't want to stop. I turned around and offered my back. "Jump."

He obeyed immediately, leaping on my back. I caught him, and he wrapped his legs around my waist. "Onward, trusty steed!" Hollister giggled.

He sounded so happy, I started laughing too, and we

kept that up as I carried him to the car. He stayed on my back, and I handed him one bag, the lightest of the bunch.

"I can take more," he whined.

"You can, but you won't." I'd discovered something wrong with this position: it was harder for me to kiss him when he was behind my head. I grabbed the rest of the groceries, including the bag with Hollister's present, and brought us back inside the house.

Hollister slid down but stayed by my side as I went into the kitchen to put away the perishables. Hollister liked pancakes in the morning, but I'd learned the rest of the day he was more of a grazer than someone who sat down for meals. He liked to snack all day, and I'd needed to up my supply of celery, peanut butter, apples, and cheese. He liked nuts too, but not peanuts, so I'd searched for a blend without peanuts.

Hollister snagged the container off the counter. "Cashews!" He ripped the lid off, and I couldn't help my grin. Hollister must have felt my gaze on him because he paused suddenly and looked up at me. "I mean, do you mind if I—"

I put my finger against his lips to silence him. "You were right the first time."

His cheeks went pink as his pupils dilated. Though we'd had sex, nearly nonstop, since we'd arrived, Hollister's hair-trigger libido hadn't changed. All I seemed to need to do was touch him, and his mouth would soften as his cock grew hard. The desire ran both ways, but if I was going to get what I wanted, I needed to let him keep his clothes on a little longer.

He popped a handful of nuts in his mouth and crunched on them as I put the rest of the groceries away. "So where is it? My present? There isn't one, is there? It's a prank."

I snorted. Of his many virtues, patience wasn't the strongest. "It isn't a prank, but it does require an exchange." I held five plastic DVD cases behind my back.

Hollister puckered his lips as his eyes narrowed in suspicion.

Before that suspicion could grow into anything else, I brought my hand around, flashing the DVDs like playing cards.

"*Twilight!*" he shrieked, bouncing over the foot of space between us. "The whole saga! You got them all? I thought you hated sparkly vampires." He reached for them, but I tugged the DVDs out of his reach.

"First, we negotiate."

Hollister leaned his butt against the kitchen counter and crossed his arms while I resisted the urge to pull his arms back down. I hated how his arms muffled his heart, though I could still hear it pounding strongly. "What are your terms?"

"If I'm going to sully the good name of vampires in my mind and my home—"

"Sully?" That got his claws out.

He could act as outraged as he liked. Vampires. Didn't. Sparkle. "—then I'm going to want something in return."

"What more could you ask for than ten hours of perfection?"

I looked from Hollister to the movies. Ten hours? I hadn't read the back of the DVD cases when I'd bought them, though it looked like the movies were about three people, two guys and a girl. I assumed the guys didn't end up together—though I might have looked forward to the movies more if they did. My entertainment during the movie marathon was going to be Hollister. "While we're watching the movies, I want complete control over your body."

He froze in the middle of attempting to jump after my hand. "Complete control?" His voice lowered, making me extremely aware of how heavy my cock felt.

"Complete."

"What if I need to use the restroom?"

"You ask."

"What if you say no?"

"Why would I say no?" I wasn't into water sports.

"I don't know why, but what if you did?"

"Then you'd obey. But more likely than not, that scenario would end with me pausing the movie until you got back. I don't want to torture you, Hollister. I simply want complete control of your body."

He jumped like I'd surprised him. I couldn't tell if his sudden nerves were from fear or arousal, though thanks to my heightening senses I had a hunch it was arousal. "Will you be tying me up? Let's talk limits."

I attempted to not let this small display of distrust get to me. Allowing yourself to be bound and helpless had to be scary at first. But I didn't want Hollister afraid during the movies either. "No bondage. You simply do as I ask when I ask it, and if I ask you to do something that is outside of your limits, then just say stop. I'll respond to a safeword if you have one, but if you don't, all you need to say is stop."

He nodded absently as his eyes flitted from the DVDs to my face. He must have really loved these movies because he lifted his face, and with a serious tone, he replied, "Okay, I agree. But we have to start now, or we won't have time to finish them all!" He jumped up, likely to steal the DVDs, but I caught him and carried him and the movies into the entertainment room. I set him down on the white faux-fur rug.

Pillows piled along the edge of the rug, and Hollister immediately began laying them out, preparing our spot like a bird preparing a nest.

By the time I'd put the first disc into the player, Hollister had our spot looking cozy. He watched me walk out of the room where I snagged some tools I would need to make this movie experience one I would never forget. At some point, we'd make popcorn. If we really watched all ten hours, then there would be more than enough time for meals.

Hollister watched me reenter the room, and his eyes fell to the cloth bag I carried as his lips parted with anticipation. His curiosity burned bright, but he didn't ask the question I knew was brimming on his lips. He only looked up at me with round, innocent eyes.

He was the only person in the world I'd call devilish at the same time I called him angelic. Hollister was everything, but right now, he was waiting for my instruction and just happened to be wearing entirely too many clothes. "Strip."

———

I LET him keep his boxer briefs, but only because the fabric clung so nicely to his package. Except for some light petting, I let Hollister watch the first movie undisturbed. He'd acted as my personal narrator, explaining things he thought might be confusing as well as pointing out the many differences between the books and movies.

I'd known he was a fan, but I hadn't known he was such a nerd about it. I pictured him a few years younger, devouring every page of the books—of which there were four; I knew that now, thanks to Hollister—while he waited for the movies to release. I already knew my boy wasn't a patient sort. Waiting must have been torture.

And as I sat down after putting the second movie on, anticipation was what tortured him now. His dick had gone hard the moment I'd asked him to strip, and whenever he'd softened throughout the movie, I'd run my fingers up his thighs or tickled his tummy, and he was hard again. Since I'd left him mostly unmolested for the whole of the first film, he was left to wonder what I had planned.

Before sitting back down, I rearranged the pillows so that I could sit up with Hollister's back to me, his body snuggled between my legs. His back was warm against my chest, and there was so much skin available to me in this position, it would have been easy to lose my way. But I was focused, even if Hollister wasn't.

"What happened to my Hollister commentary?" I asked as the characters on the screen were throwing a birthday party.

"A demon started distracting me," Hollister growled. His nipples were two rosy, tight nubs against his chest.

I reached down, pinching a nipple between my fingers and making Hollister hiss. "I'm doing nothing of the sort. Watch your movie." I danced my fingers to the other side of his chest, teasing the other nipple with the edge of my fingernail.

The movie continued, but I wouldn't be able to tell anyone what had happened. My attention was on Hollister. He was all the entertainment I needed. Watching his stomach suck in the moment I squeezed his nipples was as erotic as the small sounds he'd started to make.

He began to squirm. His hips lifted off the ground like

he was searching for friction against his cock, but we were a long way from that.

"Settle," I growled, and though he sighed loudly, Hollister laid back against me.

"I thought *control over my body* meant you were going to fuck me during the movie or something."

Oh, I planned to. But we had approximately ten—now eight—hours left. "Control means just that—control." I caressed him from thigh to shoulder.

"But I'm still wearing my underwear!" he whined.

"For good reason, too. Look at you. You'd be leaking everywhere without them."

Hollister sucked his bottom lip between his teeth. "Sadist."

I chuckled and settled my hand dangerously close to the tent in his briefs. "No, Hollister, I'm here to bring you pleasure. But on my terms. When I want to. You know what to say if it's too much. We can stop if that is what you want and continue watching the movies."

"I don't want that," he mumbled quietly.

I smiled and brought his back against my chest. "Tell me what's going on right now in the movie then."

Without needing to look, Hollister said, "Bella got dumped, and now she is sad. She's about to buy a motorcycle."

"And does she use it to ride off and find her own happiness?"

He shook his head. "She tries to move on but can't."

I understood that feeling a little too well. I hadn't expected to see myself in any of these movies, and I didn't like it. I reached over, feeling Hollister's eyes on my arm as I plunged my hand into the cloth bag and grabbed the lube.

Hollister let out a sharp sigh that sounded a lot like, "Finally."

If he thought the teasing was done, he was going to be disappointed. I drizzled a small amount into my palm and used my fingers to work the slick flood around my hand.

Hollister's lips were parted as he watched me. I didn't think he took a single breath the whole time. That was, until I slid my hand under the elastic of his briefs and cupped his erection. A cage would have been helpful in a moment like this, but I would have to improvise.

Hollister's hips jerked like crazy as he thrust himself into my hand.

"Settle," I ordered with my hand down his underwear and my lips against his ear.

"You ask the impossible."

For as much fussing as my pet did, he definitely liked my touches. His shoulders were tight as well as his stomach, and even now, when I'd done no more than settle my flat hand over his penis, he moaned as if staying still were the hardest task in the world.

Pride exploded in my chest. Even though it was difficult for him, Hollister still tried to do as I asked. I gripped his dick tightly at the base while squeezing his nipples with my other hand.

"Oh, fuck, fuck, fuck, cock-sucking fuck!" Hollister cried out, pressing the back of his head into me as he looked upwards.

I released my grip, and Hollister grabbed my arm like he was trying to keep it where it was.

"Please, just let me come a little bit, and then I can concentrate better."

I made a tsking sound. There would be no coming *just a little bit* when I finally allowed Hollister to explode. He knew that. "I think you're right. It's time to transition," I said, and Hollister let out a hopeful gasp. "Take off your briefs."

He moaned. That clearly hadn't been the outcome he'd been hoping for. Still, he slid his briefs down. I held my hand out. He wouldn't need that particular covering anymore. In fact, I enjoyed this so much, I pondered making the cabin an underwear-free zone from here on out.

I was still long enough for Hollister to let out a shaky, resigned exhale. He settled back against my chest, still hard and leaking, but he'd yielded to the unchangeable truth that he would come when I was ready. And not a moment before.

As the second movie continued, I kept Hollister dancing on the edge of release. By the end of the second movie, Hollister's skin had grown so sensitive, it didn't matter where I touched. His dick twitched as he squeezed his ass muscles.

As the credits rolled, Hollister's stomach growled.

"Are you ready for an intermission?" I asked.

"Oh yes," he purred, spinning around like fluidly as he stretched to kiss me.

I held his face back the second before his lips found mine.

Hollister's eyes were already closed, but as I held him, I watched his frown turn into a pout. He opened his eyes, holding my gaze with his. "Please, Aver. I can't concentrate like this. I'm hardly enjoying this!"

That was a lie. In the moments between caresses, when I'd allowed him time to calm back down, his attention returned to the movie, and within minutes, he'd started quietly reciting the dialogue. I kissed his forehead and grinned at his scowl. "You know what to do, pet, if you want this to stop."

He let out a human version of a growl. "I don't want you to...*you know*. I want you to put something inside me! Mouth or ass, I don't care."

If this was him pouting, it was as cute as everything else he did.

"Okay, I'll put something in your mouth." I got up, lifting him with me. I carried him into the kitchen and set him down on the counter as I gathered a tray of snacks.

I pulled out a bag of popcorn when Hollister groaned. "This isn't what I meant!"

While he glared at me, I put the rest of the tray together, adding a few string cheese sticks to the mix. Wyatt always included that item in the meals he made for Kansas because it was easy and fast to eat. And it was one of the few foods Kansas liked almost all of the time.

Hollister wasn't a picky eater, but right at that moment, he was an angry one.

I brought the tray into the entertainment room first, returning to the kitchen to pick up my crabby pet. When I picked him up, he suddenly decided to change tactics, rolling his hips over my body like he was a stripper on a pole. He made sure my hands were on his ass before he started to bounce, sliding his dick between our bodies at the same time.

We were there before he could make too much progress, and I set him down to put the third movie in. His body was stiff, but he let me pull him back into my lap. Hours had passed since we'd started the first movie. It was no longer morning outside but afternoon, and we still had several movies to go. At this point, Hollister likely believed I would make him wait all five full length features before I let him climax.

The idea had crossed my mind, until I'd come up with

one I favored a little more. As the third movie started in a dark alley, I fed Hollister. He ate from my hand without question or protest, and I quickly learned why. I slid a kernel of popcorn into his mouth, and he grabbed my wrist, keeping my hand where it was as his cheeks hollowed around my finger.

I pulled free, slowly shaking my head as I did. Thankfully, he'd been sitting up just then because if he hadn't, he would've felt my cock jerk against him after that stunt. I didn't torture Hollister alone. I *ached* to watch him come. There wasn't a sight I liked more than his toes curling, his thighs trembling, all while his mouth parted in a perfect O as he climaxed.

"I was just getting the last bit of salt." He batted his eyelashes.

I just barely stopped myself from smiling. He'd been naughty, but I'd liked it.

He sat back without having to be told as if he was trying to say he would be good now. I didn't believe that for a second. But I also didn't want Hollister to be *good*.

The movie continued. Somehow, this kid still went to a high school everyday, even though her life had been flipped around on its head. If I'd been through what she'd gone through so far, at the least, I would have considered online schooling options.

I surrounded Hollister's cock with a loose grip.

His gasp was nearly silent. That was unlike Hollister. The range of pleasure noises he made was one of my favorite things about him. Experimentally, I tightened my fingers around his girth. Again, Hollister's noise of pleasure sounded restrained.

So that was his plan now. If I withheld his orgasms, he

would deprive me of his noises? I had to admit, it was diabolical. And also, a very dangerous plan to have.

I gripped his dick roughly, and he moaned before biting his lip to block the sound. He'd likely assumed I would stop there, since my caresses had, so far, been brief. When I gripped him a second time, he cried out as his hips shot forward. Before he could fuck my hand, I released him, settling my palm against his upper thigh.

"No! Fucking Aver! No!"

"No isn't the word you need to say if you want this to end, Hollister. We can stop right now and make sundaes. I bought all the toppings. It's your choice."

"I am not your super fan," he rasped. "I used to be! No more."

I kissed his cheek, and he didn't pull away, so I decided not to let my feelings get too hurt. "You wanted to keep a part of you from me, didn't you, Hollister?"

He looked down, ducking his chin in the very picture of guilt.

"I can't have it, pet. I need all of you."

His breath hitched, and I palmed the front of his throat, wrapping my fingers gently around the curve before applying the slightest bit of pressure.

Slight was all he needed. My other hand found his dick, and I stroked him at the same time. His hips shot off the rug, pumping like a piston in the air. Again, I settled my palm flat against his thigh.

"I'm sorry, I'm sorry, I'm sorry," he crooned. "I'll never do it again, please, just let me come."

His ragged breaths warmed my cheek. I gripped the base and squeezed hard, stopping right before the pleasure became pain. He howled, flopping on top of me like a fish out of water. I wound my legs around his, holding him down and effectively ceasing his ability to hump at the air.

"Aver." My name had never been spoken so desperately nor so sweetly. "Aver, please."

My hand slid up his precum slick dick. But that time, I didn't stop. On my downward stroke, I whispered, "Tell me what's happening, Hollister."

"I'm cumming!" he wailed. "Shit! Shitting, shitter, shit, shit!" His dick was like a fountain, spurting up before falling down in great splashes. His moans grew faint, but I continued to pump. Hollister had more to give. He cried out sharply, squeezing his fists as his orgasm continued. By the time I let go of his shaft, he had covered my hand, his thighs, and all of his chest with his release.

In all my planning and plotting, I had to admit, I hadn't considered cleanup. Personally, I liked Hollister this way, but the liquid would cool, and the appeal was in the desire, not the presence of fluids. This beautiful mess would need cleaning up with care. Hollister panted and shook; I couldn't imagine the rush of endorphins he was experiencing. Or the crash that was to come. When it did, I'd be there with my arms around him.

———

As THE DAWN's rays filled the window, I watched Hollister cuddle with a pillow. I preferred it when he cuddled me, but as I'd watched him sleep through the night, I'd come to an annoying conclusion. I had to face my real life today. If I did, I'd be able to get at least a few more days before anyone tried contacting me again.

Hollister would need to rest today anyway. We'd spent much of the night cuddling as we finished all five movies. I didn't think either of us had caught much of the last one since I'd forced orgasm after orgasm out of him, stroking his dick and fingering his hole until he'd passed out with pleasure.

I would have given anything to do those same two things at that exact moment, but the Aver everyone else knew had a motto: work hard, play hard. It was the type of thing he would've said on a Sunday morning when he woke up early to mow the lawn.

I'd always needed to keep active either moving or learning. It was the only way I could survive. Today, I needed to be that Aver. I didn't think I could unpack him as I always had. Not right now and definitely not when I was so close to Hollister. But I could pretend well enough.

I texted my father, confirming he would be home. I didn't want to mix with any more of the pack than I had to. I didn't want to be gone long either, so I told him not to plan any sort of meal. I was just there to talk. And that was the most pathetic part of all. Though I was a grown man, an *alpha*, a better person than him by far, his approval had been and still was my ultimate goal. For him to be proud of me, *even though I was gay*, I could finally put this bullshit behind me. I'd only ever wanted to prove him wrong, to make him see that his homophobic beliefs had been hurtful, but more importantly, *wrong*. If either my mother or father found out I was gay, it wouldn't matter what I did. I could singlehandedly stop a meteor on a crash course for the planet, and he'd find something wrong with it.

My father replied that he was available soon after I pressed send. It was too much to hope that he wouldn't. I reminded myself what this day would bring me in return and tapped Hollister's shoulder.

"Yes, Daddy! Please let me come!" Hollister whimpered into his armpit.

I didn't hate the name and didn't care what that said about me. But I couldn't explore that kink at the moment.

Already, the restraints of my alter ego chafed.

"I have to go, pet. I'm sorry. I don't like leaving you anymore than you like being left." I'd thought I was the only one who had experienced discomfort at leaving the other's side. But after he'd explained how he'd felt, the reason he'd put on my sweater—because at least then he'd have my scent around him—I realized his reactions had mirrored my own. "I'll be back as soon as I can. The house is yours. The land is yours. Rock hound in the creek nude if you like."

He'd confessed one of his favorite things to do was get out into nature and search for pretty rocks. He would look like a fairy or forest nymph with his chin-length blond hair and slim body.

I cupped his cheek softly, and he smiled in his sleep. "Stay with me," I murmured quietly. "Stay with me forever. Never leave. Never want to go home. I don't know if I could let you."

Hollister was clearly out, and I got out of bed because if I didn't then, I never would.

After taking the world's shortest shower, I went out to the car, filming a video that I sent to Hollister explaining everything I'd tried to tell him. I might have said the words to him, but he'd been in no condition to remember. And a handwritten note felt insufficient. I sent the video to his phone but hoped it would be hours before he watched it. I wanted him to sleep for much longer, wake up refreshed, and have me return soon after.

I just had to get through a few things first.

My speed down the gravel driveway, heading away

from Lawrence, was a snail's pace compared to how fast I drove when coming home. But, once I hit the winding highway, I sped up, realizing the quicker I got this all over with, the quicker I could go back to doing the only thing I wanted.

I made it to pack lands faster than I ever had. Normally, driving to the side of the island that I'd called home for eighteen years of my life felt like stepping back in those confused, angry shoes. I'd known nothing back then. I'd had no idea why I felt so much internal rage all the time that I knew now had been the start of my repression. I hadn't understood the powerful urges I suddenly couldn't avoid.

Nearly twenty years later and I was still dealing with the fallout of my shitty upbringing. There were days I'd nearly given up. My parents were never going to be proud of me, I was never going to prove them wrong, and my whole life would end up nothing more than a sad, cautionary tale.

As I pulled up to the opulent mansion my parents live in, I smirked. Though Lawrence didn't have as many rooms as my parent's home did, it had a larger square footage, and I was just petty enough to be extremely pleased by that.

But on my way to the front door, that smirk dropped. The door opened before I could get to it, and my father strode out.

"Aver, my son, I apologize, but I've just been called to *pack business*," he said importantly.

I growled but then remembered who I was supposed to be. "I texted to confirm."

His eyebrows lifted briefly. "You did, and I apologize. You know how those things are, very sudden."

I didn't because he hadn't told me what *these things* were. And since Delia Walker wasn't around to meddle in our lives, John—Wyatt and Nash's father—was still recovering after being dumped spectacularly by his wife, and my parents were scrambling daily to keep up with the pack until a suitable Alpha and Elder families could be found, there wasn't anyone to try to pull us into pack life. For the first time ever.

"What's going on?" I sounded grumpy, but that would have to be fine. Aver could be grumpy.

"It's just a family in need of support. You know how running a pack is. You're only as strong as the weakest of you."

Never mind the fact my father had never uttered an expression like that in his life. I knew this moment for what it was: a trap.

I guess that meant only Branson, Nash, and Wyatt got a break from Elder manipulations.

Still, the people of the pack weren't my parents. For the most part, the shifters who lived on this side of the island had grown up in this pack. Generations of shifters had been born and grown up here. And we'd had transplants as well, those who had come from other packs that were less compatible with them. And those people were the ones who would suffer during all this confusion with leadership.

"Is it serious?" I asked, keeping in step with my father to his Range Rover.

"Not yet, but I think it could be. A recent pledge came with her children. She's a single mother and very ill."

My father didn't know a thing about caring for children or the ill. He likely planned on getting there and writing a check to make the problem go away.

"I'll follow you," I growled.

Again, his eyes widened, but he quickly blinked the expression away. "If that's what you want…"

I didn't bother answering the not-actually-authentic question but got in my car and turned around, following my father's car to a small manufactured home. A few toys lay scattered in the small yard, but the windows and blinds were shut. In the driveway, Paul's car was already parked in the vacant space, so I parked behind my father on the side of the street.

Paul was a relatively recent member of the Walker Bay pack who had quickly become indispensable both here with the pack and over at my own home with my cousins and their mates. I hadn't known he was already here, and if I had, I wouldn't have come. I trusted Paul to be able to care for both kids and the ill.

The front door opened, and Paul came out carrying a large plastic trash bag. When he spotted the two of us, he froze but recovered quickly. "Is something wrong?" he called out. "Something with the pack? The cousins?"

Paul didn't know *where* to lay his concern, but he was ready nonetheless.

"No, no, nothing is wrong, Paul," my father boomed, sounding much too jovial for a man on a sick-call. "I'm here to help, and I believe my son would like to help as well."

If he spoke any louder, those who lived in the homes surrounding would flood out of their houses to see what all the shouting was about. I hastened forward to get inside before he could show me off like a prized pony. Inside, the home was clean, if not a little cluttered. Three children sat in the living room watching cartoons while the mother sat hunched over the dining room table. Tyrone, another new pack member, stood behind her, his thick brown fingers deftly braiding the woman's frizzy hair back off her face.

"Thank you so much, Tutu. It feels amazing just to get it up," the woman said with a tissue to her glowing red nose.

My gaze met with Tyrone's, and I arched a brow at him. *Tutu...*?

"It's what my niece calls me," he grunted. "It's starting to stick."

"Hush now, Tutu," Paul called from the other room. He returned into sight with a baby on his hip. "When you finish there, I've got one more dirty diaper where this one came from."

Until that point, my father had stood, ashen-faced, near the front door. I smirked at how out of his element he looked, but then he jolted forward. "What can I do to help?" he asked.

Paul and Tyrone both stared at each other. Paul was the first to recover. "Um, yes, Interim Alpha Walker, after diapers, I was going to start some soup, then lunch and naps. Basically, if you have a hand and time to help, I'd appreciate it."

I was sure the mother was getting a kick out of four grown men needing to come together to do the job she normally did on her own. But even though the kids were quiet now. I knew how loud they could be when they wanted.

Even though Kansas and Wyatt's child was just almost old enough not to be considered a newborn, when those four children combined their forces, they could scream the roof off.

I fully expected my father to counteroffer and agree to manage or some bullshit like that. Instead, he rolled up his sleeves and went into the kitchen. I watched him move, wondering if I was seeing the same man I'd known all my life. My father never cooked. In fact, he hated doing things he could just as easily hire someone else to do.

Paul went with him, quietly giving him directions on

how to get started, and as my father began cutting an onion, I realized if I didn't help, I'd be the one standing around.

If there was one task I knew I could do that would help those around me the most, it was changing diapers. I turned to Paul, coming out of the kitchen with the baby still on his hip and a horrible smell floating around them. "Let me handle this little guy." I said. "You're a better supervisor anyway." He didn't seem lost or unsure but calm and confident.

Paul shrugged and handed me the baby.

———

SEVERAL HOURS PASSED, and though I'd noticed each one —my skin itching to return to Hollister—I couldn't leave while there was still care to be given. We got the children changed, then fed. After that came the process of putting those of nap-age down for the afternoon. Once they were asleep, I felt confident I could leave without detriment to anyone.

The biggest surprise of all was that my father was still there, helping where he could. He didn't interact with the children a lot but stayed busy in the kitchen cooking lunch, cleaning, and then starting something for them to heat up for dinner.

One day of not being an entitled, homophobic asshole wasn't going to erase a lifetime of distrust.

"I need to get going, Paul. Is there anything else I can do before I do?"

Paul looked around for something that needed doing. "Maybe just take the garbage out on your way? I just took that trash out." But with diapers, tissues, and other extra garbage, it overflowed once again. "We'll stay here until everyone gets down for the night, so don't worry about us."

I grabbed the trash bag, replacing the can with a new liner before finding my father. "I'm leaving now, Father. I'll be leaving into town for a bit on business."

I didn't wait for his reply. The children were all quiet, or sleeping like their mother, so I left silently. The moment I stepped out of the house, my steps lengthened, bringing me to my truck. The urge to grab my phone and check to see if Hollister had replied was strong, but if I did, I wouldn't be able to stay away longer, and I needed to make one more stop before I was free. I'd already been away from him longer than I'd ever intended. The fury I felt at missing those hours with him wasn't something I could tamp down, so I didn't try the entire drive over to my cousin's home.

My home.

Except, as the beautiful bayside cabin came into view, I didn't feel the same contentment as I once had. Now, if Hollister were inside, safe and secure, waiting for me to return home, that would be something else entirely.

I opened the door and stepped out, convincing myself I *could* smell Hollister's scent. It was wishful thinking. He wasn't here. He couldn't be.

I tried to shake away some of my simmering anger at being away from Hollister. My cousins didn't deserve my temper, and neither did their mates or children.

At the front door, I nearly knocked until I remembered I lived here.

Mr. Boots, Kansas's cat turned guard dog, meowed fiercely. Another thing disappointed I hadn't been around. I gave him a scratch between the ears, but Mr. Boots could hold a grudge, and he jumped out of reach, sprinting for the forest like he was being chased.

I turned the knob and pushed open the door. "Hey everyone, I'm ho—"

Hollister's scent hit me strongly enough to leave me with no doubt. He was here.

I couldn't wonder how or why. My alpha nature demanded only that I find him and make sure he was safe.

What could have pushed him from the cabin? A fire? Intruders?

No one was in the living room, but I heard laughter toward the kitchen and took off down the hallway.

Had he been trying to leave me? I'd stayed awake for nights wondering how I would handle that moment when it came, but for all my planning, the only thing I could do now was growl.

"Hollister." I found him in the kitchen, gorgeous eyes rounded with surprise as he sat at the small circular table with Riley, Phin, and Kansas. The children must have been sleeping. Though the sight before me had been the exact one I'd fantasized over, I couldn't enjoy the moment because I had no fucking clue how it had come to pass.

"Are you hurt? What happened? Why did you leave?" I hurried forward, aware that Branson and Nash were coming in from the patio, but I didn't care about a single other person in the world at that moment, only Hollister.

"Hey, Aver, I was wondering when you'd crawl back home." Branson smiled.

I didn't take my eyes off Hollister. I couldn't. Inside, my mind roared, snapping and snarling at any idea that wasn't gathering Hollister in my arms and taking him back to the safety of my cabin. "We need to go."

I hurried around the table, lifting Hollister from his seat.

Hollister frowned. "Aver? These people know you?"

I couldn't imagine how confusing this must all have been for him. I didn't understand a single thing myself except the fact that I wanted him out of here, fast. I wasn't ashamed of Hollister, not in the slightest. But the man I was when I was with him didn't match the man I was here.

And with Hollister, I never wanted to be anyone but who I *truly* was.

"What is wrong—" Riley pushed back from the table.

"We're leaving." I carried him to the hallway while Nash and Branson looped around the other side, meeting me head on before I could reach the door. "Move," I growled, not seeing my cousins, but two alpha shifters challenging my claim.

Branson took a step back, but it seemed more out of shock than anything else. "Not until you tell me why you're carting Riley's new friend out of this house."

Riley's new friend? Clearly a lot had happened while I'd been gone, and I was eager to hear what, but alone with Hollister, as we were meant to be. I tightened my hold around Hollister. "Get out of my way, Branson."

"Or what, you'll kick my ass? Nash's ass? Is that what you want to do? Because that's what it looks like. You've been gone for days, hardly call, leave me high and dry at work, and this is how you come home?"

He couldn't know how much I had to restrain myself. Right then, I did want to kick his ass. Nash's as well. My muscles swelled large with untapped strength, and as far as my alpha nature was concerned, these two shifters were keeping me from protecting Hollister. And that was unforgivable.

A sound of warning rumbled from deep in my chest.

Hollister wiggled. He wasn't trying to move out of my arms, but he rotated so he could see into my face. He cupped my cheek and waited for my eyes to find his before speaking.

"Don't," he whispered sadly, shaking his head. "I have no idea what is going on here, but don't do whatever you are thinking. I ran into them at the coffee shop, and we got to talking. They offered lunch. I figured since you were still out..." He frowned. "These people are nice."

I knew that. These people were my family. But right now, these people were crowded around both ends of the hallway, staring at me like I was a stranger.

6

HOLLISTER

Waking up without Aver had been jarring, even with the video he'd sent me. It wasn't long before the warmth I usually felt in his presence began to fade. I'd tried distracting myself, but the longer we remained apart, the worse the feelings grew. My skin had felt too tight, ready to break apart and slide off my body. When I touched Aver, the world was brighter and my dick harder, and the world in general felt like an okay place to be. But I'd begun to suspect the opposite reaction was also true. When we were apart, the world was dark and dreary. My dick still ached, but with no release in sight.

I'd thought I'd been lucky to find some nice people to hang out with while I waited for Aver to return, but clearly, I'd stepped into tumultuous and unfamiliar waters. I wanted to understand what was going on. Before I did that, I needed to try to calm Aver down enough so he stopped sounding like a cornered wild animal, preparing for the attack.

"Is there someplace we could talk privately?" I asked, directing my question at no person in particular.

"That sounds like a great idea," Riley said. "Aver, why don't you take him to your room? There's soundproofing there."

Soundproofing? I was on a quest for answers, but so far, I just had more questions. Like why hadn't Aver told me about this home he obviously lived in? Or any of these people...

"You're his cousins," I blurted out. When I'd seen the others' husbands, I'd thought they looked similar to Aver, but I'd just figured they cut their men from sturdier stock in these parts.

"I'm not sure what we are." Branson wasn't talking to me but Aver.

Aver inhaled, exhaling a slow, shuddering breath. "My room is down here." He didn't let me down but carried me past Riley and the others down another hallway. He carried me through a doorway, shutting the door immediately after.

He didn't let me down. Instead, he carried me to a wide bed, neatly made with a blue comforter turned down to show the flannel sheets. On the wall in front of us, there was a shelf of trophies. Some looked to be from his youth, trophies awarded for exceptional performance in baseball, football, and golf. But many of the awards looked newer and higher quality. He'd won awards for his dedication to maintaining a planet-conscious business, giving to the community, and one that looked like it had the mayor of Seattle's name on it.

"Aver..." I brought my hands up against his chest and pressed.

His arms squeezed. "Let me explain—"

"...who are you?"

A double life sort of situation had occurred to me. Aver was so perfect; it would be my luck that he actually had a wife and kid at home. But, the time we'd spent together in the cabin had convinced me I'd been suspicious for no reason. When Aver was with me, he wasn't distracted scrolling his phone or doing something only he enjoyed. He was *with* me, watching me, engaging with me, and just generally *there*. Present.

"I'm the man you know," he said roughly. He released the hold he had on me and stood, leaving me sitting on the mattress as he paced back and forth. "How are you here right now? Did something happen?"

At the time, it had felt like something was happening. The longer I went without Aver there, without *anyone*, I'd felt like screaming and pulling my hair out all at once. I didn't like thinking about it now, nor the fact that the itchy wrong feeling that had started when I woke up alone hadn't truly gone away until I was in Aver's arms again.

Meeting the others had been a distraction, but one I didn't need now. I was warm again. "You were gone for a long time," I said, feeling like a petulant child. But I hadn't done anything wrong. I wouldn't be ashamed. "I couldn't handle the solitude. I remembered you said there were bikes, so I decided I'd try to ride into town. Do some sightseeing."

This was supposed to be a vacation, after all.

Aver's body had gone very still. His face looked carved from marble, stony and unchanging. "You rode a bike? The cabin is at least a two-hour bike ride to town."

I pushed my hair back with one hand. "Yeah, I realized that an hour in, but then someone drove by and asked where I was heading."

"You *hitchhiked*?" The longer I explained what had happened, the stiller Aver became. If he'd been marble before, he was as unmovable as a mountain now.

"What? I've hitchhiked before. The guy was nice, and he gave me a tip to go to the cafe where I found Riley, Phin, and Kansas."

Aver winced as I spoke those three names.

I'd been waiting for this feeling, the one that was like having your heart torn apart slowly while your head was being shoved under water. I nearly reached out to touch his skin, if only so his carnal warmth would distract me from this feeling. "I'll go, okay? I'm sorry. Clearly this place is not a place you wanted to share with me. This life isn't something you ever meant for me to see. Hold nothing back? Isn't that what you asked from me last night, Aver?" I would have given anything to stop the angry tears from burning my eyes. I didn't want to cry in front of him. I would be crying, but later when I was alone to blub in peace.

He moved so quickly he was like a blur, stopping in front of the door. "Hollister, wait."

Was he blocking my exit? Fear made my throat squeeze, but I didn't need to be afraid, right? This was Aver, the man capable of keeping me on the edge of orgasm for hours. The man who tended to my every need when we were together. But that had been before I knew about his double life. Did I know Aver at all?

"Are you keeping me here?" I asked quietly.

"No," he growled, but he didn't move. "You are free to make your own choices, but please, let me try to explain."

From somewhere outside of Aver's bedroom, a baby started to cry. The sound allowed me to hold back my sobs for a little bit longer as angry curiosity replaced despair. "Are you married?"

He glowered

What—the fuck—ever. If he wanted to live two lives, he could handle my suspicion.

"I'm not married. I don't have a partner."

"Is that kid yours?" I nodded toward the wall that faced the rest of the house.

"No."

No partner, no kids. I exhaled just a little.

"You live here, though? I mean, I guess I knew you didn't live in Lawrence. You said he was a vacation-hobby home. I could have done more due diligence there, but... you live here? Right?" I lunged for the wall with the trophies and grabbed the first one my fingers touched. "You can't really lie even if you wanted to. This room literally has your name all over it. See, right here. Aver *Walker*?"

I couldn't believe it even though the proof was literally in front of me.

"You're a Walker? Like Walkerton? Walker County? Walker Lake? Walker Bay?"

Aver scratched his chin, looking down and to the side. "There's a Walker Street too. And the Walker Memorial."

"You're not making it better." I wished I could growl like he did. Any of my attempts would just be pitiful in comparison.

"I'm sorry, Hollister. I've said as much already, and I'll say it however many more times you need me to before you believe me. I didn't want you to know about this part of my life because..." He let out a ragged breath. "I don't like the person I am here."

"Why?"

This had been what he'd held back when we first met. He didn't look all that thrilled to be talking about it now either. But we'd gone past the point of waiting for him to be ready. This man had been inside my body. He'd changed me in a way that I didn't know if I could reverse, and the real reason I'd left the cabin was because I'd been hoping to run into him. Leaving him without leaving a piece of myself was already a hopeless endeavor.

So the only thing that makes sense, buddy, is to leave before you can lose anymore of yourself.

Could I? Or was I that far gone?

"It's complicated, but basically, in Walker County, I am in the closet. Sort of. Everyone in this house knows."

Relief came over me. "Thank fuck." I didn't want to think about what would have happened if they hadn't.

"A few other people in my life know, but the majority doesn't. My parents don't."

"Do your parents live here too?" It was a big house, but for me to live with my parents at the age I was now, that house would have to be a palace.

"No." He snorted, and I hated how good it felt to see that he could still smile.

I was supposed to be angry and deciding if I was leaving. I lowered my brow, trying to look the part. "But they come by?"

"No. They've never been here either. But they live on the island. On the other side of the bay. I visit them occasionally. It's complicated."

I believed it was for him, but I was finally getting the puzzle pieces I'd needed. I wished he would've told me some of it ahead of time. Mostly, I was uncomfortable with the parts that made me feel like I was the dirty secret. What Aver chose to do with his private information was fine, but I'd spent too much of my life learning to accept every part of who I was to spend time with someone who was ashamed of me. And he hadn't seemed all that excited to have me here with his family. What other reason could there be?

But, when I'd offered to leave, he hadn't seemed pleased with that idea.

"Riley seems nice. They all did, actually. They were in the coffee shop when I walked in. I got a coffee, but when I went to find a table, they waved me over."

His lips twitched. He'd moved out from directly in front of the door but still looked ready to tackle me if I went for it. "Riley got Phin here almost exactly the same way."

"Kansas is a hoot. I haven't met his husband..."

"Wyatt."

"Right, Wyatt, he said that. I hear he's a character. They said he was coming back any minute." There. If Aver had a problem with me being here with his family, that should be enough for him to show his true colors.

Aver didn't say anything. He sighed, dropping to his knees in front of me. He grabbed my hands so slowly I had ample time to refuse.

I didn't.

"I'm not mad that you met them, Hollister. They're lucky. Their lives will be better now that they know you."

Damn, why did he have to be so smooth while also knowing what I was thinking? That couldn't be legal. "I thought I was the king of compliments."

"You still are."

As slowly as he'd moved when he'd grabbed my hands, he lifted the back of my hand to his mouth just as slowly. I still didn't take the chance to pull away, and he brushed his lips along my knuckles, sighing with obvious relief. Was it possible the gift that made him sexual catnip to me went both ways? That would be a new development.

The longer we held hands, the more I wished we could sneak away and back to Lawrence and pretend this all hadn't happened. But, as much as that was what I wanted, I knew I would never be able to. "Does the version of you that you are here in this home want me to be here still?" The question hurt my head, and I was pretty sure I'd asked in the most confusing way possible, but I was trying to be sensitive to his needs.

"I don't care." Aver shook his head. "I can't be anyone else but who I am when I'm with you. If you still want to go out there and stay to chat, I'll go with you, but as me. It will be strange, but more for me and my cousins."

I worried I was pushing him into something he wasn't ready for, but he sounded so confident of his decision. Then again, Aver always did. Before he'd barged in and gone bananas, I had been having fun talking with the guys. "Okay. I wouldn't mind talking more."

Aver smiled, flashing me his perfect white teeth.

If he wasn't ashamed of me, and we didn't have to hide who or what we were in this house, then the majority of my concerns with the situation had been alleviated. Moving forward, my focus could be on supporting him as he needed.

Except I wouldn't be able to do that for very long since this was a *vacation*.

Aver grabbed my hand and led me out, squeezing my fingers the moment before we walked back into the kitchen where everyone waited. I understood the reassuring squeeze better. They were an intimidating group to stand in front of, scattered throughout the kitchen. And they'd begun replicating. Either that, or Nash's twin had returned.

Aver stood a little bit ahead, letting me stand a little bit behind. "By some random chain of events, you all already know each other, but, everyone, this is Hollister."

Kansas waved while he munched on a baby carrot. His husband, Wyatt, stood beside him, holding who I assumed was their baby. Branson and Riley stood behind the kitchen island with Bran sitting, assisted by his father, on the countertop. Phin sat at the table with Nash standing behind him, both holding a baby. These guys sure did have a lot of kids. Since none of the fathers could stop gushing about their children for very long, I felt like I already knew them all too —Bran, Madison, Patrick, and Calvin. I'd liked being near so much pure joy. I might have snuck a touch on Phin's watchband, after they'd invited me back to their house, and the only thing I'd felt was happiness.

"The kids just got up," Phin said as he wrestled the child trying to wiggle out of his arms. "But, after diapers, we're going to have dinner..." He made a face. "I should've phrased that differently."

I laughed. "Diaper dinner, huh? On second thought..."

Phin's eyes widened, and he shook his hand at me. "No, no, don't let me scare you. It's food. Real food. That we...will eat." He looked over at his husband like he wished Nash would put him out of his misery.

Dinner sounded fun, but Aver had specified a chat. Was that because that was all he was ready for, or because it was the first thing that came to mind? I tugged on his hand, and when he looked over at me, I whispered, "Is that okay? Can we stay?"

Aver smiled and kissed our joined hands. "Of course, pet."

For a reason I didn't want to look at too closely at the moment, I loved that he'd called me that pet name in front of the others. So far, the name had only been spoken between us two.

We turned back to the group together. Every eye was on Aver, and each of them looked shocked. "Hollister will be joining us for dinner," Aver announced.

"I'd say so," Riley murmured, fanning his face. His husband, Branson, grabbed the waving hand and kissed it.

Nash stood forward, holding one of their children on his hip, and with his other hand in Phin's back pocket, he guided his family forward. "I'm not sure what's going on here, but I am a fan."

"But not a super fan," Aver whispered in my ear, and my cheeks went red.

I glared at him, but he just smiled proudly while we both pictured the same moment from the night before.

"Clearly, you're good for this one." Nash jerked his forehead toward Aver. "He's returned a new wolf."

Aver stiffened while I frowned. That was a weird word choice. Aver was like a lone wolf, but then, living with three relatives and their families didn't exactly paint the picture of a lone wolf. "What do you mean? What sort of wolf was he before?"

Aver's lips arched down as his eyebrows dipped with worry.

The sudden mood swing didn't make sense, but the tension still thickened in the room. I hadn't needed to touch anything to see that; it was obvious. It felt very much liked I'd somehow stepped into another field of landmines, but I didn't understand why.

Suddenly, no one seemed to know what to say. But I didn't want an explanation from anyone—I wanted it from Aver. At least he wasn't avoiding my gaze like some of the others. "What is he talking about?"

Before he could reply, Kansas butted in. "We definitely don't all turn into wolves."

Aver sighed.

"Smooth, baby," Wyatt said with one hand reassuringly squeezing Kansas's shoulder.

If this was their version of a prank, it lacked the believability factor. Were they honestly trying to convince me

Aver turned into a wolf? That they all did? I looked back at Aver. He held my gaze, but the tightness in his eyes hadn't been there a few minutes ago. So he was in on this too?

I laughed, but it sounded airy and high-pitched. "You're all shi—shooting with me right now, right? Is this an initiation thing? Aver?" I was still waiting for his reply and was positive he'd say something to make the whole situation make more sense.

"It wasn't something that came up, pet. And it wouldn't have changed anything about how I felt about you."

Was the implication that he was worried how it would've changed how I felt? And what exactly were we talking about? I'd partied with a wide variety of people— general kinksters, vanilla couples, furries, adult babies, and so many more—but this didn't feel like that. It didn't feel like they were explaining a kinky lifestyle where they all acted like wolves. "Okay, I'm getting scared. What didn't come up?"

"Aver, I can't believe you wouldn't—" Branson started to say.

Aver snarled over my head at him. "Really? Because you were so forthcoming. Riley had to force the truth out of you."

"Accidentally!" Riley chirped.

The bickering felt familiar, an argument between two people with a lot of history. But what they were arguing about was impossible. Right?

"It wasn't something I purposefully hid from you, Hollister. But, like my sexuality, this is a secret that only few know, and it must stay that way."

I pulled my hand free, and that time, he let me. "How many more secrets do you have, Aver?"

"This is the last one, but—" He grimaced. "It's layered."

I threw my hands up, putting a few feet of distance between myself and everyone else crowding the kitchen—including Aver. "Okay, fine. You turn into wolves. Show me."

Having pushed this joke to its natural conclusion, I expected them to start laughing. Instead, they looked at each other like they were silently deciding which of them would get the task. My vote was for baby Bran. I mean, if I was about to see the impossible, they could at least make it the adorable impossible.

But it was Branson who stood forward while everyone else held their breaths.

I looked him up and down. He was a sturdy man, over six feet with a muscular build. The picture-perfect definition of sexy lumberjack. "Do you need to say a spell or—"

Branson dropped so suddenly, I gasped and lunged forward. But my hands reached for a wolf standing on all fours, not Branson. An actual wolf. I fell back and would've landed hard on my ass if Aver hadn't zoomed to catch me.

I searched the ceiling and the floor around the wolf, looking for wires, a trapdoor, something that explained what I was seeing. In the blink of an eye, the wolf disappeared, and Branson stood once more in that spot, wearing the same clothes he'd been wearing.

More than anything else, that seemed to be the fact that broke my brain. Where did the clothes go? How was this possible? If there were people who could turn into animals, what else was true about the world? Fairies? Gnomes? Singing trolls? My head felt light, like I'd gotten up too quickly after laying down.

"Do you have any questions?" Aver's question came from closer than I'd anticipated, and I realized I'd frozen in the same falling position he'd caught me from. Most of my weight braced into him, though he didn't look or sound like holding me up was very difficult.

Did I have any questions? A zillion. Did I know how to verbalize them? No.

"Can I...have a minute?" I said quietly. Something like this required at least a few minutes of quiet contemplation. "Maybe outside? Alone?"

Aver tensed, and I anticipated him rejecting my request, but then Branson cleared his throat, drawing Aver's gaze that way. I didn't know what passed between them, but the result was Aver guiding me through the group of wolf-people to the back patio. "You can stay out here as long as you need." He let go of me, and it looked like the action had been difficult for him.

Now that I'd learned what I had about Aver, I wondered if his intense protective nature was a byproduct of what he was.

"Just...please stay where I can see you," he asked, his eyes tight.

I nodded. I didn't know what to say any more than I knew what to think. I needed time to process everything I'd seen and hopefully figure out how it was all still a prank. Walker Bay stretched out before me, and though the choppy surface and serene forest backdrop was beautiful, and the water churned white with activity in a way that was awe-inspiring, I couldn't concentrate on any of it for very long.

I looked back over my shoulder to where Aver had gone inside. He'd shut the glass door. I hadn't expected him to do that. The others stood around him in a half circle. I could only see bits and pieces of them around Aver's frame, but their mouths moved as they talked heatedly. About me? Probably.

My phone chimed, bringing the surreal moment full circle. We were still in the same world. I was the same person. My phone was the same; so was the ringtone. In fact, most of what I'd known about the earth was still true. Only a fraction had changed. But whoo boy was it a hefty fraction.

The text was from Sprinkles. Thank goodness. I'd been worried when Sam had told me they hadn't seen him since the night I met Aver. And right now was the perfect time to hear from him. I could use some nice, normal, good news.

Call off the hounds! I found my soulmate, and he lives in Ballard! Don't worry. I'll stay in touch. XOXXOX

I replied, letting him know I was excited for him and chastising him for not letting someone know where he was. People disappeared all the time, and a young, gay man in a city he was still learning... it wasn't a chance I wanted him to take.

And make sure you check if he turns into a wolf.

I didn't really type that part, but I thought about it. I hadn't known to put that on my list of things to watch out for.

Was it, though? The fact remained: before the wolf thing, I hadn't gotten a weird vibe from any of them. I hadn't checked them all, but I didn't feel like I had to. These were good people. They loved each other. They loved Aver.

Thinking about the man made it impossible not to turn around again. He stood where he'd been before, but with his back to me. I could tell from the bits of faces I could see around Aver's body that the conversation was tense. I got to my feet, my first thought that I should be there for Aver.

I stepped slowly back to the door and grinned. Aver had

left it cracked open a little, but not enough that I could tell from where I'd been sitting. That little turd.

From my angle and with how close Aver stood to the door, I couldn't see the others from my position, which meant they couldn't see me either.

I didn't want to eavesdrop, so I reached for the door quickly.

"And when were you going to tell him he could get pregnant?"

I froze, my hand falling silently to my side. That voice had sounded like Branson, who hadn't struck me as being a real big joker. Nash and Wyatt, yes. But not Branson.

What the ever-living fuck was going on? It was a truth universally acknowledged that eavesdropping rules did not apply when the conversation was as batshit as this one, so I held my breath and listened on.

"He won't," Aver growled.

Why did that hurt?

"I'm very careful, and besides, he could only get pregnant if he were my mate, and he doesn't have any special ability or power. I would've known by now if he had."

The words popped out of me, both in defense and because I had an innate urge to be helpful. "Yes, I do."

Aver turned. Our eyes met. I'd spent several days learning those eyes, and the look they had now was one of complete shock. "You do?" He'd only whispered two words, and yet, I'd heard caution, hope, fear, and love in equal measures. "What can you do?"

Aver stepped aside, and I entered the kitchen. Everyone was still there. The twins had been put in their highchairs, facing each other. That made sense when I watched Madison pick up a chunk of banana and hurl it the few inches to her brother's tray. He laughed and popped the chunk in his mouth.

Meanwhile, baby Bran was on the ground standing like one of the grownups around the island, but it looked like he was a little wobbly, so he kept his pudgy hands braced against the island wall.

"I don't turn into a wolf or anything." I suddenly wondered if what I could do would really even count in present company. At any other party, I'd be the guy with the coolest trick, but I couldn't completely transform my freaking body. But everyone was still staring, so I had to tell them something. "When I touch things... well, I basically already told you, Aver, when I told you about telling fortunes. Except I read more than the room or the person. If you remember, I ask them to let me hold something important to them. Certain items have memories. Powerful emotions, life-changing moments, times of happiness and sadness, it can all get left behind." When nobody said anything, I figured my explanation had been insufficient. I tried again. "Basically, when I touch certain items," *and recently certain people*, "I feel a person's aura or the emotional memory of what a thing has been through."

I'd been unconsciously using my gift since meeting Aver. When I touched his things, I felt his desire and passion. I'd told Aver I liked standing against the walls inside Lawrence, but really, I liked *touching* the exposed logs of the wall because I felt the hands that had touched them. The passion felt wild, uncontrollable... basically, rubbing the logs gave me a log, and that was a weird thing to admit in any company.

"What...What do you feel when you touch me, my things?"

I'd never heard him stutter.

I also didn't want to admit to the way I felt when I touched Aver or anything of his in front of near strangers. They were his family, but my extremely nice but new acquaintances. "I can prove it. Test me. Something you wore during an especially emotional or poignant time in your life. It can be anything."

Aver frowned while the others started looking, searching their pockets and the space around them.

"I have something," Branson said. "But for this to prove anything, everyone has to try their hardest not to let any reactions show beforehand."

A smart suggestion. People didn't think about how much information they conveyed with just their expressions or body movement, and sometimes, I didn't even need to touch an item to know what I was going to say. Telling fortunes was as much about confirming the past as anything else. People didn't want to be told they were going to be rich someday as much as they wanted to feel connected to someone or something again, if only for a minute.

Everyone schooled their faces into blank masks, and Branson removed a white ribbon from his pocket. A circular medal dangled on the loop, and there was a wolf carved into one side. The item didn't look mass-produced like a cheap trinket might be but genuine. A good luck charm of some sort?

That was my guess, at least until I actually grabbed the item from Branson. I nearly dropped it, gasping against the rush of fury and injustice. This was not a good luck charm. I closed my eyes. It wasn't even an item Branson liked. "You hate this. I can't tell you why, but it's an item you despise. It makes you feel like a prisoner, powerless." With my eyes still closed, I took a breath and let it out slowly. "But I also feel determination. Like it's beginning to hold a new purpose for you."

I opened my eyes, meeting their shocked faces. Aver's was the closest. He didn't look shocked, but worried.

"Did that hurt you?" he asked, cupping my face gingerly. "You gasped. Did it hurt?"

My lips curled. "I do feel the more powerful emotions and memories. But that's mostly just jarring or uncomfortable. It isn't usually physically painful unless a memory was attached to a particularly violent event."

Aver's worry never budged. He wasn't relieved by my answer.

"Why did you keep it?" Nash asked Branson.

I handed it back to him, glad to be rid of the anger. Branson looked at the medal in his palm, caressing the flat edge with his thumb. "I wear it for my mom. Whenever I start to feel sympathy that she's rotting in prison, I pull it out and look at it. I remind myself of *bowing*, and that's enough to keep me searching for evidence that will put her away forever."

That answer must've made more sense to the others because they nodded while Riley moved to touch Branson's arm.

Nash turned to Phin, who stood near the twins—both now with as much banana on their face and heads as was smeared across the trays.

He reached for Phin's fitness tracker watch. Phin curved his eyebrow questioningly but nodded to his husband.

"Try this one," Nash said, handing the watch to me.

After what had just happened, I was a little hesitant. That had been a *powerful* rage. But there was an excited gleam in Nash's eye that piqued my curiosity enough I put out my hand, palm up. He dropped it without touching me with his skin. My fingers curled over the watch. I closed my eyes and smiled. *This* was a much better emotion. "This watch has seen *very nice* days." I opened my eyes. As before, Aver's was the first face I saw.

He took one look at my face and snagged the watch out of my hand, flinging it back to Nash, who laughed wildly. "Not funny," Aver growled.

"What?" Kansas asked. "Fill the rest of us in!"

"It was a gift," Phin said, red-faced but smiling. "For our six-month anniversary. The day he gave it to me, and I wore it for the first time was an..." He cleared his throat. "Enjoyable time for all."

"Ooooh, Nash used Phin's watch to make Hollister horny," Kansas said, patting Calvin's back as he lay against one shoulder.

I laughed along with everyone but Aver, who snarled loudly.

"Gosh, okay, jeez." Nash threw his hands up in surrender. "I won't make your mate horny again, I promise. Intentionally, anyway. I have no control over how other people react to my body."

I understood. I often felt the same way about myself. At the moment, I was only joking along with them because it was clear that Phin was fine with everything happening. More than fine—he'd been in on his husband's joke.

"I don't know how I feel about this new version of you," Nash said with a rudeness that could only come with familiarity.

"What do you mean?" I asked. "How much differently did Aver act?"

Aver groaned as the other's began to grin.

"Oh no, I know how much you Walkers love torturing

each other." Riley had his hands on his hips. "If we're going to *finally* be able to tease Aver, then I'm going to make sure we have enough sustenance."

"I thought you were a friend," Aver grumbled.

The group started to move, children were gathered as the migration to the other room began, and frankly, I was feeling a little underexamined. "That's it? You all just believe me? I'm telling you I can sense emotions of the wearer when I hold things, and you're all okay with it?"

"You proved it," Wyatt said, snagging a few bottles of beer from the fridge to bring into the dining room. "What more are you supposed to do?"

I snorted softly. I wasn't looking for their encouragement. I guess I'd expected a closer examination, more disbelief. "No one has questions?"

"I can think of some," Phin offered helpfully.

My shoulders slumped with gentle defeat. Why was I pushing this? These people wanted to accept me while I seemed bent on proving how strange this should all feel. "No, that's okay."

Phin looked relieved.

Wyatt stood, offering Aver and me beers. I shook my head along with Aver. This was strange enough. I didn't need to get tipsy on top of that. "Kansas can steal your energy, Phineas can heal most injuries, Riley compels people to tell the truth, and we all turn into wolves." He looked at my face and must have decided I was disappointed because he added, "But I like what you can do, too. It's very subtle."

Now my head really spun. Clearly, this conversation wasn't over, and I would have to deal with the very strange feeling of not being the coolest guy at a party.

————

Hours later, my belly was full and ached but from laughter. The guys had been ruthless, painting a very different picture of Aver than the one I'd known. To them, Aver was cautious to the point of frustration. He was quiet, a worrier as a child, and, from the sounds of it, that trait hadn't let up into adulthood.

The man I knew only to be bold, commanding, and dominating, they knew as reticent, unassuming, and passive. At least I understood a little better how his *double life* operated. The person at the foundation of it all was caring—I believed that with all my heart. He just showed that care in different ways.

"Are you planning your exit?" Aver asked quietly so he wouldn't disturb the frogs' singing.

He held me in what I would call his favorite position, with my back to his chest, snuggled between his legs—or on his lap—with his arms around me.

"No." I nudged him playfully with the back of my head. "But I am wondering why me? This thing you did, going off into the city to be one person so you could return to Walker County and be another—what made you stop? Why bring a stray home this time?"

Aver's growl shook from his chest and through my back. But it was comforting by now, not scary. "You aren't a stray."

"But why me? Why bring me back—" My throat closed in an instant, blocking any other words from being spoken. They couldn't make it around the dam of jealousy and uncertainty that suddenly flooded me.

"What? Did you see something?" He moved behind me like he was searching our surroundings.

"No, I..." I didn't want to ask, but if I didn't, the question would eat at me. This was why I was always honest and open: because not knowing was worse and would drive a wedge between us faster than anything else could. I didn't want that to happen, so even though I felt uncertain, I asked, "Am I the first? I just assumed...but I guess you could have brought men that didn't get so stir-crazy and ruin everything with a bike tour of the island."

"While I hope the next time you want to go for a bicycle ride on the highway, you'll tell me so I can go with you, no, Hollister. You ruined nothing. You're my one perfect thing in this mess, but you must know that this was a mess of my causing. I created this. Not you."

I exhaled shakily. I'd been more worried about that than I'd let show. Jealousy also wasn't a common emotion for me. I didn't believe love always flowed one way between two people. Love was an entire system of rivers, stretching and branching, coming together before splitting apart. Love was fluid and changing, taking an infinite number of forms.

I still believed all of that. But I also didn't like the idea of Aver having shared things that had become sacred to me with other people. It was a selfish emotion but not something I could change at the moment.

Aver exhaled, tightening his embrace and blocking me from much of the cold air.

A late cover of clouds had drifted in, blocking the moon and stars. The bay stretched out in front of us. The rolling, inky surface now looked sinister when it had once been inviting.

"I never liked leaving the city. The person you spent our first days together with, that's the real me."

"Then why not share the real you with your close family?"

Aver sighed before resting the side of his face against

my head. The man I'd been with for the past couple of days had been passionate and sexy, but he hadn't displayed this sort of sweet vulnerability. I liked seeing that he could be both.

"It's difficult to explain, but a lot of it was fear. That and uncertainty. When the four of us left the pack, we were four hormone-fueled, testosterone-ridden, eighteen-year-olds—"

"I think I've seen that porno."

Aver tried masking his laugh with a growl. "I don't doubt it. But believe me, there was nothing sexy about us at that time. We were a confused, stinky mess. I'd been hiding my nature for years then. My parents had made it clear from before I'd even thought of sex that there was a right and wrong way."

Now, it was my turn to growl. Aver kissed my head, but it didn't feel patronizing, more like he understood completely.

"My body changed, and as I grew into being an alpha, it was obvious early on that, despite every attempt not to, I'd turned down the *wrong way*. So I hid it. And to hide one, I had to hide the other. And then our eighteenth birthdays came, and our parents took us to that field, and the years got muddy for a bit. But instead of taking the chance to spread my wings and test my limits, I drew inward.

"I hated and loved my parents. I wanted to never see them again, but I still wanted them to be proud of me. Somewhere along that path, I'd settled on proving them wrong. The plan became work, keep out of trouble, and prove to them that I could make them proud. Then I was going to come out in a blaze of glory..." He sighed. "It all sounds so juvenile now that I'm saying it out loud. A man, nearly forty, still looking for his parent's approval."

That wasn't at all how I would've described Aver's situation. "That's an exaggeration but I get it. I was adopted. My parents chose me to be their son, and then they chose for me not to be."

"I'm sorry, pet. Here I am, complaining when you've gone through the same thing. But you stayed true to yourself."

I turned my upper half around so I could see his face and cup his scratchy cheek. "We can't all take the same road. Besides, your situation is completely different. You had roots. I don't think I ever really took root at that house. I mean, you've seen my place. And if *that* was preferable to their house, it gives you an idea."

Aver frowned, but I thought it was because he was picturing my house again.

I stretched my neck to kiss him, planting my lips on his sturdy chin. "I understand the why now, but not what changed. You seemed to have a working system." One that was slowly chipping away at his soul, but that didn't mean he hadn't been able to keep the parts of his life portioned away from each other, like a picky eater making sure the foods on their plate didn't touch.

Aver kissed my lips. "You, pet. It was you. I saw you at the club, and it was all over for me. Even if I didn't know it yet. I couldn't put who I was away anymore. That ability broke the more time I spent with you. But, even though this started because of my reaction to you, I think now it's me who has changed irrevocably. Kiss by kiss, you extinguished the fire that fueled my desire to show my parents how wrong they are. I was never going to convince them otherwise. It took about a week of time with you to see that."

"You're giving me too much credit. I didn't even know the situation. If anything changed, you changed it." I kissed him so he couldn't disagree.

As was his way, he quickly took over the kiss, slipping his tongue through my lips. This day had marked the longest time we'd gone without having sex with each other, and my body was beginning to protest.

But I still had questions. My dick twitched in protest. *Believe me, buddy, I know.* There were a few topics that were still more important than getting naked. "Now that you know I have powers like the others, what does this mean? Does it make me your..." What was the word they'd used? It had sounded barbaric while also feeling like a hug. "Mate. Am I your mate? Am I allowed to ask that?"

When Aver didn't immediately respond, it was as if he'd unleashed bubbles of anxiety inside me. I didn't understand what *mate* meant in this context. Maybe it was something he didn't want me to become. Even though I didn't understand the word, that Aver could not want me in any capacity was a fear I was only then facing. Love was fluid, but this had felt permanent. Unless it only felt permanent for me.

I leaned my weight forward, out of Aver's arms. He let me go but only so he could spin me around, maneuvering me so I sat on his lap with my thighs cradling his.

"In our culture, shifter culture, mate means something like marriage. It's something that is chosen, just like with regular people. I don't think that's what we have."

Oh good, he'd wanted to turn me around to break my heart to my face.

He cupped my cheeks, bringing our faces closer together. "We have something more. But we just met, and I've been trying hard not to scare you."

"Something more? What's more than mate?"

"It's not exactly more, but different. An omega. That's a little harder to explain."

"Is it how the others became pregnant? They were omegas?"

Aver shook his head. "One doesn't immediately cause the other. Before Riley and Branson, there had been generations of alphas choosing omegas where nothing out of the ordinary happened. Omegas are much more common than blessed births. But they are still very special. Only an alpha can take an omega, and the omega is granted protections and security they wouldn't have otherwise within the pack. They're sacred." He stopped speaking so suddenly I knew there was something more he wasn't saying. Instead of pestering, I waited, letting him find the words.

"The way I feel about you is...intense. If I'm not around you, I want to be. If I am around you, I need to be closer. I know it is a lot to handle. And the last thing I want to do is frighten you away."

I smirked because I understood completely and sighed because it was a relief to hear him say it. "I'm not one of those easily spooked horses."

I popped up as a thought hit me like a lightning bolt. "Am I pregnant right now? Because you didn't know?"

Aver shook his head. "We were careful, every time. You aren't now. But, if we have sex without protection, there is a chance you could become pregnant."

Which meant there was also a chance that this was all a coincidence, that I just happened to have powers like the others, but that I wasn't the man Aver was looking for. That hurt so much, and I didn't want to think about it. But becoming pregnant shouldn't be something that just happened, if it could be avoided, so I couldn't block this whole conversation from happening, even if it hurt.

"Do you want that?" Did I? I lived in a single room in a house of drug addicts. That certainly wasn't a place to raise

127

a child. And how could I afford to provide for a tiny Hollister on a fortune teller's salary? You'd think something like that would remain predictable, but it wasn't. And I couldn't actually tell the future, so I never knew when people were going to be willing or not.

But I wouldn't be pregnant alone. I'd consoled enough pregnant teen runaways to know it took two to make a baby the old-fashioned way.

"Hollister, I can see I need to make this part very clear. I want *everything* from you. I want to be *everything* for you. But you're a person, with your own emotions, opinions, and dreams. I won't take those things from you, and I can't make this choice."

I settled into my position on his lap. He was hard, and feeling his erection only made me harder. I wanted to make whatever choice made us naked faster, but at the same time, this was an important conversation. Possibly the most important conversation I'd ever had. "What are you asking, Aver?" I whispered. Despite my best efforts, my hips wiggled, rubbing our dicks against each other.

The area around us grew silent. The frogs had stopped their croaking, and other than the short waves lapping at the shore, there was no sound. It was as if the world knew that this moment was important and wanted to take away any other distraction.

"Stay with me, Hollister. I don't want to vacation with you. I want to live with you. We can stay in Lawrence, not for just a few weeks, but for the rest of our lives."

"You aren't needed here?" I didn't want to become a homewrecker.

"Yes, but I was trying to convince you to stay. I couldn't say move in with me and my ten roommates. We could split our time, or make a schedule, or whatever you want. You know everything now, all the important stuff anyway."

While Aver had been talking, his hands slid to my upper thighs, where he made lazy circles with his thumbs. I'd already had a hard time concentrating through my lust, and his touch made it all the more impossible.

"Are you listening to me, pet?" His voice contained that roughened sharpness that I'd grown to love. "Or are you too distracted?"

My hips hadn't stopped their rocking. I was all but humping Aver on the shores of Walker Bay. We couldn't be seen from the house, and the bay would cover most of our sounds—I'd learned Aver and the rest of them also had heightened senses—so we were secluded where we were, but being outside, in the open, made it feel dangerous.

Aver pushed me back so he could look into my face. "You need me," he said with sultry concern.

If that wasn't the hottest way to say, "You're horny right now," I didn't know what it was. And he wasn't wrong. This conversation was important, but my body felt conditioned. It had grown used to constant loving, and now a few hours felt like a drought.

"You can't answer when your head is clouded." Aver's eyes wrinkled with concern as his hands dove between our bodies. He reached into my pants and gripped my dick with such sureness, you would've thought they were his pants. And his dick.

"This isn't going to help," I moaned, while attempting to roll my hips into his grip. My ass stuck out with every retreat while my back bowed with each advance. By now, Aver thinking of my dick would make it hard. And he was doing so much more than thinking about it.

Despite my moan of protest, Aver continued his strokes.

The way was slick, thanks to his spit and my precum, and it wasn't long before my balls tightened, preparing to blow. "I don't want your decision swayed by desire, pet." He chuckled, and the warm sound stroked my spine. "That, and it has been far too long since I've touched this cock."

In that, we were agreed.

If someone were to come upon us in that moment, there would be no question about what we were doing. Between Aver's passionate kisses, expert dick-handling, and the way I humped him, what we were doing was obvious. I didn't care, though. And that was probably why Aver wanted me to come before I decided what to do. Right then, I'd do whatever kept his hands on my dick.

I climaxed, bringing an explosion of color that erupted behind my eyelids.

Aver kept our mouths together, swallowing my moans so they wouldn't drift up to the house. Pleasure made my limbs light, and as I breathed through the intense orgasm, clarity did indeed return. I circled my arms around his neck, hugging him tightly. With my face buried against his neck, I could see now there'd only ever been one choice for me.

Aver.

I still wasn't sure about people turning into animals and knew there was a whole lot of baggage I still needed to understand, but I wasn't choosing any of that. I was choosing Aver.

So, I whispered the only words possible in that moment. "I want to stay with you. Wherever you are, Aver, that's where I want to be."

7

AVER

Saturday mornings pre-Hollister had been like any
other of the other days. The days all ran together before
him. My tasks never changed; needing to hide didn't
change. The only time I'd looked forward to a set of days
was when I had a Seattle trip planned, and now, the
thought of going into town as I once had held zero appeal.

My focus was on Hollister now and always.

"In my mouth," Hollister mumbled, draped over my bare
chest while still very much asleep. And dreaming, clearly.
"Put it in my mouth."

This wasn't the first time I'd overheard Hollister sleep-
talk during a sex dream. It was something he'd done often
and never failed to make me jealous. I knew my pet couldn't
control what he dreamed about. I could only hope anything
that made him sound that excited involved me.

"Mm, yes, so good, dark, definitely not blond, stranger..."
Hollister murmured.

His breathing had changed, so I knew he was awake and
teasing me. "Nice try, pet."

Hollister opened his eyes, stretching his arms over the

top of me. "What? Huh? I'm just now waking up," he said with mock innocence.

He stretched out the stiffness from a night spent in deep sleep. After our time on the shore, I'd been eager to get him into a shower, and then he'd looked too sleepy and comfortable to make him drive back to Lawrence.

Hollister lifted his head, looking around like he was only just noticing our location. "I'd convinced myself that yesterday was a dream. But it wasn't. You're a wolf. There are more people than just me that can do impossible things."

"And I love you."

The apples of his cheeks rounded as he smiled. "And you love me." He pushed off my chest like he was trying to leap off the bed, but I grabbed him around the middle.

"And?" I was fishing, but I wanted to hear him say it again, if only so I could convince myself last night hadn't been a dream. Hollister hadn't only accepted who I was, but he hadn't looked at me like I was weak, or less of a man, like I'd been expecting.

"And you're stuck with me now," he said.

I flipped him over, making him squeal. Nestled in the pillows, he looked up at me, and my chest felt tight. I wasn't *stuck* with him. He'd set me free. All this time, he'd been the catalyst I needed to move on with my life and finally accept something I should've a long time ago. And now, I needed to thank him.

He must have seen what I had planned because his pupils darkened as his lips parted.

"Aver! You up?" Branson yelled while pounding on the door.

"You would be now if you weren't," Hollister joked before suddenly darting his eyes to the door. "Dang! He heard that, didn't he?"

The pounding stopped long enough for Branson to laugh and knock more. "I did."

Laughter came from somewhere behind him; it sounded like Phin.

"Riley is at work, and I'm going to take Bran to the house to keep searching. Do you want to come?"

No, I didn't. I wanted to stay in bed and make love to Hollister. But my pet's eyes gleamed with excitement. He was eager to see other shifters and more of that world. He'd been given only the highlight reel the night before. "When are you leaving?"

Maybe I'd be lucky, and he'd say after lun—

"In ten minutes. I'll meet you in the rig."

He was gone before I'd agreed, and without enough time for me to do anything about the throbbing need between my legs. Hollister had been so deliciously needy the night before. His eyes had gone unfocused, hazy with desire. Seeing him come apart in my hands had been my second favorite moment of the night. My first was the moment right after that, when he'd agreed to stay.

We hadn't talked about making the move, but he'd already packed most of his belongings anyway. They'd fit in a backpack and large duffel. His friends were also important, so I needed to figure out how to make sure he kept those interactions, while also fulfilling his need to help others.

When our gazes met, Hollister bit his bottom lip, sucking it between his teeth. I inhaled, but the smells were just all of Hollister and his need. After a steady exhale, I kissed the tip of his nose. "To be continued."

. . .

"Do you ever mess with people? Turn into wolves just to scare them?" Hollister asked, his face plastered against the window.

I smiled, remembering he'd been that way on the ferry. Filled with curiosity and wonder. Seeing his passion for the world and everything in it stoked my passion. Before Hollister, things had been black and white with minute shades of gray. Now, my world was in color. But I didn't want to stare at the window, just at Hollister.

"I've never," I said from the front seat while baby Bran kept yelling 'Tree!' over and over.

He'd been picking up words quickly these days. We had to be much more careful about what we said around him.

"Neither have I, but we were taught that humans were mostly to be ignored."

"Harsh," Hollister replied.

Branson turned down the driveway that led to his childhood home. As the two-story brick mansion came into view, Hollister turned his attention from his window to the windshield.

"Okay, so everyone is loaded here. That's not at all intimidating or anything."

Branson's old home was impressive, but it was impossible for any of us to look at these homes without thinking of everything else that came with it.

Thankfully, the driveway was empty. Only Delia's town car sat in front of the house. Someone should've move it into the garage, but Delia and her butler had been taken too quickly for either to give the order.

And after she'd tried to kill Riley and kidnap Kansas, there wasn't a prison cell dark enough for her. I could forgive the lifelong meddling and manipulations—if not forgive, then forget. But none of us could allow someone who had proven themselves dangerous to any of the mates to remain in our lives.

Branson opened the door. There was no need to lock houses on pack lands. Not that crimes never occurred, but when they did, the culprit was normally located and dealt with quickly.

"I've been coming here searching every room since she was arrested, but other than the safe, I haven't found anything of note and nothing I could use to prove her guilt. If I knew what to look for..." He looked down at his son, walking alongside him on unsteady feet. Branson exhaled slowly, releasing the tension that talking about his mother brought him. "I'll find something. She wasn't dumb enough to write down her evil plans, but there is proof in this house, and I will find it."

We split up to cover more space. Branson and Bran took the top floor while Hollister and I searched below. But, if Branson didn't know what to look for, then Hollister clearly couldn't be expected to either. He mostly walked around the room, careful about what he touched. We'd told him enough about the type of woman Delia was that he didn't want to touch any of her things unprepared.

We worked through the downstairs study and then over into the dining room. There weren't as many places to hide things in the dining room, so we quickly moved into one of the sitting rooms. Hollister stood in front of the window, looking out, when he suddenly stiffened and backed away.

"There's someone here," he said, returning to my side.

I grabbed his hand, walking us both to the window. "It's my father. Someone most likely told him they'd spotted us."

Hollister pulled his hand free, and I thought he wanted to walk behind me instead, so I didn't question it. This hadn't been how I thought I would come out to my parents, but it was a good a time as any.

I opened the front door before my father could knock.

"Aver! I heard you were here," he boomed happily. "Someone said they saw people they didn't recognize, so I thought I should come check it out."

On the surface, nothing he said sounded odd, except for the fact that my father wasn't the type to check out sounds or noises. He sent people to check out sounds and noises.

If he wanted to keep this charade up, that was his choice. "I'm helping Branson search." I wouldn't say any more on the subject until I could be more certain how much of this helpful interim Alpha act was fake.

"After what Delia did to the blessed mates, I support any action that leaves her in prison. Let me know how I can assist you."

If he thought that would make me happy, he would be disappointed. The situation was simply too layered for me to know. In general, our parents hated each other. My father had always hated that Patrick was born an alpha and not him. That hatred had extended to Delia and Branson. But he also hated Wyatt and Nash's parents. At the same time, if the reward was great enough, our parents were known to work together.

"We won't be needing any assistance," I told him, part as a test of how he would react and because I wanted him to know I wasn't buying this act. Maybe the old Aver would've played along for the sake of keeping the peace, but my thoughts on the situation would've remained the same.

I inhaled, not afraid, but ready. I angled to the side. "Father, this is—"

There was no one there.

"Hollister?" I called out, trying not to give into the

immediate urge to tear the home down in my search. When he didn't answer, I ran back the way we'd come, following his scent. We'd been down here for at least an hour, though, and his scent was everywhere.

Tracking him wasn't as difficult as it once would have been, and I followed his scent up the stairs. I didn't know where my father had gone or if he was still even at the door waiting. I didn't care.

All I could focus on was that Hollister was missing. And that was unacceptable. "Hollister!"

Branson poked his head out of one of the doors down the left side of the hallway. "What's going on? Is your dad here?"

"Yes, but I can't find Hollister." Keeping the snarls and growls from my voice took great effort.

"Can't say I blame him. I wouldn't want to meet Glendon either."

That was funny, but I wasn't in the mood to joke. I needed to know Hollister was safe; I couldn't function otherwise, and while he was missing, he wasn't safe.

And the longer he remained missing, the larger the possibility of danger.

I followed his scent trail down the right side of the hallway. "Pet, if you can hear me, I need you to say something."

"I'm here." Hollister's resigned, quiet voice sounded from behind the door to my left.

Branson's old room.

I opened the door but couldn't see Hollister.

"Here. In the closet."

I would've found him moments later anyway; his scent was so strong. I opened the closet door slowly. Hollister sat on the floor on his bottom, sitting against the back wall. The clothes hanging in front of him gave him some camouflage, and his feet lined up perfectly with a line of shoes. But the shoes on either side of his feet were much larger.

Inhaling, I exhaled the rising panic. He was here, safe, in front of me.

I still wanted to know why he was hiding in the closet.

I pushed aside the hanging clothes closest to him, and he peered up at me, hugging his legs tightly. "Is he gone?"

"Who? My father?"

He nodded. "I'm sorry. That was close. I know what he looks like now, though, so—"

The snarl that came out of me had nothing to do with Hollister, but he was the one who gasped at the sound. He was the only faultless person in this whole messed-up situation, and though I was furious with myself for making Hollister think this was what I wanted, this wasn't the time for me to deal with my fury.

Leaving the door open, I stepped into the closet, shimmying my much larger body into the space beside him. I stretched my legs out, so long my feet stuck out through the doorway.

Immediately, Hollister dropped his head to my shoulder. I took his right hand, holding it tightly in my lap.

"I don't want to hide who I am, but I also don't want to force you to reveal something you aren't ready for." Hollister's lips turned down, and his voice was soft. "You didn't know your father was coming. You didn't have time to prepare."

"And so you hid." I'd filled in the blanks before that point, and the thought simultaneously warmed and broke my heart. "For me." Because unlike me, Hollister could never pretend to be anyone but who he was.

He didn't say anything, but he didn't have to.

"I was ready," I said, not to make him feel worse, but so

he would know to never feel like he was something that needed to be hidden. Maybe our days in Lawrence had led him to believe he was my secret, but really, it was the rest of my life that I didn't want tainting him. Pack life was shitty on the best occasions, and recently, it had gone fully septic. "I turned around to introduce you, and you were gone. He probably thinks I'm crazy," I laughed so Hollister would know that didn't upset me in the slightest. This could work in my favor, and he could let up on the requests to visit that had increased tenfold since Alpha Walker had died. Though the allotted time he was allowed to stand as interim dwindled, they were still no closer to getting a Walker alpha to take the position of pack Alpha. And if they couldn't have that, no one knew what they would do. A pack without an Alpha was a pack primed for destruction.

Hollister sat straight, turning to look at me. A sleeve from one of the hanging shirts fell over his head, and he pushed it back impatiently, shoving his blond waves askew at the same time. "You were? I ruined everything."

"No. Clearly, it wasn't the right time. I don't want to make you uncomfortable, though, so I won't come out with you around if that's what you would like."

"Not at all! I want to be there for you. I guess...we hadn't talked about it, and I feel like I'm barely treading water here. This is all a lot to deal with, and I once put on an entire drag-queen fashion show for charity with only five hours of preparation."

I didn't doubt him for a second and was certain they raised a lot of money thanks to his efforts. "I understand. You've had your knowledge of the world challenged. But don't worry. Coming out won't be anywhere near as difficult as a fashion show."

My phone chimed, and I assumed it was Branson

checking in on us. It wasn't. My father's text said he'd left since he had interim work to do but asked that I come to dinner in the coming days and bring any *new friends* I may have.

I tilted the screen so Hollister could read it at the same time. "Is that weird?" he asked.

"Very."

"Do we trust it?"

Not if we had any sense. "No."

"Are we going?"

Our eyes met, and the world drifted away. Did I want to put Hollister in a potentially uncomfortable situation? No. But I was eager to put all the facades behind me, and I trusted Hollister to be honest about what he could and couldn't handle. "What do you think?"

He sighed and pursed only the corners of his lips. "If you want to, we should. You don't have to worry about me. I once agreed to play Jorge's new boyfriend when his ex came in from California. Those were some very uncomfortable dinners, but I'd told Jorge I would act the part."

I cocked my head to the side. "Do I want to hear the rest of this story?"

Hollister beamed and shook his head. "Probably not... actually, *definitely* not. I was *very* convincin—"

I kissed him. It was rude. He'd been talking, but he kissed me back, proving he'd mostly been teasing. If I had to live in a fantasy world to keep believing that, then I would.

Besides, I had a dinner to plan for.

8

HOLLISTER

My stomach would not stop flip-flopping. Later, in the evening, Aver and I were supposed to go to his parents' house. I didn't know what they were serving, but I knew what Aver would be doing, and I was as scared as I was excited for him.

I wasn't scared about what his parents would think because fuck that. I did hope Aver could let any negative opinions roll off his back just as easily. Mostly, it was the unknown that had me full of nerves.

That was why, earlier, I'd been drawn to the happy sounds and playful laughing outside.

Aver was in the home office a few rooms over, trying to get a handle on all the projects that had marched on in his absence. I was glad that at least he could work more easily now that all the cats had been dumped from their respective bags. He was glad too, though he wouldn't say as much.

Mostly, Aver wanted some alone time in Lawrence, and I did too, but he'd let the projects in his life slide to pay attention to me, and I wouldn't let that keep happening.

I wasn't sure where anyone else was, and though I'd

only ever been welcomed in this home, I still tiptoed from Aver's bedroom to the glass doors in the kitchen.

The laughter was louder now, but I still couldn't see where it was coming from. Water splashed as a baby laughed. I crept over the patio stones around the house toward the sound, though I could have stomped and still not have been heard.

I peeked around the corner.

Riley, Phineas, and Kansas were in the hot tub. The jets were off, and the water must have been cool because they had the children as well. Madison stood with her chubby fingers gripped to the edge of the tub as she babbled at Mr. Boots. If the cat wasn't careful, he was going to get a bath. Bran stood next to her holding a plastic book.

The moment after Mr. Boots ran away—finally wising up to the dangerous position he'd been in—Madison made a swipe for Bran's book, prompting the other child to yank it out of reach. The book slipped from his fingers and fell with a splash behind his head.

Riley ducked beneath the water, emerging almost immediately with the book. "How about I read it to you both?" he suggested.

Patrick crawled out of his father's arms to stand with the other children for story time, and Kansas angled Calvin so he could see too.

The sun shone overhead, though they were saved from direct light by a cleverly placed table umbrella. Each of them were smiling, and the children were—for the most part —happy. The seven of them painted such a beautiful picture. Although I wanted to turn the corner and ask to join in on the fun, I worried I'd be stepping in on a moment that wasn't actually mine. I didn't have any kids. Aver and I hadn't talked more about the possibility of me becoming pregnant after I'd made the decision to stay. We hadn't had sex without protection yet, though, so I assumed he wasn't ready.

"Come on." Aver grabbed my hand.

I jumped, feeling like I'd been caught doing something I shouldn't. He tugged me inside and through the kitchen while my heart pounded.

Aver was simply so perfect. I kept waiting for the other shoe to drop. For him to get angry and lash out.

He stopped suddenly in the hallway and turned around, backing me into the wall. With his fingers spread, he placed his palm against my heart. "Why is this pounding, pet?"

"I'm sorry I was snooping."

He frowned. "You weren't snooping. You're my mate. You belong here as much as anyone else."

I beamed. We'd talked about it, but hearing him say it released a heavy worry I'd carried for a few days. When he'd told me that mates were chosen, I figured he was saying it wasn't something he chose for us. He'd said I was his everything, but I still hadn't believed that meant he wanted us to have labels.

That was another thing I wasn't normally so hung up on —what people called each other. Why did titles matter if everyone was having fun and knew the score? But with Aver, it mattered.

Aver had his eyes on me while I thought through my concerns. His eyes tilted, and he leaned in, kissing me sweetly. "I screwed up again, didn't I?"

"No, no, it's fine."

"If you don't know with confidence that your place is with and beside me, then it isn't fine. I keep trying to soften aspects of our lives, but every time I do, it blows up in my face. For good reason, too. I won't shield you from what you mean to me anymore. When I do, it has the opposite effect."

I'd been staring at the button of his shirt when Aver angled my face upward.

"I'm helping you find a swimsuit, so you can join the others. If you still want to, that is... ?"

My right foot popped up, rotating in a circle with my big toe against the ground. "If you don't think they'd mind..."

Aver hauled me over his shoulder and down the hall. He dumped on the bed and disappeared into the closet, emerging with several pairs of swim trunks. "You'll have to try some of my older ones. Kansas or Phin might have a pair that fits you better, but..." He scratched the back of his head, looking at me from under his lashes. "I don't like the idea of you wearing someone else's things. It's a shifter thing, or a me thing. Probably a me thing."

These tiny moments of indecision were so precious. So often when we were together, Aver knew what to do and when to do it.

"That's okay. I don't all the way understand, but I understand enough."

Aver's shoulders relaxed as he picked through shorts he'd gathered. In the end he held up two options for me to decide.

"The blue ones."

Aver grinned. "These were my choice too." He reached for my shirt like he was going to undress me but then stepped back. "I should let you change on your own, or neither of us will get where we're going." He went to the door but stopped. "Do you want me to go with you?"

Yes. I did. But that was silly. Riley and the others were some of the nicest people I'd ever met. "I'll manage. Got to get my feet wet somehow." I smiled at my pun and turned toward the bed, when Aver grabbed my wrist and twirled me around.

I leaned into him, his hands cupping my ass as his tongue explored my mouth. That was familiar territory by now, and yet each kiss felt new and exciting. As my body stirred, switching from being nervous to turned on, Aver leaned back. "Tease," I growled, the sound still not as impressive as when Aver did it.

Aver just laughed down the hallway, leaving me to put on a swimsuit like a grownup.

I hated being grown up.

I changed quickly, nearly sprinting back outside to the corner of the house. They were all still there—I'd worried they'd finish before I could get back. I took a deep breath, remembered I was a shiny unicorn full of splendor, and walked forward.

"Hollister!" Phineas called out. "Thank goodness! I've been having a horrible time wrestling these two. It doesn't help that one always seems to be trying to drown the other."

He was exaggerating, but I appreciated the invitation, nonetheless. I climbed the steps and dipped my toe as the others scooted over to give me room. The water was room temperature, as I'd suspected. Not cold, but not anything I would call hot. Instead, the water was that perfect temperature that required no period of adjustment.

With the exception of Calvin, who was still working on rolling over independently, the children stood on the same bench the rest of us sat on. They could shuffle around without the water going too high, and if anyone of them did go off the step, one of us would be near enough to grab them. At the moment, Bran was the strongest walker, but Madison and Patrick were eager to become mobile.

"When these niblets learn to run, that will be the death of me," Phin said.

"We need to work on our herding skills," Riley suggested. "If a border collie can keep hundreds of sheep in check, I think three wolves could manage four children."

"Five, soon!" Kansas chirped.

The other men looked to me, their heads turning at the same time.

Kansas sat back. "Unless you don't... I mean, you don't have to. No one expects you to...your body, your choice!" By then, his face was blazing red.

I smiled so he would know I wasn't offended. But I was curious. Patrick stood to the right but grabbed onto my arm, working his little body around where he crawled in my lap.

I felt chosen, like when a stray or friend's pet chooses to trust you enough to sit on you. Patrick seemed to have a plan, though, and grabbed a finger on both of my hands. I pulled, guessing he wanted to be on his feet, and he squealed out his happiness. "What is it like? Does it feel weird?"

"Definitely," Riley said.

At the same time, Nash said, "It's a little strange."

A little? I'd thought it would be a lot strange. "How does it happen?"

Riley held Bran under his arms in the deeper part of the tub so he could kick his legs. "Well, when two people love each other very much..."

Warmth spread out from my chest at the gentle teasing. I liked that they felt comfortable enough with me to joke around. The bond these three men had not with each other, but with each of the Walker cousins, was intimidating.

All these men, living together, loving and caring for each other, it wasn't a situation I'd seen before, and I didn't think I ever would again. What these men had was unique, and I didn't want to do anything to disturb their bonds.

But I so desperately wanted to be included.

"They call the pregnancies blessed. And, according to shifter history, it has happened before, but not often. Riley becoming pregnant was a miracle. When me and Kansas also did, it was like nuclear levels of miraculousness. But no one knows exactly why it is happening or how we all can do what we can do," Phineas explained.

"What other similarities do you all have?" Patrick grew bored of standing on my thighs and tried to climb over my shoulder.

Phineas reached forward for the plastic book and handed it to me. "You don't have to read it, just open the pages. Books are about the only thing I've found that makes either of these two rascals slow down."

I opened the book, and Patrick turned, settling into my lap like magic. He grabbed the book from me but kept it open like he was reading a newspaper.

"We all have abilities. That's the obvious one. And we all came from less than ideal backgrounds," Riley said.

I was two for two at the moment. "I was adopted."

"Is your birthday June twenty-first?" Riley asked with a knowing smile.

"How did you... ?"

"June twenty-first." Phin raised his hand.

"Here too," Kansas added.

"The others were all born on the same day in December too. At the same exact moment, well, give or take a half a second."

It felt like we were on the edge of figuring something out, but I didn't know what that thing was.

"Don't break your brain over it," Phin said. "We haven't been able to figure it out either."

Did that mean I would definitely become pregnant? And if that happened, I'd turn into a shifter too. At least, that seemed to be how it went. I'd have to cross that bridge when I came to it. "Aver called me mate today. It was the first time. It feels..."

Riley sighed while Phin's cheeks went pink.

"It's amazing, isn't it," Kansas whispered. "I mean, we can never tell them this, but I swear, all Wyatt has to do is call me mate, and there's just something so primal..."

Riley nodded. "It's like *pow*, right to the penis."

"Penis!" Bran shouted.

Kansas burst out laughing, which was the wrong thing to do in the moment because it only made Bran scream *penis* louder and louder searching for the same reaction.

"Branson Evelyn Aver Nash Wyatt Walker Junior," Riley said, but to no avail. The child continued screaming the word, making it hard not to laugh. "Great, now the rest of the children are going to start." His words seemed annoyed, but he didn't sound that way.

He sounded happy. They all did. Deliriously happy. No one here had been forced into anything, and this, more than anything else, convinced me of what I wanted.

Was the world ready to handle a tiny Hollister-Aver hybrid? I didn't know the answer to that question, but my hope was that we'd find out.

9

AVER

EVER SINCE HOLLISTER had returned from his time in the tub with the others, he'd been quiet. I'd assumed he was nervous about the coming dinner. I wasn't nervous as much as I wanted to get this part of my life over with.

It was strange how I'd held on to something for so long, but now, I couldn't wait to get rid of it.

"At any point, if you want to leave, just tell me. We'll leave." I pulled the car around the driveway so that when it was time to go, we could drive straight out. Planning an exit strategy off pack lands had become common practice for us cousins. We'd had more contact recently than we'd ever had with the pack since we'd left, and I didn't see that changing while everything was still up in the air. Ideally, the pack would get to a place where they were self-sufficient, and we could continue to maintain healthy separation.

While Delia had tried to use pack law to force us in, since her arrest, the shifter council had decided that the blessed mates needed to be protected, above all else. No one understood why the blessed pregnancies were happening,

149

but there was one fact most shifters agreed with: they needed to be protected.

I had to let go of Hollister's hand while we both got out, but his palm was in mine as soon as I could get to him.

"Are you sure?" Hollister asked, staring at where we were joined. His voice was steady and his eyes clear.

"Positive. I've held this back for too many years. I'm done doing that."

Hollister grinned. "If that's what you want."

I had a hunch that not only was Hollister not scared, but he was looking forward to this. If there was any part that he was nervous about, it was likely how this was all going to affect me. But I didn't want him worrying about that either.

My finger barely pressed on the doorbell when the door opened to reveal Glendon and Clarice Walker. Both blond like myself, my mother's hair was more platinum, while my father and I shared a darker tone.

My father smiled, while my mother's face was stony. "Aver, my son, come in. Who is your...friend?"

"Hollister is my mate," I corrected him. There were more subtle ways of coming out to your parents, but if this was where the dinner ended, then so be it. I wouldn't let anyone address my mate as less than what he was. The fact we hadn't had an official ceremony meant nothing. He was mine.

"So that's been the difference I've noticed in you. Having a mate suits you, son. Welcome, Hollister."

Even though my father sounded happy, my mother had yet to blink. Either Glendon hadn't told her what to expect, or she knew and was still unhappy. But, when I looked into my mother's eyes, green like my own, I didn't feel any uncertainty in my decision. This woman could withhold her love for all eternity, and it wouldn't make Hollister any less of my mate.

Clarice had yet to speak, even though her husband looked at her, clearly waiting. "Thank you for coming home," she said stiffly, stepping to the side to let us in.

Hollister squeezed my hand. "Thank you," he said, though with an edge that made me think he was enjoying this discomfort now that he knew I wasn't going to be hurt by it.

Instead of leading us into the parlor like I'd seen her do countless times with important guests, she walked to the dining room. She spun, slightly lifting the hem of her blue cocktail dress. "While drinks before dinner would be customary, I believe we're all eager to eat." My mother must have had the same plan I did: for us to get out of there as soon as possible.

The table was already set, the dishes prepared and waiting in warming trays in the center.

"Tonight, we're eating roasted duck with a rustic mix of locally harvested vegetables and quinoa." She lifted the lids with a dramatic flourish.

Hollister made an impressed sound. "This looks delicious, Mrs. Walker."

My mother barely kept herself from pursing her lips. "Thank you."

We sat, and Clarice launched into serving. I assumed that was so she could have something to do and not be expected to talk.

"Aver, it's good to have you here," my father said. "And I'm glad you were able to bring your fr—mate. I guess I never realized how like your cousins you truly are."

The serving spoon *slipped* from my mother's hand and landed against the glass rim with a clatter.

"You mean gay?" I asked.

Hollister squeezed my hand, but I couldn't tell from his expression if he was urging me on or cautioning me.

"It's just—you never mentioned these...feelings," my mother said, her mouth as tight as a rubber band that had been stretched to its limit. "You never said anything when I set you up with all those nice young women."

Hollister snorted, and my mother's face turned red.

Served her right. She was clearly trying to stir up trouble, bringing up the blind dates.

"You're right. I never said anything. But, at the time, that was easier. I didn't enjoy any of the dates other than the handful of times we'd had interesting conversations. And that, I believe I did tell you. After each one." At this point, I didn't blame her. It had been my responsibility to speak up.

She'd finished serving, and with nothing left to do, she sat down, smoothing her dress as she did. "I just wish you felt like you could be more honest with me. At least that way I wouldn't have wasted all those nice young women's time."

"I agree," Hollister said. I turned to him, waiting for the rest. "You could have saved Aver's time too."

My mother's eyes dropped to the table as she clenched her jaw.

At the same time, my father looked between Hollister and me with an expression I didn't trust.

"Let's begin," he said brightly.

Clarice grabbed her fork with a white-knuckle grip. "Gladly."

Hollister took a bite. "This is delicious. As good as it looks."

"Thank you," Clarice replied tightly.

I cleared my throat. "Which one of your servants made it?"

Hollister coughed to hide his laugh, and I patted his back.

"Here, drink your water." I lifted the glass rim to his lips and poured as he drank. When I set the glass back down, both parents were staring. It was probably odd for them to see me so attentive to someone who wasn't my cousins or their mates.

"How long have you two known each other?" Clarice asked. She wasn't white-knuckling her fork anymore, but she had a grip on her wine glass that wouldn't easily be broken.

"Not very long. But I didn't need very long to know." I turned to look at Hollister, the one shining, bright spot in this dreary room.

I'd grown up in a house of repressed dreams and unattainable goals. It had started when my father who, while being born first, wasn't an alpha, making him ineligible to lead the pack. Then Patrick—Branson's father—had been born, and his anger had truly set in.

I didn't know what my mother had lost in her life, but I knew she'd treated me like an issue to be resolved for most of my childhood. I hadn't known how cold she had been until I'd witnessed my cousins and their omegas interacting with their children. The unconditional love and acceptance they had was awe-inspiring and eye-opening.

"And where do your parents come from, Hollister?" my mother asked.

My instinct was to jump in and answer first, saving Hollister any embarrassment or worry, and before today's conversation, I might have. But, Hollister was made of stronger stuff than that. Hell, he was made of stronger stuff than me.

"Washington. Though that's just an assumption at this point. We haven't spoken in many years."

"And what do they do?" my mother asked like she hadn't listened to a word of his first answer.

"Sudoku? They like to watch football. Well, my dad did. My mom just liked to cook and drink in the kitchen during the games."

"I meant, what do they do for a living?" my mother clarified, but from his sly smile, I assumed Hollister had known that.

"I'm not sure, really. My dad left for an office. I don't know what he did there, and he didn't talk to me about it. My mom was a part-time sub for a nearby grade school."

Clarice brought her glass to her mouth. She'd need a whole lot more red wine if blacking this night out was her goal. "I see. So you met my son days ago, and you have no family. Where do you live? The streets?"

"Clarice!" my father boomed. "Apologize."

My mother stood, throwing her napkin down but keeping her wine glass. "No, Glendon, I will not. If you are fine with our son being tricked by this—"

"Choose your words carefully," I warned quietly.

"Aver." Hollister shook his head. He was probably trying to tell me this wasn't worth it, that him being called names wasn't a reason for me to speak out.

He'd be wrong.

My mother's mouth dropped open. She wasn't accustomed to me opposing her, and certainly never in front of guests. She closed her eyes, her nostrils flaring as she breathed steadily, in and out. When she opened her eyes, the fire behind them had been extinguished. She smiled sweetly at my father before shooting Hollister and myself a regretful expression that was eerily convincing. "My apologies. I was up very late last night preparing, and I think I may be coming down with something. You must excuse me for the night."

She walked around the table, kissed her husband on the top of the head, and left the room.

The three of us remained silent for a few seconds before my father spoke. "She's getting used to the change, Aver."

"This isn't a change, Father. You just didn't know this about me."

He rose his elbows to the table, steepling his fingers in front of his face. "I—yes, that's true. She will adjust. Just give her time. I know," he said brightly. "We could plan a mating party for you two. The pack will enjoy the distraction."

Don't ask, Aver. Don't you dare fucking— "Distraction? From what?"

"Forgive me for bringing it up. These are the pack's problems, not yours. The interim period ends in a few short months, and we are no closer to agreeing on a new Alpha. If there was an option who had Elder families already poised to care for a pack, things would be easier."

He meant someone like me. Except he wasn't usually so subtle. It wasn't like he'd been silent about wanting me to lead the pack before.

"But that isn't for a few months, and it is not your burden to bear. Let me talk to her. She loves planning parties, and given time, she'll be ecstatic to help plan this one."

This felt like classic Elder parent meddling, but that didn't lessen the desire to present my mate to the world. There wouldn't be a pack member who wouldn't know who Hollister was and that he was untouchable. And a mating

party meant we could easily have an official mating ceremony. But I was torn between wanting to keep distance
between myself and my parents and wanting to claim
Hollister in every way possible.

I looked to Hollister, who shrugged. "I like parties. But
something casual though, right? I look good in anything, but
I don't feel good in a suit."

"You could wear whatever you want," I said, noticing the
way my dad's eyes tightened.

I preferred my parents when they were both one
hundred percent horrible. This version of my father was
strange, and I didn't trust it. "I want to be a part of the planning," I said.

"Of course," he replied quickly.

I looked for my napkin, feeling a sudden urge to wipe
my hands clean. My plate was untouched, while Hollister's
food was mostly gone. If he was finished eating, this was as
good a time to leave as any. "I'll call you about the party. You
don't need to call me."

My father's eyes widened but only briefly. "Of course,
son."

———

"That was fun," Hollister said less than an hour later as
he flopped down on the couch.

I'd taken us to Lawrence instead of the main house,
figuring we could both use some quiet time to process what
had just happened.

Hollister reclined back, propping his feet on my lap. "I
mean this in the nicest way possible, Aver, but your mother
is creepy. That pod person face swap? I felt like I was in a
movie."

156

I played with Hollister's toes as he spoke. "Welcome to my childhood. Without the parts where I stood up for myself."

Hollister massaged my thigh with his heel as he frowned. "I'm sorry. Your life was like...physical and mental warfare."

He was spot on with the mental warfare. "Not so much the physical. I was a timid kid." Anytime Nash or Wyatt had ganged up on me as kids, Branson had been the one to step in.

"But it's over now. All done. Here I thought I needed to be there for support, but really, I needed to be there to hold you back. I don't understand it, Aver. You've held onto this secret for so long, and now suddenly, you're done."

"And glad to be rid of it."

Before he could ask why, I slipped out from under his feet and crawled up the couch, covering him with my body. I kissed his lips, but only for a short time before my lips continued traveling up his jaw and then down to his neck. His pulse fluttered beneath my lips, and I stayed that way, letting the gentle rhythm wash away any residual discomfort from the day.

At least this was a response I was used to. Coming to Lawrence was like shutting the door on the world and sitting in my own room for a while. Now, that room belonged to me and Hollister.

He cupped my face, pushing so I'd stop kissing and look into his eyes. "You won't regret this? Me?"

"How do you regret a piece of yourself?"

Hollister let out a low whistle. "Smooth, buddy."

He released my face, letting my lips continue with their task. I didn't know how long we made out, laying on our couch in middle of the forest. I didn't want to stop, but Hollister's hands pressed against my chest.

"Are you uncomfortable on the couch?"

"No," Hollister replied. "It's not that. I just want to say this before I convince myself not to, or that you don't want to hear it or whatever reason I come up with that won't actually be true."

The seriousness in his tone made me lean back and give him space. When Hollister copied me, pulling his body up into a sitting position, I reminded myself that this was my mate, not my parents. He didn't use his affection like a weapon, and I didn't need to be so immediately concerned. But though I knew all that, my body responded like he was trying to run.

I forced my limbs to stay motionless as Hollister shoved his hair back and off his forehead. What could he have to say that made him so nervous? The only possibility I could think of also happened to coincide with my worst fear.

"Aver, we haven't been together that long."

"I didn't need long to know you were the one."

He looked over at me, smiling briefly. "And you're so damned smooth..."

I bit my tongue. Clearly, I didn't have any idea what he was about to tell me, and the result was that I was prepared to defend against any reason he might have that he needed to go back to his old life.

It would be fitting that an evening with my parents was what pushed him out of my arms and into—

"Will you please stop imagining the worst? If I'm not supposed to, you can't either." He flashed me a smile and moved, slipping to sit on my lap facing me. "This position seemed to work in the past for conversations."

If I remembered correctly, this position had ended with

him orgasming in my hand. But that couldn't be what he wanted. If it was, he would've just come out and said it.

He smoothed the skin on my face with his hands, likely attempting to work out the worried lines I couldn't quite mask. "So, I know we're always safe," he began, ensuring now I really had no idea where he was going with this. "But I didn't know if that was a for-you thing or a for-me thing."

Was he more confused about the situation than I thought? Where had we gone wrong in explaining it to him? "Pet, if we have sex without protection, it could change you in ways I have no control over. You'll get pregnant."

"I know."

"Exactly, and I know that it doesn't seem like a possibility, but none of the others thought it was a possibility for them too, and... you know?" It took me an idiotic amount of time for my brain to catch up with what he'd actually said and not what I'd thought he would say.

His lips lifted slowly. "I know. I could get pregnant. I could become a shifter. I'm telling you I want that."

A primal snarl caught in my throat. I'd known this conversation would come up, but I'd never dreamed it would come so early. I also didn't have any idea how meeting my parents had made him want to stick around more, but while I might have been slow, I wasn't completely brainless. "You want to try? It might not happen right away."

"That's okay. And I know. I talked it over with the guys. I feel so selfish."

That made absolutely no sense. "How are you selfish?" There wasn't an angle a person could stand to look at Hollister and see a man who thought only of himself first. He was confident, and he voiced his needs, but he was anything but selfish.

"Because you all had this pocket of joy. The relationships that you all have with each other, I mean. It isn't like I don't have friends. But what you all have is something special. And I wanted to be a part of it. I want to have a part of you inside me."

"You already do, pet."

He settled his finger against my lips. "Don't say your heart," he teased.

"Well, I guess I should say you will."

Hollister grinned, understanding what I meant immediately. He pushed off me, and though I should've had no problem snagging him before he made it, I'd been so distracted with the blood rushing to my dick, he was already on his feet. He spun, running down the hallway, laughing his head off with every step.

"You'll have to find me first!" he yelled over his shoulder.

The kindest thing would've been to remind him that I had super senses and would've been able to track him with my eyes closed, but since my reward was getting my dick where it wanted to be most, I didn't.

I should have indulged him, made it seem like finding him would be at all difficult. But as long as I knew that when I found him, I'd be able to finally touch him without barriers, there would be no slowing down or drawing this out. I sprinted down the hallway reaching Hollister's position just as he opened the door to the bedroom. I caught him, pushing off the ground as I lifted him and landed us both on the bed.

Hollister squealed as his hands scrambled for my clothing. He ripped open the two sides of my shirt, flinging buttons in the air as he did. His lips found my nipples, and he bit down.

I hissed, my dick twitching in the next second. "You're a wild animal," I growled, realizing the irony of my statement.

"Takes one to know one," Hollister replied, reaching for the button of my pants.

He managed to free my dick before I picked him up, spinning him around so that he was on his hands and knees, straddling my body while his head hung somewhere between his legs. I gripped the waist of his pants and pulled them down slowly, revealing his smooth ass.

"How is a man supposed to be sane with this waiting for them?" I pulled his cheeks apart reverently. Hollister was a gift that never stopped giving. His pucker winked at me as my pet moaned, sending hot air across my erection.

At the same time my tongue flicked out, finding his sweet center, Hollister opened his mouth and lowered his head. He took me entirely, all at once, not stopping until his breath came in sharp whooshes and his nose was buried between my balls.

My cock jerked, spurting precum in Hollister's waiting mouth.

Enjoying the feast before me at the same time Hollister's lips were around my dick brought out the most basic of my urges. But I didn't just want to fuck Hollister, though I did plan to rut against him. The end result was still my dick, uncovered and sinking deep into his sweet heat.

Hollister hummed before the sound was cut off by my dick sliding down his throat. I longed to see his round eyes looking up at me, but getting to dine on his ass was no consolation prize.

I flexed my tongue, turning it rigid before spearing his tight ring.

Hollister's howl was muffled, but there was no mistaking the desperate way his hands kneaded my thighs. His frantic sounds continued as I bobbed my head, fucking his hole with my tongue in the same way I would be with my cock.

He grabbed my balls, fondling the heavy sack. It was clear Hollister wanted this to be a race, but he forgot one thing. He was *my* pet, and I knew exactly how he liked being scratched. I continued to plunder his hole as I reached around, barely touching Hollister's cock when he threw his head back and howled.

"Fuck yes. Aver! Fuck me with your tongue. I'm so fucking close."

I grinned; my sweet mate had such a filthy mouth. But usually only when I had him where I wanted and was doing what I wanted to his body. Unfortunately for him, I didn't want his orgasm coming and taking off the edge. I had no doubt Hollister would be ready for round two almost immediately after, but I wanted him dancing that line of desire so that when he finally did plunge, we fell together.

Removing my hand prompted Hollister to let out a string of curse words so filthy, I didn't dare repeated a single word in polite company.

"Tsk, tsk, that's a dirty mouth. I might need to wash it out."

Hollister looked over his shoulder. "As long as you wash it with your cum, *mate*."

Any restraint I still possessed evaporated against the heat of passion that one word stoked inside me. I'd heard the others address each other that way, never thinking I'd ever be able to do the same. I hadn't dwelled on it, accepting that as my cross to bear. It took Hollister to show me I had more than support to offer someone.

I'd had to become worthy of the title of mate before I could be called a mate. And now that I had my other half, it was time to show him just what the word could mean.

I sat up, lifting Hollister from his position and spinning him around so he straddled my dick. I held his ass suspended in the air, tantalizingly close to the tip of my cock. "The lube," I growled, using the last of my control to make sure Hollister wouldn't be hurt. "Grab it."

Hollister didn't need to be told twice. He stretched to the side since I wouldn't let his bottom half move in any direction that took his ass farther away.

My desire boiled, gathering strength the longer I remained outside of his body. And even though Hollister was moving as fast as he could, I was too impatient to feel him without anything separating us. I took the bottle away, tossing it to the other side of the bed as I lifted Hollister by the hips and brought him down, plunging my dick to the hilt.

Sitting up like I was, Hollister could hug my neck, holding on as I brought his body back down.

Up and down, I lifted and let him drop, delving so deep inside him I knew he'd feel me there the next day. That thought made me smile, not for any discomfort Hollister might feel, but the reminder he'd have of this night, this moment.

I knew I'd never forget how good his body felt, how hot his channel was, or how tightly his inner muscles clung to me.

"You're mine, Hollister. Forever," I snarled, setting a pace that would be brutal for any other man. But any other man wasn't Hollister. There wasn't a thing I could throw at him that he couldn't handle. And if there was, he would tell me. Knowing that gave me the freedom to make love to Hollister without reservations. He didn't need coddling from my desire. In fact, if I tried, he'd likely call me a few choice words.

"Yes, Aver! Fill me up! Please!" That was a rare, non-expletive filled request that I had no intention of denying.

I'd known this would be quick, but we had the rest of our lives to have every other kind of sex. My fingers never loosened as I brought Hollister up and then back down with a roar.

Hollister climaxed, his head back as he howled and rotated his lips. Cum shot from his dick in a beautiful arch.

At the same time, my balls tightened. Pulse after pulse shot from me, and it didn't stop. I'd never come so long or so much in my life, but when I was finished, I was still hard as Hollister collapsed, trembling against my chest.

"Holy shit, Aver, that was—"

I wasn't finished. Though I didn't enjoy cutting him off, that first orgasm had only left my dick throbbing and left me nowhere near able to speak calmly. I moved his hips, pumping my own to drive me harder and deeper. I felt possessed, like a demon. Hollister had been right all along.

Now that I'd gotten a taste of how good this felt, I couldn't stop. I roared, unable to vocalize beyond primal grunts and growls. My balls tightened at the exact same moment Hollister bit down on the soft spot where my shoulder met my neck.

I didn't think he knew how much of a shifter thing that was to do, but it was exactly what I needed to push me into the abyss a second time. His teeth held on as I unloaded everything I had. But it was more than ejaculate that I let go. It felt like a door had been opened, one that had locked so long ago I'd forgotten that door was even there.

When I looked back into Hollister's face, it was like seeing him for the first time. I pushed his hair back, wiping the sweat from his forehead. "I love you, mate." My hips continued to pump, though there wasn't more to give. "I love you, Hollister."

Hollister smiled a tired, content sort of smile. "That's good," he whispered. "Because I love you too." He let his head drop, clearly exhausted from our lovemaking.

Already, my cock swelled for a third time, but my pet was tired. And I could afford to at least let him have a nap before going again. I lifted him from me, setting him on the mattress beside me where he quickly snuggled into my side.

"We need to clean you up, pet," I whispered, smiling at how much he looked like a kitten, curled up after a long day. The ejaculate would cool along with his skin, and I didn't want him getting cold.

"I don't want to," he said with his eyes closed. "Let me keep you in me, on me, just a little longer. Please."

Who was I to say no to that?

———

I'D WAITED for Hollister to fall asleep before slipping out of bed and getting a warm washcloth. While he slept, I cleaned his body gently, making sure he wouldn't wake up a sticky, flaky mess. He never budged, not even to sleep talk, so when I was finished, I let him be and went out to the kitchen for a glass of water.

Out the front window, a shadow sprinted by. We had bears, coyotes, and bobcats up here, but I didn't think the shadow was any of those things. It had moved like a shifter.

At once, the warm contentment I'd found in the bedroom disappeared. My mate was asleep and relied on me to keep him safe. I turned off the lights, stalking to the side door. For a few minutes, nothing happened.

I flung the door open, running and shifting in the same

moment. I hit my mark, and the body beneath me fell hard as I found its throat with my jaws.

"Aver!" Branson's voice was one of the only things that could've kept my jaws from snapping closed.

I jumped off and shifted. "What the hell are you doing here?"

Branson scowled at me, rubbing his neck and shoulder. "Fuck man, you almost killed me."

Branson's voice may have brought me from my rage, but his presence here in my sanctuary had the opposite effect. Especially with my mate sleeping inside. "What the hell are you doing here?"

"Oh, I don't know, coming to talk to you after I had to hear from Paul that you went to your parents tonight? What the fuck is that about? I thought we agreed if we had to go to pack lands, we'd go together."

For the most part, that had been the rule, but I wasn't going to ask Branson's permission when the situation had changed. "It was just a dinner. I came out."

"Fuck," he whispered, though, beneath the confusion, I heard pride. He'd been wanting me to come clean to my parents for decades, but only because he had seen how much trying to please them messed with me. "How'd it go?"

I shrugged, cocking my head to the side as I focused on the sound of Hollister's steady breathing. "Hollister was amazing. My parents were... my mom was how I expected. But my dad is..."

"Up to something," Branson finished for me.

I didn't disagree, but that was exactly why I couldn't hide what I'd agreed to. "He wants to throw us a mating party."

Branson started to laugh, but it died when he saw I wasn't joining him.

"It would be good for the pack. I plan on taking over the planning so there will be no surprises."

"You already failed on that account," Branson snarled. "What is going on with you, man? I get you keeping stuff from your parents, but us? Me? I had no idea what you did when you went into Seattle."

None of them had; that was the entire point. But Branson had always been the cousin I was closest to, both growing up on pack lands and after. I didn't mean to hurt him, but I hadn't seen Branson as someone who could understand what I'd been going through. He'd always been out, proudly, and had no trouble telling his mother what she could do with any opinion she had on his sexuality. And then he'd found Riley, and it seemed like his life had truly come together.

Of course I hadn't wanted to share my pitiful problems with him. Since I couldn't go back in time and confide in Branson, I focused on the thing I could change. "The pack shouldn't suffer because our parents are assholes."

"Each person in the pack is free to leave. If they stay, that's their own choice."

I stared at Branson, wondering when he'd turned into someone I didn't know. "Is that really how you feel?"

He crossed his arms. "Abso-fucking-lutely."

I clenched my jaw. "Then we disagree."

His eyes widened with brief surprise. "I guess we do."

I wasn't the same Aver to him, that much I understood. That Aver had been agreeable, even when it went against his own thoughts and opinions. "Every one of you were given a moment to present your mate to the pack. And yet you want to deny me mine, after everything?"

"That isn't the same, and you know it. We had to, to keep our mates safe. You just want to flaunt your—"

My fist moved, colliding with his chin. I barely felt the impact. In all our years of knowing each other, I'd never once hit Branson out of anger. We'd wrestled, but even then, I almost always conceded or lost. But, when it had sounded like Branson was disrespecting Hollister, I'd seen red.

I tensed, preparing for a retaliation that never came.

Branson stood several feet away, rubbing his chin as he growled in a low continuous hum. "I'm going now. I want you to think about the people who have been in your life since the beginning. The people you respected and trusted... at least, I thought you did. I don't know what kind of person you are anymore."

He didn't wait for my reply. I didn't know what to tell him. I was still the same person. The same shifter. But parts of me had changed. Branson and the others had accepted who I'd been when I'd been miserable, why couldn't they accept me now that I was happy?

10

HOLLISTER

"HOLD STILL," I said, frowning as Aver continued to move. If I didn't have a huge razor against his throat, I wouldn't have cared. Aver had been letting his beard grow since I'd told him I liked the roughness of his bristly facial hair against my skin.

He'd agreed to let me manscape the curly dark blond hairs, but now he was doing everything he could to get me to cut his throat.

"How do I hold still when you're standing pressed against me? That's unreasonable." He lifted my shirt and proceeded to lick my stomach. This wasn't behavior I should've rewarded, but I laughed anyway, setting the razor down on the counter before I cut my own finger off.

"We could get one of the others to do it," I suggested, waiting for his reaction.

And I got it, a slight wince before he gained control of his facial muscles. At first, I'd thought that unlocking the next stage in our relationship was what made him reluctant to go back to the main house. Now that several days had passed, I *knew* something else had happened. But as for what it was, Aver was tightlipped. "They're busy. I don't want to bother them."

On the surface, that sounded reasonable. With kids, jobs, and everything else, the Walker household always had something to do. I'd been brainstorming ways I could help, pitch in and earn my place, but Aver had insisted I didn't need to earn anything.

I knew my place next to him was secure; he told me often. But just because Aver loved me didn't mean his family had to.

And I wanted them to. Part of that desire surely stemmed from me knowing those people were important to Aver, but really, I just liked them. They were good and teased each other so much, there was always laughter in the house.

Since I didn't know how to explain to Aver that he was enough and I loved him wholly, but that I wanted a relationship with his family as well, I let the issue fall back. When I'd thought of the best way to bring it up, then I would. In the meantime, I'd see if I could stop his beard before it grew out of the sexy lumberjack phase and into the I-have-an-underground-bunker phase.

"I need the scissors. Wait here." I ran into the bathroom, finding the scissors. By the time I got back, Aver was on the phone.

"Yeah, I understand. I agree. It's probably nothing," he said. "We will. I'll let you know, thank you." He put the phone down, and I set the scissors down next to it.

"What's going on?"

Aver lifted his arm, and I hurried to step under it. Whether he needed the embrace or he thought I did, I took any chance to touch my sexy alpha. "That was Julie.

170

Someone spotted some movement up at Nana Walker's place."

"Do you think she's back?" The only things I knew about Nana Walker was that she was a very important matriarch figure, but not only to the Walker cousins. And, she was still gone, grieving the loss of her son, Alpha Walker.

Despite news of Nana's return being a good thing, Aver shook his head slowly. "No. I think I would feel it if she were. But that just means someone else is up there snooping around."

I ducked back into the bedroom to grab my pants. When I came back, Aver eyed the clothing warily.

"Why are you getting dressed? There's no reason we both have to wear pants."

That had been said jokingly, but I knew Aver better than that by now. I buttoned up and stood straight, looking him in the eye as I spoke. "Either we both drive over there, or you drive and I run after."

Aver's jaw went tight. "Pet, if there's danger..."

"Do you think there is? That same part of you that would know if Nana is back, does it know if whoever's up means us harm?"

"I don't hear spirits like Nana. It's just a feeling." He sighed, his eyes gloomy. "No, I don't. But we still need to check it out." He looked me up and down. "You'll need a jacket. It's a little bit colder over there."

I grinned, snagging my jacket on the way out. I'd worn through the clothes I'd packed until I was sick of every pair of pants, shirt, and sweater. Since then, Aver had been enjoying supplementing my wardrobe, though he always chose things that emphasized his most favorite bits. Namely my ass. But I'd never been one to hide what the good Goddess had given me.

"Why did Julie call you?" I asked, hoping he knew my question wasn't meant to be as rude as it sounded. But, if I was remembering this all right, Julie was Nash and Wyatt's mother. But she'd called Aver's house phone.

"That's not a question so easily answered, pet." Aver lifted me into the rig even though I was capable of getting in myself. "A few days ago, I had a disagreement with Branson. And I think they are nervous."

My relief that Aver had confided in me was short-lived. The storm that had blown into his eyes flashed with restrained fury. "Nervous of what?"

"My loyalties likely. I imagine Branson filled the house in, and one of the twins told their mother. I suspect she called me in an attempt to keep me in the loop, so to speak."

My stomach dropped to the floor. I hadn't expected Aver to say that and had been unprepared for how it would make me feel. I could only use the evidence before me, and the truth was, they'd all seemed fine with Aver, until I'd come around. Looking at it that way, the only reasonable option was that I was the reason they believed him disloyal. Because he was spending so much time with me? That wouldn't be fair. It wasn't like I could tell Aver what to do. I could suggest, and I could plead, but if it didn't have to do with my own personal boundaries, then Aver did only what Aver wanted.

"Stop it, Hollister." The growled command brought me out of my mental pity party. "Their issues have nothing to do with you. Not really. It's the pack. Like always. The fucking pack."

He wasn't in the mood to explain more, and I decided not to push him. If thinking about the problem made him that angry, then it was best to only think about it in small doses.

"I'm excited to see Nana Walker's place. It will be like one step closer to meeting her."

Aver grabbed my hand and brought my knuckles to his lips. "I hope you get to do that one day soon too."

The drive ended up being under fifteen minutes before Aver turned off the main highway and onto a gravel road. The branches had grown into the road and smacked into the windshield so hard I gasped each time.

He turned a corner, and the road opened into a clearing. An adorable wood cottage sat straight ahead with a large front porch. Parked in front of that was a four-door sedan that looked like it had seen better days. Seeing the car made Aver's shoulders drop, so I assumed it was someone he knew.

The yard surrounding the house wasn't one of those neatly manicured lawns but looked like it belonged to a person who knew how to work the land and knew how to get the land to work for them. Further from the house, there was a small barn with a fenced area next to an empty chicken coop. Both barn and coop doors were open, but I assumed that was because the animals had been relocated while their owner was away.

A young man walked out the front door, clearly checking to see who it was he'd heard coming. He had wide shoulders and a tapered waist, but he wasn't as muscular as some of the other shifters I'd spotted.

Of course, in the normal world, he'd be considered fit, but not here in bizarro muscle land. Still, the calm determination with which he searched the driveway told me he wasn't one to easily lose his head. "He's cute," I said.

Aver frowned. "He's Paul."

"So that's Paul. I'm glad I get to meet him too! The other

mates told me so much about hi—what?" I turned my head to see Aver smiling at me.

"You said other mates. You included yourself." He grinned again, but that time, I thought the smile was more for himself than me. "That makes me happy. That's all."

I pushed him away playfully, getting out of the car after. "Hi, Paul! I'm Hollister, Aver's mate."

Paul blinked a few times before he found his words. "Hi, Hollister. I didn't know Aver had a mate. Just like I wasn't supposed to know he was gay."

"He is. He does."

Aver watched our conversation like he was watching a tennis match.

Paul nodded. "Well okay. Good to know."

"I got a call from Julie. Someone called her saying they saw movement up here," Aver said.

Paul left the door open as he walked into the house. "If the call came about an hour ago, it was me. I've been here trying to find the dried herbs Nana used for her medicinal teas. We're near to running out, and I never realized how much we relied on her teas for day-to-day illnesses."

"Are people sick?" Aver asked, leading us into Nana's house.

"No, not how you're asking. But you know how shifters are. And the pack doctors can't see every case. Most low-level illnesses, stomachaches, headaches, insomnia, we used Nana's teas first. But now..." He sighed and looked around the room. "At least I found her ginger." He lifted a Ziploc bag full of golden tan powder.

I'd heard so much about Paul; it wasn't that I felt like I knew him, but that I knew he was a good person. "We can help," I offered. Perhaps I should've asked Aver first. We'd come up here to answer a question that we'd already answered.

But Aver didn't look upset—the opposite. "I know she keeps some in her desk," he said, going to an old-fashioned wood desk. The surface was blocked by a rolling lid that he carefully maneuvered up.

While Aver searched the desk, I tried putting myself in the shoes of a woman I'd never met, until I remembered I didn't have to do that. I looked around with a new mission to find something that might give me a clue or two.

While I searched, Paul sighed, letting a little growl escape with the sound. "I don't know how much more of this I can take," he said to no one in particular. "Today, it's the teas. Yesterday, there was a backup in the trash service because one of the trucks broke down, but a majority of the pack's finances are tied up in this Delia thing. I thought that text would be enough proof, but I guess not. She's going to drag this out until it's as painful as it could be."

I didn't understand all of what he said, but I knew how to let someone vent when they needed to.

"Branson has control of the company's stocks and finances now. He could... on second thought, maybe not."

Paul's lips pressed together in a grim line. "I know a lot of shitty things happened to you guys a long time ago, and I don't ever want you to think I'm making light of it, but right now, the pack is suffering, and the people I would turn to for help are either missing or don't want to talk to me."

"What about the interim?" Aver asked like he wasn't asking about his father.

"The people don't trust him. They didn't know him before he assumed the role, and they still don't. He's trying harder than I thought he would, I'll give him that, but it isn't enough yet."

"Sounds like you get called a lot now," I said, hoping I was understanding the situation correctly.

"I do, and I don't mind. This pack saved my life. I mean that. Despite everything—the Elders, Delia—it's still better here than in my old pack. When the system works here, it really works. But when it doesn't, there is no backup plan. I wished we would've thought of something like this happening before it happened. If we could pivot from expecting our care to come from Elder household incomes to something like a pack-run company, then when there are changes like what we're going through, it wouldn't mean our way of life coming to a stuttering halt." He rubbed his face tiredly. I saw the same fanatic gleam I sometimes saw in Sam's expressions. Both men clearly had huge hearts that they used to serve others.

"Have heart, Paul." Aver clapped his shoulder reassuringly. "You aren't alone. Next time, call me."

Paul smiled. "Thank you, Aver. I like your mate too. Good choice." He shot me double finger guns.

I hadn't been finger-gunned in years, and it felt good. But, now that both shifters were staring at me, I turned under their gentle scrutiny. "I'll keep looking."

The home wasn't messy as much as it was the home of a person who preferred function over form. I put my hand out. Sometimes in these sorts of situations, I could feel where an item with a strong memory was located in a room. Maybe that item would lead us to more of her herb reserves.

Right then, every sense I had directed me to a book sitting on the coffee table among several others. This one was old, the pages yellowing and tattered. It lay open, and the paper had been written over with pen. On closer look, the extra writing looked like corrections to the recipe on that page.

I grinned. I might not have known the woman, but I knew this wasn't just hers, but she'd spent a lot of time with it. I bent over to pick it up, gasping the moment my fingers clutched the cover. The book didn't feel like anything I'd touched before. I wasn't even sure what emotion it was that raced through me, only that it felt *good*.

But all Aver could hear was my gasp, so he ripped the book from me, shaking me by the shoulders. "Hollister, what is it? What did you feel?"

I opened my eyes, having to work to focus on Aver's face.

"What happened?" he asked when our eyes locked.

"Nothing. It's fine. It's more than fine."

"What did he feel?" Paul asked, I supposed with the company he kept, he caught on to the strange and unusual pretty quickly.

"Peace." I smiled. "Nothing but peace." My smile fell. "I'm sorry. That doesn't help us, does it?"

Aver exhaled, though his hands still clenched into fists. "Yes it does. We know the herbs aren't in the book now. Why don't you get some fresh air, and I'll be out there soon?"

"Watch out for the devil," Paul called over his shoulder while he was bent over searching beneath the kitchen sink.

"Who?"

"The goat," Paul said. "We tried relocating him to a farm nearby. He had a huge field to run in and everything. Damn thing escaped every time and ran up here." He let his weight fall back so that he balanced in a crouched position on the balls of his feet. "Julie and I decided to just let him stay here. But he has free rein."

Now I really wanted outside. Goats were up there with

narwhals in my opinion, magical creatures that needed scritches. "Don't worry. Animals love me."

"Be careful anyway," Aver called to my back.

I waved over my shoulder. It wasn't like I thought for a second he would actually let me do something as daring as walk outside without him watching every step. His constant attention might have been annoying if it was any other man in the world. But with Aver, I knew he was looking out for me. He wasn't watching me to gather evidence he could use against me later; he was learning how to better care for me. And how could that be annoying?

I tiptoed through the yard, Paul's warning making me jumpy. I, of course, headed right to the barn, but the inside part was empty as well. Behind the barn, there was a stream at the bottom of a short ravine that looked like it ran the length of the property.

"The land is steep there, Hollister," Aver called out through the window.

I turned my face and grinned. I might have liked his overbearing care, but he didn't have to know how much I liked it. "Don't worry," I called back. "I'm very—"

"Hollister!" Aver yelled a moment before I was struck from behind.

I shouted and fell forward, turning in time to see a goat watching as I fell down the short ravine. The creek was cold but shallow enough that I didn't have to worry about the water rushing over my head.

I tried to call out to Aver to tell him I was okay, but my voice wouldn't work. It felt funny, like—

"Hollister!" Aver came to a skidding halt, freezing at the top of the ravine just like the goat had done. "Hollister." He said my name again, but this time, it wasn't spoken in fear, but reverence.

Again, I tried saying I was fine, but I couldn't get my mouth to work. I gathered my legs under me, trying to stand, but I couldn't do that either.

I looked down and spotted the problem immediately.

I didn't have feet.

Aver slid down the slope, gliding like a surfer to the bottom where he picked me up. Water fell from me in streams, but it didn't feel as cold as it would normally if I had nothing but bare skin. I had fur now.

Fur, four paws and, if that black thing at the end of my face was my nose, I knew I had one of those too.

"Hold on." Aver's tone hadn't changed, except that it held less worry. "You need to see you." He carried me to the truck, and I tried to make sense of our reflection.

I was a wolf. My fur was golden, like my hair, and though it was wet now, I was sure when it dried, it would flow in the wind.

"Can you shift back?" Aver asked gently. "It's okay if you can't. This process has been different for each—"

I knew when I'd done it because Aver had to adjust his hold. He let my feet hit the ground and waited for me to gain my balance before letting go. "Did that really just happen?"

Aver's smile couldn't have been wider. "Yes. That happened."

"I'm a shifter now?" That part was obvious, but, if my journey followed the same path as the others, then that meant... I looked down at my stomach, frowning when it was still flat. Everything else had changed so quickly; I thought maybe that would too.

"Is everything okay?" Paul asked from the porch.

"It's fine," Aver replied. "Will you please call Branson and tell him that Hollister has shifted?"

There was so much pride in his voice—why didn't he call Branson? I only needed a single extra second to answer my own question. Things still weren't settled between them, but Aver was still proud enough that he wanted his family to know.

My heart twisted, and I swore the next thing I'd do was figure out how to repair any damage my presence had caused. Well, after I explored my new skills as a freaking wolf!

Aver looked at my face and grinned. "You want to go for a run?" He shifted. His wolf was darker than I was and much larger, but that meant I'd be faster. Aver threw his head up, launching his front feet in the air in a gesture that I took to mean, *jump on in; the water's fine.*

I closed my eyes, but when I opened them again, I was still me. The human version. I huffed and closed my eyes again. Aver stepped near, licking my hand and starting a reaction that made my body feel like it was made of fluid. This time, when I opened my eyes, I was several feet lower.

I looked to Aver, swallowing rapidly at the feeling that came over me. Something in me recognized Aver's wolf on a different level than I had before. My front legs bent as I bowed until I was laying on the ground in front of him.

Aver's ears perked up, and he padded forward, sniffing my face. He licked my cheek, and my tail wagged. The feeling was so strange I had to look back at it. My tail was *fluffy.* Much fluffier than Aver's. I tried to move it, finding I could maneuver my tail as easily as I'd been able to move my parts in my human form.

Aver barked before taking off into the forest with a wolfy grin.

My predator's instinct kicked in, and I took off after him.

———

IT TURNED out I wasn't faster than Aver. Not even by half. Even though I could run faster than I ever had on my four legs, it was never fast enough to catch up with him, unless he let me.

We wound through the forest, jumping over logs and into puddles. Animals scurried away, keeping their distance as their tiny claws scratched into the dirt. As we ran, it was as if the world had opened up. I could smell scents I'd never smelled before. I heard sounds that had been too quiet for me to hear as a human. I imagined the moment could have been overwhelming if I hadn't had my alpha to guide me.

I'd realized as I ran that that had been what I'd felt. Aver's alpha nature had been not much more than a title to me before. Now, I understood better what it meant.

Aver turned, and I followed, jumping and propelling myself off a tree as I did. I tried to shout with joy but ended up making a yipping sound. Ahead, Aver leapt over a fallen tree, his powerful body having no trouble clearing the obstacle. I jumped after him, grazing my back claws against the bark, but I made it.

If I'd been a human, I would have gasped at the sight in front of me. We were in a large meadow, encircled by tall pine trees. The grass had grown several feet, and among the blades, there were tiny purple flowers that stretched as far as the meadow.

I followed Aver's scent, finding that just smelling it gave me a sense of comfort that I hadn't had before. Was this how Aver felt when he smelled me? I wasn't sure how to ask that question, but to do so, I'd have to find Aver first.

I sprinted forward, but the grass was too tall. Whenever I'd gone with Sam to help him with outreach, we had a rule that if we got separated, I would stay put, and he would come to find me. I decided that was a good a plan as any and skidded to a stop, whining softly in the sudden stillness.

Aver came out of nowhere, making me think he'd had an eye on me the entire time. In my fear, I shifted, but so had Aver, and when he landed next to me, he wrapped me up in his human embrace. "You are amazing," he murmured, kissing my cheeks and down to my mouth.

"Amazing," I panted. "And out of breath. I thought shifters were naturally athletic."

"They are, but you're blessed."

"So what? Does that mean I stay wimpy?"

"No, pet. You just need time to grow into your new body."

The words *grow* and *body* in the same sentence reminded me of the other thing this might mean. "Do you think I'm... ?"

Fire burned in his gaze. "We'll need to get you tested to be sure, but if you are, it is very early. With Riley, he became pregnant and then shifted, but Phineas shifted before they knew he was pregnant." Though his words were informative and slightly clinical, his hands had gone for my pants.

"Where do the clothes go?" I cried out.

"Shh, don't question it," Aver soothed. He picked me up, laying us both down on the tall grass.

"You don't tell me what to quest—oh fuck!"

Aver's wet mouth encircled my dick. He drew me deep in his mouth, using his tongue to swirl around my shaft.

After our forest run, my adrenaline still coursed through me, colliding with the endorphins Aver's skill had rapidly released into my body. My dick swelled, aching despite the attention it was already getting.

I didn't only need to come. There was a part of me that needed to submit to Aver more than anything else. He'd been my one-night stand and lover, boyfriend and mate, and now, he would be my alpha in the truest form of the word. He was my beginning, and, as I came with a shout, spilling jet after jet into his mouth, I knew he would be my end as well.

We lay there after, Aver holding me as I continued to catch my breath. When I sighed, he stirred.

"Time to go?" I asked quietly. The grass surrounded us like the walls of a nest. I didn't want to leave. I wanted to move in.

"After I do what I need to do first," he said.

I frowned, not trusting that tone. "What do we need to do first?"

"I need to take care of that devil goat."

I dug my feet into the ground, grabbing his wrist to keep him from moving forward too. "No, Aver! That's Nana's goat, and I think she'll be mad if you—"

Aver kissed me with an amused look on his face. "You're right. She would be. Fine. He's saved. This time."

11

AVER

No MATTER how many different events we gathered in the ceremonial fields to witness, I'd only ever see the rectangular expanse of land with its torches and tables as one thing. Branson sat ahead with the other mates and children with him. The mates had turned and waved when we'd arrived, but Branson remained with his face forward.

I never liked coming to this place, and I liked bringing Hollister here even less—especially after we'd taken several at-home pregnancy tests that had all come up positive—but the event we were here to witness was important enough that both were necessary.

It had taken Julie Walker nearly twenty years to gather the courage to leave her mate. Alpha Walker, the true Alpha Walker, had absolved their mating before his death, but it was Councilman Knoakes who would make it official with the shifter council.

Nash and Wyatt stood at the front of the crowd; the rest of us sat at the tables facing them. Their mother, Julie, was with them, as well as the councilman. The only one absent was John. The ceremony could be performed without him, so he wasn't holding anything up. He was just being a dick. Like usual.

"I don't want everyone to have to wait," Julie said quietly to her sons and the councilman.

"Mom, this is your divorce. It's okay for people to wait on you," Wyatt replied, dropping his arm over her shoulders.

"Don't." Nash tugged him off. "You'll wrinkle her dress."

Julie smiled shyly, and joy shone in her eyes. We hadn't found out until later that she'd needed help, that the actions of the both of them were truly only the actions of John, who forced his wife to do what he wanted. But now, she was standing next to both of her boys, and they were fussing over her.

For as much as she went through, it looked like she was getting to a place where she was rediscovering herself.

"She's glowing," Hollister whispered.

I hadn't been back to the house. Hollister and I had remained in Lawrence, and though the others knew of Hollister's transformation, they hadn't yet spoken to him about it in detail.

He'd want to. It was obvious how much Hollister liked the others. At times, it made me jealous, but that was not the sort of jealousy that was meant for Hollister to know about. It was for me to deal with on my own.

"Maybe after, people will want to come over and see the place? We can throw Julie a Freedom Party. I had this friend, Justine, who wanted to spend the first night of her divorce the exact same way she'd spent her bachelorette party, except that time she had sex with as many dudes as she wanted."

I grimaced. "I don't know if Julie..."

Hollister laughed. "No, of course not. The party must fit the person. That's the first rule of party planning."

Usually, I planned a party by agreeing and purchasing whatever the other person also planning the party told me to buy.

That was going to change with our mating party. I'd taken over all of the preparation. That night, I'd present my mate to the pack, but I would also present myself to the pack, as the man I truly was. I wouldn't leave something that important up to my mother.

"Aver! Look!" Hollister turned around to the gravel road, where two cars drove into the clearing, kicking up dust as they went.

The first car parked, and John stepped out, dressed like he was on his way to a meeting. He was clean-shaven, his hair combed and styled. He didn't look at all like a man bereft at losing his mate. If anyone needed any more proof that John didn't deserve Julie, then they just needed to see this.

He sauntered through the tables, head held high. He smirked as he walked, like he was glad he'd annoyed everyone this one last time.

But it truly would be the last time for Julie. She was able to keep her position as Elder as well as continue to live and be a part of the pack she'd spent her life in.

"Apologies for my lateness," John said to Councilman Knoakes and *only* Councilman Knoakes.

"You don't need to apologize. You just need to stand here," the councilman bit out.

I smirked, turned my head to the side, and saw Hollister doing the exact same thing.

"I see no need for you two to join hands again. Normally we would unbind the hands, but it's clear these hands haven't been bound in a while." He pulled a long silver chain from his pocket. "This chain is a symbolic representation of the chain used to bind these two shifters together. As this chain breaks, so will this mating."

"It was broken long before this," Nash mumbled, earning a sharp glare from his father.

The councilman handed one end of the chain to John first, who held it like it was a piece of trash. He handed the other side to Julie, who wasted no time in yanking her end back, snapping the chain in two.

The councilman did a double take, staring at Julie once and then again before his lips twitched in a half-smile. "It is done. All goods shall be divided, all assets separated, and any children—"

"We go with our mother," Wyatt said.

"I meant *young* children," the councilman said as people laughed quietly. "But you are free to choose how you like."

While everyone else watched the humor passing between Wyatt and the councilman, I watched John. He wasn't scowling or doing anything I expected. His suit and appearance hadn't been that shocking, but his lingering smile was suspicious. This was a man who had officially lost his two alpha sons and mate. He was still an Elder and had his trucking company, but in shifter terms, he'd been stripped of nearly everything today. All but his title.

So why didn't he look that way?

"Is this finished?" John asked the councilman, receiving a nod in return. John stormed back the way he came. His door had barely shut before the driver took off, flipping around and driving back down the gravel road.

It was odd that my father wasn't here, but there wasn't anything for him to do officially as interim. He didn't have the authority to end a mating, just like he didn't have the authority to approve an omega. As interim, he was important but not all-powerful.

"Aver," Hollister whispered, jerking his forehead forward where Branson and Councilman Knoakes were headed for our table.

I stood, draping my arm over Hollister's shoulders as we waited for them to finish their approach.

"It's good you came," Branson grunted. "Nash and Wyatt weren't sure."

"Even if I was angry with Wyatt and Nash, I would have come. This day was for Julie." The woman stood at the front still, but this time with a circle of well-wishers around her. I darted my eyes to the councilman; they wouldn't have both walked over here to thank me for coming.

Though it was the councilman I looked to, it was Branson's gaze that I found. His mouth set into a grim line, and the vein in his forehead throbbed. That only happened when he was upset without a way to release his anger.

I tensed, instinctively holding Hollister tighter. "What is it?"

"Delia," Branson said without emotion. "Always."

The councilman sighed. "As I was telling Branson, though Delia is being held in a maximum security location, I believe she still has contact with people on the outside. Her defense has suddenly claimed that Delia was framed, and they say they are working on a case that will prove her innocence. In any other situation, with any other defendant, I wouldn't be worried."

But this was Delia Walker. A woman slipperier than a bar of soap in a lube factory.

"That's why we need to ignore everything else and keep searching," Branson said. "We're going to the house right after this."

Hollister had wanted people to come over, but when I checked in with him, he shook his head. "I want to help," he said, though he didn't look at Branson when he did.

"Branson," I growled, wanting to put an end to one thing right here and now.

Branson's cautious expression turned to me.

"This fight between us, does it have anything to do with you not liking Hollister?"

Hollister squeaked and hit my arm before looking at the ground as if he were shy. My pet wasn't shy. He didn't know the meaning of the word.

"Of course not," Branson replied before adapting a gentler tone to address Hollister. "The issue between us has nothing to do with how we feel about you, Hollister. You are welcome and accepted. I hope that hasn't been what has kept you both from *your home*." The implication being where we were was not home.

"We'll help you search." I let my arm fall so I could hold Hollister's hand. Things were simply easier when I was touching him, and since he didn't mind my touches, it worked out. "After, I'm inviting you all to Lawrence."

Branson's eyebrows bunched together. "Lawrence?"

"My home, the house. Lawrence is his name."

Branson didn't say anything to that, and the councilman cleared his throat, drawing our attention to him. "I must return. The moment you find anything, Branson, let me know. I believe the entire world is a safer place without Delia Walker walking free."

He left, his spot in the grass replaced by Riley holding Bran's hand.

"Are you guys coming to help?" Riley asked brightly.

"Yes," Hollister replied before I could. "And then everyone is coming over to our place for a party."

189

"Cool." The two were in total agreement.

Branson's gaze met mine, and though things still weren't okay between us, we shared a moment of amusement. "Seems it has been decided," Branson replied gruffly.

"Seems it has," I responded in a tone that matched his.

Hollister shook his head, wrenching his thumb my direction. "Alphas... am I right?"

Despite the fact that he hadn't really said anything, Riley nodded. "So right."

———

THERE WERE TOO many children that had grown entirely too mobile for us all to concentrate on searching Delia's house. Hollister and the other mates ended up going outside, where they made a round grassy space in the shade for the children, while the rest of us, Paul and Julie included, searched the interior.

By this point, there wasn't a room in this house I hadn't already looked. Either Delia had known her home would be combed through for evidence or there wasn't any.

Outside, a small crowd had gathered. The blessed mates, particularly the blessed children, were still something of an attraction for the other shifters.

"One of us should be out there," I growled when I noticed four more had shown up. So far, they were chatting, and a few of the pack children had gone into the circle to play.

"Don't worry," Paul said while he was on his hands and knees searching beneath a huge dresser. "I sent Tutu out there. He's a puppy, but he looks like a dragon."

Tutu—Tyrone, that was—did look menacing. He had a large, broad chest and tapered waist. He had thick biceps, and with his shaved head and unblinking stare, he put on a good show. But right now, his niece rode his shoulders while the other children took turns clinging to his legs. He could fit almost three on one leg.

I'd been about to rush out there and at least bring the mates and children inside when I paused and truly looked at the sight outside. None of the Elders, except Julie, were around. It was only pack members who had come, and they were all chatting peacefully. The mates were all smiling, and the children played happily.

The longer I looked at the scene outside the window, the more I wished we could see this more often. I didn't know how to convince the others that this pack wasn't dead, that we shouldn't turn our backs on it and leave the members to dwindle and suffer.

I looked up, feeling eyes on me, and I found Branson standing against the same wall but through the doorway and on the other side of the foyer. He stood in front of a window as well, but he was staring at me.

We don't have to fight. I don't want to be fighting with you. The old Aver would've been able to say those words without issue, but though I felt stronger and more capable in every other way, in this, I lacked.

I sighed, my gaze drifting from Branson's face to the picture hung on the wall next to the window. The paper backing had peeled, but something looked odd about the way it bulged. As if the area beneath it wasn't completely flat.

I lifted the painting from its hook and set it glass-down on the nearest armchair.

"What is it?" Paul asked, getting back to his feet.

I pulled out a utility knife and sliced carefully along the vertical edge. I didn't need to peel the rest of the paper away to see there was something under there. Yellow, like a large envelope.

"Branson," Paul called out as I carefully slide the envelope free.

Branson joined me, and I handed it to him. "I thought I looked behind this one," he said as he unbent the tabs keeping the upper flap closed. He pulled out a sheet of paper that was thicker than regular printing stock. From the backside, it looked more like an official certificate.

Paul had called Nash, Julie, and Wyatt from upstairs, and they entered through the doorway the same time Branson said, "It's a death certificate. For Patrick Walker."

"But I thought that sort of pack stuff was kept in the Alpha's mansion?" Wyatt asked.

"It should be." Julie frowned. "In fact, I know there is one."

Branson's eyebrows dipped as his mouth turned down.

"What is it?" I asked, crowding in.

"This isn't right," he whispered, unable to tear his eyes from the yellowing sheet of paper. "This information. It isn't the right day. It isn't the right cause of death."

"What does it say?" Julie asked.

"Drowning. It says he drowned. But that..."

That wasn't what any of us had ever been told. Not like people had been eager to speak about Patrick Walker after his death. That event, more than any other, had been what plunged the pack into decades of backstabbing and scheming.

"I don't... I don't know what to do with this information. It doesn't help me. It doesn't help the case." Branson growled loudly. "Even in prison, that woman is *fucking* with me." He picked up a decorative vase from the nearby table and threw it against the wall. The blue-and-white glass shattered before the pieces scattered across the floor.

Moments later, the front door opened, and Riley ran in, followed by Tyrone, Hollister, Kansas, and Phin.

"What happened?" Riley asked. "What was that sound?"

"Just more unanswered questions," Branson replied, breathing slowly in an attempt to calm down in front of his mate. He angled the paper for the others to see while Riley slid under his arm, hugging one arm around his chest.

But when Riley saw the paper, he froze. "That date. That wasn't the date you told me before, was it?"

"No. It isn't what any of us were told," Julie said. "Why? Is that date significant to you?"

Every eye was on Riley, but it was Hollister's face I watched. He stretched his neck to get a good look at the paper before the color drained from his face.

"Hollister?" I held my hand out and he took it.

"That date, it isn't..." Hollister looked up at me, confusion making his features heavy. "That's the day before the police dropped me off at the hospital. When I was a child. I don't really remember it, but that date is on my adoption paperwork. I'm sure of it."

"That's the day my parents died," Riley added.

Branson passed the certificate around. Phineas took one look and nearly dropped it.

He nodded at the rest of us, but I wasn't sure if he saw us in that moment or if he'd gone back to that night in his head. "If we look at those newspaper clippings again, they'll confirm this was the date...and almost the exact *time* my parents died."

Everyone turned to Kansas, who held Calvin tightly while he stepped behind Wyatt's back. "I don't know," he said quietly. "I don't remember. We could ask my uncle..."

"Absolutely not," Wyatt growled, turning to embrace his mate rather than forcing him to stand in front of everyone.

Suddenly, Branson yanked the paper out of Nash's hands and folded it in half, shoving it in his back pocket. "That's enough. We've learned something new. Dwelling on it will just make us crazy. I'll come back and look again, but we're leaving now. All of us. We have a housewarming party to attend."

Hollister squeezed my hand excitedly. "And a Freedom Party for Julie!" he said brightly.

"And a 'congrats, you're a wolf' party for Hollister," Kansas added.

"Then let's get the hel—ck out of here," Branson said.

———

"This place is gorgeous," Riley said, letting his fingers drift along the outside wall. "You made this? I mean, I know you guys build things for a living, but this is..."

"It's beautiful, right?" Hollister effused. He'd started talking in the car ride from the pack lands back to Lawrence and hadn't stopped until the others had showed up.

They came with coolers of meat and beer. We had supplies enough to put together a couple side dishes, and once the barbecue had been fired up, the party got started. For the most part, I manned the grill, answering any questions about the house that Hollister didn't already know the answer to.

"You should try rubbing the walls inside," Hollister said with an airy, dreamy quality.

I darted my eyes, but he shook his head and hands at the same time. "It's a powers thing," he explained, but by the way his cheeks went red, I made a mental note to bring this up again later.

"So you had this place the whole time you lived with us?" Nash asked. He sat in a plastic lawn chair that was angled so he could talk to us at the grill while also keeping an eye on the kidlets playing in the grass.

Kansas sat on a blanket with Calvin laying on his tummy in front of him.

"Not the whole time." I took a swig of beer. "But I was working on it that whole time. I had to buy the land, clear the land, put in the foundation, wiring, plumbing." And all mostly by hand and between my actual work projects. "It took a while."

While Branson had put the beef between us behind him until this point, I knew by the tilt of his eyes that he was growing upset again. "We all could have helped you. I think I know a thing about building houses."

Hollister rubbed my leg but said nothing.

"I know you do, Branson. But this place...it was where I went when hiding who I was became too difficult." Before, I had nothing to take out my aggressions on. But when I started building this place, there was shoveling and demolishing to do, hammering, lifting. I'd come up here ready to peel my own skin off but would leave calm enough to believe I could make it for a few more days. And then, every few days, that cycle repeated.

Branson didn't reply, though that was partly due to the sharp look he'd received from Riley.

"I agree that your home is beautiful," Julie said. "And when Nana comes back, she'll agree too."

We were quiet for a moment after that. I assumed the others were wondering the same thing I was. When would Nana come home? I couldn't deny everything we were dealing with would've been made better by Nana. But a mother needed to grieve, and Nana had experienced so much more loss.

"So, Nana is everyone's great-grandma, right?" Hollister asked.

Julie shook her head. "She's my grandmother-in-law."

Hollister reached for a chip he popped in his mouth. "Who was your mother-in-law?"

Julie squished her face like she'd just remembered she had to do her taxes when she got home. "Celeste Walker was beautiful, but never warm. I'm not sure why Alpha Walker chose her, and Celeste and Nana never got along. But then Celeste died, and Alpha Walker took it harder than anyone could've guessed. He aged that day. I think that's why he always seemed so much older than his mother. I didn't understand Celeste, but Alpha Walker must have loved her."

"And then Patrick died and then her son, Alpha Walker," Hollister added sadly. He wasn't trying to drag out uncomfortable memories as much as he was trying to understand the tangled web that was our lives.

Julie lifted her face, shaking the gloomy mood from her shoulders. "Nana is strong. She said she'd be back. I trust that she'll come back. The woman has never lied to me yet. Besides, I thought this was a housewarming-freedom-becoming a wolf party. And I haven't seen anyone become a wolf."

Hollister grinned like he'd been waiting for the right time for someone to ask. He got to his feet, smoothing his clothes out like he was a performer taking the stage. He winked at me and then looked up at the rest of them. "Watch this."

12

HOLLISTER

MY STOMACH BULGED like I'd swallowed a bowling ball. I pushed Aver's arm to get his attention.

"Aww, when is the little guy due?" Aver asked, pressing a single finger into my stomach.

The pressure was too much for me to hold, and air rushed out of my mouth as my stomach shrunk back to its normal size. "I thought I'd be bigger by now," I complained, holding my breath so I could stick my stomach out again.

"It will be big enough in due time, just you wait. When Phineas was pregnant, I don't think he could see his feet for most of it."

I didn't think I'd ever get to a point in my life where talking about becoming pregnant or being pregnant, like it was something that was possible, would ever not be strange. But just because something was strange didn't mean you couldn't enjoy it.

I saw what the others had, and I wanted it. The kids, the mate. I'd never been the type to settle down in Seattle. The opposite—I'd enjoyed living free. Those days were behind me, but the people I'd met weren't. I stayed in touch with

Jorge and Sam—Sprinkles's last text had been a week ago, claiming he was still deliriously happy—who insisted they meet Aver again at some point to give their approval.

Aver didn't need their approval, but I'd played along anyway.

"It's still early, pet." Aver pulled me into his lap after first setting aside the stack of paperwork he'd been going through.

I turned the opposite direction to look at the baby monitor. While Branson was on site and Riley at work, I'd agreed to watch Bran. Aver needed to do work, and I was eager to fix any of the bridges that had begun to crumble between him and his cousins.

"What if I'm not actually pregnant yet? The tests could've been false positives."

Aver leaned in, inhaling like he sometimes did. He claimed I was the sweetest smell in the world. Before I'd shifted, I might not have believed it. But I did now because it was the same for me. It wasn't his body wash or cologne or any other hygiene product. The scent was just Aver. Woodsy, strong, clean. No matter the distance, it attracted me like a cartoon character to a pie cooling in a window. "One or two could have been, but we've taken several, pet. They've all said the same thing. I think you're gonna have to come to terms with the fact that you're carrying my child."

Goddess, he couldn't look any prouder when he said that.

And I couldn't have—secretly—loved it any more. We were still in the early weeks and hadn't gone to the pack doctor yet, but Aver said he wanted to wait until he understood the new pack climate a little better. I'd heard that Nana had acted as midwife for Riley, while Nana and Julie had helped when Phin went into labor, and I suspected

Aver was hoping his nana would return in time to help with mine.

"If it would make you feel any better," Aver began huskily, "I guess I could try again to be safe. And again. And again." He lifted me as he spoke, spreading my legs so I sat upright on his lap facing him.

I pressed my palms to his chest but didn't push. "We can't. We're watching the baby."

"Mate, we're going to have to get used to it eventually. I don't plan on stopping making love to you when we have our first child."

I hit him with a loose fist. "That is so domineering," I said, leaning away while his hands pressed into the small of my back. "Maybe I'll want the break, huh? Ever think of that?"

Aver just kissed my nose and smiled. "You won't. I know my mate. When it comes to exploring each other's bodies, you're as insatiable as me, pet."

I rolled my hips, rubbing our penises together through our pants. He wasn't wrong. We would need to learn how to still be mates when we were parents. I brought my lips to his, and, in a rare release of power, he let me guide the kiss. It was my tongue that plundered his mouth, and my growl—still not as impressive as his—that vibrated between us.

An alarm beeped softly.

"That's the perimeter," Aver said, his mood changing in the span of a single beep. He slid me off his lap, settling me on the couch before he stood to go to the window. "It's Riley. I thought you said he worked all day today?"

"He does." I got up to stand next to him. Riley's car tore up the driveway. He threw open his car door and slammed it shut. "Something must've happened."

Aver grabbed the monitor, and we both went out to meet Riley on the path.

"What is it?" Aver asked, searching the forest behind him.

I'd never seen Riley so angry. But he was only angry, not upset or scared. Just mad. Which meant this didn't have anything to do with one of the cousins or his mate.

"I got suspended," he said, spitting the word out of his mouth.

Riley was the only social worker to serve the rural but large county. "Why? Who are they getting to take over while you're away?"

Riley shrugged. "Jake is going to let me know when he hears something. This is Delia or one of the Elders. I know it."

We went inside to the kitchen, where I made Riley tea, and Aver sat him down at the small table.

"They said there'd been complaints about me from all over the county. My director even showed me the reports, all anonymous, all negative to me specifically. There were hundreds of complaints, all of them claiming to have met with me in the last month. I couldn't have even met with that many clients in the last month. The director agreed with me, but they can't ignore what looks to them like an unprovoked attack. I can't explain my evil mother-in-law wants me dead, and Delia knows that."

I'd dunked the bag of tea in Riley's mug the moment the door opened again. This time, Kansas and Wyatt stormed in with Calvin.

Wyatt went straight for the fridge and pulled out a beer.

"What's going on at the bar?" Aver asked while Wyatt worked on chugging the first beer.

"We got shut down," Kansas said. I was pretty sure the

only thing keeping his tone so calm was Calvin. "He'd just got down for a nap when they came too. I'm going to try again, Wyatt." Kissing his mate's cheek, Kansas went down the hallway.

"Shut down?" Aver prompted Wyatt.

"The Health Board came. Claimed I had over a hundred sick people claiming my bar was the last place they ate. There's no way. I know every single person who walks through that door, and if I don't know them, I at least remember them. None of those people could have visited The Greasy Stump. I told the health inspector that, but they can't let me reopen until they perform an investigation." He put the beer bottle back to his lips, but when he turned it over into his mouth, it was already empty. Wyatt turned back to the fridge but seemed to think better of it, pausing at the island instead. "Will you make me one of those, Hol?" he asked, jerking his head at the tea bags.

"Of course. Extra calming, coming up."

Riley sipped on his tea, exhaling out his anger after each swallow. "It had to be Delia there too. She failed trying to manipulate Branson, she failed trying to use pack law against us, and she'll fail with this new plan too. I'll make sure of it."

I dropped the teabag in Wyatt's mug. "What's her goal here? Just to cause chaos so we won't have time to search the house?"

Before anyone could answer, the door opened again. Branson stormed through the kitchen doorway. His eyes widened briefly as he took in the rest of us. "Delia?" he asked, the word a pure snarl.

Riley nodded, as well as Wyatt. "What did she do to you?"

"Permits. All of a sudden, the county says they don't

have them. I know they do." He looked to Aver. "For the Gallows' job?"

Aver thought about it before nodding. "Those were approved before I left for Seattle. They should absolutely have them on file."

"Well, they don't, and until they are found, or I get new ones approved and paid for, we're dead in the water, and the Gallows have a hole in their yard where they wanted their pool to be."

This was my first time experiencing the phenomenon I'd been warned so much about. John's lame-ass power play when he showed up late to the ceremony had been one thing. This was a whole different level of meddling.

The door opened again, and the five of us turned toward the kitchen doorway. Nash walked through first, followed by Phineas. Both had been smiling, each holding a twin. For a second the room was silent as they stared at us and we stared at them, both groups waiting for the other to explain.

"Well?" Wyatt prompted.

Nash frowned and scratched his chin. "The doctor said they're growing fine?"

I breathed out a sigh of relief. "Oh, that's right, you had the twins' check-up today."

"And they're both in perfect health." Phin beamed.

"But you all aren't—what's going on?"

Branson, Riley, and Wyatt launched into an explanation while I continued to make tea. We'd need a bigger pot if this was going to keep happening.

"If you're doing drinks, Hol," Nash said, "Can I get a coffee?"

Aver frowned and joined me on the other side of the island. "You aren't a barista, mate," he said quietly while we both had our backs turned to the group.

I grabbed a pod for the coffeemaker, checking to make sure it wasn't decaf. "I know that, Aver." I kissed his cheek. "I like to help people. I can't do anything to make this situation go away, but I can be of service during." I closed the top of the maker and pressed the right buttons. The hairs on my nape tingled, and I turned, seeing Aver doing nothing but staring at me. "What?" I looked down like I was afraid my pants were unzipped.

"Nothing," he murmured. "Just, that you are amazing."

"That settles it," Branson said. They'd been plotting while Aver and me had been talking. "Nash, check in with the fire station. Make sure nothing's been said against you. I'll go with Riley to file a formal complaint with HR, and then after, we'll visit City Hall and see if we can't figure out more about the permits. They had them at one point. There has to be record of that."

Wyatt put his empty mug in the sink and then headed down the hallway. "And I'll make this shitty lemon day into amazing lemonade," he said as he headed toward his bedroom.

As quickly as they'd come, the group dispersed. Nash took his coffee to go, leaving with Phin and the twins. In seconds, it was just me and Aver again, alone in the kitchen.

And they said life moved fast in the city.

My gaze found Aver's, and we stared at each other, both realizing the same thing at the same time. We were alone again. Maybe not quite as alone, but Kansas and Wyatt sometimes slept when Calvin did, which meant we could get back to what we'd been doing before everyone came home.

Aver lifted me up on the island and nestled between my legs. "Where was I?"

I clenched my thighs, squeezing Aver's middle section. "You're where you belong, *mate.*"

Aver growled before claiming my mouth. Riley had been right. That word worked both ways. *Pow,* straight to the penis.

13

AVER

If Delia thought her traps would slow down Branson's search for evidence, then that woman truly did not know her son. Without the permits, he couldn't work. And without work, he had nothing to do but search his childhood home.

We'd taken down every painting, tearing the backings off them all. Then he had us searching and removing anything with space inside to hold anything. We'd removed vases, small trinket boxes, and every single dish, pot, or utensil from the house. Every piece of furniture had been taken apart and searched. And so far, we'd found nothing. Other than a death certificate which seemed to do nothing but give us all more questions.

Branson was a few short steps away from demolishing the home completely, so I offered to join him the next time he went.

I didn't want Hollister in that house. I definitely didn't want him touching anything that belonged to Delia. He'd said that bits of the emotional memories lodged inside him, that if the emotion was powerful enough he would sometimes feel ecstatic or furious for days after. I didn't want any part of Delia staying with him. So far, he'd been the only one of us who had escaped her latest scheme, but that was only because Hollister hadn't been around when Delia had been arrested.

Clearly, the councilman had been right, and Delia had outside help. It was only a matter of time before that outside help told her about Hollister.

I turned and offered my hand to Hollister, walking up the path behind me. His stomach had grown just like he wanted, though he'd only just begun to show.

He'd been attractive before, but with the glow of pregnancy and the confidence of a shifter, he was breathtaking. He was also unhappy with me.

"I'd be careful, Aver."

"No, pet."

"Aver." He said my name like he was trying to get my attention, but I was already looking at him.

"Yes, Hollister?"

He stuck out his bottom lip. "Please."

Fuck I loved this man. His strength, his sweetness, his vulnerability, and his boldness. Quietly, I'd continued planning for our mating party. Things would be close. As it was, the party would be a few short weeks before the interim Alpha period ended and the pack met to decide their new Alpha. With any luck, Hollister would go into labor well before that day. "I'm only trying to protect you. That woman is poison. I don't want anything of her inside of you."

The door opened, revealing Branson on the other side. "I agree with Aver, if you guys are talking about what I think you're talking about."

Hollister pouted harder. "You can't keep me from helping." He lifted his chin in defiance.

Branson smirked my way. "I won't make you do anything, Hol." He turned back into the house.

"What does that mean?" Hollister asked, close on Branson's heels. "Branson? What does that mean? I won't make you?"

Branson just laughed, and I tugged Hollister back into my arms. "He means me. Your alpha, remember?"

Hollister blinked rapidly and lowered his face. "Yes. I remember. And I normally love it, Aver. But I have an ability. And I could use that ability to help. Not helping is killing me."

Branson appeared at the top of the landing. "I have an idea, if Aver is okay with it."

I would have to be now. Hollister looked too pleased at the prospect of helping.

We ended up in Branson's old bedroom. The bed had been lifted and dismantled along with the rest of the furniture. Only the safe remained, nestled in a carefully cut hole in the floor. "If I'm going to go through the trouble of trying to pry this thing out, maybe you can give me an idea first if you think it's worth it?"

Hollister almost fell forward in his desire to help. I caught him before he could, and he shot me a sheepish smile.

He leaned down to his knees, holding his hands over the safe first. "Hm," he frowned. "I'm not sure. But then, this house is already full of emotions." The way he winced made me believe not all of them had been good. "This was under your bed, right? This was your room?"

Branson nodded.

"Did your mother visit you often? Was this a space she frequented?"

"Never. She wasn't what I would call warm."

That only made Hollister frown more. He looked up at me, round eyes pleading. "I can do it. If something weird happens, just yank me off it."

I gained no comfort from that. If I had to yank him off anything, that meant the damage had already been done. But he was right to think this wasn't a space Delia would think of. Her son had only been a burden, until he'd become an asset.

"Maybe we shouldn't," Branson said, his eyes flitting between us. "If this will harm you in any way..."

Hollister turned his face away from us both, pressing his hands flat against the safe.

I stalked around him, dropping to look into his face as he did his thing.

His eyes moved rapidly beneath the lids. He said he never saw anything, but it seemed like he did.

His mouth opened, but not to gasp in horror. To sigh. A happy, resigned sort of sound. "Love, urgency, fear, devotion. *Power*." He opened his eyes. "This did not belong to Delia."

If it wasn't Delia's, and it wasn't Branson's...

Branson dropped to his knees, and I sat down, tugging Hollister closer.

"This was my dad's? How could he keep this under my bed without anyone knowing? My mother couldn't have known. She wouldn't have let it remain here if she had." Branson wasn't talking to either of us directly as much as he was thinking out loud.

As a child, I'd envied him. He'd had a father he didn't know, which shouldn't have made me jealous. Branson's father had been a good man. No one but a few of the Elders disagreed on that.

Branson hadn't been able to talk to his dad or learn life's

lessons as my child would from me. But I'd still been jealous as a kid because he'd had a dad he could look up to. He could wish and wonder how his life would've been different if Patrick hadn't died. I had my father. I couldn't pretend if he were around, things would be better.

Until recently, I'd only ever believed him able to make things worse.

"What do you think the combination is?" I asked.

Hollister shook his head. "I'm not sure. I did feel a lot of love. Not sexual love, but pure love. I assumed it was for you, Branson."

Branson's face turned into stone, unmoving as he thought over what Hollister had said. He blinked several times, leaning forward to look over the top of the safe.

He had an idea, and Hollister and I barely breathed while he worked it out in his head.

"Do you think... ?" Branson smiled before it dropped suddenly. "No, that's stupid. A kid's wish." He pushed his hand through his hair, tugging so hard he pulled a few hairs completely out.

"You're never too old to hope your father loves you," Hollister said, finding the perfect words. "What's your idea?"

Branson didn't answer. He leaned forward again and began to spin the lock dial. He counted in his head, spinning one way and then the other. At the last number, he twisted the lever, and the door opened.

"What was it?" I asked.

Branson looked up at me, and for a moment, all of the issues dividing us fell away. He wiped his eyes, clearing the tears. "My birthday."

The moment stretched on too long for Hollister's curiosity. He leaned over my thighs toward the safe. "What's inside?"

Branson reached down, looking as though he was reaching through the floor, and pulled out a stack of papers, folded and bound together with thick twine. He flipped through the first few. Some had envelopes and looked dated, while others looked like scraps of notebook or drawing paper. "They're... letters."

He carefully pulled the envelope that sat on top. The flap hadn't been sealed, so he only needed to lift it and pull out the paper within. "It's written by my dad. This is his handwriting. This letter was written to me. It looks like they all are." He cleared his throat, reading directly from the page. "I had a talk with Glendon today. He remains unable to look past his hatred. If I thought it would make the pack stronger, I would gladly give him the title, but I fear as this wedge grows between us, he is becoming less of the brother I used to know."

I leaned away. The words Patrick had written so long ago were too similar to what was going on at the moment between me and Branson.

Except this was a short disagreement. I didn't want Branson's place; I simply wasn't ready to turn my back on an entire pack based on the actions of a few. This wouldn't end with us hating each other. It would end with us punching each other until we weren't mad anymore.

Branson flipped through the rest, too excited at this peek into his father's life to see the same parallels as I did.

"I wonder if Nana knew these were here?" Branson asked. He pulled out the remaining papers from the safe, a second stack of letters, and a black bound notebook. He opened a second letter, scanning the lines quickly before he scowled. "Listen to this. Written to me, but it's dated more than a year after the first one. *Things have not improved with the pack. Father insists a Walker alpha has always and will always hold power. But, it is you, Branson, that I worry about. You're just a child. Growing so fast. You and your cousins should be given the opportunity to grow into whatever you want. I wish I had the power to take your alpha status away. At least then, you'd always be safe."*

14

AVER

"I DON'T SEE why we shouldn't invite a few of the nearby pack representatives to your mating party." My father rested his elbows on the table after sliding several sheets across the table like we were in the middle of contract negotiations.

In a way, that was what planning Hollister's and my mating party felt like. The list my father had put in front of me was more than two pages long, and there wasn't a single actual Walker County pack member on it yet. If we let everyone come who my father wanted to have come, this would be the biggest open event a pack had held in years.

"That looks like a lot of people," Hollister murmured. He reached for a fry off my plate and popped it in his mouth after loading the end with ranch and barbecue sauce. "I thought this was going to be a more intimate thing. I don't even know these people."

"And with the mating party so close to the end of your interim period, that would send the wrong message." I pushed my plate over the tablecloth so Hollister could pick from it. He'd already eaten all of his own food. And Alexis had came and gone with the dessert. There was still chocolate sauce smeared on the inside of Hollister's cheek as proof.

I wiped the smear with my thumb.

"Is it all over my face again?" Hollister asked sheepishly.

I could only grin. In a little while, Hollister would be too large to take out of the house, unless we were traveling to a short list of locations. As the pregnancy progressed and his body changed to adapt to the life growing inside him, his appetite had changed as well.

"I know I eat like a trash compactor these days." Hollister's eyes dropped to the table.

I leaned over, kissing him chastely on the cheek. A small peck shouldn't have made me feel so mighty or my dick so hard, but after decades of hiding, it did.

"You two are so cute," Alexis said, coming by with a pitcher of water to fill our glasses.

I dropped my arm over Hollister's shoulders. "Thank you." I was done wondering what my actions would make my parents do.

"Will the other Walkers be there?" Glendon asked.

My arm stiffened as Hollister settled his palm on my thigh under the table. "No. They don't wish to attend."

"I know they are reluctant to attend pack events because of all we put you through. Can any of us be blamed for believing our own sons were the perfect candidate for Alpha?"

"If you bring that night up again, this party is over."

My father sat up. "Of course. I understand."

Hollister leaned in. "What if we change the venue to one with less history? The cousins' house maybe? There's more than enough room outside to put up chairs. They might feel more comfortable if they were on their own turf."

That wasn't a bad idea at all.

"I wish, Aver's mate, but many of the party supplies have been ordered or reserved."

Hollister's right eyebrow dropped as the other rose. His cheeks dimpled from how he was biting them from the inside. "Reservations can't be changed?"

I studied my father's face, waiting for a muscle to tic or any other expression that would signal his annoyance, but I found only patience. "They could be. But at a cost. And as Aver wisely suggested, we should be keeping this party within a strict budget at a time like this."

I couldn't decide if the pack would be bitter about a party or appreciate the distraction. If I knew the others were coming, Branson and the rest, then I might not feel so troubled. Really, I was just putting myself at the bottom of the pecking order, again. At least at the bottom, I wasn't challenged, which meant I didn't have to fight my instinct nearly as often.

The hairs on my nape stood up, and I turned as my father stiffened.

Hollister turned as well, but his reaction at seeing who had just come into The White Otter was much more relaxed than my own. "Riley, Branson!" He waved and smiled.

Riley spotted him, copying his smile and wave.

They weren't alone. Sheriff Maslow was with them. Riley still hadn't been cleared to go back to work, though he'd been told the clearance was coming soon. The investigators hadn't been able to locate a single one of the people who had sent in complaints. We all knew it was because those people didn't exist, but the investigators had to dot every *i* and cross every *t* anyway.

"I should be going anyway. Think about the guest list. Even if you only wish to extend an invitation to a few of the representatives." He stood as the others reached our table.

"Afternoon, Mr. Walker." Sheriff Maslow extended his hand forward.

"Good afternoon. You'll have to excuse me. I was just on my way out."

"No worries. I just wanted to take my old coworker out for lunch." The sheriff threw his thumb over his shoulder toward Riley.

"I'm not your old coworker," Riley replied, like this wasn't the first time the sheriff had made that joke. Riley looked directly at my father as he said, "Just an annoying clerical issue that will be dealt with and then forgotten. Forever."

"O-kay." Sheriff Maslow looked from my father to Riley and the rest of us.

"I hope the issue is resolved swiftly," my father said before nodding his goodbyes.

With him gone, Riley's face brightened considerably, though Branson had still not stopped scowling. He couldn't still be upset that I'd punched him, so it had to be him seeing me here with my father, planning the party he thought would ruin everything.

We all had hated the idea of Branson presenting Riley as his omega to the pack, but he'd done it anyway. And we'd accepted his decision.

"Were you two leaving as well?" Riley asked. His eyes darted from my now-empty plate over to the two empty dishes in front of Hollister.

Hollister just shrugged. "I could eat more."

Alexis came by to clear out the old dishes and set places for the three new people. After ordering, the sheriff went to the bathroom, which left the four of us alone at the table.

The list of prospective guests still sat where it had been on the table in front of me.

"You're still going through with it?" Branson tore his eyes from the guest look to glare at me.

Hollister grabbed my hand under the table and squeezed. I understood the motion to be both reassuring and a warning not to blow up in public. Or to punch my cousin again. While people were watching anyway.

I returned the squeeze. "I never said I wasn't."

"Can we just talk about something else?" Riley suggested. "Anything else?"

The sheriff returned then. He eased back in his chair, his head swiveling to each of us. "You Walkers. I always feel like I've stepped in the middle of your plans to dominate the world. Why so serious? Is something wrong with Riley?"

Hollister frowned. "No. He's fine." His confusion shone clearly, and I cursed myself silently. We'd forgotten to let Hollister know about how the sheriff had been led to believe we had a dog named Riley. But that was only because the sheriff had shown up at the house while Riley had been in wolf form and unable to shift back.

"Are you guys planning a party?" he asked, likely hoping he'd found a safer topic.

Not even the sheriff could miss the way the air thickened with tension.

"Yes." I smiled. "An engagement party for myself and Hollister."

There was nothing but happiness on the sheriff's face. "Congrats, guys. That's great. When is it?"

"You don't want to go," Branson growled.

At least *I* managed to keep my growl silent.

"Branson!" Riley hissed.

At the same time, the sheriff asked, "Why do you say that?"

Branson didn't immediately answer. That seemed about right: act recklessly; cause a problem; wait for steady, calm Aver to come clean it up. Not this time.

"I'm sorry, Sheriff Maslow," Hollister said, his voice sounding loud in the awkward silence. "You see, Branson wanted it to be a *My Little Pony* party, but Aver is strictly a *Filly Funtasia* type of guy."

Riley burst out laughing. He turned to his mate's face, seeing the same utter confusion as was on mine and laughed harder.

Alexis arrived then with the food. I hadn't ordered anything, but Hollister had gotten an order of onion rings— as *dessert*, he had said. Technically, they were his second dessert, but I wasn't dumb enough to bring up that fact either. I also didn't care. Hollister could eat a thousand desserts—as long as he got the vitamins and nutrients he and the baby needed at the same time.

The sheriff leaned back from the table patting his stomach after inhaling much of his meal within the first thirty seconds. "I can't give any advice. I was more of a *Power Rangers* guy myself."

———

LATER THAT EVENING, Hollister and I were at Lawrence. I'd built a fire that kept the room comfortably warm while we reclined on the couch. Hollister read a book while I switched between reviewing the variety of plants, shrubs, and trees we offered and going over the guest list, striking out the names of the people I definitely knew I did not want to come.

Anyone from Paul's old pack or Tyrone's old pack had been crossed out first. From there, I used what I'd heard of the other packs and my own experiences.

But, while I was juggling the two sides of my life, Hollister had been reading the same page for the last ten minutes.

"What's wrong, pet?"

I'd assumed his reluctance to speak after the lunch had been because of me and Branson. But, if that were the case, Hollister wouldn't have shied away from bringing it up. Which meant he had a concern that he wasn't sure how I would react to.

Hollister blinked rapidly, looking at the open page like he was seeing it for the first time. He set the book down without bothering to mark his place, telling me he hadn't been paying attention to what he'd been reading since he'd sat down.

"I'm worried," he said, keeping his tone even.

I rubbed his foot, concentrating on the arch, where he held most his pain. "What are you worried about?"

"I don't know." He shook his head, rubbing his temples.

I hated seeing him upset or worried. I wanted to immediately fix the problem, but Hollister didn't get upset about small things, and the things he did get upset about weren't easily fixed. "Is it safe to say your concerns stem from today's lunch?"

He could have been upset about how I acted to Branson or how quickly I'd wanted to leave after. Or it could have something to do with the party. I hoped it was Branson.

"Your dad," Hollister said slowly. He wouldn't look at me, choosing to stare out the window instead. "When you kissed me at the table..."

"Did that make you uncomfortable?" I wouldn't have done it if I had any suspicion that Hollister would mind.

"No, not at all. But, you were looking at me, and I watched *him*."

My muscles tensed, and I forced my hands to keep moving in a steady, soothing motion against his feet. "Did he signal something to you?" Already, my body was tight, my veins flooding with wasps, buzzing as they searched for a release.

"He didn't know I was watching. He was looking at you. And I mean, he didn't frown or looked grossed out, but there was... I don't know how to explain it. Like, a void."

I'd known my parents had a void in them since I was born. It had been located right where their hearts should have been, but recently, it seemed like that void was getting smaller. Perhaps Hollister had just seen what I'd known was there all along. Or he'd sensed something new. "Did you use your powers? What else were you able to feel?"

He shook his head and pulled his feet from my lap, moving to sit straight up beside me. "It wasn't my powers. Just a feeling I got in that moment. Not happy or sad or angry, but... nothing. Like he was purposefully trying to feel nothing."

I wouldn't defend my father to my mate. If Hollister said he felt something strange, I believed him. "I don't doubt you felt what you felt, Hollister. And I believe I know why that worries you. Before I brought you back, my parents acted very differently toward me. They didn't ask me to do things, they told me, and I could either do them and keep the peace, or not and fight them as well as my nature. It was easier to keep the peace, and I ended up doing a lot of things I didn't want to do. I won't do that again." I draped my arm over his shoulders, and he let his head fall against my chest.

His other hand settled over his stomach. "If anything feels wrong, or off, that's it. I'll cancel the party. I am not the same Aver they took advantage of, and I won't let them again."

"That isn't my concern." He buried his face against my chest. "I can see that you have complete control over your party."

My eyebrows furrowed. "Our party, pet. This is our party."

Hollister sat up, pulling himself out of my embrace and his face off my chest. "This isn't my party, Aver. I don't know anyone who is going. The only people I do know won't attend. I can't say I understand all of that completely, but you also won't budge. Not with Branson, not with your father. You're enjoying seeing him dance for your affection. This party is nothing but a giant fuck-you to your parents, and that's it. I'm fine with huge fuck-you parties. I love fuck-you parties, but not when they hurt more than the person intended."

I inhaled slowly, adrenaline pumping through me as if danger stood in the room, pointing guns to our heads. But there was no danger. It was just me and Hollister here, and now that I'd installed the perimeter alarms, I'd know if any danger was approaching as well. "No one will be hurt by this party, Hollister. Branson's feelings are hurt, but he'll get over it. We all did when he made a similar choice. And after the party, you will know everyone on that list." I tore the guest list my father had given me in half. "The guests will all be immediate pack members."

"I don't know them either. Except Paul, Julie, and Tutu."

"But that's the point, pet. That's my reason for wanting this party. After that night, you will know them, and they will know you. My hope is that this turbulent time will come to an end. An Alpha will be selected and—"

220

"Will it be you?" Hollister asked quietly.

My first instinct was to blame Branson or one of the others for getting inside of Hollister's head, but Hollister wasn't like that. He wasn't easily swayed or naive. And he deserved my honest answer, so while I wanted to deny what he'd asked, I couldn't. "Would that be so bad?"

Before, I wouldn't have been fit for Alpha because though I'd been born an alpha—with a lowercase A—I'd never allowed myself to feel or act like one. But now, I could already see the good Hollister and I could do in the pack. The peace we would bring.

"That will kill your cousins."

My chest twisted like the two sides of my ribcage were trying to break apart from each other. Again, Hollister wasn't wrong. I still thought that if I took the position, and they saw how normal everything remained—not normal, *better*—they would see that they'd been afraid for nothing. "It isn't a for-sure thing. And the interim period isn't for weeks. The party will have come and gone by then."

Hollister didn't look any more relieved.

"You said that people would be hurt by this party. Will you be hurt?"

He looked confused but also suspicious. "No. I'm worried about you, Aver. For you."

He let me draw him back against my chest. His shirt rose over his round stomach, and he settled his palm over the roundest part.

"You are my main concern, my only concern. I can't control how the others feel, pet. And despite what you believe now, this party is about you and me. Ensuring your protection "

"And rejecting nearly every idea your parents have..."

"That part was just a bonus, and I'm sorry if I got a little

221

overzealous. We'll keep it small, only the pack will be invited, and after, if my cousins really don't attend, we can have a second event at their house." If Branson allowed it. "Would that help?"

He nodded, but his frown remained. "I wanted to bring up Sprinkles."

"Your friend from Seattle?"

Hollister nodded as a wrinkle formed between his worried eyebrows. "His texts have decreased to almost nothing. He still says he's happy each time. But that's suspicious, right? Even we've had our ups and downs."

"Is it possible Sprinkles is a private person? They could have had arguments that he just didn't mention to you guys."

Hollister nibbled his bottom lip. "Maybe. I just..." He rotated his upper half and tilted his head back to look into my eyes. "Could we make time to go to Seattle soon? Sam, Jorge, and I would all feel better if we could see him. He hasn't even wanted to meet up to chat."

When I'd found Hollister, I hadn't wanted to share him either. If he hadn't rode off that one day, we might still be alone at Lawrence. "It's too soon to the party now, but we will go. Afterward, I'll book us a hotel, and we will stay until you find him. How does that sound?"

Hollister bobbed his head up and down, but I could tell he was distracted. He pressed his hand harder into his stomach as he waited.

He gasped.

"What happened?"

Hollister beamed, the worry from minutes ago forgotten. "I think the baby moved. Earlier, I thought it was gas, but now... Oh!"

Hollister grabbed my wrist and smashed my hand over

the spot where his was. At first, I felt nothing but warm, smooth skin. I stared at his bellybutton, smiling at the way it stuck out, when there was a tiny flutter against my palm.

"Did you feel that?" Hollister whispered. That was as loud as he dared to speak. Neither of us moved, too afraid to break the magic of the moment.

"Yes," I breathed.

"Can we sit here a little longer? See if it happens again?" he asked.

There wasn't anything else in the world that I wanted to do.

15

HOLLISTER

I STUMBLED, my feet heavy with sleep and because they were swollen, again. When I'd thought about all the reasons I wanted to try to have a child with Aver, I hadn't taken into account the hunger that only ever ended so I could be nauseous for a bit. Nor had I thought about the way my hands and feet would swell until I couldn't put on regular shoes without help.

Normally, Aver was there to do everything I needed to do anyway. He cooked for me, fed me—on occasion when we didn't mind spending the next several hours in bed—helped me bathe, and got me dressed for the day.

Today was the day of the party, though, and he'd left early to start setting things up. He was supposed to come back later in the afternoon to help me get dressed. I'd been left with strict instructions to sleep in and take it easy.

So far, I'd already failed on the sleeping in part. Aver accidentally woke me up when he'd gotten up, and I'd pretended to be asleep until he left. He must have been extremely distracted for my ruse to work. Normally, he knew when I was faking it.

I was up now, though, well before any time any normal person would call morning. I was ready for this day to be over with. The stress and tension this party had caused hadn't made the event worth it in my mind, but I knew this all meant so much more to Aver. I wanted to be there for him. I would be. I just wasn't as eager about tossing everyone out of our train as we raced toward an unknown future.

Accepting or requesting the position of pack Alpha would devastate the others. No matter what Aver said, that much was obvious. My only hope was to use the time from today to the meeting to make everything right.

I could do this. I'd acted as mediator before. Once, I'd gotten stuck in a janky elevator with a couple who had decided that day to get a divorce. We'd been trapped in that metal box for almost three hours, but when we were rescued, the couple wasn't fighting, and they'd decided to try therapy.

None of these people were stuck in an elevator, so I already had a leg up.

My phone chimed in the other room, and I grinned. So Aver hadn't been as fooled as I thought. I waddled back to the bedroom, but I could tell from the doorway the text wasn't from Aver.

It wasn't from a number I recognized, but I knew Sprinkles had sent it.

HELP ME

I called Aver. It was early. We could get on the ferry and at least get the search going before we had to come back. There was time. There had to be time.

Aver didn't answer, and I immediately dialed a second time.

I checked the text again, like I'd thought the words had

spontaneously changed. *Help me.* There wasn't a message clearer than that. Sprinkles was in trouble.

I called Jorge. "Hello?"

I'd known I was going to wake him up. Either that or he hadn't gone to bed yet.

"Did you get a strange text? I did just now. It says *help me*. I think it's from Sprinkles."

"Sprinkles?" Already, his voice was clearer. "Did you tell Sam? We spent all day looking for him yesterday. The address he gave us was bogus. We walked up and down the streets of Ballard, but no one had claimed to have seen him. I didn't want to call you because I know you're going through your stuff, but we're scared. Even if he was still happily living with his dream man, someone would have at least seen them walking around."

"What about the police?"

Jorge cursed in Spanish. "They won't do anything. They said that until we had proof he was missing or being held against his will, there was nothing to do. He isn't underage, and the cops think we're just being overprotective."

There were many truly amazing police officers who patrolled in and around Seattle, but there were a handful of some not-so-great ones too. And the not-so-great ones were often the ones we interacted with. "I should be there. I need to help." If anything, I'd provide more eyes to search, and together we would cover more ground.

Jorge didn't respond at first. He sighed heavily. "I want to say no. To tell you to stay. But I can't. I was already scared, and now that you got that text, I'm terrified for him. He's an adult, yes, but he was still new to the city. All Sprinkles wanted was to find someone to love him. A place to belong. He was easy prey."

My stomach twisted into knots, for once the feeling not

caused by my pregnancy. That reminded me. I had a huge belly now. Most people would look at me and think I drank a twelve-pack of beer a night, but anyone who looked long enough would be able to tell that wasn't what was going on.

But I wasn't so large I couldn't hide it.

I looked to the clock. Ferries ran every hour during the tourist season. "Wait for a bit. I'll call you when I've figured everything out. We'll find him, Jorge. I promise. And with any luck, he will be deliriously happy, and this text will have just been a ridiculous coincidence."

Jorge hung up after, and I dialed Aver again.

"Hello?" a woman's voice answered. "This is Aver Walker's phone."

I knew I was saved as MATE in Aver's phone, which meant the person I spoke to was his mother messing with me. I hadn't seen the woman since that dinner, but she would fuck with me like that. "This is Hollister. I need to speak to Aver. My friend—our friend is in trouble, and—"

"My son can't come to the phone right now. He's busy setting up *your* party. Now you want him to drop everything to help you find a human?"

Until that point, I hadn't seen any true hate from shifters towards humans. There was tons of indifference, but that had seemed to be where it ended.

"This is more important than any reason you might have to dislike me, Mrs. Walker."

"That's Elder Walker, and there is no reason more important than that. Goodbye."

She hung up, and for the first time, the growl that erupted out of me would have rivaled Aver's. Of course no one was here to hear it.

I had a few choices. Do nothing and hope or get to Seattle and help search. As long as I kept my eye on the clock, there was no reason I couldn't get back in time for the party. I wouldn't be able to change first, but I could change there real quick. Aver would understand. He had to.

But I wouldn't know if he did until I talked to him, and that wasn't happening anytime soon. I couldn't risk the time it would take to get a ride out there and then get back to the docks. By that point, it really would be too late. I wanted Aver with me. I wanted Aver's arms around me telling me everything would be okay. But I wasn't going to get that, and I needed to deal with that fact quickly so I could find my friend.

I picked up my phone, calling the only other people I could think of.

———

"My investigator buddy said the number you provided pinged in the northeast sector of this tower. That means, at the least, your friend—if that text was from your friend— sent the text from somewhere between these streets." Nash pointed to the corresponding section of the grid on the map he'd unrolled over the hood of the truck.

I, Riley, Phin, Branson, Jorge, and Sam watched Nash mark out the areas we needed to search.

"These streets have nothing but apartment buildings," Sam said. It was strange to see the two sides of my life standing so closely together. I'd never realized how short Sam was.

Or how freaking broad-chested all the Walker men were.

Jorge had noticed the same thing. Despite his worry, I'd seen that gleam in his eye dampen when he found out everyone was already paired off.

I checked my phone for contact from Aver. It had only been a few hours since we'd left. Riley had answered on the first ring. I'd worried I would be waking the whole house up, but they were already awake, and in minutes they'd mobilized. Kansas and Wyatt had stayed home with the kids and to answer any questions Aver had, while the rest of us had gotten on the Fast Ferry from Walker County to Seattle, which cut our time on the water in half but still didn't give us a lot of time to search. We needed to find him quickly.

"Do we split up? Canvas door to door?" I asked. Even with more than half of our search party possessing enhanced senses, that could take days, but I didn't know that we had any other option.

"Maybe that's how you would have done it," Nash said with a smirk.

"I don't like that face," Phin murmured. "I don't trust it. He has a bad idea."

"I have a great idea, mate," Nash replied with a cocky grin.

Jorge audibly swooned.

"Assuming your friend isn't locked up in one of the luxury apartments, we can narrow our search to this section here..." He pointed to the map. "These are still large apartment buildings, and searching just one would take hours. But each of those buildings will have a fire alarm system—"

"You want to pull it?" Sam asked.

"Yes...but I won't take resources and trucks from the local fire department. We do this systematically. Pull the alarm. I'll call it in and tell them it is a false alarm. The FD will have to send someone out to reset it, but that's a lot better than a whole team."

"And everyone inside will be forced to evacuate," Phin said. "I wonder where you got this idea from?"

I was pretty sure it had something to do with how they'd met.

No one could think of an objection, and even if they could, there wasn't a better option. Time wasn't on our side. The location wasn't on our side, and the authorities wouldn't believe there was even a person to look for. The best case scenario would only prove them right. But I didn't think that would happen here.

It wasn't just my gut that told me, but I sensed it. Just like I'd sensed something was off...or *missing* in Aver's father earlier that week.

I double-checked that Nash's jacket was still buttoned all the way. His had been the only one big enough to fit me and hide my stomach. "I don't think any of us are eager about this, but if Sprinkles is inside one of those buildings, being held against his will..."

Riley dropped his arm around my shoulder. "We'll find him. And when we do, I have services lined up here in Seattle to help with the emotional aftermath. If your friend has been held against his will, then rescuing him will be only the first step to recovery."

Riley hadn't needed to tell Sam and Jorge that. They knew all too well. I hadn't shared with the others what Sprinkles had already gone through in his short life. It wasn't my story to tell, but knowing definitely made this all more painful.

"Let's get started," Branson said. His eyes scanned up and down the road. Being off the island made him twitchy. "Have you heard from Aver?" he asked me.

I shook my head. I was both happy and glad about that and had a feeling when the first of the calls did start coming in, he would be upset.

But we didn't have time to drag our feet.

"Let's go."

We set off on foot to the first of the buildings that Nash had sectioned off on the map. If Sprinkles wasn't here, it would be easier to walk to the second location than it would to try to find parking again. Nash sauntered across the street while the rest of us waited behind a parked van.

"He seems certain he'll get in," Sam commented.

"He's just certain," Phin replied.

"Of what?" Jorge asked.

"Everything," Branson, Riley, and Phin said at the same time.

By the time we looked back across the street, Nash was gone, having already gained access. A few minutes later, the door opened as a trilling bell sounded loudly. Nash was on the phone, reporting the false alarm as he strode back across the street, meeting us behind the van.

"Now, we wait." Nash put his phone in his pocket and turned to face the building. The first of the residents had begun to stream out, each of them looking either angry or confused.

"Do you see him?" I asked the others while trying to look between the bodies funneling out.

"No," Sam said. "Maybe they won't come out?"

"Or he isn't here," Jorge added.

Fifteen minutes later, the stream of people coming out had slowed, and we had people standing on either side of us, none of them Sprinkles.

"He's not here," I whispered as a SUV from the Seattle Fire Department parked in front of the building.

"That'll be the guy to reset it," Nash said. "I'm going to fireman hell for this."

"He's a fireman too?" Jorge whispered.

The trilling stopped minutes later.

"Why aren't we going?" Riley asked.

"Because the fireman has to leave, or he'll get to the next false alarm before he's even driven out of the area." Nash lifted his arm, and Phin slid into the space. "Just a couple minutes longer. He'll get the paperwork signed, and...there he is."

Using a megaphone he pulled from the SUV, the fireman explained it was a false alarm and told everyone it was safe to get back inside. When he got in his car and started the engine, Nash led the way down the block to the next apartment building.

We waited across the street, this time huddling in an alley as Nash went in, bells rang, and he walked out.

"Are we not worried the authorities will use the same tech you did and find out you were the one who called both times?" Riley asked.

"They can't afford our friends," Nash replied, the cocky arrogance thick.

"Hollister," Sam whispered urgently. "Look."

I followed his gaze to the sidewalk across the street. A man stood with another man, shorter and smaller than he was. The shorter man stood close to his side, his head down so I couldn't see his face. "Is it him? Is that the guy keeping him?"

Branson moved to my side, peering across the street. I wished Aver was here, not just so he could be my support, but because I knew leaving on the day I had was going to hurt him. But he would understand. Just like how he believed the others would understand after he became Alpha, he would have to understand that I'd gotten a call for help, literally. And I'd tried contacting him. His mother must've still had his phone. I wondered if she was crafty enough to delete the evidence of my calls.

"Do you have something that belonged to your friend?" Branson asked Jorge and Sam. He knew I didn't. I had only had my phone and was wearing Aver's pants with a belt that kept them over my stomach and one of his t-shirts.

"I do," Jorge said, unwrapping the cloth square he had tied around his wrist like a bracelet. "I thought if I wore something he'd given me, it would bring us luck." He handed the cloth to Branson, who sniffed it.

I watched Sam and Jorge, and while they might not have known I could turn into a wolf or could smell the shot of tequila Jorge had taken before coming out to join us, they were good with not making other people feel weird.

Jorge frowned only briefly. "Can you...smell him?"

"It would've been impossible trying to search the hallways, but out in the open, maybe." Branson handed Jorge back his makeshift bracelet and turned around to where the two men stood, his nostrils flaring. "That's him."

We tore across the street. People jumped out of our way until there was no one between us and the man. They were facing the building, the older man saying something to the other. Before, I wouldn't have been able to hear the hissed whisper.

"Say nothing. Do nothing," he snarled. "They're saying it's a false alarm. Don't mess this up."

Though we were still several feet away, Sprinkles's whimper found my ears, and I saw red.

I forgot I was pregnant. I forgot we were trying to keep a low profile. All I could think about was that my friend was being hurt, and I was *finally* strong enough to tear the aggressor apart. "Get away from him," I ordered. My growl drew the attention of those around us, but the people were smart and gave us room instead of crowding in.

The two turned our way. Sprinkles's eyes found me, and

they widened with relief before darting up to his captor. He looked back at me, shaking his head fearfully.

He was trying to save me. Save us. From the man standing beside him.

That was the only thing I needed to see to know that this wasn't the first time this man had made Sprinkles whimper in fear. He was trapped. He wasn't deliriously in love, and this hadn't been an overreaction. I couldn't enjoy being correct as much as I normally did.

"Excuse me? Who are you? Do you know these people, honey?" he asked, looking down.

My stomach turned. I couldn't think about what Sprinkles might have been through, only that we were here to help him now. My phone rang, but I pushed it to silent.

"You have our friend," Sam said, coming to my right while Jorge took the space to my left. "We're here to take you home, Sprinkles," he said gently, offering his hand forward.

The man jerked Sprinkles back and against the wall. "Your friend is my boyfriend, and he doesn't want to—"

Nash and Branson breezed through our standoff. In a coordinated maneuver, Nash grabbed the other man by the arms while Branson lifted Sprinkles gently, prying the two apart like they were nothing more than opposite pieces of Velcro.

Branson deposited Sprinkles in our circle. "I'm sorry. I'm sure you would've gotten him to do what you wanted, but we don't have time."

Nash still held the other man, who now fought uselessly to get free while he screamed for help, drawing the attention of everyone waiting on the street.

"What am I doing with this one?" Nash asked like he

was holding an item we were all deciding whether to sell or keep.

"Throw it away," I told him, wishing I could instruct Nash to do much worse. But we had an audience. "Only Sprinkles can press charges. We can't do anything now to jeopardize that." I didn't want this dipshit getting off on a legal technicality.

Sam had his phone out, taking a close up picture of the man's face. "I have you now, fucker. There won't be a bar in this town that doesn't know your face. Try picking up a victim again with your picture plastered all over your hunting grounds." Sam had the means to make good on his threat too. He'd developed many connections over the years, and his social network spread across the country.

Sirens wailed in the distance as my phone rang again.

"Someone called the police," Riley said. "We should leave this area."

We didn't have time to stand and chat, and I hadn't thought as much about what we would do after we found Sprinkles. We hurried down the street, putting Sprinkles's attacker and all those people behind us before I asked, "Are you in pain or hurt? Do you need to go to the hospital?"

He shook his head. "He didn't... It wasn't like how you're thinking. It was..." His breath shuddered as he inhaled.

"It's okay." I touched his arm. "You don't have to talk about anything until you're ready. I'm just glad we could find you."

Since we only had the one car, we piled in, Jorge and Sam sitting on either side of Sprinkles in the back while Phin, Riley, and I took up the middle row.

Though no one had pushed him for information, Sprinkles started filling in the blanks of what we already knew. "I thought he was nice, you know? I met him at the park the day after we all went out. We just sat and talked for hours. Those first texts I sent were actually me."

Which meant the others hadn't been. I cursed silently. I'd known something was wrong. I should've come out here sooner. My phone rang again, and though I sent Aver's call to voicemail, I texted a reply telling him what we'd had to do. I told him his mother had answered his phone but wouldn't give him the message, and I told him I was here with his cousins, who had made sure everyone remained safe the whole time.

He called back immediately after. I wanted to talk to him, but we were driving back to the docks, and I wouldn't be able to talk to my other friends after that. This was the only time we had for a face-to-face conversation.

"I've got our way back booked," Phin said. He patted Nash on the shoulder. "You had to pay extra since there was only one car slot left."

"What are you guys rushing back to?" Sprinkles asked.

"My engagement party," I said, receiving double-looks from my Seattle friends. I rushed to explain before any of them could get their feelings hurt. "It isn't a normal one. That's why I didn't invite you guys. It's like...a Walker County thing."

I shrugged, trying to make it seem like there was nothing odd about what I'd just said, but Sam watched me the entire time and for several seconds after.

I didn't want to waste this time making Sam worried for me. For the first time ever, I was thankful for Seattle traffic. Every time we slowed to a stop, bumper to bumper on the busy road, that meant more time to find out what had happened to Sprinkles and to make sure he was okay. Or would be.

"He took my phone from me one day, saying he wanted

to change something in the settings. I don't remember. It was a lie anyway. When I asked for it back, he convinced me I spent too much time on social media and that I'd never make real connections that way. He'd said that was why I was still having trouble making a lot of friends. He never gave it back and kept it locked up, checking the phone periodically. Whenever the texts from one of you sounded particularly worried, he would ask me what to say, paranoid that I was trying to send a secret message. He gave me too much credit. I didn't have any fucking clue what to do. I didn't even have your numbers memorized. So that's what I did. Waited for him to text one of you again and memorized the number, waiting for my chance. I unlocked his phone with his thumb and sent Hollister the text while he was sleeping."

Sprinkles's face fell as the tears came. "I wasn't being chained or tied up. He was always near, but I could've run. So many times. I could've—"

Branson looked back at us through the rearview mirror. "I don't know you, Sprinkles, but as someone who has been manipulated and fucked with his whole life, I can tell you nothing that happened was your fault. Not running wasn't your fault. Not knowing your friend's numbers wasn't your fault."

Sam grinned and picked up where Branson had left off. "You did just what you needed to. Stayed safe, kept your head. But even if you hadn't, there isn't an aspect of what happened to you that is your fault."

"Thank you," Sprinkles said with a watery smile. "All of you."

. . .

GOODBYES WERE ALWAYS TOUGH, and this one was no different. Sam and Jorge would take Sprinkles back and talk to him until he was ready to report what had happened. Though his body hadn't been beaten black and blue, I knew Sprinkles's wounds ran deep. It would be longer now before he trusted anyone, and that fact alone made me wish we could've done more to that man.

But any vigilante justice we sought now would hurt Sprinkles's case later.

"I love you guys," I said, dragging the three of them into a group hug.

Jorge kissed my cheek. "Don't take this the wrong way, Holly Golightly, but did you develop a dessert habit?"

On instinct, I sucked in, but there was no place for this belly to hide. "No, I..." I sighed, looking to Riley, who frowned sympathetically. "I'll call you guys, okay?"

Sam was the last to let go. "Are you sure you won't be sending me a *Help Me* text in a week?" he asked quietly, but not quietly enough that the others wouldn't hear.

I laughed, but Sam did not join me. "If I do, will you come?"

Though I'd meant it as a joke, Sam's concern remained. "Of course. I—we will always be there for you. Just... be careful, babe."

The ferry horn blasted. If we didn't get on, it would take off without us, and then Aver really would have something to be mad about. "I will."

After one more round of hugs, I got in the car and shut the door as Branson drove us into the belly of the ship.

———

I'D TEXTED Aver during the trip, telling him we'd found Sprinkles and were coming back. I was excited to see him and eager to explain my side of things. When I reviewed the events of today and how they'd happened, I couldn't see a different option. Now, Sprinkles was safe, surrounded by people who would help and support him, and we still had two hours before the mating party.

Still, I knew Aver would be upset. If for nothing else than that I'd left the island without him. I hadn't liked doing it either. But I hadn't gone alone. I'd brought his family.

Branson drove us off the ferry and to the street. I spotted Aver's rig ahead.

"He's there." I pointed.

"I know," Branson replied. I didn't understand his wariness.

I was back now. The issue had been handled. Everything was fi—

Aver got out of his rig, and even though the windows were tinted, he stared directly at me.

His lips pressed in a tight line. His gaze, unblinking. He stomped up to the car, reaching for the door when Branson pressed the lock.

"What are you...?" I tried to catch Branson's gaze, but he was looking at Aver.

I understood why now. I'd never seen Aver so angry. He shook with fury, his hands tightened into fists on both sides. His neck muscles corded, bulging beneath his skin.

Aver yanked on the door handle like he was trying to tear it off. "Open the door, Branson," he snarled, the words barely words. "Do not stand between me and my mate."

I put my hand on the door. "Guys, it's fine...I'll just—"

"It isn't fine, Hollister." Nash turned around in his seat. "I can hear your heart pounding. It's been getting quicker the closer we've gotten to home. Tell me honestly, are you nervous?"

"Aver would never hurt me."

"Those shouldn't be words you have to say." Branson turned his head to the window. "I'm taking your mate to our home," Branson said calmly through the glass. "If you want to calm down enough to talk, then follow behind." Branson didn't wait for Aver to reply; he drove forward, rushing through the yellow light and down the road.

I turned, watching Aver run to his car and tear out behind us. There were two sheets of glass and a few feet of road between us, but I still felt his eyes on me. I'd known he would be mad, but this was something else.

My stomach fluttered, and I held my tummy. "It's okay," I whispered, unsure if I spoke to my child or myself.

I could only hope I wasn't lying.

16

AVER

In the hours since I realized my mate was not safe in our home where I'd left him, I'd imagined Hollister dead on the side of the road—killed by a rotating carousel of possible horrors.

Arriving home and searching room after room built a panic in me that would not fade for a long time. I'd imagined him lost in the forest, trapped under a fallen tree, crying out for me. And then, when I'd called and my calls had gone straight to voicemail, I was sure he'd run. Bolted at his first chance to get away from me to a place where he wouldn't be protected.

By the time I received Hollister's text telling me he was unharmed and they'd been successful, there wasn't room in my brain to be reasonable. *Find, protect, claim.* Those were the only words that I could concentrate on, and only because they repeated on a loop.

The only time I knew Hollister was safe was when he was by my side. That he had left, this day, *of all days*, without telling me a single thing—the pain burned brighter than my anger, but it was my anger that everyone saw.

I slammed to a stop within inches of Branson's bumper. I was already out by the time their doors opened.

The tiniest sigh of relief hissed out of me as Hollister climbed out, using Phin's hand to help steady him. I couldn't be comforted yet that he was here in one piece. I'd pictured the worst for so long, I needed to see with my own eyes. I wouldn't relax until I'd searched every inch of him.

My eyes were on my mate when an east wind brought his scent to me. I inhaled, trying to find the calm I knew I needed. *There it is.* Hollister's scent was like a balm, until I picked out the other scents clinging to Hollister. Smog and oil from the city, saltwater from the ferry. And something else.

No. Not something. *Someone* else. I stalked forward, my way blocked by Branson and Nash.

"What the fuck is this, Branson?" I'd never felt anger the way the others had. When I'd watched them fight to control their tempers, I hadn't understood just how difficult it was. With my alpha side locked away, it hadn't been all that difficult, and when it was, I'd had Lawrence to get out my frustrations. But right now, with two alpha wolves standing between myself and my mate, I didn't care if they were my cousins. I'd fight through anything to get to my mate.

Branson glowered. "You need to calm down."

The dick was enjoying this. Without his help or support, I'd gone forward with the mating party, and he'd been unable to get me to do what he wanted. Now, he was making me pay for it.

We stood nose to nose, chest to chest, unblinking, like two angry cement walls, neither near to crumbling. "You need to step aside."

Nash leaned in and spoke quietly. "Aver, take a breath, man. We can't let you—"

242

His scent was unavoidable at that distance. It hit my nose, setting off a chain reaction inside me that I had no control over. While I was hurt and confused, my alpha side wanted only anger. And to my alpha, the puzzle pieces of today's mystery were falling into place.

Hollister had disappeared suddenly.

Hollister placed himself under the protection of not only other shifters but other alphas.

Hollister carried Nash's scent.

I leaned away.

Branson looked over his shoulder where the others waited. "We just all need to bre—"

Leaning away gave me the leverage I needed, and with a snarl, I slammed my head forward, knocking my forehead against the ridge of Nash's nose.

Instantly, blood poured from his face as the others shouted. I didn't know what they said. Adrenaline, testosterone, and pure alpha rage kept my vision tunneled. I could see only Hollister. Could smell only Hollister.

Except that wasn't true. I smelled Hollister and *Nash*.

"Take off that fucking jacket," I snarled over Branson's head.

Hollister's eyes were wide, his mouth open in surprise and shock. My beautiful mate who I'd left snuggled in bed this morning was now being urged toward the house by Riley and Phin. Kansas stood in the doorway as Wyatt rushed out to help.

"The kids are all fucking sleeping," Wyatt growled.

Even through my rage, I could be thankful for that. But on the heels of that thought came another. Only Branson, Nash, and Wyatt's children were safe inside sleeping. Mine had been unwillingly carted off-island and taken on a journey that could have easily gone wrong.

"Hollister, take off the jacket." I paid no attention to the others holding me back. I didn't fight Nash or Wyatt as they grabbed an arm.

The fear in Hollister's eyes faded. I didn't understand what I saw in him now. "You want me to take it off? Fine? I'll take the stupid jacket off. I was only wearing it to hide this." He framed his stomach with his hands. "What is wrong with you, Aver? I told you Sprinkles needed help. I tried to call."

What was wrong with me? I had a lifetime of not learning how to control impulses that burned hotter than the sun. I couldn't blame all of my reactions on my nature, though. If he hadn't left on this day, with these people, wearing that jacket... I was hurt. But it was easier to be angry. "Fine. We'll talk about it on the ride home."

"Yeah right," Wyatt grunted. "You guys aren't planning on letting them go, right?"

Letting? I angled my elbow, sending the pointy side into Wyatt's stomach. He grunted, his hold loosening enough for me to get loose and turn on Nash. By then, Wyatt had recovered and jumped on my back as Nash and I went down. We rolled over the gravel and onto the grass. Nash got in as many punches as I did, but when we finally settled, Nash had his back to the lawn, and I had my hands around his throat.

I didn't remember telling myself to do that.

"Stop it!" Hollister yelled. There wasn't anger in his voice but fear. He was afraid.

Instantly, my fingers loosened, and I rolled off. Panting, I sat on the grass, attempting to control my temper. I didn't have a temper. Not normally. But I'd also never been in this sort of situation. Hollister had never been on the opposing side. He was against me. Like they all were.

Now you know you're fucking crazy.

The paranoid thought was like a jolt to my senses. Hollister was against me? That was bullshit of the highest order. Bullshit lit with neon that clearly illuminated every wrong move I'd taken since realizing Hollister was gone.

"Maybe you should go, Aver. Take a walk and calm down. I'll wait for you," Hollister suggested softly.

Conversely, Branson's reply boomed, "No. You don't have to go with him, Hollister. You can stay here for as long as you want, and Aver can go fuck himself on pack lands." He angled to face me. "That's what you want, right? That's where you were when your mate needed you. With your parents. *Not* being manipulated." He nodded as if agreeing with himself.

I didn't growl in reply. As quickly as my rage dissipated, shame replaced it. But though I couldn't bring myself to look at my mate, I also couldn't leave him. Unless I knew that was what he wanted. I could only be sure Hollister was safe when he was near. I would not leave the area without him. "I'm not going anywhere. I won't abandon my mate."

Branson stepped back, joining Wyatt and Nash. The four of them—Hollister included—stood on one side of the driveway as I stood on the other. "Then you can sleep outside, in the woods. I don't want the children to see you. You're only still conscious right now because they weren't awake to witness any of this."

Before realizing Hollister was missing, I'd spent the day strutting, ordering my father around, and smirking when I watched him scurry to obey. I'd felt mighty, but that feeling had been false. Hollister was right. I wanted the party to protect him, yes, but I had enjoyed vetoing every suggestion from my father or recommendation from my mother. It was like the more I rejected them, the harder they worked for my affec—

I was an idiot.

But I was still a mate. Getting to my feet, I brushed the grass off my pants and found Hollister's gaze. "Tell me to go and I will, Hollister. But if you don't, then I'm staying. You're pregnant with my child—with our child—and I won't leave you now. I couldn't. Not unless you tell me it is what you want."

"You'll miss your party," Hollister snapped.

I deserved that.

"I don't care. I'm not leaving unless *you* want me to."

Hollister's bottom lip trembled. I would've given anything to be able to comfort him, but I was the thing he needed comforting from. Branson was right. Every horrible thing he'd said about me was right.

"I'm sorry..." Emotion clogged Hollister's throat.

My heart tore in two.

Hollister looked up at Branson and the others. "I'm sorry. I can't do that. I don't—" He took a deep breath and closed his eyes, centering himself. "I can't."

"It's okay, Hollister," Wyatt said comfortingly. "He'll stay outside then. If he doesn't want to go, that's his choice. But we don't have to let him in."

The four of them walked to the house, Branson keeping watch on me until the other three had gone inside. He followed them in, closed the door, and locked it.

———

The hours went by, but the door never opened. I retreated back to the forest line so I wouldn't frighten the children when they woke up. My clothes wore torn from the fights, and my face ached. I'd bruise, but it would heal quickly. Like Nash's nose.

My lips twitched at that. The circumstances around headbutting him made me feel like shit, but actually head-butting the man after nearly years of his teasing had felt good. When the others would get wound up, they'd go in the yard and fight it out. After, they'd come in with bruises and cuts but smiles, like punching each other had been all the other needed.

I'd never joined in. Never had an anger that I thought would be fixed by pummeling another.

My phone rang, and my chest felt light, filled with effervescent bubbles. Maybe Hollister wasn't ready to forgive me, but he was at least ready to talk on the phone.

Except it wasn't Hollister, but my father. I answered.

"Aver, did you lose track of time? The guests are arriving, and you are not here."

It looked like I really would get the fuck-you party Hollister told me I was planning. Only not in the way I thought. "The party's off."

"I think the connection cut out. It sounded like you said the party is off? What do you mean off? Do you need me to postpone?"

"No. You need to cancel it. Or have it anyway, I'm sure the pack members will enjoy the food and music without us there."

Mr. Boots padded over the fallen leaves and sticks, coming from the direction of the house. He stopped three feet away from me and sat on his hind legs before lifting his paw and beginning to groom himself.

I was supposed to be surrounded by friends, proudly showing off my mate as we danced, drank, and laughed. Instead, I was sitting on my ass on a log, my mate didn't want to look at me, my cousins never wanted to see me again, and a cat was licking his nonexistent balls in front of me.

"I didn't pay all that money for the pack to dance and eat lobster," my father snarled.

I snorted at his anger, the sound dissolving into laughter.

"What's so funny?" he hissed.

I wiped my eyes. "You. Me. All of this. I'm the stupidest alpha on this island, aren't I?"

My mother's voice whispered in the background.

"Why didn't Mother tell me my mate had called?"

My father sputtered something before covering the phone with his hand. Their conversation was muddled, but I could still hear the urgency in their tones. "She said it was a misunderstanding. She thought it was a prank for your mating par—"

"That's enough," I growled. Despite what I'd thought, I still had the capacity for anger. But now, I was finally directing it toward the people who deserved it. "Do what you want with the lobster. Throw it into the bay. I don't care. But you should give it to your people." I hung up, setting the phone on a pile of sticks in case Hollister did try to call.

Time marched on. I noticed with a detached sort of interest when the time for the party came. I didn't know what my parents had decided to do, but I'd meant what I said. The pack deserved a party.

It grew dark and cold, but I remained where I was in the woods. My legs hurt from sitting in one spot for so many hours, and I was starving, but I'd made this mess, and now I had to clean it up.

I'd forced my mate away. Not Branson or Nash or

anyone else. Me. My anger and unwillingness to listen. Hollister had once called me a demon. My cousins had always joked I was a puppy.

I needed to learn how to live somewhere *between* demon and puppy. If I didn't, I really would lose Hollister. I searched the front of the house through the trees. My bedroom light was on, and that gave me comfort. I was cold and hungry, but Hollister was warm and safe, and that was all that mattered.

AT SOME POINT I'd fallen asleep. I opened my eyes, and the morning sun streamed through the trees. A warm, furry body snuggled against my back. I spun over, coming face to face with the slightly cross-eyed stare of Mr. Boots.

"Did they kick you out too, buddy?" I asked.

Mr. Boots got to his feet and hissed softly. Maybe he had a thing about morning breath.

My stomach growled. I could've left for food or even hunted, but I worried about what might happen when I was away. "Think you can get us some food?" I asked.

I could fall no lower. I was dirty, cold, and banished to the woods, and now I was talking to a cat.

Mr. Boots padded off without a backwards look. I checked my phone, but the battery had died sometime in the night. That was for the best. I'd only have a thousand voicemails from my parents, and I would have to go through and delete each one just to check to make sure Hollister hadn't left one somewhere in the middle of theirs.

Sometime later, Mr. Boots returned, dropping a dead bird at my feet.

"Wow. Thanks?"

When I didn't immediately dive in to consume the tiny

robin, Mr. Boots gave a huff and picked it up, dropping it near the tree, where he began tearing it apart. I wasn't squeamish, nor was I above hunting to eat, but the robin was so small it would be like sucking meat-flavored toothpicks.

While Mr. Boots ate, I did what I could to clean up myself. I didn't have much on me, but I rolled my sleeves up, leaving my jacket to hang on a tree branch. I rolled my pant legs too, the ends tattered and caked with mud.

A branch snapped, and Mr. Boots and I both whipped our heads to the sound. A wolf stood among the trees, staring at me and the cat with cautious, yellow eyes, wearing a backpack.

"Which side sent you?" I asked.

The wolf's form shook, as the shifter transformed. "No one," Paul said. "I came out here to see what the heck was going on. Last night, Interim Alpha Walker dropped off containers of food at my doorstep, instructing me to pass it out to the pack. Wasn't that your party food?"

I nodded. At least the pack had eaten well last night.

"Kansas called me this morning. He said that you guys had a fight, and you were roaming the woods like Bigfoot."

"That sounds like Kansas," I grunted, turning to check on the house. The light in my room had gone off somewhere around midnight the night before. I hoped he was still sleeping. He'd looked tired yesterday.

Tired and scared.

Paul walked to my side, sinking down to sit on the log. "What happened?"

"I was an idiot."

Paul gasped sarcastically. "No way, a Walker alpha did something they regret? That's unheard of."

He had a point, but all the times before, I'd been able to sit smugly on the other side of the issue. "I freaked out. I was so scared and angry and hurt..." I looked over at Paul. We'd never been what I called close. We didn't call and chat like he did with some of the others, but close or not, he was here trying to get both sides of the story.

But if he thought my side of the story would absolve me of guilt, he was wrong. I'd had a lot of time over the night to play back every mistake I'd made, every wrong choice. My alpha nature hadn't been what propelled me; my own insecurities had.

"Do you remember how hung up I was on Wyatt when I first got here?"

When he first got here and several months afterward, but I didn't mention that. "You're young. You have an excuse."

"Maybe, but that's not my point. I was so twisted with the idea of Wyatt and me getting together. Even after it became painfully clear that there was nothing between us, I held on and did some pretty embarrassing things too." His mouth stretched in to a cringe as he remembered those days. But, at some memory, his lips curled into the ghost of a smile. "And almost the whole time, Tyrone stood near, waiting for me to be ready to see what was right in front of me. And even though I'd done some truly cringeworthy things, he didn't tease me. He wasn't angry I didn't recognize who he was to me more quickly."

My stomach growled. "What are you saying, Paul?"

"That we can act like idiots and the people who love us, who matter, will be there when we're done and have learned from our mistakes. Kansas said Hollister couldn't tell you to leave."

That had been the case last night, I didn't know how he was feeling now. "He still might."

Paul shook his head. "Nah. He's smart. Too good for you

by far." Paul smirked, elbowing me softly in the stomach. He stood, shaking off the sentimental moment. "But you can't starve to death before that happens, so here." He handed me a square Tupperware container he'd pulled from his backpack. "Julie is the one who put it all together, so don't thank me. I was just the messenger."

I had a feeling Paul had been playing *just the messenger* for a long time.

"Thank you, Paul. For the food and...everything."

"Just thank me for the food," Paul said. "I'm headed in there next." He jerked his head toward the house.

"Don't worry. You're still allowed in," I said to his back.

He grinned over his shoulder, jogging the rest of the way to the door. When it opened, I kept my gaze down. I wouldn't search for Hollister in the sliver of space the open door allowed me to see. I opened the Tupperware instead, pulling out a sandwich wrapped in plastic, some fruit, jerky, and nuts.

Branson had made his stance clear. He didn't want me inside. He didn't want me near the kids. And, looking at my actions since meeting them on the dock with clarity that could only come with time, I understood why. But I also couldn't beg. To no one but Hollister anyway.

My only choice was to wait and hope for my mate's forgiveness.

———

TWO WEEKS LATER...

I wiped my mouth, leaning back as Mr. Boots continued to chew his meal of venison. In the days since I'd been banished outside, the cat and I had grown close. Besides Paul, Mr. Boots was the only person to visit me, so when footsteps approached, we both froze to check out the visitor.

We'd been visited by bears and natural wolves, deer—like the doe I'd taken down the day before—and a large number of small forest critters. But this was the first time we'd been visited by a wild firefighter.

"Your nose looks good," I grunted.

"You look like shit," Nash replied. "I'm not here to let you in. Branson's putting his foot down."

Our eyes locked, silence stretching between us, but that didn't mean the air was calm. Nash wore a t-shirt and joggers, and he smelled like soap. I hadn't showered in weeks—other than my freezing cold creek dips— but it didn't really bother me, until I faced someone who had. "How is he?" I asked tightly. Not being near him for this long was killing me. I could still feel him, smell him. That was better than nothing.

"How do you think? He's pregnant, ready to pop, and his alpha is camped out in the woods outside his house."

I lifted my chin. "Did he send you out here to ask me to go?"

Nash stared at me, the time seeming to race by though it could've only been a few seconds. "No," he said finally. "He didn't. He won't. For some reason, he loves you."

My chest tightened. The only thing I wanted to do was rip the door down and carry my mate out, but I forced myself to remain on the log. I stretched my legs out, crossing them at the ankles. "Is he being cared for? Does he need anything?"

"You know he doesn't. Who better to anticipate his needs than three men who have already gone through what he is going through? Riley, Phin, and Kansas have been tending to his every need, barking at us only when they need more chocolate or movies." He pretended to be annoyed, but the irritation didn't reach his eyes.

"His checkup was yesterday. Did someone..."

Nash arched a brow. "You weren't in the woods watching?"

No, I knew I wouldn't have been able to see Hollister and still stay away. And since Hollister clearly wanted me out of his sight for a bit, I'd gone hunting instead.

"We all took him," Nash said. "Well, everyone but Wyatt and Branson. They stayed with the kids."

I would've liked to have seen that. Nash piled in the car with the mates, everyone doting on Hollister.

Like a punch to the gut, my shame took my breath away. But I could concentrate on how shitty I felt, or I could be comforted by how well my mate was being taken care of. I chose comfort. Out here, it was the only kind I'd see.

"You could make a fire," Nash suggested out of nowhere. "At least then you wouldn't be cold."

I'd thought about it, but as the days marched on, I looked at my time here as a payment, penance. I might not ever be forgiven, but I would always try for it. I shrugged.

With a sigh, Nash pulled out a plastic bag of trail mix. "If you get tired of raw deer...here. It's stale," he grunted, clearly hoping I didn't get the wrong idea from his kindness. "And I spit on a lot of the pieces of chocolate before mixing them back in the bag. That's for trying to kill me and breaking my nose."

That was the first I'd heard of it being broken. His shifter healing would've made sure he hadn't been in pain for too long. I took the bag from Nash. "I'm sor—"

"Don't apologize," he barked. "Breaking my nose was the coolest thing I've ever seen you do. Don't ruin it with remorse."

"I was going to say I'm sorry the mates had to see that. Next time, I'll drag you into the woods first to kick your ass."

Nash took a step back, his eyes widened before narrowing with excitement. "I change my mind. I like the new Aver."

He left me with my trail mix, and I waited until I couldn't hear his footsteps again before peeling the lid off.

There was a lot of chocolate.

———

In the days that followed Nash's visit, I started receiving visitors at least once a day, though not all of them stayed to chat. And not all of them stopped by when I was in that spot.

Every morning I left to rinse in the creek. A few of those times, I'd returned to find food, a new pair of clothes, or some flint for a fire. After the flint, they dropped off matches. Then a lighter. But, other than the basic needs I had to meet in order not to die, I didn't think I deserved comforts, and I never built a fire.

The pointy, hard ground I slept on was a reminder of what I was out here for, as was the crisp air that bit my nose at night. Sometimes, Mr. Boots came out to lay on me. I allowed myself that warmth since it was what the cat wanted.

For the most part, I sat, thought, and thought some more. I went through my whole life, from birth to now, reliving every moment. They hadn't all been bad, but the one thing my happiest memories all had in common was my family. Not my parents, but Branson, Nana, Nash, and Wyatt.

I spent a lot of time wondering if Nana would ever

come back. She couldn't know what was going on. If she did, she would have been here. But that was where the problem rested. Nana knew everything. Between the wisdom of living a long life and her spirits, she had to know about this.

Which meant she stayed away for a reason. Because she wasn't done grieving? Or because this was a problem we could only handle on our own? Wondering and supposing only sent my head in circles.

"Your parents have been calling for you. Constantly, actually," Branson said, stepping out of the trees like a phantom.

"You didn't tell them?" If these weeks had a bright side, it was that my parents had no way of contacting me.

"I haven't answered. But Paul must not have told them either. You can't live out here forever," he grunted.

I lifted my chin. I didn't want to fight, but I wouldn't be pushed from my mate when he needed me most. "I'm not leaving until Hollister tells me to." If he wanted to be angry about that, he could be, but it wouldn't change anything.

"I know. But I don't know if it helps Hollister or is hurting him. He spends most of his days looking out the window."

"Is he afraid to come see me?" Never had I asked a question that was so difficult to push out of my mouth.

"I won't let him."

I growled, clenching my hands into fists as I leapt to my feet.

Branson took a cautious step back, but he didn't respond. He just watched and waited.

"Are you keeping him against his will?" I growled.

I waited for his anger to rise and match mine, but he leaned back against the nearest tree and crossed his arms instead. "What happened, Aver? The shifter I thought I knew would have never asked me that. The shifter I thought I knew would have known that there was no way I would step between him and his mate unless I was positive there was cause. You were in no mood to talk calmly with Hollister, not with your rage where it was at. And you responded with further violence. You left me no choice."

Put that way, I didn't have a leg to stand on. So I sat down.

Branson sat down on the log across from me. "It was like you left, and then *you* never came back. You don't trust me or us. Not with your mate, not with what's going on between you and the pack. It's like you found your alpha side and became..."

"A dick."

Branson's grin was fleeting. "You said it first."

"Meeting Hollister was like having someone sit me down and explain clearly what my purpose in life is. I never doubted what I was meant to do with Hollister by my side. The clarity brought the cocky and then some. The party was a mistake. It wasn't ever only about presenting him as my mate. Deep down, so deep I couldn't see it, my pain was what fueled me. They were so agreeable, even after I told them I was gay, and it felt like my life was falling into place on my terms. I only ever wanted to make them hurt like they'd hurt me, but instead, I hurt you. I'm sorry, brother."

Branson beamed, the tension washing from him. "I've been going through the letters my dad wrote me," he said, watching my face.

I'd forgotten all about those letters, other than the way they'd made me feel the first time he'd read one out loud. "Have you found anything out?"

"Not really. Most of it isn't about the pack. It's just

thoughts he had that day or things he ate. He talks about Nana a lot and his brother. Later in his letters, he talked about you."

If Branson's late father was talking about me and my father, it couldn't be good. Maybe Patrick Walker had seen early on where my life would lead.

"My father is why I'm out here, actually. That and because you're too stubborn to make a fucking fire."

"You were the one leaving the flint and stuff?"

Branson scratched his head, shoving his legs out so they matched my own. "Not at first. I realized after a few days we were all sneaking out here and leaving you things. I don't know what you've been through these weeks, but inside that house, it's not the same. Just—let my father say it. He does it better." Branson reached into his pocket and pulled out a square of paper. He unfolded it carefully. The creased lines looked soft from how many times he'd folded and unfolded it before now. "This was the oldest of the letters I found. He wrote it before I was born. Right around when he met my mother." Branson cleared his throat and began to read. "I spoke with Alpha Walker, wishing the whole time he'd just let me call him father. I'm meant to take over, to lead the pack forward, but there is a difference between people telling you you are a duck your whole life and being thrown into a lake to prove it. I'm worried, son. I'm worried I won't be enough. But mostly, I'm worried I'll lead with too hard a hand. Like becoming leader will rip a monster out of me that I didn't know was there. The concept certainly drives my brothers crazy. They can no longer even be in the same room when Alpha Walker wishes to speak about me taking over. I wish they wouldn't hate me for something I can't change. But that is not why I'm writing this letter. I don't know that these words will be read, or if you are a person who will ever end up existing, but you must know: a pack is only as strong as its weakest link."

I cringed, having heard that line over and over growing up. But, with my parents, it was used with derision, as an insult.

Branson watched my face. "I thought the same thing. Until I kept reading." He looked back at the letter. "I don't think that means what everyone says it means. A pack is as strong as its weakest link, yes, but it isn't the pack's job to cull the weak, leaving them behind to wither and waste away. It's our job to lift the weak. To bring them to a place where they do not feel so down, where they know they are loved. That they matter. If you remember nothing else, my future son, remember that you will be strong, you will be powerful, and you may even be an alpha, but you will never be better than anyone else."

Mr. Boots meowed, and I took that to mean he agreed.

"So what do you say, Aver, *brother?* Will you act like a duck with me?"

I laughed, deciding we could be a little cheesy at a time like this. I leaned forward to clasp his elbow as he did the same to mine. "Quack, qua—"

A scream split the air, and I needed no extra time to know whose mouth it had come from. I leapt to my feet and sprinted forward, lowering my shoulder to bust the door down. It opened at the last minute.

Riley stood there, eyes wide. "It's Hollister—"

17

HOLLISTER

"Branson will talk to him," Riley said with confidence. He bounced Bran on his knee, making the child giggle each time his bottom lifted in the air. "He'll bring him back safely."

I closed my eyes and nodded, hoping I looked worried and not in the pain that I was in. My baby was fine; the doctor had confirmed that the day before. Dr. Tiffany had told me she expected me to go into labor any day now, and I just barely kept from sobbing.

This wasn't how it was supposed to happen, with my mate locked outside. I knew why it had needed to happen. I'd never witnessed rage like that. But, after a few days of staying apart, the cold had set in, and it had only gotten worse.

There wasn't a thing I could do to warm myself. The only time I didn't need to fight not to shiver was when I was in Aver's bed, and the memory of his body surrounded me. I stayed there a lot because of that, staring out the window in his room.

But things still got worse. Sudden bright lights or

sounds made my head hurt, and sitting in a room lit by more than a window made my eyes sting and water. At least my nausea had gone away—replaced by a gnawing hunger that couldn't be sated. No matter what I ate or how much, I was still hungry.

I knew it wasn't food that my body wanted. But I couldn't only think about myself; I had to think about my baby. Except I *was* thinking about my baby, and everything in me told me Aver was still my safe harbor. What had happened those weeks ago could not be swept under a rug and forgotten, but it could be forgiven.

Nash's nose had healed in a day. Jorge and Sam had stayed with Sprinkles as he reported what had happened to him, and that time, they told an officer willing to listen. They'd arrested Sprinkles's attacker the next day, and he was still in jail waiting on kidnapping charges. Sam suspected he could've been charged for much more, but they could only do as Sprinkles wanted.

The night of the mating party had come and gone without a splash. I'd worried not going would create a huge wave that was just going to make everything worse, but it didn't, not when it came to the Walker cousins anyway. None of them mentioned it, not that day nor the days following. They were all amazing, but the mates, Kansas, Riley, and Phin, had known what to suggest even when I couldn't verbalize what I needed.

But they weren't Aver. And Aver was the only thing my body wanted.

"They've been talking a while." I brought the plush gray throw blanket tighter around me, drawing my knees against my stomach.

Riley slipped to the floor, handing Bran blocks of different shapes, textures, and colors. He looked at each thoughtfully and I wondered, which characteristics of an item did young children take notice of. Mouthfeel?

Riley handed Bran the whole container and got to his feet. "Do you want lunch? You didn't eat much of your breakfast."

I tore my face from the window. "Are you hungry?"

Riley smirked. "I know what that means. Keep an eye on Bran. I'll be right back."

The moment his father left the room, Bran lifted himself to his feet, the process needing a few extra seconds for him to find his balance. He turned his head to the hallway Riley had disappeared down and then over at me.

He toddled over, solemnly handing me the last block that Riley had given him. A blue star. Bran placed the block in my hand; our eyes met. For a crazy second, it was as if I could see the universe unfolding behind his gaze, thousands of years of wisdom, trapped in a tiny body. "You know more than you let on, don't you?" I rubbed his cheek affectionately.

"Penis," Bran whispered seriously.

I hadn't laughed in a while, but I couldn't stop myself then. Riley had no chance of ever getting Bran to stop saying the word if we couldn't stop laughing every time he did.

It felt good to laugh, especially once Bran began laughing with me. The two of us shared the chuckle before Bran stopped suddenly and stared at my stomach.

"Time," he said.

"Time? For what? A change?" I leaned over the edge of the couch with the intention of checking Bran's diaper, but I never made it that far.

I felt a stabbing pain and then a ripping sensation. Something was *wrong*.

"Riley!" I yelled. "I think something is—" I bent over, clenching my teeth against the wave of pain. For once, I felt hot, but it was a sickly flush that didn't reach my toes or fingers.

"Don't panic." Riley's voice sounded like it came from far away, though I could see him standing a few feet away. He held Bran and pedaled back to the hallway where he yelled for the others.

Nash kneeled at my side, my wrist in his hands. "His pulse is weak. Phineas, call Dr. Tiffany. Tell her to come right away." Nash cupped my cheek, patting it lightly, but I couldn't figure out how to open my eyes for more than a few seconds. "No, no, Hollister, don't fall asleep. Not right now." His voice came more quietly. I figured he'd turned his head. "What happened before this? Did he complain of anything?"

"No. We were talking about Aver and Branson, and then I stepped out to make lunch..."

This wasn't Riley's fault, and I attempted to tell him as much, but my lips were so cold they refused to work. My teeth chattered uncontrollably.

This was all wrong. I was supposed to feel warm and happy. My mate was supposed to be here. I wasn't supposed to be scared and cold. I wasn't supposed to feel like I was slowly dying, my life force fading away.

Nash lifted my shirt, touching the smooth skin of my stomach. The moment his hand lay flat against my skin, blinding pain exploded behind my eyes, releasing bursts of colorful light that I couldn't enjoy.

I'd tried to stay strong. I'd tried to stay quiet.

I opened my mouth, back bowing off the floor from the pain. I didn't recognize the ear-piercing scream that escaped me.

My body collapsed with a thud. I couldn't have moved if I wanted to. The door slammed open, and someone growled. Many someones. While they fought, I was dying. I grew weaker by the second, my entire body starved for sustenance. My tongue stuck to the roof of my mouth, dry and thick. Thirst and hunger bickered like unhappy siblings, each vying to be the thing that killed me. And though I knew I was starving, it wasn't for food. The hunger was for something I couldn't describe.

Like two fingers snapping together, suddenly, the pain was less. I sobbed with that small relief as warm fingers brushed my tears from my cheeks. Heat blossomed on my face, and I turned into the feeling, wishing I could crawl inside of it. In that space, there was warmth. Just as I'd known I was dying, clinging to life with tired fingers, I knew that what touched me now could be my salvation.

"I have you, pet. I'm here. I'm so sorry. Thank you for making me sit out there and think. I was being vindictive and stupid. I love you so much."

Aver's voice only made me cry harder. I didn't want to believe it was real. I couldn't. If I opened my eyes and he wasn't there...

"He can't sleep, Aver," Nash said over my head. "I don't know what's wrong with him, but he has to stay awake. Dr. Tiffany is on her way."

Stay awake. I had a goal. And the longer Aver held me, the more able I felt to meet that goal. I turned into him, but there wasn't skin, only cloth.

"Need...touch..." I rasped, hoping he would understand what I meant.

I thought someone lifted my shirt, but I couldn't be sure until Aver's hands cupped my stomach, and he rubbed the skin gently. His touch sent arrows of heat and life. With every caress, every embrace, I could breathe a little easier. The chattering stopped.

I opened my eyes.

"Aver?" He wasn't in front of me, but I had heard his voice. Nash had spoken to him.

"I'm here." He cupped my chin. I'd been pretty sure I was laying on the floor, but now I sat upright, cradled between Aver's legs with my back to his chest. His legs hugged my body as his hands rubbed my exposed belly, and his lips caressed my cheek. Everywhere he touched, my body thawed, the hunger lessened.

When Nash dropped down, I shied away with a hiss. His touch had felt like knives. I didn't want it happening again.

Aver rubbed my arm as Nash waited, crouched on his heels.

I tried turning my head, but my vision spun. "It hurt me," I whispered. "His touch."

Aver kissed my cheek, but I wanted his lips. He brought my face around and lowered his mouth to mine. His kiss felt like a spring breeze, blowing away the frost of winter.

I realized my arm was out; someone touched my wrist. But this time, it didn't hurt. All I could feel was Aver.

"Back to normal," Nash said.

"Aver's touch," Riley whispered. "He needed Aver's touch."

I'd always known that.

"Aver." Riley's tone had grown panicked. "If you weren't here. If you weren't as close..."

Branson held his mate and son as Riley's shoulders shuddered.

Apparently, I hadn't been the only one who knew I was about to die.

I turned my face up toward Aver. He kissed me gently, reverently. For long weeks I'd been so worried and unsure, but those feelings were gone now, replaced by certainty.

I sighed, the air shimmering around me as my body felt like liquid, dissolving and reforming like icicles. The next I knew, I lay, transformed, over Nash's lap, all four of my furry legs braced across his thighs.

"Look!" Phineas gasped, pointing at the floor between Aver's knees. I turned my wolf head, my heart melting at the tiny poof of fur laying on the ground.

I frowned or tried to with my wolf features. The puppy wasn't crying. Nothing but a ball of fluff, it lay motionless on the carpet. On instinct, I licked the puppy, repeatedly rubbing my tongue up the hair along his spine.

Her spine.

The tiny fluff whimpered, and I shifted, the puppy shifting with me before letting out a cry that was unmistakable and beautiful. I drew her into my arms, and together we slumped against Aver, his body acting as a shield for us both.

"You did it, Hollister," Aver said softly. "I knew you could. I knew you'd be perfect."

I turned my face against his neck and smiled, hoping he could feel it. This day had been far from perfect, but I liked Aver saying as much anyway. Mostly, I just liked that Aver was here with his arms around me again.

"She's beautiful," Phineas said.

"I'm here!" Dr. Tiffany burst through the door. "I'm here! We need towels, hot water." She rounded the corner, medical bag swinging wildly on her shoulder as she pulled her hair back into a ponytail before skidding to a halt. Her round eyes took in the serene scene before her. "Oh fudge it!"

If she'd come just a few minutes earlier, she could've witnessed me writhing on the floor, hungry for Aver's touch.

"I'm sorry. That isn't what I meant. I'm glad you've given birth successfully. I just..."

"You wanted to help?" I asked.

"Just once!" she cried out, her exasperation both endearing and funny. She set her bag down, pulling out a sheet of paper. "I may have missed the exciting part, but there's still work to do. Nash, will you get Hollister's vitals?"

Nash moved into place beside me as Dr. Tiffany held her arms out. I appreciated her waiting for me to be ready. She gathered our daughter against her chest, wrapping her in a soft blanket Riley had gotten for her.

"What is her name?" Dr. Tiffany's face turned toward ours, expectant.

"Uhh."

"Umm."

Dr. Tiffany nodded. "Unusual." She looked at the baby and smiled. "Hello, Uhhumm Walker."

No, that would not be my child's nickname. Suddenly, I understood how Tyrone felt.

"What about Autumn?" I asked the room, though Aver's opinion was the one I was truly after.

Aver hugged me from behind. "I love it."

"Autumn Walker," Dr. Tiffany said. "Welcome to the world, Autumn Walker. Let's see how much you weigh."

"Why would that matter?" I snapped, furious that the doctor would instill her own body prejudices on—

"It's for her health records. We'll need to monitor her weight gain closely, so we need a base measurement," she explained.

I'd known that and sheepishly dropped back down against Aver's chest.

"I'll wait a few minutes for your blood pressure." Nash laughed.

Thankfully, it didn't take Dr. Tiffany very long to proclaim Autumn in perfect health. Aver lifted me to the couch but didn't leave my side, and a few minutes later, Dr. Tiffany settled Autumn back in my arms.

Her skin was creamy, not mottled as I'd been expecting. But then, she hadn't been pushed from my body in the same way most newborns were. She'd been propelled into this world by something I could only call magic. But that suited her. She was magical.

"Aver, have you ever seen such a thing? She's perfect. How did we make this perfect thing?"

I felt Aver's grin widen against my cheek. "That's all you, pet. I just chose wisely."

"Pfft, like you chose." I'd been joking at first, but as the words left my mouth, the truth of what I'd said settled against my bones. So much of what had occurred between us felt predestined. I'd been given a choice the entire way, but by Aver. I had a feeling the universe had already made its choice.

With the hard part done—Dr. Tiffany's words—she finished quickly, lingering after when Riley offered her coffee.

He ended up bringing an entire tray into the living room, passing out cups to those who wanted any.

Phin and Kansas set up a play area in the corner for the children, but they were more interested in the new little person in the room than they were their toys. Bran, Madison, and Patrick climbed onto the couch and sat on the cushion next to me and Aver, peering at Autumn with their chubby hands braced against Aver's leg.

"Hey, you guys, this is your new cousin, Autumn.

Autumn Walker," I said, lifting my daughter so they could see her better. She was asleep, her perfect eyelids closed around her perfect eyes as she slept perfectly.

Madison and Patrick lost interest after that, returning to the play area where they played their favorite game of waiting for one of them to choose a toy so the other could try to take it away.

But Bran remained, sitting on the couch properly with his back against the cushion and his legs out in front of him. "Tum," he said, patting his legs. "Tum."

"I am going to die of cuteness," Riley whispered as his son patted his legs quicker—the baby version of talking louder to someone you think doesn't speak your language.

Bran's legs weren't quite large enough to hold Autumn, but he could with my help. I settled her into his lap, holding her top half so I could support her head and neck. Bran met my eyes and beamed.

"Tum, tum, tum," he sang with a smile.

The room gave a collective "Aww."

After Bran had his fill, the adults wanted their turn meeting Autumn. Thankfully, they seemed to sense I wasn't quite ready to let her get too far away, so they all took turns sitting where Bran had.

At some point in the early evening, Dr. Tiffany left, but Julie replaced her, arriving with flowers and a gift basket full of bottles, formula, onesies, and pacifiers. The whole time, the others lingered in the front room, leaving for a minute, but each time, they returned quickly, reluctant to separate.

There'd been a rift dividing this unit since I'd met them, and now for the first time, I truly saw who they all were and what they meant to each other.

There was teasing and jokes, but also unconditional

love. They were a family, a pack. The first time I'd come to this house, I'd loved Aver, but now, I'd fallen in love with them all.

THREE DAYS WENT BY, but no one was eager to return to their normal lives. We slept in our rooms or in the living room, watched movies, napped, talked, and ate together. Aver gave me tips on diaper changing, while Kansas told me the tricks that had helped with bottle feeding. Phin and Wyatt had tips on burping, while Nash reviewed the steps for baby CPR with everyone.

I called Jorge that first day—Sam and Sparkles were there when I called—and told them what I could, and they promised to make the trip over soon.

I had to tell them I'd let them know the best time.

While in the Walker home we'd remained nested in a pocket out of time and without worries, the world had gone on, and today was the final day Aver's father could act as Interim Alpha. No one knew what to expect, and no one was eager to bring it up either. But as the final hour drew near, we couldn't ignore the problem any longer.

———

"WE DON'T HAVE TO GO," Aver said to the others sitting around the dining room table.

The Walker men looked so similar: backs straight, elbows on the table as they either tapped their chins or steepled their fingers. Maybe it was an alpha thing, but it was yet another trait that linked these four.

"What message would that send?" Wyatt asked.

"Do we care?" Nash countered.

"There are more factors to consider," Branson said. "Whoever becomes next Alpha, we'll need to build a relationship with. If not a relationship, a rapport. Skipping the naming ceremony might not put us in the best light."

While they'd encouraged our opinions, the four of us mates stayed mostly silent. This was a moment decades in the making, and the decisions they made today would influence the rest of their lives.

The cousins stared at each other, none of them speaking for several minutes until Branson suddenly said, "So we're agreed?"

Riley's look of confusion matched my own.

"How?" Phineas mouthed silently.

Aver grabbed my hand, squeezing it under the table. "Unless there are objections, we're going to the ceremony as a pack."

No one disagreed with him.

I was glad we had a plan now, but the last few days had been so amazing. I understood what the group had meant about the Elder's manipulations. They were like poison, infecting and reinfecting their children anytime one of them was the slightest bit healed. I hoped that after today they would no longer be the Elders of anything.

Though I was eager to see that happen, I sighed because it still made me nervous. "I guess we march off to face the asses."

"Do you mean masses?" Phin asked.

I shook my head. "No."

18

———

AVER

WE'D FINALLY REACHED the day when we could not all fit in the same car. There was room for either car seats or bodies. So we'd split up. I drove with Hollister, Autumn, Calvin, Wyatt, and Kansas, while the others piled into the work van.

According to our plan, we didn't drive straight away to the Alpha's mansion but toward the regular pack housing. Most shifters would be at the naming ceremony, and for good reason. This night was going to change how their pack operated. Even the smoothest of transitions required a time of adjustment. Many shifters were nervous and wanted to be there as the Alpha was selected.

But it was for that reason we couldn't bring the children. We needed to be there, but without knowing how the pack would react, it was too dangerous. Thankfully, Tyrone's grandmother and Mrs. Boxer—Phin's former neighbor—had become friends in Nana's absence, and together they had over a hundred years of experience raising children. Both women waited at the door with open arms.

The moment Bran was released from his seat, he took off in a stumbling run, jumping into a hug at the last minute.

"You are sure you don't want to attend the ceremony?" Branson asked Tyrone's grandmother. Mrs. Boxer wasn't a shifter, but no one ever mentioned that fact.

"No, I've seen Alphas come and go. I've seen them rule kindly, rule with fear, with blood. I've seen them fall and rise from the ashes. And yet my life remains the same."

I scanned the walls of the living room as Tyrone's grandmother spoke, stopping on a framed cross-stitch that said, "That's What I Do...I Knit and I Grow Things."

"You all go. It's important for you to be there. Nana told me," Mrs. Boxer said.

We all looked at her. None of us had heard from our great-grandmother since the funeral.

"In my dreams, of course," Mrs. Boxer continued. "She visits me nightly."

I couldn't be the only one who was wishing in that moment that Nana had visited them in their dreams. These past few months wouldn't have happened how they had if we'd had Nana.

Maybe that had been the point.

But I didn't have time to think about that now. We needed to get going to the Alpha Mansion. "I'm leaving the work van," I told Tyrone's grandmother. "If you end up needing it and there is an emergency, use the vehicle's security system. There is a button that will call 911 directly."

After a round of kisses that immediately set off a second round of kisses, the eight of us tore ourselves away. I hooked my arm around Hollister's waist, drawing him close.

"It's for a few hours, and then we'll be right back."

"But...I just got her... What if she forgets who I am?"

Hollister's face was turned down toward the ground. A tear dropped from the tip of his nose to the ground.

"She can't forget you. She spent the last three months protected inside of you. And that might be short for a human, but it's long enough for a shifter. She's got your scent. Our daughter will always know who you are."

Hollister sniffled and looked up at me. "Really?"

I nodded. "Really."

He didn't look happy, but at least he stopped crying. I hated seeing Hollister cry.

As we pulled up to the Alpha's mansion, the road was lined with parked cars along the shoulder on both sides. The gates to the mansion were still open, so we drove in, parking in the lawn near the exit. This way we wouldn't be separated from our fastest means of escape.

Since the fire that had destroyed a large amount of the Alpha's mansion, the pack had come together, rebuilding and restoring the home into its former glory.

The front of the home was lit up. Huge four-paned windows glowed with warmth, but from the sounds of things, the real ceremony was outside, behind the house. Hand in hand with our mates, we walked in a line, Branson with Riley, then me and Hollister, Nash with Phin, and Wyatt with Kansas.

The moment we cleared the back corner of the mansion, we found ourselves standing in front of a large group of people. And not all of them were familiar.

More troubling, some faces were familiar—but weren't ones we'd ever wanted to see again.

Everyone sat in white chairs arranged in rows that faced the back of the house. Paul and Tyrone sat at the end of the front row, Paul's face ashen as Tyrone held his hand tightly in his lap. A raised platform had been installed in front of the chairs, where my father and mother sat with John. Julie sat on the stage as well but on the other side. The divide between her and the other Elders was as obvious as the physical space between them.

I'd wished we'd come earlier, if only so Julie hadn't had to sit alone while the others glared at her. We wouldn't be sitting on the stage with her, but our presence would be comfort enough.

"There are chairs in the back," Riley murmured.

But, as we diverted to go around those already seated, my father stood, clearing his throat. "We hoped you would come, but since you didn't respond to our RSVP, we didn't know. Your chairs have been held for you," he said, and though he smiled, I couldn't trust it.

The last time we'd spoken had been the day of the failed mating party. At that time, his plan had been to open the role of Alpha up for discussion with the pack. But not all of the people in attendance now were even a part of this pack.

"We can sit where there is space," I replied stiffly.

"Nonsense, they were just placeholders." Glendon twitched his hand, and the shifters in the front row—Paul, Tyrone, and the unfamiliar faces excluded—stood to sit in the chairs we'd originally spotted.

I narrowed my eyes at the open seats. Front and center. My father had a plan, and I was in the unfortunate position of having no idea what it was.

The moment we sat, my father stood and cleared his throat. "I wanted to begin this evening by thanking you all for accepting me as Interim Alpha. It has been my pleasure to serve—"

Nash snorted loudly.

My father scowled but tried to ignore it. "It has been my pleasure to serve each of you, but as I am not an alpha, I don't have the authority to remain your leader, nor do I have the authority to decide on the new Alpha on my own. This must be a pack decision..."

I sighed silently, relieved he'd stuck with his original idea. My father was technically correct: a shifter needed to be an alpha to be *nominated* as Alpha of the pack, but once nominated, a pack Alpha was basically all powerful.

Our grandfather, the late Alpha Walker, could have appointed anyone he wanted to follow him. But he'd clung to his power until the very end, refusing to name anyone who wasn't a Walker.

"...and as a pack you have appointed us, your Elders, with the duty and responsibility of making decisions for the welfare of us all. For that reason, we've decided that it is time this pack experienced a change. It's time we grow and dust off the spectacle and tragedy these years have become. It's time we say goodbye to old dreams and greet our future. Better. Bigger. Stronger."

The lump in my throat grew the longer my father spoke. I wasn't going to like what he said; I knew that much already. My hand trembled with restrained fury. Hollister squeezed my fingers, but not even he could soothe me.

My mate and daughter were my life. My family—my true family—were a close second. But this pack, the people who lived and relied on its strength, they weren't nothing. But they were the ones who would be harmed. Their lives would be the ones disrupted.

"Steady, Aver," Branson said from the corner of his mouth. "It's a trap. Like every other time."

I nodded once curtly. I had no doubt that this was a trap, but this time, they'd finally constructed one we couldn't avoid.

One *I* couldn't avoid.

"The Elders and I came together before this meeting and voted, taking the majority opinion." His lips curled into the ghost of a snarl.

I was sure Julie was the reason he'd said *majority* opinion and not *unanimous*.

"We've been in close contact with our friends, allies, and neighbors. We've discussed our best options and have come to terms with the fact that our numbers have been dwindling for some time. A once mighty pack has dimmed into shadows of its former glory. We must adapt or be over-run. For this reason, and so many others, we have decided to join forces. Starting tonight, the Walker County pack will be a subsidiary to El Paso County. We will be led by their Alpha, Harold Woody. For the sake of unity and clarity, his best man, Jeb, will act as the Alpha's official representative. But don't worry. We will all be staying on as your Elders. *We* would not *abandon* you in a time of so much need."

His emphasis was meant for me alone, and I felt each word like a stab to my gut.

Hollister cursed and straightened. His thighs tightened like he was ready to run. I held onto his hand, not in an attempt to force him to stay but to reassure him.

I understood Paul's expression perfectly now. The El Paso County pack had been the very one he'd escaped from when he came here.

I recognized Jeb now too. He'd been one of the shifters who had come to Walker County when Delia had put a call out for auxiliary support. He'd promised to return to his Alpha and report the chaos he discovered. Paul had belonged to his brother, though their process of mating didn't sound anything like ours. It had been an unhappy union, and when he'd died, Paul had taken the first chance he had to run. He'd barely been of age when he'd arrived in Walker County.

According to our pack laws, Jeb had zero claim on Paul, but as mouth of the Alpha? Everything could change.

"Fucking evil," Nash breathed.

The crowd began to murmur, the noise growing into a buzz as anger and fear collided.

"Can they do this?" a shifter behind me hissed. She hadn't been talking to me, but to anyone around her who would listen.

"What choice do they have?" another responded.

What choice did they have...

Every choice. But this was the one they'd made because my father knew I couldn't allow it. I might not have agreed with them in that a Walker alpha must rule the pack, but I couldn't let them hand it over to a monster.

All I had to judge Harold was the people who came from his rule. Paul was one of the best men I knew, and he'd run from Harold's pack. On the other hand, Jeb was a steaming pile of shit, and now that pile was going to act as mouth of the Alpha?

My chest rumbled. My growl began quietly but grew the longer I watched Paul's face.

If Nana were here, she would've stood up, put a stop to this. As mate to the former Alpha, her words held weight, especially with the people of the pack—unlike the words of the Elders. The Elders had only ever been a source of income for the pack. And it wasn't like any of them tried to change that over the years.

They'd turned themselves into royalty, and now that they faced a ruler who might not have been on their side, they were scrambling.

Many in the audience stood. I wasn't the only one growling.

Jeb sneered at the crowd, likely memorizing the faces of those who had spoken out. My father remained silent, letting the pack whip themselves into a frenzy.

"You can't do this!" someone shouted. Paul was a loved member, and he wasn't quiet about where he came from either. The pack knew what this decision meant.

At that, my father lifted his hands. "I know some of you are afraid. We've heard stories about the El Paso County pack that have put them in a less than favorable light. But, in reality—"

"There is no light that makes child marriages okay," Paul snarled.

Jeb didn't deny what Paul had said. He just looked at him, his smile widening like the jaws of a shark. "You are grown now, Paulie."

Tyrone snarled, lunging forward. Nash and Wyatt went for his arms, holding him back as Jeb continued to taunt him.

But as the pandemonium grew, I watched my father watch me. His eyes were dark, soulless, unblinking, and *victorious*.

I sensed the choking fear that plagued my mate. The shifters around us bickered and argued. Jeb's people formed a protective line in front of him, daring any to cross it. Feeling another set of eyes on me, I turned to Branson, and our gazes collided.

"Don't," he whispered sadly. "Please."

How couldn't he see that we no longer had a choice?

I cleared my throat, wishing my vocal cords would suddenly snap and save me from what I was about to say. "I volunteer as Alpha."

19

HOLLISTER

I CLOSED MY EYES. My breathing sounded loud in my head, and though there was more than enough noise around me, I could hear only my shuddering breaths. Each inhale a prayer, each exhale a plea.

All went unanswered.

Not even I had suspected this. But, I realized now, that was because I'd been able to imagine the depths these monsters would sink. They didn't care about their people; they cared about power.

The only thing Glendon Walker wanted was his son as Alpha. Whether Aver ended up hating him in the process was of no concern. This hadn't been about Aver for a very long time.

"He volunteers!" the first of the cries began, spilling into the night like dawn, chasing away a night of darkness.

"Aver Walker volunteers as Alpha!"

Glendon Walker didn't even have the decency to hide his smirk, but Jeb wasn't nearly as pleased. I guessed they'd never told him he was just a pawn.

"The decision is done. I have my Alpha's acceptance

here, sealed until it is to be read at midnight." He lifted a scroll bound closed with a wax seal.

"And midnight is when this will go into effect, unless we have a better option for our people." Glendon gestured to where I stood with Aver. "Do we, son? Do we have a better option for our people?"

I wanted to tear his eyes out and make him eat them.

Aver kept a tight hold on my hand, but I wouldn't leave him now. I hated every second of this, but I'd also watched it all happen. This wasn't what Aver wanted.

His hold never loosened as we stepped through the crowd, people parting before us to make a direct route to the stage. We stood furthest from Jeb, near Julie, who smiled sadly.

"I didn't know. They kept this plan from me until right before this meeting. I voted against it." Her voice trembled with emotion.

"I know you did." Aver used his free hand to clap her shoulder. He squeezed reassuringly. "This was always going to happen."

That didn't sound correct. This wasn't like the fate that had bound us; this was all due to meddling. We stood where we did because of greed. Not destiny.

Aver caught my eye. His green gaze glittered, asking me to do one thing. Trust him.

I didn't want to. I wanted to fight. I wanted to bring down hellfire and vengeance. I wanted the Elders hurt like they'd hurt so many others. But my alpha was asking me for trust, so I remained silent. I remained by his side. I had faith in our love and in him.

I didn't cower when we turned to face the crowd. I held my chin high.

"The Elders must decide!" John Walker yelled, remaining on Jeb's side of the platform.

"Of course, brother," Glendon replied. "Majority rules, as was decided earlier today." He angled so he addressed both the stage and the crowd. "My son, a true Walker alpha, has volunteered to lead us. Is there any who oppose?"

"I do!" Jeb barked.

If I didn't hate Glendon so much, I might have enjoyed the derisive stare he sent Jeb's way. "Any who officially belong to this pack at this moment? Does anyone meeting that criteria oppose?"

"I do!" John snarled. He might have given up on ever seeing Wyatt or Nash standing where Aver was, but he wouldn't let go of the promise of power.

"That makes one Elder opposed," Glendon said smoothly and turned to his mate. "Dear?"

Clarice hadn't looked at me once and still didn't. I could only assume the next plan those two had was to get rid of me. *They could try.* She folded her hands tightly in her lap and spoke with a soft, gentle voice that in no way matched the soul within. "I vote in favor."

"Julie?" Glendon barely glanced her way.

Julie's face crumpled. Her heartache was like a physical thing, weighing her down. But, she lifted her head, finding her sons in the crowd as she said with a clear, loud voice, "I vote in favor."

Glendon floated on the high of victory. His wide smile bared every one of his teeth, but I saw only fangs. "Then it is decided. Thank you, Jeb and the El Paso county pack, for offering to help in our time of need, but your services won't be needed after all." His voice boomed over the crowd.

Branson, Wyatt, and Nash stood tall among the rest, each of them fighting the urge to run. Aver must have asked silently for their trust as well, and it was only that trust that kept them from bolting.

Glendon stood beside his son and lifted his arm into the air. "Welcome your new Alpha, my son, Aver Walker."

The shifters pointed their faces to the sky and howled. Each was still in their human forms, but their howls combined, merging and harmonizing into a single unified sound. The warbling note was eerie but also hopeful. These people had been toyed with tonight, dangled over a fire as bait. But now, their savior was here. Aver. The Alpha.

"Do we need to wait until midnight before I am to take control?" Aver asked stiffly to both the pack and Elders.

"As current Interim Alpha, I don't see any reason to wait," Glendon replied, stepping back while waving his arm in a sweeping gesture in front of him. "You are in control. Lead us."

"Remove the outsiders from our territory," Aver commanded.

Instantly, a group of shifters, Tyrone included, jumped forward. The outside shifters must have known they were up against unbeatable odds because they left with only a slight scuffle.

Jeb screamed threats over his shoulder the entire time. Even when they'd disappeared to the front of the house, his screams echoed. "My Alpha will hear of this disrespect! He will not let it pass unchallenged!"

A group stayed with them to escort them off the territory while the rest returned. The excitement in the air was palpable. These people were ecstatic, and for a second, I couldn't hate what had happened, not when so many lives had been improved so rapidly.

That excitement didn't extend to the other Walkers. They stood huddled, mates tucked behind them as they faced the others. They wanted to run, but if they did, their family would never be the same. If they abandoned one of their own now, there wasn't any going back from that.

Tyrone took his place beside Paul, who at least had color in his face again.

"Talk to your people," Glendon murmured eagerly. "Reassure them."

"I know how to lead," Aver snapped.

Glendon's mouth tightened, but his gaze dropped with respect. "Yes, Alpha."

Aver stepped forward, continuing until the two of us stood on the very edge, looking out at the sea of anxious, hopeful faces. Aver took a deep breath. "I bet we never thought this would happen, huh?"

The conversational tone made it seem like they were sitting down for a chat. He didn't sound anything like how his father had, with that over-exaggerated boom. Aver's words were quiet and unassuming, like a true leader. A few in the pack chuckled.

"Hell, I'd never thought I'd be here." Aver scratched the back of his head. "But they did, right?" he wrenched his thumb over his shoulder.

Glendon scurried forward to murmur in Aver's ear. "Son, it's good to keep the people on your side but—"

"Silence," Aver commanded. "Your opinion has not been asked for. I'm speaking with my pack, not the Elders."

Glendon had no choice but to obey, his face burning red the entire time.

Branson smirked as Nash elbowed Wyatt in an *I told you so* sort of way.

"You may be wondering right now why I've chosen to volunteer now and not during any number of times when the fate of this pack had seemed bleak. I'll be honest. I didn't want control."

Clarice gasped, but she couldn't speak up either. Glendon had given his authority to Aver, and he was Alpha now.

"But sometimes, we don't get what we want. Take me. I wasted a lot of my life trying to prove to these people behind me that you could be gay and successful. That I deserved their pride. But they never deserved mine. Thankfully, I have a mate and a family who helped me let go of my bitterness. And Elders Glendon, Clarice, and John, I hope you can do the same one day."

Glendon's face burned an even brighter shade of red. All of his scheming, years of plotting and planning, was going to be for *nothing*. I felt no pity. He'd made the bed he was lying in. And he could stay there.

I let my lips curl, my heart pounding in breathless anticipation. My mate had something up his sleeve. I knew it. I could sense it as clearly as I could feel him standing beside me. The others knew it as well. Riley beamed while Phin shot me a thumbs up. But mostly they looked relieved to not be where I was.

"But I won't wait for that to happen. Only a shifter born an alpha may be considered by the Elders, that is true and what my parents were counting on. But the *standing* Alpha of a pack, can..." He sighed and sat down at the end of the stage, gently leading me down to sit next to him. "...basically do what he wants, right?"

That got actual laughs from the crowd. They hung on his words, as starved for a true leader to guide them as I'd been for Aver's touch.

"Paul, will you stand please?"

Heads turned to the end of the front row, where Paul

had remained with Tyrone. He rose to his feet, his eyes wide and wary. "I'm here, Av—Alpha Walker."

Aver smiled. "Do you love this pack?"

A fraction of his wariness faded. "Yes, with all my heart."

"You are not an alpha, correct?"

Paul frowned, but he trusted Aver enough to continue answering, though he clearly wasn't sure where this was leading. "No, I'm not, Alpha Walker."

"And though you are not an alpha, you've spent these months—and longer if we're all being honest—working for the pack, not the Elders. Delia was your sponsor, but when you obeyed her, who were you really obeying?"

Paul shrugged like the answer was obvious. "The people. The pack is the people. The Elders are meant to support the pack, not rule it."

"Insolent little—" John began.

"If you cannot be quiet, you may remove yourself," Aver snarled, his alpha's authority reverberating through the outside space. But, when he faced Paul again, the anger from seconds ago was gone. "So you've been arranging meals, tending to the sick, scheduling the watch to keep our territory protected all while being not an alpha?"

"I can see where you're going with this, and I must *respectfully* object, Alpha Walker," Glendon spat the words out through clenched teeth. "Paul isn't an alpha, but more importantly, he has no Elders. I certainly won't be following if this is the direction you intend—"

"Your objection has been noted." Aver addressed the people. "By us all, right?"

Many nodded while more simply glared at the Elders.

Every inch of Aver screamed confidence and poise. He sat at the edge, his feet balanced on the ground as he leaned forward, making it appear as if this were a casual conversation between friends. The whole time, he kept my hand in his, sometimes massaging, sometimes squeezing. "As my father has kindly pointed out, you all see where I'm going with this, so I'll shorten the lead-up. I am open to concerns and objections, *from the shifters in the pack*, but the final decision will be mine. I nominate Paul as Alpha of the Walker County packs. And I appoint myself as his first Elder." Aver made sure his voice carried over his shoulder.

"That's just one," Glendon snarled. He'd dropped all pretense of respect for his son. The number of times he'd been asked to remain silent was proof of that. "You need more than *one* Elder to support a pack this large, or else the pack will wither. You will face threats. Your people will get sick. And there will be no money. *That* is what a pack relies on, more than gentle leaders or a united front. It's money."

"I'll remain as Elder," Julie spoke up. "If Paul will have me."

"She isn't as rich as she was." John stood, gesturing to his ex-mate while his skin turned red and mottled. "We are no longer together. Her fortune isn't even half of what it was. My lawyers—"

"Were very good, yes," Julie agreed. "But you assumed you knew where I kept all of my money. My cup may not overflow, but there's more than enough in there to pass around. I've got to spend it on something. Might as well spend it on creating the pack I'd always wished this one could be."

"Then it's decided," Aver said. "If Paul becomes Alpha, he has two Elders already."

"Three." Branson's voice carried easily over the sea of heads. "As half-owner of Walker Construction and majority shareholder in my father's company, I would be proud to be an Elder for Paul."

"Me too," Wyatt said with a sigh. "But I'm not paying pack taxes," he added obstinately.

Kansas elbowed him.

"Us as well," Nash added. "I don't make a ton as a fireman, but my sugar-daddy over here writes bestsellers."

Phin's face burned while those around them laughed.

The change in this space from now to just thirty minutes ago seemed impossible. They'd been on the verge of running or rioting—their mutiny would have spread destruction. Now, they were laughing, smiling. There was hope.

In front of us anyway. Behind us, there were only sour faces. That didn't matter because no one but me was looking at them anyway. They all watched Paul, who had yet to say a word.

He was young, yes, but you didn't need age to be a backbone, and that was what Paul had become to this pack. I'd been here the shortest time of anyone and knew that. He was the first name people brought up when they needed to help, and he was the last person to leave when there was a problem. He cared about every member, no matter how long they'd been members or how much influence they had.

"You're asking me to be Alpha?" Paul blushed but kept his head high.

"I could order you," Aver joked. "But yes, I'm asking you, and I'm asking the pack." He looked to his family, sharing a silent moment. "We will not abandon you, but we don't want to lead. None of us has ever wanted to lead. I don't know that Paul really wants to lead either, but he loves this pack and will do the best by it. I'm sure of that."

Suddenly, Tyrone threw his head back and howled.

Others joined him, the noise not as singular as it had been before. This time, it was clearly a combination of voices, different notes, volumes, and tones, coming together in support. Branson and the others tilted their heads back, joining in, and I looked to the sky, letting my howl release into the heavens.

Aver hopped off the stage, leading us both to stand in front of Paul. The tips of his cheeks were pink, and his eyes glittered with unshed tears as he took in the sight of his friends and family howling their support. "Do you accept the role of Alpha, Paul Tyson? This isn't a short-term thing. You won't be an interim. You will be Alpha, until you die or appoint a suitable shifter to replace you. Today's decision will have an effect on the rest of the shifter world, but I promise you, you won't face it alone."

The howls stopped abruptly, and the pack waited to hear his reply.

Paul scanned the crowd silently. He looked into each face before replying. "I accept."

We turned toward the stage as one, but only Julie remained. The others had likely scurried off when they realized their plan would fail.

"Then take the stage, Alpha." Aver stepped aside, but Paul didn't move. Not forward at least.

He turned to Tyrone. The man was so much taller than him; Paul had to look up to see into his face. But it was a face full of a warm, loving smile and proud eyes. To Tyrone, Paul had always been special, and now he wasn't jealous or worried but happy. He clearly loved Paul now as much as he had before he'd been named Alpha. "If I'm going to take the stage, I want to do it with my omega by my side."

Paul grabbed the collar of Tyrone's shirt, yanking him down into a kiss that Tyrone had already been racing towards. Their lips collided with all the passion and fire of two people who had found the one they were meant to be with and were poised to spend the rest of their lives together.

"Can he claim an omega if he's only an Alpha by title?" I didn't see who had asked the question, but from the expressions on the other faces, it was something many were wondering.

Aver lifted his shoulders, letting them drop. "I think he just did."

———

WE WERE all eager to return to the children, but some celebrations couldn't be rushed. Paul had moved the party into the Alpha's mansion, his new home.

The former elders had disappeared, all but Julie, who smiled as widely as the rest. She sat with her sons on either side of her as they discussed what it would mean to be Elders. Wyatt had been under the impression it was mostly writing checks.

Branson and Tyrone were in the middle of a deep—and not at all extremely boring—conversation regarding foundation beams for the new school building they hoped to break ground on in the coming weeks.

I had a feeling there would be many changes in our future, but this time, it wasn't something I needed to dread.

I hadn't suffered for as long as the people around me, but it felt as if their happiness soaked into me. Maybe my power wasn't all that different from Kansas's, but instead of energy, it was emotions. I stepped through the crowd, pausing to bask when the joy was particularly bright.

I found Aver and Paul in the sitting room speaking

fervently with their heads drawn toward the other. It sounded as if the ideas Paul had shared with Aver to help improve pack life were only been the tip of the iceberg. He'd been brainstorming ways to improve pack operations since he'd joined and had realized it was home, and it seemed he'd finally found the shifter eager to hear every one of them. I didn't want to interrupt them, at least for a few more minutes. I could give them that much.

Floating through the pockets of people, I was a butterfly sipping joy like it was nectar. In the kitchen, I found more people celebrating but also preparing food for the rest. "May I help?" I asked.

"Of course. We we're just about to pass out drinks," said a woman with sleek blonde hair and bright blue eyes. "Will you grab the mugs from the cupboard?"

I went to the cupboard she pointed to and began pulling cups from the shelves, arranging them on a tray she'd handed me. In no time, it was nearly full, and I stretched to grab the last mug. It was further back than the others, and I had to jump to get my hands around it.

My fingers clasped the mug handle, and I felt as though I'd been shot through the heart. I fell back, slamming against the floor. My head bounced against the tile with a sickening thud, and my vision dimmed, the edges tinged with fire. Hatred. Anger. Disdain.

Murder.

"Murder," I screamed, my throat raw and ragged. I didn't recognize my voice as it screamed the same word, over and over. "Murder! Murder! Murder!" My body shook. Spittle shot from my mouth as my limbs flung out of my control, connecting with the bodies and furniture standing around me.

I needed to let go of the cup, but my fingers were frozen.

The emotional memories were too strong. Especially when I hadn't prepared myself for the onslaught, and I was helpless to do anything to stop the endless waves of hatred soaking into me, filling me with a loathing so deep it eclipsed all else.

"What happened?" Not even Aver's voice could put a stop to the assault.

"He was filling the tray with cups," the blonde shifter replied. "He was fine, until—"

"Move aside," Aver ordered, dropping to the tile.

But though I could see him, it wasn't with my own eyes. My brain wasn't all mine. It housed ghosts, echoes of whoever had imprinted on the cup. And whoever that was couldn't stand the sight of him. "Don't touch me, *disgraced* alpha!" I growled, not meaning a single word I said. This feeling wasn't mine; it didn't belong to me.

As quickly as the attack came, it left. But not completely. Aftershocks of anger made my body twitch, and I wiggled my hand, my fingers touching nothing but air and then Aver's hand. I cried out, flying into Aver's arms as quickly as he hauled me against his chest.

"It was the cup?" Aver asked with his lips against my ear. He wasn't confused about what had happened; none of the guys would be.

I shook my head, relieved I could do that now too. "Where is it?" I asked, as if afraid someone would thrust it in my hand again.

"Bring him here," Riley said. "I have some water. He should sit."

Aver lifted me from the floor and brought me to the small table. The others circled around, Paul, Tyrone, and Julie included, while the rest of the pack crowded together, spilling out the back of the small space.

My gaze dropped to Paul's hands, and I hissed, attempting to climb over the back of my chair.

Paul looked down, quickly placing the cup behind his back.

It was a sweet gesture, but I could still sense it. I didn't know how I'd ever missed the vibrations. Now that the connection had been made, I felt the cup throbbing with malice.

"Someone needs to explain what's going on," Paul said without anger. "I know you have an ability, will you please explain it again?" His words were urgent but in a way that clearly indicated he wanted to know so he could help.

"I have this trick..."

"Trick or curse?" Paul asked.

"Trick. It isn't a curse, not normally." I shuddered. Before this moment, I hadn't known a person could feel a hatred so strong.

"He feels memories from objects. The stronger the memory, the stronger the feeling," Aver explained more to the crowd than Paul.

"And this one was a doozy."

"How can we tell who put the memories in the object?" Paul asked, proving he had an advanced ability to learn new information and roll with it.

Normally, people handed me the things that belonged to them. I didn't have to try to figure out who had left what. I was confident I could, but not without touching it again. Parsing through the different kinds of hate would be like separating them into flavors, deciding between jealous hatred and violent hatred.

There wasn't a part of me that wanted anywhere near that cup a second time, and though I felt a little silly fearing such a mundane object, I knew it had been used to do something awful. I leaned into Aver, stealing some of his strength. My alpha had enough to spare.

"You don't have to," Aver growled. "No one is making you." His face lifted, his words half promise, half challenge.

No one disagreed.

"Does he even need to?" Nash asked. "*Disgraced alpha*, is that only ringing a bell to me? And this is the Alpha's mansion. The Alpha was last person to die suddenly in this house. Everyone knew Alpha Walker drank tea in the evening. Many of the blends were given to him by his own mother."

"So you're saying Nana killed her son?" Wyatt asked.

"Don't be dim, Wy. I'm saying we know who was poised to benefit from Alpha Walker dying."

"But he died of natural causes," Julie said. "I saw the report."

Nash wasn't convinced. "Raise your hand if you don't think the Elders would lie about how Alpha Walker died or doctor an official report to suit their needs."

No one raised their hands.

"So we save Hollister the heartache and go take care of them," Nash addressed the crowd. "They must have scurried home, oblivious that Hollister was able to do what he can."

Most nodded their agreement, but not Paul. "We have to be sure." His face twisted with regret. "We can't just assume and grab our pitchforks. I wouldn't be a very good Alpha if that's how I allow the pack to find justice." He spoke loud enough for the room to hear. "We must be positive, but when we find the person responsible, they will pay."

My head pounded, making it difficult to keep up with the conversation. If I hadn't been a shifter, I likely would've split my skull open falling as hard as I had, but I'd heard enough to know I would need to touch that cursed thing again. If that cup had been used to kill someone, I would have to touch it again.

Paul grabbed the table, crouching to look me in the face. "I won't force you, Hollister. We can do this a different way."

I shook my head as Aver tightened the grip he had on my shoulder. "I'll do it."

20

—————

AVER

"WE AREN'T THROWING it in his palm and seeing what happens," I snarled, though no one had suggested as much. The entire pack, all those who had stayed for the naming ceremony, crowded in the kitchen, spilling out into the hallway and sitting room beyond.

I'd assumed my father's sudden absence after it was clear Paul would be Alpha was because he'd left to pout with my mother. Now I wondered if there hadn't been a more sinister reason.

"Paul, should we send guards to the former Elders' homes? Just in case?" I attempted to ask quietly enough that only Paul could hear me, but the room was too crowded for me to be very effective.

Paul shot me a grateful smile anyway.

I was confident in my decision. Paul was the best choice this pack had for Alpha, but no one could be expected to act perfectly from the first day. "Kyle and Del, go to Glendon and Clarice's. Do nothing but stand out of sight and watch. Ben, Tyrone, will you go to John's?"

The four shifters, Paul's new omega included, nodded and headed out.

"The children," Hollister whispered in my ear. "I'd feel better if Autumn was here."

"Wyatt, Nash?" I asked without looking away from my mate's face. I didn't like how pale he still was. He'd just given birth three days ago. It was a magical labor, but it had taken a lot out of him.

"We're on it."

Slowly, the rest of us migrated from the kitchen into the study. It was the largest indoor space—asking anyone to clear out at a time like this would only cause more fear—and the room was carpeted. I'd be there to hold him this time, but I wouldn't risk Hollister cracking his head again like he had. I'd heard that sound before I'd heard anything else, and though I'd been two rooms over, I'd known it was Hollister. I'd felt it.

Paul turned in a slow circle as he spoke. "I understand you're all scared and want to get to the bottom of this, but please give Hollister space. What he is about to do comes at a cost that I am asking him to pay, for us. So please, remain, but stay quiet and do not move. Does everyone understand?"

"Yes, Alpha," they chorused.

"What do you need us to do, Hollister? How will we know if it's too much?" Paul asked.

Hollister sunk down on the maroon velvet settee with his palms resting open on his lap. "Just, keep me from knocking my beautiful face into anything." My pet tried to joke, but his lips trembled, ruining the effect.

"You don't have to do this," I growled. He'd been told already, but I wanted him to know, mostly because I was hoping he'd decide he didn't want to. The Aver who hadn't spent a few weeks stewing in the woods and in his bad choices might have forbidden this from happening entirely. While I'd seen the error of my ways, I didn't ever want Hollister in pain.

He smiled, but not even he could hold the expression for very long. "I know. I'm ready. I can do this." He spoke to himself as much as us. "I'll tell you if it's too much. I'll just say *stop*, right?" His lips twitched into a smile, bringing back memories from a night that felt like it had happened years ago.

I kissed his forehead. "That's all you ever have to say."

Paul had the mug in his hands. "Just say stop," he said again, looking into Hollister's eyes and waiting for his nod before he lowered the white porcelain into Hollister's waiting palms.

The effect was instant. Hollister's fingers curled into a white-knuckle grip as his spine went rigid, and he sank into the settee. His lips twisted in a grimace before his mouth opened, and he spoke as if he had no control over the words or volume. "Hatred." That one word was breathy and shaky. "He grieves for an injustice. An inadequacy. He's never enough."

Hollister might as well have painted a picture of my father. It couldn't have been any clearer who he was talking about. He grimaced, squeezing his eyes tightly closed. The vein on his forehead throbbed, while his neck was so rigid the tendons looked as if they were trying to escape from under his skin. "She wants revenge. She wants the world as it was, the future as it had been."

That could've been either my mother or Delia, but it proved that more than one person had come in contact with this mug, which meant more than one person was responsible for the murder it had been used in.

"Death," Hollister growled, sounding so unlike himself I searched his face to make sure my mate was still there. "Death and rot...vengeance."

Hollister shook all over. His teeth clanged together while the muscles in his arms tightened, his fingers pressing so hard into the mug he snapped the handle off, and yet he continued to cling to it, rocking back and forth as he whispered too quietly for me to hear what he was saying.

"What is it? Who does he sense now?" Branson asked.

I shook my head, dropping to my knees in front of Hollister as I attempted to discern the words he whispered.

It wasn't words. It was a word. S*top.*

"He's had enough." I grabbed his wrist, but his grip was too strong. He'd cut his palm on the jagged edges where the handle had been, and though he bled, he refused to let go. He chanted louder, the word growing more panicked with each repetition.

"Stop, stop, stop!"

"Get it out of his hands!" Branson shouted.

"I don't want to hurt him." I couldn't pull any harder. If I did with the grip he had, his fingers were liable to snap off.

"Find something to pry under his fingers," Paul urged, searching around his person.

We didn't have time for that. I covered Hollister's hands with mine, easily overlapping his fingers as I pressed in, distributing the weight evenly around the mug. It crumbled beneath our combined strength. As the pieces fell from our hands, Hollister slumped forward.

I caught him, holding his trembling body tightly. "Get the doctor."

"No," Hollister whimpered. "I'm okay. Just give me a second." He exhaled roughly. "That was—whew. More than one. More than two."

"And you think each person you sensed had a hand in the murder?" Paul asked.

Hollister didn't need time to think about it. "Yes. If not directly responsible, then they helped. I'm pretty sure he was poisoned." He grimaced. "Over a period of time, if that makes sense."

No one was eager to connect the dots Hollister had given us out loud.

Except Paul. "The Elders murdered Alpha Walker?"

"I had no idea," Julie whispered. "I swear. I have served Alpha Walker tea, hundreds of times. Most of us had. When Alpha Walker died, I lived with Nana. I'd been all but excommunicated from the Elder council by that point."

"No one suspects it was you," Paul assured her.

Outside, a car approached quickly. The tires had no sooner stopped than did the doors open, slamming shut immediately after.

"Paul!" Tyrone yelled. "Alpha Tyson!"

I carried Hollister with the others to the front of the house where we met Tyrone and Ben.

"Is he gone?" Paul asked before Tyson could speak again.

Tyson stopped suddenly, confused at how Paul already knew what he'd been about to tell them. "Yes, Glendon and Clarice as well. Kyle and Del went to search the forests around their homes, but I don't think they even went back there after the ceremony. Their scents were weak."

"Aver," Hollister whimpered, confirming he felt the same dread that had come over me.

"Wyatt and Nash will return. They'll—"

A howl ascended above the forest in the distance. At the same time, the white work van tore down the driveway.

I caught Branson's eye, and the truth of what had

happened passed between us. We didn't need Wyatt and Nash to jump out and tell us anything. The children were gone.

The children were gone, and so were the Elders.

––––––

"THEY COULDN'T HAVE GOTTEN FAR. This is an island," Paul said, arranging the pack in groups of four. "They're panicking. We'll start here, continuing in an overlapping grid that will spiral out. If one of you picks up on their scent, alert the others and follow it. No matter where it leads you. The blessed children are our only concern right now."

Hollister sobbed into my shoulder, and he wasn't the only one. Kansas, Riley, Phin, and many of the shifters were crying too. Wyatt and Nash had brought Mrs. Boxer and Tyrone's grandmother with them. They'd been easily over-powered and had no idea where our parents had planned on taking the children.

I shouldn't have been surprised our parents could sink so low. Repeatedly, they'd proven I'd yet to witness the truth depths of their greed. Our parents would always have a leg up for that reason. None of us could even fathom the things they were capable of.

But they'd made a mistake taking the blessed children. They were miracles, every one of them, but more than that, they were a sign of hope for the pack. The ex-Elders had stolen that hope.

"If you spot them, keep your eye on them, but do not approach unless you are positive a blessed child is in imme-diate danger," Paul instructed.

The crescent moon shone weakly over his head. But we

wouldn't need light to search. The Elders couldn't have gone far—we'd realized their deception too early—but underestimating them was a mistake, one we made over and over.

"What if we reach the end of pack lands?" someone asked. "Do we continue?"

Paul nodded decisively, his omega standing like his bodyguard beside him. "We won't stop until we find them."

Though we were a pack more than a hundred strong, the territory was vast. Searching pack lands wouldn't be so bad, but searching all of Walker County required more than the numbers we had to search thoroughly and quickly. If we were lucky and caught a scent early, that would be one thing. But I couldn't chance our children on luck.

I wasn't the only one who had come to that realization, either. Wyatt, Nash, and Riley had too.

We couldn't find them like this. Not without a miracle.

"Look!" Kansas cried out, pointing to the forest line at the edge of the lawn.

A figure emerged from the trees, the steady, purposeful gait as familiar as her wild silver hair. *Nana*.

She was barefoot and wore a simple brown dress. She raised her arms as we sprinted toward her. Branson reached her first, hugging her tightly, but the rest of us couldn't wait and simply added our arms to the mix. I couldn't be sure she was really here until I touched her.

"You're back!"

"The children are gone!"

"Where have you been?"

Everyone spoke so quickly their words overlapped. Nana listened, never once looking surprised or shocked. "I came as quickly as I could," she said.

Hearing her voice, after spending so long wondering if I

ever would again, should have been a joyful time. When I'd imagined this moment, it had been followed by hours of calm conversation where we caught her up on all that had happened and she let us know all she'd faced out in the woods. But, if she was here, that meant the spirits had told her what was happening.

"Do you know where they are?" I asked.

Nana closed her eyes. With the heavy lines on her face, she seemed like the old woman the rest of the world saw, but I knew there was a fire in her that made her something magical. "I've seen it. The children are safe for now. I know where they're keeping them. I know what the Elders have done. To the blessed ones and to my *son,*" she growled the word out. "We go together. As a pack."

She blinked, turning her head like someone had called her name, though no one had. "That is, if our Alpha allows it," she added with the barest hint of a smile.

"Nana, you don't need to ask," Paul said. "Wherever you lead, we will follow. A united pack." He raised his voice to be heard throughout the yard. The chilly night air made each word its own cloud. "They have taken something that belongs to us all. The blessed ones are ours to protect. We will find them. And we will avenge Alpha Walker's murder." He shifted immediately after, letting his wolf's howl carry into the night.

The ex-Elders may have been able to hear Paul's howl, but they had no idea what was coming for them.

———

WE CUT THROUGH THE NIGHT, a wolf pack of enormous proportions. There wasn't a man, woman, or child belonging to the pack who wasn't among us. All those who hadn't

303

attended the naming ceremony joined the herd as we ran by their homes and through pack lands.

No one had wanted to spend time wondering what our parents had planned for the children. Why they'd taken them in the first place. Or how long they'd had this plan tucked away in case of an emergency.

With them, it was always greed or power. And a blessed child would bring them both. They had five of them.

Though it would have been easy to fall apart, once the chase started, Hollister and the mates funneled everything they were feeling into a single driving purpose. We never slowed. Our direction never wavered. With Nana at the lead and the spirits leading her, there was no doubt that we were on the right path.

The forest split before our might. Growling barks, baying, and howls echoed in the air around us. Our parents would know we were coming. They would know, and they would be afraid.

All claws, teeth, and murderous rage, we'd become a nightmare, the thing that people feared when they searched the darkness. Our pack had been stolen from, the treasure we cared about most ripped from our arms. Perhaps our parents had assumed only the Walkers and their mates would care and that we'd be easily manipulated. The idea that other people would care for children that were not their own had never occurred to them.

Whatever force drove a person to do the right thing, even when no one watched, didn't exist in them.

They didn't understand devotion or unity. But they would see it. And soon.

Ahead, the forest thinned around a small log cabin. At Paul's yelp, the pack split in two, the right funneling around the front of the cabin while the left circled around to the back side. A dim glow shone from the front window, and there was movement, shadows flitting behind the thin curtains.

I shifted, joining Nana, Paul, and the other Walkers at the front of the howling horde.

"They know we're here," Paul said dryly.

"Good," Nash snarled.

"You are surrounded," Paul yelled. "Release the blessed children, and we may show you mercy."

The curtain moved, but that was the only indication we got that they'd heard us. Perhaps they knew what we all did. After what they'd done, it didn't matter how they groveled. Mercy was not on the menu.

"Are you ready for what has to be done?" Branson asked me. There wasn't judgment in his question as there might have been a few weeks ago, but he needn't have worried.

"Absolutely." My growl was joined by Hollister's.

I didn't want Hollister in there. Not because I thought he couldn't handle himself, but because we would not walk away from this with clean hands. I'd carry the stain of parricide for the rest of my life. And I didn't want that darkness spilling over onto him.

I angled to face him, but he already scowled.

"No, you can't keep me out," he snarled.

I knew his anger wasn't meant for me. I just stood in the way.

"Pet, I will bring you our daughter. I swear it. But you are not going inside. I won't make you bear this burden. It isn't meant for your shoulders."

The others were explaining the same thing to their mates, each as equally adamant as Hollister that they be allowed in.

"Look, someone's standing there," Tyrone said, gesturing toward the curtained window.

My mother. I caught her scent but would have known her silhouette without it. We were well off pack lands, on the southern edge of the island. Perhaps their plan had been to hide here, believing our search wouldn't take us this far before they were able to secure a private boat off-island. Or maybe they didn't have an exit plan at all. It was possible I gave them too much credit.

Their town car was parked out front, the tires slashed. It wasn't like they could use the car to get away. This was an island. There was no place to run. Wherever they went, we would follow, and they likely had come to that same conclusion.

Branson faced the mates. "If any of them slips by us—"

"They won't have their arms for long," Kansas snarled, spinning to face his mate. "Wyatt, let me drain them. I can do it. I'll drain them dry." He sounded like a man who had been pushed to his limits, but instead of falling, he pushed back.

"No, love. I don't want any of them inside you. Not even if you drain and release. Besides..." Wyatt's smile held no humor. "My father has had this coming for a long time."

"We'll kill them!" my mother suddenly shrieked from inside. "This moment. Starting with the littlest. I will kill every last one of—" She let out a bloodcurdling scream, and the four of us surged forward.

Paul, Tyrone, and Nana nipped at our heels as the pack closed the circle behind us. Branson took the lead. He jumped, feet first, and shifted in midair. When his paws hit the rickety door, it croaked open under his weight and slammed against the inside wall with a loud thud.

Directly ahead, there was a hallway, but my mother

stood in the living room area to the left. She scurried toward the corner, clutching a bloody hand to her bosom.

The children were on the ground behind her. Autumn and Calvin whimpered, laying on their backs with their blankets open, doing nothing to fight the chill in the air. They weren't crying, but I wished they were. I'd never forget the sound of their soft, helpless whimpers. Bran, Madison, and Patrick crouched before the younger two, each snarling at Clarice's backside as she stumbled away from us.

Bran let out a sharp barking sound, his teeth still bloody from where he'd bit my mother. That must have been why Clarice had screamed.

From down the dark hallway came the sounds of a scuffle. There was grunting and cursing, and then the back door slammed shut.

"They're everywhere! John has abandoned us!" Glendon screamed, running into the front room and skidding to a terrified stop when he saw me standing with the others. "Son, I told John not to do this."

"Silence." The word could hardly be called that, but, for once, Glendon shut his mouth. "For once in your life, stop lying."

Nana had broken off to walk around the couch. She approached Clarice slowly with her hands stretched out in front of her. "My child, this doesn't have to be your path. Are you truly willing to hurt children? Babies?"

"Shut up, you old hag!" Clarice snarled, as unhinged as I'd ever seen her. "Our lives would've been perfect without you. You gave our son a place to stay. You allowed him to leave the pack. If it wasn't for you—"

Bran lunged forward with a swiftness I'd never seen from him before. His teeth found my mother's ankle, and he bit down, blood spurting from the wound. She shook her leg, screaming as she dislodged Bran, sending him back to the other two. They patted him as if telling him he'd done as much as he could.

Branson snarled and stomped forward, driving Clarice back. At the mouth of the hallway, Glendon stood frozen until John, driven back inside by the pack waiting outside, slammed into his backside.

"This was an idiotic plan. I should've done as Delia asked and killed you both along with Alpha Walker."

"Killed *us*?" Glendon howled back. "We allowed you to live. Your weakness brought us down. Imagine it, a man unable to keep a single woman in line." My father wasn't winning any husband-of-the-year awards, but the two men fought with each other anyway, seemingly oblivious to the death sentence that stood before them.

Paul shook his head with disbelief, deciding the children were a higher priority than watching two grown men squabble. "Step away from the blessed ones," he ordered.

Clarice didn't move.

"As Alpha of this territory, I order you to—"

Clarice leaned forward, her hatred jumping from her like a living thing. "You are Alpha of nothing, you piece of trash. Delia took you in for one purpose, and you couldn't even do that."

Clarice's taunts bounced off Paul like pebbles against a stone. "You leave me no choice, Clarice Walker. I sentence you to death by the pack. Do you have anything final to say?"

Her eyes narrowed, her chin high. "You wouldn't dare—"

Nana shifted, leaping on the woman before she could finish her sentence. She dragged her, screaming, by the head behind the couch where the children could not see.

But I did.

"Take the children," Branson told Tyrone and Paul. "We'll handle the rest."

Bran tried to climb over Tyrone's shoulder, fighting to remain with his father, but Tyrone shushed him, patting him gently. "You fought well, pup. Now let your father handle the rest."

Clarice's screams turned into whimpers. Tyrone and Paul carried the children, shielding them from the violence and closing the door behind them. Nana growled once more, and Clarice's whimpers turned permanently silent.

Glendon was oblivious to his mate's demise. He still fought with John up and down the hallway. The two pushed from each other at the same time, their backs slamming against opposite walls.

As if dazed, Glendon took in the sight of his wife. He spotted me and fell to his knees, his hands clasped and pleading. "I didn't want to do any of it. Your mother...and Delia...they—"

Branson moved to my side so we stood shoulder to shoulder. "Delia will rot in prison. You could have too. You made the choices that brought you here, Glendon, no one else."

Wyatt went to Branson's other side as Nash came to mine. We were a united front, four men who were done living under the shadows of their parents.

John didn't try to plead. He'd lost any relationship with his sons long ago and must have known begging would get him nowhere.

Glendon must have realized the same thing because he stood, scowling, his moods changing faster than a strobe light. "You were a disappointment," he growled, attempting, even in his last moments, to tear me down.

"I don't care."

We shifted as one. The fight was brief, the struggle short. We were alphas after all, each one of us. And they were nothing but sad, tired monsters. Despite knowing this was absolutely what had to happen, when the brutal task was finished, not one of us was left without tears in his eyes. I wiped mine away as Branson and the other two did the same.

"It had to be done," Branson said.

None of us disagreed.

Outside, Hollister had Autumn pressed against his face as he nuzzled her like a wolf would its child. Riley, Phin, and Kansas did the same, though Julie stood with Phin, helping him control the twins, who still snarled anytime someone swayed too close.

I brought mate and daughter into my arms, needing a few moments to just stand and hold them. My cousins would need the same.

At some point, wolves circling us began to howl. One after another, the shifters let their voices lift to the sky as if they were all realizing the same things at once.

We'd found the children.

The ex-Elders were gone.

For the first time in decades, this pack was free.

21

HOLLISTER

"MADISON, you spit your brother's foot out, right now," Phin scolded.

The cannibalistic child in question rolled off her brother with a huff. The maneuver brought her closer to Autumn, but Madison's entire body language changed as she took in the younger child. She smiled sweetly into her cousin's face before bending down to kiss her on the forehead.

The twins might have liked to torture each other, but they were both protective of their cousins, particularly Calvin and Autumn.

As they grew older and more of their personalities shone through, watching the way the children interacted with the world around them was a humbling experience. We'd all worried about the lasting effects that being kidnapped would have on them, particularly Bran, but the kids had shown us just how tough they were. Issues might still arise in the future, but we all knew what to look out for.

But, for all their amazing qualities, sitting still for a picture wasn't one of them.

We'd been trying at it for the past ten minutes but were no closer to getting a shot that showed each adorable face looking toward the camera with their eyes open. We'd given up on smiles two minutes in and now would settle for one where none of them was just a blur.

"Let her establish her dominance," Nash suggested with a devilish gleam. "It's never too early to learn how to defend yourself."

"But it is too early for your son to lose a toe," Phin countered.

Nash pretended he had to think about that, which prompted Phin to elbow him gently.

"I'm here. I've brought reinforcements." Julie walked through the glass door to where we'd spent most of the afternoon outside on the back patio. She had a bag of toys that I assumed were going to act as distractions. Nana followed behind, her hair twisted back into a thick braid.

The others told me she was thinner now than she'd been, but other than that, she looked exactly the same. She'd been tight-lipped about her time in the forest. All she really shared was that when the spirits came to her, telling her the children had been taken, she'd left immediately. Thinner or not, all I saw when I looked at Nana Walker was a strong, independent woman who relied on her wisdom...and spirits.

I had yet to get a definitive answer on what people thought the spirits were. Ghosts? Angels? Her own intuition? I didn't think I'd ever get a straight answer, but really, who were any of us to question her ability? I could sense emotions, Riley made people tell the truth, Kansas could knock a person out in seconds—and he was getting better and not overloading as much, too—and Phin could literally heal people. In the grand scheme of things, what she did wasn't that odd.

"Oh good," Aver's low voice rumbled close to my ear. "Nana's here." He lifted me by the waist, unceremoniously hauling me over his shoulder. "Nana, will you keep an eye on Autumn? I need to take my mate into the woods."

My face burned, hovering just above Aver's ass. I vowed silently to make him pay for basically telling his great-grand-mother that we wanted to go bone. He'd told me he was waiting for her to arrive but not why.

"I could've watched her," Riley muttered, sitting next to Phin on the grass in front of where we'd attempted to stage the children.

They'd already scattered. Even Calvin had rolled over and was trying to army crawl toward where Nash and Wyatt were throwing the football.

"That's okay," Aver said, fishing his hand into my back pocket, where he pulled out my phone. "Keep an eye on this too. He won't need it."

I smacked his ass, but the neanderthal acted like he hadn't felt it. He turned to Nana, waiting for her reply.

"I will, son."

I couldn't meet Nana's gaze. This wasn't our first social gathering since she'd returned. It had been a month since the Walker alphas had come together to remove the pack's greatest threats, and she'd been a daily visitor since then, along with Julie and Paul.

They'd had to figure out logistics with the Walkers acting as Elders now. Instead of moving into their old homes, they'd decided to open the homes to the pack, letting them decide how best to utilize the extra space.

Not even Delia would see her home ever again. When the evidence came forward that she'd at least had a hand in Alpha Walker's death, the scales had finally tipped so far not even she could wiggle out of trouble. Apparently, having a hand in murdering an Alpha brought a swifter judgment than selling a blessed mate. The council had returned with a sentence that would keep Delia Walker in shifter prison for the rest of her life.

There'd been plenty of celebrating in the month that followed, but all of it bittersweet. No one wanted things to turn out how they had, but in the end, it was clear that the ex-Elders would never stop. Even if they'd left peacefully this time, they would've been back, again and again.

Aver clamped his hand on my butt, waving to the others with his free hand as he kept me in place. Branson howled while Nash made annoying kissing sounds. I'd have to trust Riley and Phin would make them pay. But I wouldn't be there to see it. Aver carried me around the house, taking a right toward the forest.

"Let me down, Aver!" I squealed, though my heart wasn't in it.

"I will, pet." He massaged one cheek, squeezing generous handfuls of flesh as his chest rumbled with a noise that wasn't quite a growl. It sounded more like a hum...or purr. But wolves didn't purr.

I didn't think they did.

"We don't have time to diddle in the forest. We'll never get a picture for the Christmas cards now."

"Christmas is months away," Aver countered. "But my cock is hard now."

I twisted my upper half around, looking both directions to make sure no one had been around to hear that. The house blocked the others from view. I'd just have to hope it muffled the sounds as well. I didn't care if the guys heard him but would be mortified if Nana had. Maybe her spirits had already told her. I shuddered at the thought.

"Your cock, your cock. Were you always this demanding?" I pinched his butt—the only part of him within easy reach.

"Yes," he replied without remorse.

"Well, you won't be happy with what I do to your cock unless you let me down right now!" We both knew there was no fire to my threat, which was why it wasn't surprising when Aver refused to obey.

"That's impossible. I love everything you do with my cock."

The light dimmed as Aver stepped into the forest. He kept me hauled over his shoulder like a Viking carting his plunder.

If I were Phin, I might have been able to do a ninja leap from his shoulder, shifting in the sky with a triple somer-sault, but I was still trying to master running without hitting trees. Aver lifted me from my perch, letting my weight slide down his front, where he cupped my butt just as he had when he'd carried me.

"Is it so wrong that I wanted a little alone time with my pet?" He buried his face against my neck, kissing the skin so softly goosebumps popped up on my arms.

I giggled, the kisses so soft they tickled. "No, we just need to work on your subtlety. I was told you were once very diplomatic."

Aver grinned. "That's a kind word to use. Subtlety, huh? How about next time I say we need to go find wood in the forest?"

I laughed. "That isn't subtle. And a job like that wouldn't require two people."

"It does if you find big wood." Aver emphasized his meaning with two sharp pelvic thrusts forward. His hard dick prodded my stomach, flipping that switch inside me that only Aver had access to.

"Didn't I tell you?" I peered up at him with wide, innocent eyes. "I'm training to be a lumberjack."

I shoved him back and spun around, hoping my sudden movement would catch him off guard. I didn't even make it three steps before he gripped his hands around my middle. He lifted my feet off the ground and hauled me deeper into the woods, stopping in a small clearing where beams of sunlight filtered through the sparse canopy.

I couldn't say which of us kissed the other first. One moment he'd been carrying me, and I'd been teasingly protesting. The next, we sank to the forest floor, rolling over the damp ground of moss and fallen nettles.

We kissed like it was our first time—or the last. We kissed like we hadn't spent the majority of our time within touching distance of one another.

With Aver, it was never enough. I always wanted more, which worked because he always had more to give me. But it still didn't feel right, leaving Autumn the moment Nana had arrived.

"We have to be fast," I whispered, straining to keep my mouth on his neck.

"Sexiest words I've ever heard," Aver teased, but in his gaze there was only desire.

Want.

Need.

I ripped his shirt open, tearing it in half down the middle of his chest. Aver growled, claiming my mouth as I skimmed my fingers over the ridges of his muscles. Every hard, aching inch of this demon was mine. And I still could hardly believe it. Not because I didn't deserve someone as perfectly sexy as he was, but because when I thought of how our relationship had started, I saw all the different choices we could have made. Any one of those choices could have stolen this moment away before I'd ever known it was possible.

"I'm going to put another baby in here." Aver cupped my stomach, touching me the same way one would a piece of fine art. The contrast of his gentle touch and rough words had my back bending to get closer.

"Promises," I whispered, knowing there was nothing that egged a Walker on better than a challenge.

And Aver was definitely a Walker. He grinned, winking before he threw me up in the air. I landed upright in his arms with a squeal and without my pants. He trapped me between his body and the tree, letting my feet swing, unable to find purchase. "Hold on, spider monkey," Aver rasped, nudging my legs open with his hips before entering me in a single driving thrust.

I couldn't even make fun of him for the cheesy line, not while my body raced to accommodate his length. There was no pain at his intrusion. The more we made love, the less time my body needed to prepare. Which was good, since Aver fucked me like a man possessed. With a hand at my nape and the other at my hip, he controlled the depth, speed, and angle.

He snarled, grabbing hold of my neck with his teeth as his hips moved like pistons, pinning me against the trunk. My head lolled back, bouncing softly against the bark with every forward thrust. My arms dropped to my sides, useless and unnecessary. I'd learned long ago: Aver was never more *alpha* than when we were intimate, and there wasn't much I could do but enjoy the ride.

He leaned back, pushing my shoulders against the bark so he could look into my face without me slipping. "Does my pet want to cum?" he crooned.

I didn't dare answer, afraid he'd only make me wait

317

until tonight or tomorrow before he allowed me to orgasm. He'd already talked about making a trip into Seattle, not just to see my friends, but to get me fitted for a cock cage that I could wear for long amounts of time. The idea both horrified and thrilled me.

Without slowing down, he licked up my neck and waited for my eyes to focus.

"I asked a question," he murmured, binding me with his sultry gaze.

I'd been ready to reply with a joke, but the fire in his expression burned away the memory of what I'd been about to say. I sucked my bottom lip between my teeth, nodding eagerly.

"Then my pet will come."

Aver grabbed my cock, masterfully coaxing an orgasm to the surface in seconds.

"Who do you belong to, pet?" he asked roughly. "Who does your pleasure belong to?"

"You," I whimpered. "Always you, Aver. I'm yours."

Our eyes locked, and I erupted, cum shooting from my slit in arching ropes.

I clenched my inner muscles, capturing Aver's gaze before he lifted his face to the sun and roared out his pleasure.

"Aver!"

For a split second, I thought it was me who had said Aver's name. But I was still trying to catch my breath.

"Aver!" That time, I recognized Branson's voice. He had to be standing on the edge of the forest, and though he didn't sound panicked, he wouldn't have been standing there just to tell us the food was ready.

"I'm changing my name," Aver growled. "Too many people know this one."

I smacked his shoulder, still pinned against the tree with his dick, and seed, inside me. "They'll just learn the new one."

"What?" Aver yelled with thick irritation.

"Clean up and meet us out back. We have visitors."

In another world, with another group of people, I might have been embarrassed to have my mate's dick in me while he held a conversation with someone else. Instead, I called back. "We'll be there in a second."

Aver covered my lips with his, kissing everything else that I'd been about to say away. "You are naughtier than I ever knew, pet. Talking to another man while I'm inside you."

He'd been doing the same thing! I opened my mouth to point that out, but the way his eyes burned dried my words while making my stomach flip as my cock prepared for round two. But Branson wouldn't have come out here if whoever was waiting for us at the house wasn't important.

I patted his bicep. "We better go. We'll go through the front so we can stop real quick to change and clean up."

Aver frowned and stepped away, letting me drop to my feet. "Why wait? Time is, apparently, of the essence."

Before I could piece together what he meant, he carried me away from the tree, and I screamed seconds later as cold water bit my skin.

"You... !" I sputtered. My brain short-circuited, giving me the mental blue screen of death as I crawled up Aver's body trying to escape the freezing cold water of the Lynx River.

He didn't make me stay in the icy water for long. Though I chattered my teeth for extra sympathy points, the moment he held me tightly, his body heat chased away the cold from my bones. My own personal heater.

But he wasn't a dryer, so when we stepped around the house, joining the familiar and unfamiliar faces, we were both soaking wet. Aver was still shirtless and both had the obvious flush of exertion.

Aver's body stiffened, and his hand tightened on mine. There were six unfamiliar faces. Five men and one very scary-looking dog stood in the back yard in a loose formation. While the Walkers looked like men who weren't afraid of hard work, these men looked more accustomed to illegal work. Each of them was armed, the type of weapons changing from person to person. More than half of them scowled—including the dog.

"Branson?" Aver asked, skirting around to stand with the others.

"We come in peace," the one standing closest said, grinning at our disheveled state.

Aver tucked me behind his body, out of the man's sight. "Who are they?" Aver asked Branson, acting as if the other man hadn't spoken.

Nash stepped forward, clapping the second closest man on the shoulder. "This is my investigator buddy, remember, the guy who dug up information on Phin's stalker?"

"The ones who sent those bikers?" Riley asked.

Nash nodded.

"They're a little late to help now," Aver said, moving to stand in line with his cousins while I remained with the children, Julie, Nana, and the other mates.

The one standing closest made a deep, displeased noise at the back of his throat. He stood over six feet—something they all had in common—and had light brown hair with a generous dusting of silver.

Along with being tall, the others were built as well. Even the dog was ripped. I couldn't tell what breed he was, but he had short, bristly, gray hair, a square jaw, and only one ear that stuck straight up like a tiny triangle on his head. It sat on its hindquarters at the foot of Nash's investigator buddy.

"My name is Knox," the one standing closest said. He pointed to the next man behind him, Nash's buddy. "This is Faust, and those two crazy-looking sons of bitches are Huntley and Jagger."

He pointed to the last of them, an angry, tall, muscular mountain of a man with long dark hair that matched his long beard. "And that's Diesel."

I was pretty sure Diesel had a line of explosives strapped to his chest.

Huntley and Jagger nodded our direction, both with dark hair, blue eyes, and leather straps that crisscrossed over their front. It looked like they held swords, the handles sticking up over their shoulders.

They looked almost identical, though one of them had a scar that ran across his neck from one ear to the other.

Whoever these men were, it was clear that they were no strangers to violence. I got the distinct impression they'd had to fight to be standing where they were today.

"I heard from Badger. He still isn't happy with one of you in particular," Knox said with a grin.

"Which one?" Kansas asked.

"Whichever of you can 'suck a man dry, but in the bad way,'" Knox replied.

Kansas nodded solemnly. "That does sound like me."

"If you've heard from your buddies, you know you're too late to help. What are you doing here now?" Aver asked.

Knox didn't seem at all bothered by Aver's hostility. "We got a job that brought us this way. Thought we'd swing by.

We're going to be neighbors for a while. Got a place a little further south along the coast in Oregon."

Now that I knew these people weren't here to hurt us, I looked for Nana. I turned my head, gasping when she was standing directly next to me with Autumn. "Thank you, Nana," I whispered, sighing silently as my daughter's weight settled in my arms. I understood Aver now when he said he couldn't relax unless I was near and he knew I was safe. I felt the same way about my daughter.

"Of course, spider monkey," Nana replied.

Riley snorted and handed me my phone while I wished the ground would open up to swallow only me.

Knox had been talking that whole time, explaining in finer detail what they were doing here. "We're supposed to be guarding this kid. His dad said he was last spotted near here, in Seattle. But we've searched the city. If he was here, he isn't now." Knox accepted the tall glass of iced tea Julie handed him. "Figured it couldn't hurt to swing by here and put faces to names."

Julie continued down the line of men, offering Faust his glass from several steps away since his dog growled the moment Julie approached.

"Who are you looking for?" Riley asked. "Anyone we know?"

Knox shook his head. "I doubt it. He isn't local but was known to hang around here sometimes. Jazz Whitten. He ran away years ago, and his father hired us to find him. For a price," he added, making the hairs on my nape stand up.

I barely kept from gasping when the man said a name I recognized, and though I'd kept from making a sound, my face burned. I stared at the grass, hoping no one would look my way.

"'That one knows."

I jerked my face up, meeting the gaze of the huge mountain-sized man. I forgot his name.

"That one is my mate, and you will show him respect." Aver was at my side in a flash.

Hunter and Jagger angled toward us, their gazes turning cold and calculating.

"That's enough," Knox said, standing in no-man's-land with Nash and Branson. "We all have big dicks, we know that." He turned to me, and though I wouldn't call his expression soft, at least it wasn't a scowl. "If you know who this kid is, you would be helping him by telling us where to find him."

I scoffed silently. *Yeah, sure, I'd be helping Jazz by telling a group of angry men where he was.* With Aver by my side, I found my voice, and it didn't even shake. "He isn't a kid. He's in his twenties, and I don't know where he is. The last I saw him was a few months ago." At Aver's questioning look, I added, "At the club."

"Do you have a phone number? Something we could track?" Faust asked.

I grabbed Aver's hand, clenching my phone with my other. "I do have his number, but I won't give it to you without his permission. I don't care what his father told you. If Jazz ran, he had a reason."

Several of the men growled, earning a sharp snarl from Bran and Madison. Both children looked eager to escape their parents' arms and show these men who they were dealing with. Knox's eyes widened before his lips curled into a smile. "I like them."

"Careful, this one will take a toe," Phin said.

While the kids distracted them, I dropped Aver's hand and typed out a message.

"What are you doing?" Knox asked sharply.

I'd already pressed send. A good thing since the five of them looked ready to rip the phone from my hands. My phone chimed with Jazz's reply.

"Did he just tip off our mark?" Faust asked, sounding none too pleased.

I read Jazz's reply and snorted before tilting the screen so Aver could see as well.

"Why'd we come here again?" the mountain man asked. "To make our jobs harder?"

If I'd come face to face with this group anywhere else, every instinct I had would've told me to run. But I could be as brave as I liked with my alpha near. "I'm not trying to make your jobs harder, but I don't know you. I don't know if you're lying. But I know Jazz. I told him you were looking for him and asked him if I could give you his number."

That got them cursing at one another, and the atmosphere in the yard dropped from questionable to decidedly tense.

"And what did he say?" Knox growled out.

I smiled slowly, enjoying the moment more than I should have. "He said it's fine and to give you his number. He said he wasn't scared of you, and, I'm quoting here, 'let the bastards try.' Do you have a pen?"

22

HOLLISTER

THOUGH NANA HAD INVITED the men to stay for dinner, they'd been in a rush after receiving Jazz's phone number. I'd call my friend later to give him more of the details and to ask him who the heck he was. It wasn't normal to have your father hire five men who looked like hardened criminals to chase your son.

When they'd left, the one who'd seemed like the leader, Knox, sent me a smirk over his shoulder that I didn't trust in the slightest.

I hoped Jazz knew who he'd just given his number too.

But he'd consented to me giving his number to them, so until he called again to tell me different, I'd trust he knew what he was doing.

Aver remained a growling, stalking mess for a long time after the men left, and only the children rolling around on the blanket could pull him out of his funk. Calvin was a master at sitting up on his own now, and I figured it would only be a matter of time before Autumn could as well. She'd already grown so much.

"It's getting late. Why don't we eat dinner out here?" Nana suggested, her face lit warmly by the sinking sun.

I didn't mind either way, and no one else seemed to either.

"Make yourselves useful and help me bring the food out," Nana said.

Those of us around her looked to one another, trying to decide who she was talking to.

"Nash and Wyatt," she clarified, turning on her heel as the brothers raced to catch up.

Nash returned first with a steaming tray of corn on the cob, already soaking in butter. Next to that, Wyatt set down a platter of meat. Her grill had been going for the last hour, and I was eager to finally taste the smell that'd had me drooling.

Nana came out last with a bowl of potato salad. The boys set out plates on the table, and Nana dished a scoop of potato salad onto each one. She stabbed a chicken breast with the serving fork, the tips charred from where the fire had licked at the sugary barbecue sauce.

"Do you want one ear or two, Hollister?" she asked.

"One, please," I said with a smile. I'd been secretly worried that I wouldn't feel as close to the matriarch of the Walker family as the others because she hadn't been a part of my life in the pack until very recently.

I'd worried for no reason—something Aver had tried to tell me several times over. Already, I wondered how we'd ever lived without her, and I didn't want to try again. The last time she left, this family nearly ripped itself apart.

Nana handed me my plate, turning to dish up Riley, Kansas, Julie, the older kids, and Phin before she took her own plate and sat in the grass near where the older children waited like begging puppies.

The guys had pulled the travel cribs outside so Autumn and Calvin could sleep when their bedtime had come. Both children were out, their arms and legs sticking out like tiny X's.

"Oh, we're just chopped liver then," Wyatt whined, staring at his mate's plate.

Nana shrugged and gave Kansas a look when he tried to feed Wyatt from his plate.

"Brutal," Nash muttered under his breath, though not quietly enough so that any of us had difficulty hearing what he'd said.

I didn't want to be on the receiving end of one of Nana's looks, but as a natural helper, I had to fight to keep from jumping up.

Nana settled her hand on my knee and leaned into me like she was about to tell a secret. "Every once in a while, you've got to make sure their britches still fit."

I laughed and committed the tip to memory.

The others dished up, joining us as we sat scattered in the grass, all but Branson, who stood a few feet away, watching us eat.

"Now?" Riley asked him.

I put my corn down at the exact same time everyone else stopped eating as well. A person couldn't just ask a question like that and not expect those around him to take notice.

"Are you pregnant? Tell me you're pregnant," Kansas squealed.

Riley laughed, shaking his head before pointing to his mate standing in front of us like he was about to give a presentation.

"Riley isn't pregnant, but I do have something I want to share. I think it might answer some of the questions we've had. Or maybe not?" He shrugged and threaded his fingers through his hair.

I took my cue from Riley, who clearly had some idea about what Branson was about to say. He smiled, but it was an odd type that made me wonder if I wanted to hear whatever was coming next.

"Get on with it! We don't have a great track record for surprises," Wyatt called out.

Aver sat down beside me, and I leaned into him, snuggling under his arm as Branson pulled a sheet of paper from his back pocket.

"You all know that with Hollister's help, I opened the safe under my bed, finding stacks of letters my father had written me." We hadn't had an abundance of downtime for a while, but when Branson did have an extra moment at home, he could always be found reading from the stacks of letters he'd been gifted from the past.

"Is it true? You're adopted?" Nash asked.

"Hush, you two," Julie scolded her sons.

"This letter was different from the others," Branson said, letting his thumb rub almost affectionately over the white paper. "This one he mailed to himself. It was in the stack, unopened but with the words *For my Son* written on the back."

He flashed the envelope and the message written in neat cursive.

"But it wasn't really for me. Not only, anyway. It's for all of us. I think."

"All of us?" I asked with a frown.

He couldn't also mean me. Patrick Walker had died when I was a child, very near, if not on the same day that my biological parents had died. In the bustle of pack problems and relationship drama, we hadn't had a lot of time to wonder about the coincidences and similarities of how we'd each found the other. I wasn't alone in feeling like me being here had been predestined. The others felt the same.

"I think it will be easier if I just read it," he said, lifting the letter. "To my son, Branson, and his cousins, Aver, Nash, and Wyatt, I'm sorry.

"I watched the four of you play today, and I fear it is the last time I'll see such a thing. I know this pack will witness the end of me. Whether that day is in many years, or not, my time will come to an end, and every eye will look to you four.

"If only I could live forever and spare each of you the heartache that I know lies in your futures. But as the moon wanes, every Alpha must, one day, relinquish control. On that day, try to remember moments like the one I was lucky enough to witness today. *You are family* and each other's best friends. Though you sometimes prefer making each other cry more than anything else, you carry a bond, and though others in your life may try to weaken that bond, I pray that you will always recognize it. Turn to one another. No one will understand you like your cousin can." Branson took a deep breath. The words from his father, spoken aloud, had a spell-like effect.

Aver wiped the tears from my cheek. I hadn't noticed I was crying. I wasn't the only one. Julie's plate was forgotten, and she leaned into her son, Wyatt, one arm comforting his mother while he held his mate with the other.

"But you cannot thrive alone. When it comes time to find a mate, choose wisely, sons. But since I know better than most how difficult that can be, I will make a wish to help you along. I wish for you to not only find your souls but for your lives to be *blessed*. May your mates be honest and brave. May they be healers and capable of miraculous things. And, may they be fearless and bold. They will need to be to handle you four. Whatever you do, do not settle as I did. Find your soulmates. If you do nothing but that, you will have won. No one can harm the spark that burns inside each of you. You will go on to do amazing things, I know it. But you will also face hardships. When you do, remember truth, hope, faith, and love will always see you through."

Branson let the magic of the words linger in the air like a spell. He cleared his throat and wiped his eyes. "The letter is dated June twenty-first."

"Our birthdays," Riley whispered. "Can it be a coincidence?" Riley didn't sound like he believed it was.

I turned to Aver, his warm eyes waiting as he stared at me like I was the miracle. "Didn't he die the same day your parents did?" Aver asked gently. "Isn't that the day most of you remember experiencing your powers for the first time? Coincidence? No."

He sounded so sure. I wished I could sound as sure. Could Patrick have been the one to start this whole crazy ball rolling? Had the gentle wish of a man I'd never met be the reason I could do what I could do?

"It's unbelievable," I whispered.

"That may be, but I don't know how else to explain it." Branson went to his mate, sinking down to sit on the lawn. Bran climbed into his lap and sat so he faced forward.

A little Walker if I ever saw one.

"I wished there was a way to thank him," Kansas said, absently petting Mr. Boots. "Even though my powers felt like a burden, they brought me here, to you guys. I can only look at what I do as a gift now because of that."

Aver slipped his hand in mine. "We can," he said gravely. "We'll thank Patrick by helping to create the pack he always wanted. One without backstabbing and melo-drama. One where anyone is welcome and all are accepted."

"Even Aver," Nash added as if he was being generous.

I smirked, glad that even in a moment like this, when we were faced with a cosmically insane scenario, they could still joke. I stood silently, retrieving Autumn from her crib. She didn't wake up for longer than it took her to snuggle back against my shoulder. I didn't normally like disturbing her when she slept, but right then, I'd needed her in my arms.

Kansas seemed to have felt the same. He retrieved Calvin, sinking back down to sit next to his mate. At the same time, Madison and Patrick noticed all the other children were getting attention, so they decided they wanted some too. Each took a lap of one of their parents, and for a few seconds, we just sat there, embracing the best things to ever happen to us.

"To Patrick," I whispered as the others repeated in unison.

"To Patrick."

The End

HERO: WOLVES OF ROYAL PAYNES

Mercenaries. Outcasts. Alphas.

Knox knows all the five of them have left now is each other. That, and the driving desire to find who had slaughtered their pack and make that person pay.

But investigating a tragedy with only rubble as evidence requires money and time. Knox can find one and use it to buy the other. They may be the last remaining members of their once thriving pack, but they are no strangers to taking the types of jobs that would keep lesser men awake at night.

Finding and returning some young punk to his rich, asshole father shouldn't be all that difficult.

Jazz Whitten lives as he likes, always. Since leaving home when he was young, he's operated under a single rule, never stay where you aren't wanted. Using his unique ability and the sleight of hand he's perfected over the years, life as a fugitive isn't that bad. It's lonely at times, but freedom is more important than companionship.

But when Jazz comes head to head with the latest team hired by his father, he forgets his one rule. He knows it is money, not affection that keeps the team on his tail. Their leader, Knox, is merciless and focused,but there's something else about the man. It isn't his kindness—Knox is a brute and unfortunately for Jazz, he's smart too—but Knox radiates a type of pain that Jazz is all too familiar with.

Jazz is as slippery as he is sexy and it takes every trick Knox knows to catch up with him. But when he does, how will the stone-cold mercenary ever give him up?

Chapter One
Jazz

Only in Portland could you find organic beeswax lip balm sold at a stand directly next to rows of decorative butt plugs. Some had jewels, glittering in pretty pinks, greens, and blues. Others had tails attached to the end. I paused at one that had a simple rounded cap with an image of a red X like you would see on an old pirate map.

X marks the spot.

"How much?" I asked the little old lady sitting behind the booth. From the corner of my eye, I caught sight of my hair, stained brown instead of its usual orange-red.

The woman peered up at me. She looked like she spent her weekends baking cookies for her grandchildren's bake sales. "One of my finest. One hundred percent stainless steel." Her eyes dragged up and then down my body. "It's pretty heavy and not for beginners, sweetie."

I hated it when people used pet names before they knew a person. Sweetie. Hon. Babe.

Blech.

But, this old lady was interesting, which already made her cool in my book—nothing worse than a boring stick in the mud. And she was kind. She hadn't been judging me with her warning but cautioning me. I understood. My stupidly round eyes and fiery curls made me look years younger than my actual age of twenty-three. Even though I had brown curls today, I had the body of a broomstick. Or shovel handle. Either worked. I didn't rely on my muscles to live, and it showed.

"How much?"

Before she could answer, I felt the telltale heat at my nape. If I turned my head, I'd see one of my ghosts lurking in the crowd, trying not to be seen. I couldn't be too annoyed. I'd egged the ghosts on, but how could I have known when Hollister had contacted me asking if he could give out my number that this time, this group, would be different?

Every other team my father had hired to try and find me normally didn't make it within fifty miles of catching me. And if they had, it was because I was bored and had allowed it. But these guys were relentless. I'd lived with a target between my shoulders from the moment they'd gotten hold of my cell phone number. And they were intelligent too, which sucked for me.

My father had wised up, deviating from hiring run-of-the-mill meatheads with guns to the freaking Teenage Mutant Ninja Turtles—if the turtles were angry brooding men led by a stupidly gorgeous, arrogant man.

Though the five—six, counting that evil dog that had nearly bit me the last time—were always on my heels, I'd never felt more alive than I had these past few weeks. My life wasn't about floating around and partying with the friends I had scattered over the country—while fun, a person can only party for so long. I had a goal, a purpose. Stay one step ahead, stay free, stay smart.

I dropped down to my haunches, balancing my arms on the tabletop. "I hate to ask you, but is there a man behind me staring like he's trying to drill a hole? Please don't be obvious when you look."

This wasn't her first sting operation, clearly. Her gaze slid over and then back just as quickly. "There is. He looks like a pretty strong guy. Are you in trouble, son?"

Not as long as I slip free. I knew my father hired these men to find me, but for the life of me, I couldn't figure out *why*. He hadn't especially cared for me growing up. He'd said I was the result of an impulsive night and that my mother had dropped me off on his doorstep before running. She hadn't wanted the trouble of raising a baby. My father hadn't either, but at least he had people to pay to raise me.

Our relationship hadn't improved since then.

I grabbed the slip of paper I always kept in my pocket. When I opened my hand, revealing the paper to the woman, she saw a picture of the men's leader. Knox. "Do you see this man behind me?"

She studied the illusion I projected. Though the photo

came from my mind, every detail of the man's face was perfect. I didn't know how I could do what I did, just that I'd always been able to. If I got my hands on something—as long as it wasn't bigger than a large dog—I could make it look, and sometimes act, like anything. A piece of paper became a photograph. A stack of business cards became enough money for me to have a good night out, and then some.

"I don't see him," she said. "But I think I see a few others watching you. A man with a dog."

I sighed with relief even as she spotted more men on my tail. These guys were rough, clever, and kept me on my toes, but if Knox was here, I needed to be worried.

Knox.

Only an asshole would dare to have a gorgeous name while walking around like every good boy's wet dream. I wasn't a good boy, but I could pretend for Knox.

Stop it, Jazz. You're going to get caught. He doesn't care about you; he just wants to catch you.

I was Stockholm-Syndroming myself. *How pathetic.*

Knox wasn't some guardian angel sent to make me feel not so alone. I was pretty sure he and the rest of his team were some kind of ex-military, mercenaries. They were too smart to not be.

I had to remember Knox had been hired to find me. The moment he did, he'd turn me over and move on to the next job. "I'll take the plug." I reached for my wallet where I kept my real money.

I wasn't above stealing, but not from little old ladies trying to earn a little extra cash. I stole from my father or companies nested under the umbrella of his huge conglomerate. Clubs, restaurants, hotels chains, spas—there was an endless list that stretched across the country.

"Seems odd a young man learns he is being followed and immediately buys a sex toy."

I winked as she handed me the plug wrapped in brown paper. "Odd, that sounds like me." I threw a quick look over my shoulder.

The mountain moved in. They'd spotted me, I'd spotted them, we both knew we saw the other. My plan came together as I mapped a route out of the large outdoor bazaar. I knew my weaknesses as well as my strengths. I wasn't a fighter. Any one of those men could snap me in two like a twig while I tried my hardest just to leave a mark.

But I could be slippery. I could find cracks and crawl through them. And I had a certain lovable knack for chaos. I'd been running for most of my life and had learned early on: always plan your exit, and never double back the way you came. I wouldn't be caught in a room with only one door, not unless there was a window to jump out of.

I straightened and tensed to move. "On second thought, can I get one of those lip balms too?" I asked.

The woman blinked several times but recovered. "Which flavor?"

"Pina colada, please." I'd imagine I was relaxing on a tropical beach instead of running away from men hell bent on ruining my casual Saturday fun.

I handed her the money, giving her extra for being so nice, and then slipped through the gap between her booth and the booth next to hers. One of the men said something, probably some mission code word that meant, *hurry up, he's getting away*.

I ran by a man walking several dogs of all shapes and sizes. Digging the plug from the small bag, I unwrapped it and cupped it between my hands before dropping the plug and letting it roll away on the ground behind me.

The dogs howled and barked, snapping to get at what looked like a large tabby cat sauntering by them without a care in the world. The dog walker lost control of the leashes as the dogs tugged him to the middle of the sidewalk, piling on top of their new furry friend.

By the time the dogs had calmed down and the walker got them pulled back, the cat would be gone and nothing more than a truly adorable plug, but by then, so would I.

Though I was sure of the plan, I still ran, hazarding a brief glance back where the mountain glared. His mouth moved in rapid shapes that were likely a string of curse words as he tried, and failed to get through the throng of chaos in front of him.

The one with the dog had his hands full as well. My illusions didn't just look like other things; they smelled like them as well. If I made a turd look like a pie and put it in a person's hand, they'd believe it was a pie until they put it in their mouth. Cujo was as distracted as the others.

But these guys never attacked alone. That was part of what made them so difficult. They came at me as a team, every time. Which meant...

I skidded to a stop, the Wonder Twins taking up the square of sidewalk several yards ahead. With hair as black as oil and bright blue eyes, they were difficult to miss. Sometimes, they carried swords with them. I'd spotted the handles once or twice in our time together and assumed they'd realized a crowded market place wasn't the best place to show up visibly armed.

Visibly being the operative word there.

I searched the area, spotting a police officer on top of a large brown horse. It could have been something fancy like an Arabian chestnut stallion, but to me, it looked like a brown horse.

339

Snagging the paper in my pocket, I held it, making my hand tremble as if in fear. "Officer, p-please help me."

The man on horseback narrowed his eyes at me, possibly his bullshit meter going off, but I pushed the paper closer to his nose.

"I have a restraining order. Those two men are not supposed to be within a hundred yards of me. Please, help." Sometimes, looking younger than my twenty-three years was useful.

With the proof of my story right in front of him, bullshit meter or not, the police officer looked from me to the Wonder Twins. "Wait here," he told me as he made a clicking sound with his mouth and his horse walked forward.

"Yes, of course, I'll wait..." I waited for him to get farther away, and closer to the twins, before heading off down an alley I'd spotted.

If I wasn't positive the wonder twins were going to do nothing to the police officer but be annoyed by him, I wouldn't have sent him over. I didn't want people getting hurt, or worse, killed, because of me. That had partly been the reason I'd told Hollister it was okay to send my information along. I didn't know the men at that time, but if they were asking my friend about me, they were in harming distance of him. Better they got the information they wanted and focus their attentions on the real target.

Looking left, right, and behind, I checked to make sure none of them had spotted me. It had sucked covering my red hair; it was one of the things I liked about myself. But it also made me too easy to spot. At least this way, no one had their eyes on me as I pranced down the sidewalk on the other side of the street, skipping toward the alley I knew went all the way through and opened on to the other side of the block. I pulled out the lip balm, twisting off the cap to slather a layer of fruity coconut beeswax onto my lips.

"Mmm." I smacked my lips together, sliding the tube in my pocket.

Before I could make the turn that would bring me freedom, a strong hand emerged from the darkness between two buildings and grabbed mine, pulling me into an off-balance spin. Disoriented, I slammed against a rock-hard chest as the growling man pulled my hands behind my back. His large, firm body pressed against mine while my shoulder blades smashed against the unforgiving concrete of the building behind me. Not only did he have my hands restrained, his thick fingers tightened over each wrist, and he kept my hands apart.

I needed two hands to do what I did. I knew that. I'd never told anyone else that. And somehow, this man who had been following me for months knew that now too. I must've slipped and been too obvious.

Or his relentless observation was starting to pay off.

"Getting sloppy, Jazz," Knox murmured. "Target secure. Convene to the rendezvous point." He spoke into the small headset pinned behind his ear.

While I'd thought I'd been zigzagging through them, the bastards had been herding me to where they'd wanted me.

"I'm disappointed. Diesel said this plan would work, and I told him you were too smart to fall for it." He tsked me, his grip never loosening. His voice was like a summer storm. Swelteringly hot, sharp as a crack of lightning, but also deep and soothing like thunder rumbling in the distance.

Maybe everyone wasn't soothed by thunder and lightning, but I wasn't everyone.

Though having this man this close made my body go haywire, I attempted not to let it show. "Maybe I just like getting close to you," I shot back, my voice too breathy for the tease to count.

Knox smirked. Lips that full should've been illegal on a man like him. *What would they look like curled in a real smile?* I'd never know. Knox only ever smirked or scowled when he looked at me. His silver eyes traced my face, lingering at the bags beginning to form under my eyes.

I could make most any object look like anything else, but I couldn't do a thing to magic my appearance. Not in a way that was travelable anyway. My appearance, I had to maintain the old-fashioned way with sleep, dyes, makeup, and creams. And lately, I hadn't gotten a whole lot of sleep.

"You changed your hair," he grumped. "I don't like it."

Though I wasn't a fan of it either, I bristled beneath the implication that he had a say in how I looked. I'd shave my hair off if I wanted to and was ready to say as much. But when my mouth opened to unleash a heated retort, the words that came out weren't at all what I'd planned. "How do you like me? Helpless?" I made a show of trying to tug my hands free.

His grip was too strong for me to expect to pull away, but my repeated tugging made our bodies collide softly together. My dick sprung to life, and I would've been embarrassed, except Knox's cock did the same.

Worth it.

"Is that lip balm in your pocket, or are you happy to see me?" I purred. His length didn't feel a thing like the small tube. The heat and hardness made it impossible to mistake his erection for anything but what it was.

His lips twitched in what looked like the barest hint of a smile. That couldn't be right. Knox didn't smile. I was convinced he didn't have the facial muscles for it. He eased his body back, allowing a breeze's width of space between us.

Clueless to what he was planning, I watched, breathless, as he pulled my right hand to the front of my body. He pinned my arm there with his other shoulder before slowly sliding his hands into my front pocket.

His fingers didn't linger in my pocket. He grabbed what he'd been aiming for and pulled the tube clear of my jeans. Tucking the plastic into his front pocket, he returned my right hand to my back, the grip on my wrist no gentler than it had been.

Every solid inch of him stamped against my front. I managed to keep my eyelids from fluttering and the moan from escaping, but I could do nothing about the way my dick twitched like a dog lifting its nose to a pleasant smell in the air.

"Now I know that's not lip balm." Knox let his gaze drop low between our bodies so there was no mistaking what he was talking about.

Insufferable dick. It wasn't my fault there wasn't a lot of time for loving when you were being chased by mercenaries. At this point, a well-built filing cabinet would turn me on. I couldn't admit to any of that. I wouldn't give him the satisfaction of knowing he had any effect on me. This was a job to him.

I let my eyes go round—full doe mode—and peered up at him. I had to look up to see into his face anyway. I sucked only the corner of my bottom lip beneath my teeth. "Why are you so obsessed with me, Daddy?"

A growl rumbled through his chest. Fuck, I liked that more than I should, especially since I'd never met another person who could growl like Knox. The sound wasn't an angry man's approximation of a growl; it was real, deep, and sank into my bones.

"The hissing kitten finally wants to purr?" His strong jaw and sharp cheeks loomed closer. Knox had the type of face that always looked ready for a shave. He never had a beard, but I wouldn't call him clean-shaven. His cheeks were as rough as the rest of him.

"I can do more than purr—" The rest of my taunt dried in my throat the moment my brain pointed out how close Knox's face was, how close his lips were. He watched my eyes, occasionally glancing lower to my mouth. He was fucking with me, I knew that, but my stomach flipped all the same.

My body didn't care who was touching it, just that it was being touched.

His lips drew closer, filling each of my senses with him. His scent wasn't as much comforting as it was *wild*. When I inhaled, I pictured a huge dark cloud rolling ominously over a dark blue ocean. He smelled like a storm, but there was more to it. I detected a hint of leather and the sharp freshness of cut cedar. His wasn't a scent that came from a bottle, but from his life.

Instantly, I was curious about the version of Knox that wasn't chasing me. Where did he live that he smelled like this? What did he do there? Did the five of them live and work together? I had questions—a dangerous thing when coupled with my relentless curiosity.

But even my questions were silences as his lips hovered even closer. I could've stretched my head forward and bridged the gap, press my mouth against his.

Just because I could didn't mean I should. A kiss from *this* man would only make running away from him that much more difficult. Already, alarm bells sounded in my brain. The mission wasn't as much to get out of his grasp but to stop the kiss that would surely turn my life into a tailspin I wouldn't be able to pull out of.

I did the opposite of what my brain told me to do. Annoyingly, it was also what my body wanted. Those two jerks didn't see eye to eye when it came to Knox. I went loose, limp, and pliant. Knox's grip tightened to accommodate for the way I sagged into him. I licked my lips and angled my face higher, allowing Knox open access to my mouth.

For a split second, I thought I saw something flash in his gaze. Not mean or taunting, nor arrogant or domineering. Something *possessive*.

But the look was gone as quickly as it had come, and Knox's mouth inched closer. He'd loosed his grip on one wrist; that would have to be enough. I sighed into him, but the moment our lips should've touched, my knee collided with his groin.

He didn't let go as I'd hoped, but he grunted and jerked back, giving me enough room to duck under his arms. I spun my wrists, grimacing at the burn, but it was necessary to twist my arms so the narrowest part lined up directly behind his thumbs. I yanked like they'd explained to do on the self defense video I'd watched a few days ago.

Amazingly, it worked. My wrists slipped free, stinging from the force of his hold but my own to move as I liked.

He snarled and made a swipe for my waist. I jumped back, evading his grasp but also tucking myself further down the alley and away from the street. Unlike the alley a little farther down the sidewalk, this one didn't go all the way through. I was stuck. An angry, sexy beast stood between me and freedom.

Even now, tense and stiff with irritation, he made my

insides quiver. I had a type: nice, fun-loving guys who weren't interested in anything that wasn't surface level. Knox wasn't a surface-level kind of guy. He was the type of man that would burrow under your skin and wrap himself around your bones.

He was hired to capture you.

Thankfully, my brain chose that moment to speak up before I did something stupidly insane, like fall back into his arms a second time.

Reaching into my pocket, I pulled out the sheet of paper, fashioned it into a gun behind my back, and stuck the barrel against my temple.

Knox froze, his hands outstretched. "That isn't real, brat," he growled, his nostrils flaring.

"Isn't it?" I found his gaze. "Are you certain?"

He may have been watching and figuring things about me, but he couldn't know everything. He couldn't know that while the gun was nothing but paper, it would smell like a real gun. If I pulled the trigger, it would sound like a real gun.

His uncertainty kept him from lunging forward, but he remained between me and the exit. "You'd never do it," he taunted. "You love your own pretty face too much."

That stung in an unusual way. He'd called my face pretty, which I enjoyed, but he'd also implied I was some sort of vapid kid. Little more than an unruly child throwing a tantrum.

I cocked the gun. The click of the hammer sliding into place was deafening in the muted alley. Something that looked like actual fear danced behind his eyes, gone in the next moment. My finger rested against the trigger. Though I knew the gun was fake—I'd made it— I'd begun to believe I could feel it against my head. A thrill of fear skittered up my spine.

"Do you want to risk it?" I asked softly. "Do you think you'll get paid by my father if you drop me off with a hole in my head?"

His entire body coiled like a spring poised to leap into action.

I stared him down, unsure of what I would do if he called my bluff. I wasn't in danger; he couldn't be one hundred percent sure of that. He would be next time, that was for sure. Every trick I used on Knox and his team, only ever worked once.

He'd made a decision, clear by the way Knox's body relaxed. He stepped back, placing his hands against the wall.

I stumbled forward in my haste to get free. The gun to my head, his hands on my wrists, his scent in my head—I was disoriented by nothing but *him*. This day would be a lesson in nothing but how important it was that I keep my distance. Maybe I'd been toying with them a little, lingering these passed months mostly in the Portland area. I got attached and almost got caught because of it.

I didn't breathe as I crossed Knox. Nothing stopped him from reaching for me a second time except his uncertainty. He didn't move, though, and I made it to the mouth of the alley, peeking up and down the sidewalk before I planned my getaway route.

"Jazz." Knox let my name linger on his tongue.

Don't turn. Don't listen. Just go. You don't want to hear it.

That was what my brain thought. My body grabbed the corner of the building and lingered.

"Next time I see you, I want your hair back to how it

was. And you put another gun to your head, conjured or not, and I'll paddle that ass."

———

Hero is the first book in the Wolves of Royal Paynes series. It is an action-packed, swelteringly hot, mpreg romance that introduces a world of intrigue, mystery and magic. For maximum enjoyment, this series should be read in order.

Wolves of Royal Paynes
Hero
Ruler
Lovers
Outlaw

THANK YOU!

Thank you so much for reading Love! I could not have gotten this far without the excitement, encouragement, and kind words from my readers and fans (thank you), my Writing Tribe (you know who you are—thank you) and of course, my husband who puts up with me when I don't even want to put up with myself (thank you). I'd like to give an extra thank you to Kiki's Alphas especially, Xochitl, Sabella, Kathy, Angie, and Joy! I'd also like to thank my cover designer, Adrien Rose for being so amazing, and my editor MA Hinkle of Les Court Author Services!

———

About Me

Kiki Burrelli lives in the Pacific Northwest with the bears and raccoons. She dreams of owning a pack of goats that she can cuddle and dress in form-fitting sweaters. Kiki loves writing and reading and is always chasing that next character that will make her insides shiver. Consider getting to know Kiki at her website, kikiburrelli.net, on Facebook, in her Facebook fan group or send her an email to kiki@kikiburrelli.net

Omega Assassins Club
(Wolf Shifter Omegaverse)

Wolves of Walker County
(Wolf Shifter Mpreg)

Wolves of Royal Paynes
(Wolf Shifter Mpreg)

Printed in Poland
by Amazon Fulfillment
Poland Sp. z o.o., Wrocław